Look for Sasha Summers's next novel
available soon from HQN.

For a full list of books by Sasha Summers,
please visit www.sashasummers.com.

SASHA SUMMERS

The Sweetest Thing

HQN

ISBN-13: 978-1-335-45854-4

The Sweetest Thing
Copyright © 2022 by Sasha Best

Like Bees to Honey
Copyright © 2022 by Sasha Best

For questions and comments about the quality of this book, please contact us at CustomerService@Harlequin.com.

HQN
22 Adelaide St. West, 41st Floor
Toronto, Ontario M5H 4E3, Canada
www.Harlequin.com

Printed in U.S.A.

CONTENTS

To the bees…for reminding me that determination and hard work are the only way to get results.

THE SWEETEST THING

CHAPTER ONE

"HE CANNOT BE SERIOUS." Tansy stared at the front page of the local *Hill Country Gazette* in horror. At the far too flattering picture of Dane Knudson. His long, pale blond hair pulled back in a sloppy man-bun—which should look ridiculous but, on him, never did. The skin-tight Texas Viking Honey T-shirt vacuum-sealed over what appeared to be a very Viking-like chest. And that smile. That smug, "that's right I'm superhot and I know it" smile that set her teeth on edge. "What was he thinking?"

"He who?" Tansy's sister Astrid, sat across the kitchen table, her lap occupied by Beeswax, their massive orange cat. "Who has poor Tansy-Wansy all worked up, hmm, Beeswax?" She smiled down at the cat, who was staring up at Astrid with pure adoration. "Maybe you should go cuddle with her."

"Dane." Tansy shook the newspaper. "Who else?"

"Who else, indeed?" Aunt Magnolia said. She stood, straight and tall and willowy, stacking fresh-from-the-oven lavender-honey lemon poppy seed muffins on a plate.

"What did he do now?" Aunt Camellia asked, looking and sounding the appropriate mix of outraged and sympathetic Tansy was hoping for. She wiped her hands on her apron before tightening the lid on the Mason jar full of her lavender-scented beeswax lotion.

"What did he do now?" Lord Byron, Aunt Camellia's parrot, sat on his perch close to her chair waiting for one of the oyster crackers she always had tucked away in her pocket, just for him.

"This." Tansy shook the newspaper again. "Texas Viking Honey to Help Honey, Texas, Develop Its As Yet Untapped Agri-Tourism Opportunity." She paused, waiting for the reaction.

"This is bad?" Astrid asked, leaning around Beeswax to pick up her teacup. "Why is this bad? If they're scaling back on honey, then—"

"'While continuing to produce their award-winning clover honey,'" Tansy read, then snorted, "'Texas Viking Honey, with the support of the Honey City Council, will be expanding operations and combining their Viking ancestry and Texas heritage—"

"That does sound rather impressive, Tansy." Aunt Magnolia slid the plate of muffins onto the kitchen table and took her seat. "That doesn't mean it *is* impressive."

"Impressive? More like pompous." Aunt Camellia took a muffin and joined them at the table. "All the Viking this and Viking that. That boy is pure Texan." She devoured the muffin in a few angry bites.

"The Viking thing is a marketing gimmick," Tansy agreed.

"A smart one." Astrid winced at the glare Tansy shot her way. "What about this has you so worked up, Tansy?"

"I haven't gotten there, yet." Tansy held up one finger and continued clearly now, over-enunciating each syllable as she read, "'Combining their Viking ancestry and Texas heritage for a one-of-a-kind event venue and riverfront cabins ready for nature-loving guests by next fall.'"

All at once, the room froze.

Finally. She watched as, one by one, they realized why this was a bad thing.

"But, the bees." Astrid frowned. Beekeeping wasn't just their family's livelihood, it was their way of life. But Astrid had an extra connection to their winged friends. For her, it wasn't about the honey or the beeswax or the money, it was about *protecting* them. There was one thing that made Astrid Hill upset—endangering the bees.

Two years of scorching heat and drought had left Honey Hill Farms' apiaries in a precarious position. Not just the bees—the family farm itself. They all knew this season could make or break the Hill family. None of them wanted to say the words out loud, of course, but there was an inordinate amount of pressure to win the cash prize at this year's Honey Festival—and the distribution contract with Healthy & Wholesome Markets. If they didn't, they'd lose their home and their bees...

Of course, Dane's stupid plan might run off the bees long before then.

Astrid looked crestfallen. "It's almost as if he doesn't understand or...or care about the bees."

"He doesn't care about the bees." Tansy wanted to hit something. Or someone. "If he did, this wouldn't be happening." She scanned the paper again—but not the photo. His smile only added insult to injury. "The noise and traffic and guests, and who knows what 'event venue' means? Before that, there will be construction and machinery and workers and...and destruction." She shook her head. "What is he thinking?"

"I'll tell you what he's thinking." Aunt Camellia took another muffin. "Come to think of it, he's a Knudson, so chances are he's not thinking… But, if he's anything like his father, he's determined to milk every cent he can out of every avenue available to him. This little… stunt will likely bring them a pretty penny."

"Now, now, Camellia." Aunt Magnolia held her hand out for the newspaper.

Tansy handed it over and exchanged a look with her sister. They didn't know all the ins and outs of what had happened between Aunt Camellia and Harald Knudson—only that their aunt had zero tolerance for *all* things Knudson.

On that, she and Aunt Camellia were of one mind.

She and her aunt had spent the last eighteen months perfecting their newest honey to make absolutely certain they'd win top prize at this year's Honey Festival. All the long hours and tweaking of flavors had led to the best honey Tansy had ever tasted—and she'd tasted a *lot* of honey in her lifetime. That was how Tansy knew, deep in her bones, they'd win. They'd win the blue ribbon and the cash prize and the Healthy & Wholesome Markets deal that would keep Honey Hill Farms alive and well for the long-term. But the cherry on top? Winning top honors would put the Knudsons in their place *and* avenge her aunt Camellia. Her aunt was bighearted and generous and kind to a fault. That Harald Knudson had done something to hurt her was enough to make the Hills and Knudsons business rivals. Thanks to Tansy's incident with Dane, the rivalry was intensely personal for her. Up until ten minutes ago, she'd been on a sort of high just thinking about Harald Knudson's shock as the Hill family took first place—not to mention how ecstatic she'd been imagining wiping the grin off Dane Knudson's impossibly handsome and perpetually condescending face. *Sweet victory.*

But now…this…

Tansy stood and carried her coffee cup to the kitchen sink, leaning against the counter to clear her head. Her gaze bounced around the farmhouse kitchen, taking in Granna Hazel's hand-painted bee and flower details on the pale yellow walls, Aunt Camellia's leftover lotion materials atop the large island, and the dozen or so full jars sealed and lined up beneath the window over the sink. Aunt Camellia's pups, all five of them, were a patchwork mass of fur, piled close in a long beam of sunlight that cut across the Spanish-tile kitchen floor. This room was the heart of the old house. This was where they gathered at least twice a day to share a meal, news, and work through any concerns together. Even with stacks of bee journals, magazines, books, baskets of honey, soap- and lotion-making supplies, and all sorts of bits and bobs tacked to the refrigerator and oversize corkboard by the pantry, it was impeccably clean. Aunt Camellia believed in organized chaos—that's how she described it. Tansy sighed, peering out the window at the bluebonnets and golden agarita waving in the spring breeze, beckoning to the bees that called Honey Hill Farms their home.

A home Dane Knudson is jeopardizing…

"You have to give the boy credit," Aunt Magnolia said, folding the newspaper and laying it on the table. "He has drive."

Tansy wasn't giving *the boy* a thing. As far back as she could remember, Tansy and Dane had gone toe-to-toe. From middle school spelling bees, fundraisers and

Junior Beekeepers competitions, to two publicly humiliating and painful weeks in high school that forever cemented their mutual dislike of one another. She stopped that line of thought cold. Bottom line, they'd been each other's fiercest competition. But it wasn't the competition that irked her or the time and work she'd put in to besting him, it was *Dane*. He had been—he still *was*, this article proved that—heartless. Heartless and selfish. To him, life was a game, and toying with people's emotions was all part of it. Over and over again, she'd invested time and energy and hours of hard work and he'd just sort of winged it. As far as Tansy knew, he'd never suffered any consequences for his lackluster efforts. No, the great Dane Knudson could charm his way through pretty much any situation. One thing was certain: Dane and his father were both rotten to the core.

"Drive? Or ego? Maybe he's finally bitten off more than he can chew?" Tansy shook her head. "What he's planning has nothing to do with beekeeping." If anything, there was the potential for disaster. For *all* of them. And now this…this expansion of his could cost her family their home, the farm, the bees…everything. Tansy's stomach knotted with dread.

"We should file a protest," Aunt Camellia said, taking a third muffin.

"It's his private property, Camellia." Aunt Magnolia sipped her tea, one fine red eyebrow arching. "He can do as he pleases. Besides, it sounds like the city council is on board."

Tansy didn't want to think about just how charming he'd been to manage that. *Ugh*. She took one of the still-warm lavender-honey lemon poppy seed muffins and pulled it apart. The scent flooded her nostrils and made her stomach growl. Fluffy and golden, with just the faintest hint of their homegrown lavender-infused honey. She took a bite and moaned. "Oh, yum, Auntie Mags. These are heaven."

"Of course, they are. I made them." Magnolia smiled. "But mostly because it's Granna Hazel's recipe." She winked.

Tansy spread on some of the honey butter she'd made the week before. Over the years, she learned how to balance rich flavors with a smooth-as-silk texture—making all Honey Hill honey butters spread perfectly. She took a bite, moaned again and smiled. "So, so good."

"Why not go talk to him?" Astrid asked.

Tansy almost choked on her muffin. "Me?"

"Yes, you." Astrid shot their aunt a look. "Aunt Camellia can't."

"I can't and I won't. I'm not setting foot on that man's property." Aunt Camellia nodded so vigorously that her reddish-blond curls shook. She crossed her arms over her ample bosom and leaned back against her chair, declaring, "And I won't be responsible for my behavior if *he* ever dared show up here." *He* meaning Dane's ne'er-do-well father, Harald Knudson.

"Dared show up here," Lord Byron repeated, the parrot bobbing up and down on his perch.

Aunt Camellia smiled at the parrot. "What do you have now?" she asked, retrieving the page of newspaper Lord Byron was standing on. The parrot was always taking things and hiding them away, but Aunt Camellia so adored him that he was rarely scolded—much to Aunt Magnolia's disapproval. "Little thief," Aunt Camellia all but cooed, then she fed him a cracker.

"I don't think Harald Knudson would ever think about visiting Honey Hill Farm, Camellia." Aunt Magnolia shrugged. "Which is good because we need to spend our money carefully, not bailing you out of jail. Your bird, however, could use some time locked up." She glared at the parrot. Lord Byron glared right back.

Astrid shrugged. "You have to go, Tansy. I'd only make things ten times worse, and you know it."

"I doubt that," Tansy argued, though she knew what her sister meant. Astrid would go on a long diatribe about the welfare of the bees, how beekeeping was about equity and respect and balance, before she ever addressed the very real, very legitimate concerns this expansion could cause. A whole list of worries that included things like how vehicle exhaust fumes disrupted a bee's scent signals, the necessity of an environmental study done prior to any construction—all to ensure no harm or disruption for the land, animals and bees…

Oh, how she loathed Dane Knudson—now more than ever.

He had to know that clearing or changing his property could cataclysmically alter the hives' pollen source, didn't he? Or that a queen would relocate her hive if she feared they were in danger? Or that bringing in people, people who didn't understand bees or honey or anything about beekeeping, could stress a hive and impact their honey production or have them desert their home? A real beekeeper would carefully consider all of this, plus some, before considering such a…a scheme. Since Dane Knudson proclaimed to be a beekeeper, from a long line of beekeepers, he should know of this. *He should know* better.

"Aunt Magnolia shouldn't go because she intimidates…well, everyone. That's not exactly conducive to conversation." Astrid shrugged, running a hand along Beeswax's orange-striped back. "Sorry, Aunt Mags."

Tansy couldn't help but wonder if Dane Knudson didn't need to be intimidated a little. Or a lot.

"Don't be. I love being intimidating. It's so…so powerful." Aunt Magnolia smiled. "You can do the same, Tansy. Try it, you'll like it. Put that brawny boy in his place."

"Too bad Rosemary isn't here." Astrid sighed. "She'd have the perfect talking points for him, spout off just the right numbers and present it so matter-of-factly that he couldn't argue."

But their genius little sister, Rosemary, was off following her dreams and participating in a truly innovative bee genomics postgrad study in California. *Too far away to call in for backup.*

So apparently, Tansy was it. "Unlike Rosemary, the chances of me remaining matter-of-fact are slight." *Especially when I'm face-to-face with that self-inflated, condescending, ridiculously good-looking, unethical jerk.*

"Tansy, darling, there is absolutely no reason to let him upset you so. Make your concerns known." Aunt Magnolia sipped her tea. "Stay calm and cool. Keep the upper hand."

"She's right, Tansy. He's the same bully he was in high school. Getting under your skin for fun," Astrid reminded her. "But you're older and wiser and you know how he works so he can't get to you anymore." She smiled, sort of. "Just remember what Auntie Mags said. Be intimidating."

"They're right, Tansy, darling." Aunt Camellia patted her hand. "You can do it."

"You can do it," Lord Byron squawked.

Tansy didn't miss the way both her aunts looked at her—Astrid, too. None of them appeared convinced that she could have a productive conversation with their Viking-ish neighbor. And that included herself. *But if I don't talk to Dane, then there's no chance of stopping his idiotic plan.* What choice did she have?

DANE MOVED THE boxes one at a time, checking the labels to make sure they contained the large hex-shaped honey jars they used to bottle Texas Viking Honey before stacking them onto the waiting cart. "Looks right."

"Great." One word and his fifteen-year-old brother had managed to express just how much he resented being here. If Leif had it his way, he'd be in his room right now, playing video games, texting and making plans with the same messed-up kids that'd gotten him suspended three times so far this school year.

Tough luck.

"I want to make sure everything is accounted for this time." Dane stood, hands on his hips, waiting for any indication that his brother was getting the message.

Leif glared at him. "Well, you've got the clipboard. You tell me."

He shook his head, refusing to take the bait. "Here you go." He handed the clipboard to his brother. "This barcode should match the ones on the boxes. And these specs, too." Both things he'd told Leif the last time they'd received a shipment of jars. Had that stopped Leif from signing off on forty boxes of the wrong-sized jars? Nope.

Leif took the clipboard, but continued to glare at Dane. "I get it, okay? I messed up."

"That's not what this is about." *Not entirely.* "This is your business, too. I was sixteen when I started working on the farm. You're almost sixteen now, you're old enough to work part-time and get a feel for the way things are done around here. I have faith in you and, for now, I'm only asking for a couple of hours a week."

"A couple of hours? *For now?*" Leif shook his head. "Whatever. If I got a *real* summer job, I'd get paid. I'm not getting paid for this."

Dane kept his mouth shut. He'd been exactly like Leif at that age. This was when it helped to know how Leif thought. Things like pointing out they had a roof over their head, food to eat and that they didn't want for a thing wouldn't register with Leif. He figured cutting off his little brother's internet or taking away the smartphone Leif had glued in his hand twenty hours a day would get through to him. But *actually* doing those things would make Leif even more insufferable—something Dane couldn't handle. Picking worthwhile battles had become a regular occurrence for Dane. He might not have signed up to parent his little brother, but since their father had decided to take an indefinite leave of absence from the family, it was up to Dane to step up. *And be the one to bear the brunt of Leif's temper—as always.*

Dane had enough issues with their father without bringing Leif into things. Some were legitimate, others weren't. But he didn't have the patience to sort through which was which at the moment. Like it or not, Leif needed to learn about responsibility. As it was, he had none. When the school year ended and summer vacation started, Leif would have plenty of time on his hands. If his brother wasn't occupied and productive, he'd wind up hanging out with the wrong crowd—*again*. Leif might not thank him for it now... *Hell, he might never thank me for it.* Not that it mattered. He wasn't going to give up on his little brother the way their father had given up on...everything? *Not going to happen.*

"*All* of these?" Leif asked, scanning over the paper, flipping the page, then eyeing the boxes stacked around the yard by the barn.

"Yes." Dane had already checked off the order so he knew they were two boxes short. Hopefully, Leif would catch that, too. "Questions?"

"Yeah, like, why are you being such a di—"

"Leif." He sighed, shaking his head. "You can get this done or insult me and go back to whatever it is you do in your room all day." When Leif looked ready to set aside the clipboard, he added, "Minus your Wi-Fi and phone. Your call."

"Seriously? That's not a choice." Leif shot him a final glare, then started matching boxes with the inventory list. "Whatever."

One thing his little brother was teaching him? He wasn't ready for fatherhood.

Dane headed for the barn, found the dolly and pulled it into the yard—ready to load up the boxes Leif marked with a red checkmark. He'd stacked five boxes onto the dolly when his gaze wandered to the main entry, an old truck lumbering slowly through the gate. A truck he knew.

Tansy Hill. Here?

He ran a hand along the back of his neck. Was he really surprised?

He wheeled one load of boxes into the barn, unloaded them quickly and went back for more. He started stacking boxes when the crunch of gravel alerted him to Tansy's arrival.

"Hey," Leif said, shooting a look at Tansy.

Dane nodded and took a deep breath before turning to face his neighbor and what would likely be an interesting and spirited conversation.

"You can't be serious? Like I'd ever go anywhere with you."

One look at Tansy and her razor-sharp words came back to him, just as clear as they'd been all those years ago. He could still hear the laughter in the high school gymnasium and see that smile on her face—that holier-than-thou smirk that immediately put him on the defensive even after all these years. For five seconds, it almost felt like he *was* back at the homecoming pep rally, in the Honey High School gymnasium—holding an old borrowed boom box over his head with the entire school watching while she'd rolled her eyes at him and walked away. An all too familiar clenching twisted his stomach. Instead of continuing this stroll down worst-memories-ever lane, he needed to stop thinking about their awkward, embarrassing past and focus on the here and now.

Easier said than done.

Tansy looked harmless enough in her tan denim overalls, her thick auburn ponytail swinging in time with each step. In all his years, Tansy Hill was the only woman who had ever managed to make a ponytail seem sexy to him. He didn't like admitting it, but she was. Sexy. And pretty, as always. Not that he'd ever say so. Besides, pretty or sexy or not, he knew that look. Tansy was a woman on a mission. The way she all but stomped across the gravel parking lot had him bracing for battle. *Fine by me*. Over the years, he'd learned the best way to disarm the woman was to distract, redirect and irritate. Turned out, it was surprisingly easy for him to do.

"Miss Hill. What a…surprise. You. Coming here." He held his hand out in greeting, turning on the charm. "Nice overalls. Bees, huh?" He asked, nodding at the bee buttons adorning her overalls.

She glanced between him and the buttons, once and again, then said, "Mr. Knudson." She shook his hand, her grip silky soft and surprisingly strong.

"I didn't know they made bee buttons." He upped his grip to match hers. "But you'd know." It wasn't enough that Tansy was a fanatical bee naturalist, all of her clothing had some sort of bee detail—always had. "You still have those rain boots with the bees all over them—?"

"Mr. Knudson." She tried again, her grip tightening as she attempted to steer the conversation. "I was hoping you had a minute to discuss this morning's paper?" She pulled her hand from his.

"Hmm. Hold that thought." He didn't say anything more until he'd finished stacking the rest of the boxes of jars onto the waiting cart while she stood, watching and—likely—fuming. "Good picture of me, don't you think?" he asked, reaching back to straighten his hair. He slid the band loose, combed his fingers through his long hair, then pulled his hair back through the band and into a loose knot.

She paused; her lips parted but nothing came out.

"They wanted me to take a picture shirtless," Dane continued. "I told them no self-respecting beekeeper would ever work with bees in that state of undress. In my experience, that is." He couldn't be sure, but he thought he heard Leif laughing? That's a *rarity*.

"What are you talking about?" Tansy shook her head, her right eye twitching—it had always done that when he was successfully getting to her. "Do you—"

"Regularly make a habit out of posing for pictures with my shirt off? No." He shook his head and crossed his arms over his chest. "It was flattering, though."

Leif was holding the clipboard up in front of his face now.

"I…" She broke off and regrouped. "I wanted to talk about the article."

"Which part?" Dane asked. "We're not quite ready to take reservations for the cabins, yet. Or were you just curious about the plans? It's all still in development but both the city council and the tourism department are enthusiastic about the project so—"

"No." She snapped. They both heard it. Her indrawn breath was on the shaky side but it was enough to take the bite out of her words. Even riled up and feisty, she was something to look at.

Dane *did* like looking at her.

She took a deep breath before she continued. "I'm here to discuss the potential damage this expansion of yours could cause."

"Damage?" Of course, she'd immediately assume the worst of him. *Fine*. He might as well have some fun with it. "I'm only planning on clearing one field. Maybe take down a few trees." He paused, shrugged. "Hopefully."

Her eyes widened. "But—"

"I can't guarantee we can get around paving the road but I'd rather keep it as rustic as possible." He eyed the large open yard blooming with the bee-friendly bluebonnets, pink evening primrose, giant spiderwort and golden columbine. "*Maybe*, we can use river rock— get a nice smooth surface—leading all the way down to the cabins. Cost permitting, we'll use actual river rock, want to source everything local and all that, but I'll make sure they keep things environmentally conscious." He used air quotes around *environmentally conscious*. "Like I said, cost permitting."

On anyone else, her incredulous look would have been amusing. But like it or not, from her, it got his hackles up. "And the pollinators? The flowers? The *habitat*?" Her voice was strained and brittle.

Did she really think he'd be careless with his property and his family name? Yes, he was taking a few risks and changing things and, surprise, surprise, she didn't approve. But this wasn't about Tansy Hill and she didn't have a say in this. *That's what's really getting to her.* "All of these are native flowers—it will be easy enough to plant more somewhere else," he said, beyond irritated that he felt the need to explain himself to her. "Maybe." He might not be a Hill, but the Knudsons had been in the region almost as long as the Hills. From day one, the honeybee had been just as fundamental to their family as it was hers. Who did she think she was, coming onto his property to look down her nose at him? He couldn't resist a final dig. "Cost permitting."

"But…" Her face had gone an alarming shade of red. "The bees." He watched as she drew herself upright and put her hands on her hips. "Those fragile creatures that keep our world balanced? *And* put food on your table?"

"Bees, hmm?" Was she serious? Had she even thought about how this would go? Or had her plan been to show up and insult him? If it was the latter, she was succeeding. "I'm vaguely familiar with them. I might have seen one or two in these parts." He smiled, goading her—and enjoying the way her jaw muscle tightened. "I've no intention of damaging my…" He paused, watching as she leaned forward, waiting for him to finish. "My income stream, Miss Hill, I assure you."

"Is that all that matters?" Her eyes were wide. "That's all this is about? Your *income stream*?"

No. It was about proving to himself that he had something to bring to the table that would benefit Texas Viking Honey and his family—with or without his father's approval. *None of her business.* Besides, it was easier, and more fun, to let her fume and sputter and turn red. "Yes, ma'am."

"But…" At the moment, Tansy Hill resembled a pressure cooker on the verge of blowing off its lid.

Leif ducked behind some boxes but Dane was smiling like a fool. *Bingo.* He'd hit a button all right. *Any second now.*

"Of course, money is all that matters to you." Her voice wobbled.

"Money matters to everyone, Miss Hill. It keeps you fed and clothed…and well stocked in bee buttons." He pointed at her button, shook his head and chuckled. Her wince stirred a flicker of conscience. "Why don't you take a deep breath, Tansy, calm down a little and tell me what has you so upset."

"I am calm." She sucked in a deep breath. "I'm not in the *least* bit upset."

He chuckled again.

Her mossy-green eyes narrowed. "You're not really going to—"

"Mercilessly sacrifice my bees for a dollar?" He

shook his head. "I guess you'll just have to see for yourself. And while I'm enjoying how red and flustered and not in the *least* bit upset you're getting—" he perfectly mimicked her earlier inflection "—I've got things to do. So, let's just cut to the chase. You go find something else to wear with bees on it while I get back to *work*?"

Her eyes went round and, even though he'd thought it impossible, she turned a darker shade of red. "I work twice as hard as you do," she sputtered, visibly shaking.

He shrugged. "I'll take your word for it. It's the neighborly thing to do, after all." This time, he winked. He didn't have the new business plan entirely settled yet, he knew that. But he wasn't going off as half-cocked as she seemed to think. It was on the tip of his tongue to say more—to mention the city was requiring an environmental impact study and that he consult with, and preferably use, a green architect for the cabins. He would. It was a necessary, if costly, expense. An investment he was personally sinking almost half of his 401(k) into. If he was going to make the expansion work for the long-term, and keep the city on board, cutting corners wasn't an option. Not that he'd ever planned to cut corners. Not that she'd believe that. Not that *I care what she believes*. "Thanks for stopping by, Tansy."

Tansy blinked, her complexion splotchy.

Let her go. Don't say or do something you'll regret. But he couldn't help himself. "How's the honey coming along? I've heard rumors Honey Hill Farms has some big new product in the works." He shoved his hands into his pockets, noting the twitch in the corner of her right eye. "You should know, we've got one of the best batches of wildflower honey yet. Added a little something new this year ourselves. Should make for an interesting competition at the Honey Festival this year, don't you think?"

She managed to keep her mouth shut, her jaw clenched tight.

"How about I get you a jar to take back with you?" he asked.

"No, thank you." She ground out her answer.

"Are you sure?"

"I'm sure." She shook her head. "You are a…"

"A generous neighbor?" He paused, enjoying himself. "An entrepreneur?"

Her answer was an angry grunt.

"How about a honey craftsman?" He cocked his head to the side, watching her as he pointed at his shirt. "A marketing genius." His heather gray T-shirt was emblazoned with the Texas Viking Honey logo.

Tansy was staring at his chest now, her lips pressed into a thin white line.

"I can introduce you to my logo person, if you like?" he asked, noting the increasing twitch at the corner of her right eye.

"No." She shook her head, her voice quivering as she managed, "I would *not* like."

"Did I do something to offend you?" He'd been having a hard time holding back laughter but once their eyes locked, he was done for. The mix of incredulity and anger was beyond gratifying. He laughed out loud.

Leif laughed, too, though he was still hiding behind the boxes.

She was fuming. "Stop it." She held her hands up. "Just stop. I'm leaving. I should have known you wouldn't listen to a thing I have to say—even if you should." Her voice was shaking. "You can go find someone else to ridicule." She turned on her booted heel and marched back to her scratched and dented truck, slamming the driver's side so hard it echoed in the quiet of the country.

He waved, still smiling, until her truck disappeared down the road, leaving a trail of dust in its wake.

"That?" Leif emerged from behind the boxes. "That was freaking awesome." He chuckled and went back to checking off boxes, still smiling.

Awesome, huh? Before she'd arrived, he'd been teaching Leif how important the family business was. About respect and responsibility... Then she got here and all that went out the window. "No, it was mean." He sighed. When it came to Tansy, his brain shorted out and his mouth took over. Today was a perfect example of that. "I was mean." Then again, she had come over raring for a fight.

"Whatever." Leif rolled his eyes.

But once the dust died down and no sign of Tansy Hill remained, Leif went back to scowling and sighing and being sullen and Dane went back to work. It was times like this he wished he was still in Dallas, wearing a suit and tie, and wining and dining prospective marketing clients. He'd been on the fast track.

Ancient *history.*

It wasn't the first time he had to do everything on his own—it likely wouldn't be the last. Apparently, it was too much to hope that his father would get invested in this project or that the good people of Honey, Texas, would stop spreading the completely false information his father's most recent ex-wife was happily dispersing to anyone with ears. It was also ridiculous to hope his little brother would give him the slightest break.

Which made it *beyond* ridiculous to think his interfering, holier-than-thou neighbor would ever be willing to give him the benefit of the doubt.

The best way to handle all of this? Succeed. Make Texas Viking Honey & Riverside Cabins so important to the community that no one, not even the great Tansy Hill, could ever ignore or belittle or dismiss him again.

CHAPTER TWO

"IT's TOO BAD you can't train bees." Tansy stood amongst the mesquite trees, surrounded by low buzzing. "Attack bees could be pretty awesome. Assassin bees sound even better."

"Tansy." Astrid's tone was disapproving. "That goes completely against their nature."

"A girl can dream." She stared up into the prickly branches and the bees flying to and fro in the sunlight. "I'm teasing. You know I'm teasing." She breathed deep, letting the energy and light and peace settle her. Spending time with the bees always made her feel grounded.

Normally, a bee swarm wasn't good news. It was up to the beekeeper to monitor the hives and anticipate when things were getting too crowded or when a new queen was coming. That way, they could split the hive—without worrying over a swarm and potentially losing bees. But there was no guarantee. Poppa Tom had told them over and over how bees loved to surprise their keepers. He'd said it was the bees' way of reminding us who was really in charge. Tansy didn't mind. If anything, she appreciated the focus and quiet needed for the two of them to help the bees relocate safely.

"Let me guess, the bees told you they were looking for a new home?" Tansy asked softly, teasing, watching her sister's face through the mesh attached to her wide-brimmed straw hat. Astrid, too, had her bee hat on with her veil down while they set up. But even with two layers of mesh blurring Astrid's features, Tansy recognized her sister's triumphant smile easily enough.

"Of course," Astrid whispered. "You knew the swarm was coming, too. Don't act like you didn't." She kept her voice light and airy—she insisted the bees preferred it that way—and shielded her gaze as she peered up at the swarm buzzing amongst the sprawling lower branches of the mesquite.

"Nope." Tansy placed the empty nuc box beneath the ball of bees. "I guess they like you better." The box would keep the bees safe until they were moved into the brightly painted new hive adjacent to the wildflower fields awash with color.

"Maybe they know you want to turn them into attack bees?" Astrid laughed softly and gripped the branch the bees were attached to, pausing to ask, "Ready?"

"Yes." Tansy stepped back, a stack of old wooden rulers in her hand.

Astrid shook the branch once, causing the lump of bees to undulate and sway. None fell, they were too busy protecting the queen deep inside the swarm. "Come on," Astrid coaxed. "It's only me and Tansy," she crooned, shaking the branch again. "Stubborn, aren't you?"

Tansy shrugged. "It is a beautiful day. Maybe they want to hang out in the sunshine and take a break?" Bees *never* took a break. There were times Tansy felt sorry for the little creatures. As soon as they emerged from the pampered comfort of their hive cell, they went to work. Bees were single-minded and efficient and all about taking care of each other. *A lot like us Bee Girls.* She glanced at her sister.

"Tansy thinks she's hilarious," Astrid faux-whispered to the bees. "We have a beautiful new hive all ready and waiting for you to make lots of babies and fill with lots of pollen and honey." Another shake and a vast portion of the swarm fell into the box. "That's the way."

"You sweet talker, you," Tansy said with a laugh.

Astrid shook the branch a few more times, until only a few dozen bees remained on the branch. Others flew slowly around them, stirring the air with the merry hum of their wings. "There. There she is. The queen." Without her, the bees would leave the box and return to protect their royal highness.

A bee landed on Tansy's veil, giving her an up close look at the bulging tummy. When a beehive was too crowded, the old queen would venture out with half the inhabitants—their guts full of honey to get things started in their new home—while leaving a new queen with the rest. The swarm would find a place to wait, a mass of bees that caused an alarming roar, until a scout had returned with the perfect place to start a new hive. Lucky for these bees, they wouldn't need to search.

"Poor thing looks ready to pop." Tansy bent forward, gently shaking her veil until the bee let go and drifted, sluggish, into the bee-filled box. Tansy knelt and slowly slid one ruler at a time across the top of the nucleus box. "Watch out," she said, gently pushing aside some bees with the ruler and resting it along the box rim. Tansy left a tiny opening between the last ruler and box side and stood. "Good?"

"Very," Astrid said.

Once it was dark and all the bees had returned from scouting new locations, the sisters would come back to tape up the box and move it next to their new hive. In the morning, before the Texas sun was too hot, they'd relocate the bees inside their hive. It wouldn't take long before they made themselves at home—bees didn't believe in wasting time.

"See you later, bees." Tansy waved, hooking arms with Astrid as they walked along the deer trail they'd followed along the edge of the field. "Good work, sister-of-mine."

"You, too, sister-o'-mine." Astrid smiled at Tansy. "They didn't even know we were there."

Tansy wasn't so sure about that, but they'd be happy enough once they were settled in their new hive.

It was Granna Hazel and Poppa Tom that had taught their Bee Girls the importance of interfering as little as possible with their bees.

Don't get in the way of the bees being bees. They know what they're doing, so let them do it, Poppa Tom had said. He'd also been a stickler for respect. *Respect the bees, take care of them, and they'll take care of you,* he used to say. *Treat them wrong and don't be surprised if they sting you right on the nose.* He'd tap them on the nose then, teasing. He'd had a saying for *everything,* some of them so cheesy Granna Hazel would roll her eyes and make them all laugh.

They wandered along awhile before Astrid let go of Tansy, lifted her veil and tucked it on top of her hat. "Feeling better?"

"I feel great. You know me, I love ticking off items on our to-do list." She was a big list-maker. "Not that there's not still plenty to do." There always was. They were always busy—like the bees.

"I mean about this morning. Your visit to you-know-who. I figure that's the reason you were contemplating assassin bees?" Astrid sighed. "I'm sorry it didn't go well."

"How about we enjoy the peace and quiet?" Tansy asked, pulling off her elastic cuffed gloves and tucking them into the back pocket of her tan denim overalls. Which reminded her... "He made fun of my overalls." She draped her veil up and across the brim of her hat.

"What's wrong with them?" Astrid stopped walking and turned to assess her sister's attire. "They're practical and adorable. I love the buttons."

Tansy held out the strap of her overalls out and stared down at the whimsical button and its tiny painted bee. "It *was* the buttons." He'd practically sneered at her buttons. And her boots? He remembered her bee boots? From middle school. A detail she'd forgotten until now. "The bees, in particular."

"He has no sense of fashion." Astrid looped their arms together again and started walking. When Astrid wasn't being the bee whisperer, she helped the aunties run the Hill Honey Boutique on Main Street. The shop was chock-full of all things bee-centric. From apparel to skincare, beekeeping supplies to how-to books, made-to-order quilts from the local Honey Bee Ladies Society to jars and jars of all types of honey, the shop had enough personality and unique wares to bring in a steady income stream to help offset things at the farm. *For now.*

If they didn't win the prize at the Honey Festival, they'd have to sell the farm and move into the cramped space above the shop—after it was thoroughly renovated. Just thinking about it made Tansy's heart ache. *It won't come to that. It won't.*

"Did you tell him those buttons are one of our best-sellers?" Astrid asked. "They are."

"No." Tansy had to smile then, tucking a curl behind her ear. "Are they really?"

"Yes, really." Astrid squeezed her arm. "I can hardly keep them in stock. You are a trendsetter and he's probably just jealous."

"That's me." She glanced at her sister, but Astrid wasn't teasing. Astrid didn't tease—she was too tenderhearted for that.

"I should have gone with you." Astrid looked as apologetic as she sounded.

"Why?" Tansy shook her head. "Then we'd both have been upset." *She* was upset. But Astrid? Seeing how cavalier Dane was about the potential property and habitat destruction…well, her little sister would be *devastated*.

No, it was much better that Tansy had faced that… that…infuriating, patronizing narcissist alone. *Does he not understand he's cutting off his nose to spite his face?* A face he's oh so proud of. She wasn't going to think about the hair flip. *Had that really been necessary?* Yes, it'd showcased his burly arms and his great hair… As lovely as his physique and his hair were, *he* was not lovely. She remembered his "income stream" comment—as if that was his only concern. *Jerk*.

"Were you intimidating?" Astrid asked, laughing.

"No one is as intimidating as Auntie Mags." Tansy laughed, too. "Maybe she can give me lessons?"

Their mother had died not long after Rosemary was born. When their father died years later, Poppa Tom, Granna Hazel and the aunts became their guardians. Neither of their aunts had children of their own but they'd always done their best with Tansy and her sisters. As she got older, Tansy realized how lucky she was to grow up on Honey Hill Farms. This was their father's childhood home. Being here had helped her keep his memory alive.

As children, Tansy and her sisters had been both terrified and in awe of their aunt Magnolia. She'd been stunning—she still was—tall and slender, with dark red hair and intelligent green eyes. But she rarely smiled, was on the aloof side, had a sharp tongue, and preferred to keep family matters private and the rest of the world at arm's length. To this day, there was still an air of mystery about Auntie Mags and, Tansy suspected, a scintillating secret or two.

Auntie Camellia was the exact opposite of Auntie Mags. She was five foot two at most, extra-soft in all the places Mags wasn't, and gave out smiles and hugs often and with great enthusiasm. When they'd been little, Aunt Camellia had been the one to kiss scrapes, make lunches and braid their hair. She had a big heart and was always collecting lost and forgotten things and making room for them—hence the army of cats and dogs and other cast-off animals in need of a home. But, as different as the aunties were, they were best friends.

Just like Tansy and Astrid and Rosemary. Poppa Tom had called them Tansy the Bold, Astrid the Gentle, and Rosemary the Shy. Always looking out for one another. All together, they—the aunties, Tansy and her sisters— made up Poppa Tom's Bee Girls.

I miss you, Rosemary.

They followed the trail, winding up and around until the heady scent of the Spanish lavender fields reached them. Rows and rows of blooming bushes, their tall purple stalks stretching up to the sun amidst the long, thin, gray-blue leaves and spindly stalks. Butterflies and bees flitted to and from the blooms—nature at work.

"There's nothing like springtime on Honey Hill Farms." Tansy drew in a deep breath, letting the soothing lavender flood her nostrils.

"Breathe deep. Like this." Astrid took a slow, deep breath, then exhaled. "Lavender is good for stress. After your morning visit with you-know-who? Maybe you should breathe deeper." She laughed. "Or, lay down in the field and roll in it?"

Tansy chuckled. "I'm not that stressed." As long as she didn't think about Dane. And she wouldn't. *He's taken up too much of my time this morning.* The rest of her day would be Dane-free. She'd focus on the farm, the spring breeze, the glorious day and—always—the bees flitting back and forth between the large clumps of lavender.

Astrid crouched, her hazel eyes narrowed as she studied the bees at work. "It's like a dance. Lovely." One bee paused, buzzing around Astrid before settling on a deep purple blossom. Tansy knew it was impossible but there were times Astrid really did seem to be talking to the bees. *If anyone could talk to the bees, it would be my sister.*

"You keep collecting all the yummy pollen so Tansy and Aunt Camellia can show those Knudsons who's boss and win the Honey Festival," Astrid almost sang the words.

"Yes, please." Tansy marveled over Aunt Camellia's lengthy and determined recipe-tweaking process. She insisted on getting it just right. But their new honey recipe couldn't be just right, it had to be perfect. The culmination of the drought, the cost to recoup their bee-yards and the extreme nosedive in their financial situation had Tansy assisting Aunt Camellia into the wee morning hours more times than she could count. *We have to win.* She watched as the bee moved on to the next bloom. What would her life be like—somewhere else—doing something else? Her heart hurt at the very idea. *We* have *to win.* The pair continued walking.

"Like you said, Tansy, this is our year. Texas Viking Honey won't know what hit them." Astrid sounded so confident Tansy had to smile. "You and Aunt Camellia have worked so hard on this new honey. Honey Hill Farms Blue-Ribbon Honey will win."

The name had been Aunt Mags's idea. She said it gave off confidence while intimidating the competition. Hopefully, the honey would speak for itself.

But then she remembered Dane's smile—his "I know you have a secret" smile. She stopped walking. "Dane knows. About the new honey recipe."

"How?" Astrid shook her head. "He's messing with you, Tansy. Like always." She nudged her sister. "There is *no* way he can know."

Astrid was right, and yet…she couldn't dismiss the possibility that, somehow, Dane had found out about Aunt Camellia's supersecret new honey. He could be underhanded. "Maybe you're right. Okay, no attack bees or assassin bees, but how about spy bees? Didn't they do that in a movie? Attach teeny-tiny cameras to them? We can send them in to keep tabs on Dane—make sure he's baiting me about the honey. It wouldn't be the first time he's lied through his teeth."

"Way less violent, but I think those were ants." Astrid shrugged. "I hate that he still gets to you."

I do, too. Tansy tried to shut off any further thoughts of the Knudsons. This was what he wanted, to get to her. Here she was, surrounded by the things she loved most, worked up over him? Even now, he was winning. *I'm letting him win.* She shook her head. The recipe was safe. Her aunt would win. They'd keep their home, bees and farm. And, somehow, she'd figure out a way to stop this expansion project.

"I've been thinking about Aunt Camellia and Harald Knudson and the jail comment and the bad blood *and* you and Dane." Astrid glanced her way. "What if Aunt Camellia had the same...*experience* with Mr. Knudson?"

"*Say Anything* hadn't been made yet. John Cusack probably hadn't been born. Or he was a baby. Either way, it's not the same," Tansy tried to joke. Once upon a time, *Say Anything* had been her very favorite movie. It helped that it had also been her parents' special date movie. Watching the film, in all its eighties excellence, made her feel connected to them. Teenage Tansy thought the clothes and hair and the dialogue were perfection. John Cusack, aka Lloyd Dobler, made Tansy believe that high school boys could have deep intellectual conversations and fall in love forever. She was putty every time she watched the movie—especially the scene where Lloyd stood outside Diane Court's window blasting *the* song because he had to win her back..."In Your Eyes" by Peter Gabriel. Tansy could sing every word to that song and recite every line in the movie. It had been her go-to film. Her pick-me-up happy place. Now she could barely stand to listen to the song.

Dane had to go and ruin that, too. The Tansy of today knew better. She'd never let Dane close or share something so important with him. But she'd been young and foolish, and Dane had seemed even sweeter and more sincere than her beloved Lloyd Dobler. For ten days, and one incredible kissing session, she'd let herself care about him—never knowing he'd planned to use *Say Anything* in a big, public spectacle to utterly humiliate her. He'd known the movie was special, and why. But that hadn't stopped him from breaking her heart and tainting something precious. That was why she could never forgive him.

"Similar situation." Astrid's voice pulled Tansy back into the present but did nothing to ease the ache in her chest. "I'm fairly certain no one loves that movie more than you and no one has gone to such extremes as he did. At least not in Honey."

"You think one of Harald's friends bet him to ask her out?" Tansy shrugged. "We don't even know when whatever happened happened. Hopefully, Aunt Camellia wouldn't still be this angry over a bet."

Astrid shot her a look. A "you're still this angry" sort of look.

"Fine." Tansy held up her hands. "I'll play along. I guarantee I would never go to jail over Dane Knudson. Aunt Camellia is far calmer than I am, so that can't be it."

"That's a relief." But Astrid didn't look entirely convinced. "So…what happened, then? Something pretty bad if he still upsets Aunt Camellia so much?" They stopped to check on Chicory, the abandoned mini donkey Aunt Camellia had recently rescued. He had become fast friends with Dandelion, their full-size donkey, over the last few weeks. Together, they guarded the herd of dairy goats Aunt Camellia kept. Neither donkey was overly friendly, but they were appreciative of the odd apple or carrot tossed their way. Astrid had come prepared, her pockets filled with both. "Ever since Auntie Mags said it, I'm trying to imagine it." She tossed a carrot toward the waiting animals.

"Like father, like son." But Tansy stopped there. If she kept saying Dane Knudson's name out loud, she might summon him. *We don't want that.* "I'm pretty sure Auntie Mags was joking." She shot her sister a look. "But it's not really our business. We may never know what happened." Growing up, the three sisters had whispered all sorts of fantastical and over-the-top scenarios in the large bedroom they'd shared. At the time, it had all seemed rather exciting and Nancy Drew–like. But now that they were older, they'd understood how painful the topic was to Aunt Camellia. As close as the Bee Girls were, there were some things that simply weren't talked about. Like Aunt Camellia and Harald Knudson. Tansy respected her aunt's right to privacy but it didn't stop her from being curious. "Eat up," she said, tossing the apples into the pen.

"Why do people have to make things so complicated?" Astrid added the last carrot to the pile of treats. "We could all take a lesson from the bees you know."

"Oh?" Tansy waved goodbye to the donkeys and headed toward the house.

"The strongest and most productive hives are the ones where the bees are most in sync," Astrid said, as if it was the most obvious thing in the world. "There's a collective understanding that they're all working for the good of the hive—they're all on the same team."

"If only it were that simple," Tansy murmured. But, if there was a Dane Knudson bee, she was pretty sure

all the worker bees would kick him out of the hive—
and fast. The thought had her smiling all the way back
to the house.

DANE STOPPED THE grocery cart when Leif tossed in a
fifth bag of chips.

"What?" Leif asked, pulling an earbud out.

Dane glanced pointedly at the chips.

"Now I can't get the food I want?" Leif snapped,
grabbing all five bags and shoving them back onto the
shelf with so much force Dane suspected the contents
were more crumbs than chips now.

"I didn't say that." He rolled his head slowly. "How
about two bags?"

"Forget it." Leif put his earbud back in and stalked
down the aisle, almost crashing into another cart as it
rounded the corner.

"Excuse me," Camellia Hill said, with more than a
little sarcasm. It didn't matter that Leif couldn't hear
the woman, the look of reproach on her face said it all.
She'd have likely given Dane the same look if she'd been
present when Tansy had visited Texas Viking Farms
four days ago. The thought was almost enough for him
to regret the way he'd acted... *Almost.*

Leif paused, mumbled something, turned on his heel
and hurried the other way.

I'll bet she got an apology out of him.

Petite or not, Camellia Hill had a presence about her.
Warm, energetic and practical. Dane could still remember how it felt to be showered with praise and love—
or to be on the receiving end of that look. He'd been a
handful of a kid... But he also had good memories of
Camellia Hill, the Hill home, the menagerie of animals

about the place, plus the smell of delicious baked goods and the sound of laughter spilling from the old house's kitchen. In the year following his mother's death, her loss had threatened to consume Dane and his father, until Camellia Hill stepped in. She'd taken Leif in her arms, given Dane a sense of structure and challenged his father to *be* a father. Good times—while they had lasted. But that had been when his father was welcome at Honey Hill Farms—before whatever had happened and, once again, Dane had lost everything. The one time he'd asked his father about it, his father said Camellia Hill had given him an ultimatum: marry her or stop using her for childcare. The older and wiser Dane got, the more certain he was that there was more to the story.

Camellia Hill was a good woman, a pretty woman, and his father had been fond of her. So had Dane. And little Leif? Well, Camellia was the one who got his baby brother to laugh for the first time.

Dane wasn't one to linger over what-ifs but there were times he couldn't help but consider how different things would have been if his father had married Camellia and he and Leif had had the love and guidance they'd instead grown up without.

Now here was Camellia—staring after Leif with a melancholy expression on her face. Maybe she was plagued by what-ifs, too.

Camellia drew in a deep breath, stiffened her posture and headed down the aisle—coming to a hard stop when she saw him. Her hazel eyes went round and she glanced over her shoulder then back at him, frowning.

"Camellia." He nodded, smiling, an odd lump in his throat.

"Dane." She paused, hesitating, shooting another look over her shoulder. "I… We… You—"

"Auntie Camellia," Tansy—of course it was Tansy—said, turning the corner and heading down the aisle, staring at the two bottles she was carrying. "Was it the raw garlic organic fine ground or the raw garlic organic minced?" She looked up then. "You know—" A blink.

"I'd go with the minced." He nodded at the larger jar. "Fresher taste."

"Oh?" Tansy smiled, placing the jar of minced garlic on the shelf. "The raw garlic organic fine ground it is."

Dane chuckled. "Your call. If you want to deprive your taste buds—"

"They are *my* taste buds." She grabbed the wire side of the cart and started pulling it—and Camellia—away.

"Not getting this one?" he asked, pointing at the deserted jar of garlic. "I'll put it back for you, then."

Tansy turned, that little tick at the corner of her right eye giving her away. "I'll take care of it."

"I don't mind." He scooped up the jar.

She held out her hand. "No, you're right. I took it off the shelf. I should put it back."

"You're in a hurry."

"Not really—"

"I just assumed, since you were leaving it here." He gestured at the chip shelf with the jar of minced garlic.

"Give me the garlic." Her fingers flexed. "Please."

I shouldn't be enjoying this so much. It was getting harder not to smile. "I'm headed to the spice aisle next—"

"Oh, Tansy, let the boy put it back." Camellia was glancing between the two of them. "Thank you, Dane." Did he hear laughter in her voice? He wasn't sure. With a shake of her head, Camellia Hill was headed down the aisle, around the corner and out of sight.

Tansy stared at the jar of garlic in his hand.

"You're welcome." He put the jar in his cart and steered around her, whistling cheerfully. As tempting as it was, he didn't look back when he reached the end of the aisle. He was curious, though. Was she cursing him silently or gesturing rudely after him, or had she already moved on and forgotten him? Didn't matter. Instead, he turned and headed toward the spice aisle.

"What's the deal?" Leif said.

Dane did a double take. "Where did you come from?"

"End of the aisle." Leif nodded after Tansy, looking confused. "What's her deal?"

He'd been wondering the same thing for the last decade or so. "She needed garlic advice."

"Really?" Leif ran a hand over his longish blond hair and sighed. "I thought you might be into her."

"Into?" He tried to chuckle but it stuck in his throat. "Nope." He turned down the spice aisle. "No way."

"Yeah. Okay." Leif glanced at him and then pointed at the shelf.

"Thanks." He replaced the garlic and eyed the mostly empty cart. "So, we're living on Fruity O's cereal and beef jerky this week?" By now, he should be better at this. Sitting down and planning out a week's worth of meals wasn't rocket science. With the push to have the event space ready in under three weeks, he couldn't be driving back and forth for takeout, and since Leif couldn't drive yet, that meant less eating out and more cooking. Since his father's post-divorce self-exile at his hunting cottage had just started, Dane and Leif would be on their own for a couple of weeks—if this divorce followed the same pattern as the previous two, that is. Even though he and Leif were pretty low-maintenance, cereal and beef jerky wasn't going to cut it.

With a sigh, he wheeled the cart around to the first aisle. "Let's start here."

Leif mumbled something and trailed along but his focus rarely strayed from his phone. "Getting some beef jerky," he mumbled and walked off before Dane could respond.

Dane headed to the fresh produce aisle and then the butcher counter, hoping he'd feel more inspired. Van Kettner gave Dane a wave from his spot behind the glass-fronted butcher counter.

"How do, Dane. What can I get for you?"

Dane scanned the contents of the case, then shrugged. "Whatever I can throw on the grill without screwing up."

Van chuckled. "Well, now, I'll see what I can find." He opened the case. "How's your father holding up?"

Dane shrugged. "Not so great." Van was a good guy, the sort of guy people talked to. He was like Nicole Svoboda over at the beauty parlor. They both knew everyone else's business but neither were inclined to gossip. *Though Van doesn't have Nicole's brightly colored hair or tattoos.* He tried to picture Van with blue hair instead of silver but couldn't do it.

"Well, I know folks can be mean." Van gave him a long look. "But the truth always comes out."

Dane shook his head. "Which truth are we hoping will come out? So far, I've heard my father has a mistress. That Leif is on drugs. That I'm on drugs. That my father is on drugs. Or Dad's an alcoholic. Or both? Or, my personal favorite, that I slept with my father's now ex-wife." He and his father could take it, but Leif? He was worried about his little brother. Rumors took root and spread quickly in a small town.

"Well, now. I hadn't heard all of that nonsense." Van frowned. "I don't abide by that sort of talk." He rested a hand on the counter. "And spreading it? Why that just makes it ten times worse. As far as I can tell, and you'll pardon me if I'm speaking out of turn here, you're better off without her and her trouble. Causing it and stirring it up."

Dane didn't need to ask which "her" Van was referring to. Kate, his father's most recent ex-wife, had been causing plenty of trouble and hadn't tried to pretend otherwise. Considering he'd been a grade below Kate in school, he'd known exactly who his father was marrying. But all his warnings had fallen on deaf ears—his father had been too blinded by her doting attention and movie-star good looks. *But pretty packaging couldn't make up for rotten insides.* It was one of the sayings Poppa Tom Hill had dispensed, one of many. Dane had never forgotten that one.

Van patted the counter before saying, "Everett Taggert talk to you yet? He was looking for you."

"I haven't seen him." Dane eyed the roast Van was wrapping with concern. Maybe he should have explained how limited his cooking skills were a little more clearly.

"Everett's looking for someone to help out with the Junior Beekeepers Club for a while. And the education booth at the Honey Festival, I think. Lorna Franks..." Van paused. "You know Lorna Franks?"

"I know Lorna." Lorna Franks had been Leif's teacher last year—Dane had many a teacher conference with the woman. He took the white-paper-wrapped roast Van placed on the countertop.

"She's about ready to have that baby and Everett needs coverage until she's back." Van started wrapping up some chicken breasts now. "From the looks of it, Miss Hill is willing to help out but I'm pretty sure Everett'll need all the help he can get—with the festival around the corner and all."

Don't ask. Don't ask. He took the chicken breasts. "Which Miss Hill?"

"Tansy." Van grinned, pointing. "She's a sweet girl, that one."

Sweet? Not the first word that springs to mind for Tansy. Dane glanced in the direction Van pointed. Sure enough, Tansy and Camellia were caught up in what looked like deep conversation with Everett Taggert, Regional Parks and Recreation manager.

"Those Hills are good people. Helpful and kind, always polite and smiling." There was a wistfulness to Van Kettner's voice that snagged Dane's attention. "That Camellia Hill, especially." Van shook his head. "If I was ten years younger..."

Dane was momentarily stunned by the man's admission. But once he saw the way Van was staring at Camellia Hill, he spoke up. "It'd be a shame to let a woman like Camellia Hill slip through your fingers, Van." He took the next wrapped white package Van handed him—no idea what it contained—and kept on talking, "Before someone else snaps her up." His father was single again... No. His father had blown his chance. Camellia deserved someone who'd treat her with respect and kindness. *Camellia Hill deserves a man who lit up when she walked by...his butcher block.*

But as Van's gaze fell from Camellia, his smile faded some, and he made a dismissive sound. "I'm just talking, now." He murmured. "I don't mean a thing by it. That's what foolish old men like me do."

Dane frowned. Van was many things but old wasn't one of them. Still, Dane's track record with women made him the last one fit for relationship advice so he let it go. "I appreciate the dinner help." He stared at the four packages. "I'm not sure what's what but—"

"Ribs, chicken, a few steaks and a roast," Van paused and patted his shirtfront, his apron, and then turned. "Wait a second." He turned again, searching. "Ah, right. Here." He picked up a neatly typed recipe card. "Recipe for the roast."

Dane took the card and scanned it. "Looks good." He was pretty sure they didn't have a single item on the list. Leif, who'd wandered toward the endcap and stood staring at his phone, would be thrilled to know they weren't done yet. "You have a good week, Van."

"You, too, Dane." The older man nodded. "If you've got the time, maybe talk to Everett, too. You know how important the festival is."

"If you live in Honey, you know." The Honey, Texas, Annual Honey Festival was a huge three-day weekend that brought in big tourism dollars and a whole lot of press. Located smack-dab in the heart of the Texas Hill Country made them a short—short by Texas standards—drive from Austin or San Antonio. And this year, with the soft opening of the Viking-like great hall event room planned, was even more important for him.

"Leif," he called out as his brother returned with a massive bag of jerky. He waved his brother over. "Here, I need you to get these items." He handed off the recipe card to his little brother, waited for the expected sigh, then asked, "Okay?"

Leif's glare and jaw clench were his only answer but he took the recipe card before he walked away—hostility all but rolling off him.

He could wait for Everett to finish talking to Tansy and her aunt. *But what fun would that be?*

The moment Tansy saw him, he was hard-pressed not to grin. The reaction was a long-standing pattern. She'd glare. He'd smile. She'd fume. He'd laugh. It was the way they worked. Oil and water. Make no mistake, Tansy Hill was a know-it-all who seemed to think he was a few bricks shy of a full load *and* had a massive ego. She was wrong but if there was one thing he'd learned early on about Tansy—there was no changing her mind. Since she'd decided to think the worst of him, he'd decided to have some fun with it.

"Dane." Everett was all smiles as he extended his hand. "I was planning on calling you this evening."

"Van said you might be looking for me." He shook Everett's hand. "He gave me a rundown. How can I help?" He bestowed one of his most charming smiles on Tansy and Camellia. "Ladies."

Tansy rolled her eyes.

Camellia glanced down at her shopping list. "That reminds me. I need a pork loin for the Service League meeting this weekend."

Van's day would be made.

"I'll get it," Tansy offered.

"No." The word sort of erupted out of him, making all four of them jump. *Smooth.* His brain was spinning, searching for some sort of logical reason for his star-tling outburst. "If Camellia finishes up with Van, then we can…coordinate efforts. For the Junior Beekeepers meetings? And the festival? Is that right, Everett?"

Everett was giving him an odd look but he nodded.

"Everett, I'll get you that rustic honey cake recipe soon, all right?" Camellia waited for Everett's nod before shooting Dane a hard look. She did the same for Tansy. "You two behave yourselves, won't you?" With a disappointed sigh, she pushed her cart toward the butcher counter.

"I'll email you both the Junior Beekeepers' schedule. It should only be a handful of meetings and one—two—events tops. They're good kids. None of them troublemakers or disrespectful."

Meaning, the kind of kids it would do Leif some good to hang out with. "I'm in."

Dane couldn't help turning then. Camellia stood before the counter, consulting the list in her hand, and Van had a rosy stain on his cheeks.

"Good. They're going to repaint the Welcome to Honey mural on the side of the old Espinoza barn. That's a big one—especially since it's right before the festival. And then their booth at the Honey Festival, plus the end-of-year carnival over at the high school? They'll just need a little adult supervision."

"I'm sure we can handle that. We're both adults, after all." He made a point of eyeing her honeybee earrings and shaking his head.

Tansy's eyes narrowed.

"The Honey Festival won't be too much. A couple of hours? I know you both have booths of your own so I appreciate the help. If you're willing to lend a hand, that'd be appreciated, Dane." Everett stared expectantly at Dane. "So, what did you have in mind? I'll do my best to make sure you have what you need."

"Yes, Dane, what did you have in mind?" Tansy's voice was sharp.

"Oh." The only thing he'd had in mind was giving Van a moment with Camellia. He had absolutely no idea. None. So, he smiled broadly and said, "You go first, Tansy. I'll see if I can build off whatever you're planning on doing."

Everett must have sensed he was floundering because he filled the silence. "So far, I've lined up a few groups that are willing to help out with crafts—what I need are presenters. Tansy, I don't know if you've already done your mandatory community service hours—"

"Tansy Hill…" It was too good an opportunity not to take. "Mandatory community service? What did you do? I didn't see anything in the papers."

Tansy ignored him. "I'd be happy to present, Everett."

"Hold on, now." Dane held his hand out. "If she's in trouble, are you sure it's a good idea for her to be working with kids or having her do the presentation—"

"Dane," Tansy snapped. "If you are trying to—"

"All I'm saying is we need to think about the importance of who presents since they'll act as a sort of role model? For Honey and beekeeping and the festival? That's all I'm trying to say."

Tansy pressed her eyes shut. "Everett, as you can see, it's best if you make sure that whatever roles Texas Viking Honey and Honey Hill Farms play, there's *no* overlap in the schedule." She drew in a deep steadying breath. "At all." She opened her eyes, smiled at Everett and hurried to her aunt's side at the butcher counter.

Everett Taggert ran a hand along the back of his neck. "What just happened?" He shot Dane a disapproving look. "You know I was referring to the community service hours she needs to keep her Master Beekeeper's certification current?"

"I do." Dane nodded.

"Ah." Everett shook his head and frowned. "I keep thinking the two of you are going to make peace. What's that Abraham Lincoln quote? The best way to destroy an enemy is to make him your friend...or something like that."

Dane glanced at the butcher counter. Things had looked promising until Tansy arrived, red-faced and fuming, to interrupt them. He sighed, watching as both Camellia and Van looked his way. *So much for trying to do something good.* For a second, Tansy's gaze met his—all fire and snap and, dammit, sexy as hell. But he and Tansy? Friends? Some wounds never healed. He tried to chuckle but it sounded forced, even to his ears. "That wouldn't be any fun, Everett. Why would I want to go and ruin what we have?"

Everett shook his head and sighed. "You really think you're funny, don't you?"

"You're the one talking about me and Tansy being friends. That makes you the comedian." Not that it was funny. He sighed, shoving all thoughts of Tansy aside. "How's your family? Tell me what groundbreaking things are happening in the goat farming world?"

Everett chuckled then. "Now, that is funny." But it was enough to keep their conversation Tansy-free. Too bad it wasn't enough to keep Dane's gaze from wandering in her direction.

LEIF WAS DONE. Today was sucking, a lot. First Dane dragged him to the grocery store and made him miss an online Valorant match with his team. Now, this. Text after text of total bull-crap. Leif was having a hard time not throwing his phone against the wall—or stomping it to dust. And the texts kept coming. About his family… His brother. What the hell? He locked the phone, pressing his eyes shut.

What is wrong with people? Where do they come up with this sort of BS?

He might not always agree with Dane, but his big brother wasn't a complete ass. Did Dane and their dad fight? Sure. But there was no way Dane would ever do what these texts said. There was no way—no frigging way. Just thinking about Dane and Kate made Leif want to throw up, right here and now. The two of them, together-*together*. That was wrong on so many levels. Wrong. Wrong. *So* wrong.

Dane and Kate hooked up?

Why the hell was Eddie texting that sort of crap? Leif shoved his phone in his back pocket and gripped the grocery cart handle tightly. Eddie was supposed to be his friend. Sort of. The kid was seriously messed up but Jed Dwyer was Eddie's dad so it wasn't like he had a choice. *My dad sucks but…* Jed Dwyer was a whole other level of sucky-ness. Eddie's older brothers, Clay and Donny, were big-time tools with a capital *T. They* were probably the ones making Eddie say all this crap about Dane and his dad and Kate—just to get a rise out of him. Clay was good at making people do what he wanted.

Clay Dwyer was a senior, at least until he got himself kicked out of school, which seemed like a possibility. He'd spent most of the year beating the crap out of every boy in school. Clay couldn't take on his old man, not yet anyway, so any boy unlucky enough to cross his path on a bad day wound up bearing the brunt of Clay's fury. Leif was pretty sure that Clay only had bad days. From the way Clay had been singling him out, Leif figured he was Clay's next target.

His phone vibrated with a text alert, but Leif ignored it. He didn't want to know. *Screw* all of them.

He took a deep breath, but it didn't help the weight crushing in on his chest. Sometimes it felt like the world was closing in on him. Like he couldn't breathe or think without second-guessing himself. Plus, someone was always watching and judging. And talking. That was all everyone seemed to do around here, talk about other people's business. *Lie, is more like it.*

He glanced at his big brother, who was looking back and forth between the bunches of leafy green lettuce-stuff he held in each hand. Dane didn't know a thing about vegetables and he was far from perfect but he'd never sleep with Kate. He was too busy trying to fill in for their dad and do the whole role model thing or coming up with ways to shake things up on the farm. Which was stupid. *They raised bees. It wasn't exactly rocket science.* Dane seemed to think his every idea or word was golden but Leif was pretty sure his brother just liked to hear himself talk. A lot. *All the frigging time.*

But all the talking *did* make Dane quick with kick-ass comebacks. Dane could derail one of their father's tirades with a few sentences. Their father would puff up, stutter, go red in the face and explode before storming off. Leif had to give it to his brother, he knew how to set a person off.

Kind of like the effect Dane had on Tansy Hill. Leif got the whole pissing off their dad thing but he didn't get pissing off Tansy. She was cute. Single. A beekeeper. His brother's personal life was nonexistent, so why was Dane chasing off the one woman he actually noticed? *Dumbass*.

Not that he cared. He didn't. His brother and his father were both gigantic pains in his rear. At least, when his dad was married, he left Leif alone. Dane never left him alone. Ever. He was always home, always—Leif was having to get creative when he snuck out at night.

Dane thought he was being all noble, saying crap like how he'd never give up on Leif. But Leif wasn't an idiot. People left. They always did. Dane would give up on him and he'd leave. Leif figured he might as well hurry along the process by making Dane's life hell and save them both some time.

He watched Dane put down one bunch of lettuce, pause, then trade it out—looking more uncertain than ever. Some role model. *Dumbass*.

CHAPTER THREE

"I JUST CAN'T wrap my mind around it." Aunt Camellia looked sincerely perplexed.

"All marketing, Aunt Camellia." Tansy smiled, popping the perfect palm-size bee-, honeycomb- and flower-shaped soaps from the silicon mold and onto a waiting pan. Each soap's smooth surface had a milky, pearlescent quality that was as pleasing to look at as the soap was to use.

"Sensual Honey Tea." Aunt Mags's eyebrows rose on her forehead—but she was smiling. "Whoever heard of such a thing?"

"The supplier said it was quite popular." Aunt Camellia put the pamphlet facedown on the countertop. "She thought we'd want to sell it in the shop." Her nose wrinkled in distaste.

"Of course, she did." Tansy took the brochure from her aunt. "Goodness." The image of a woman submerged in an oil-and-milk bath was…eye-catching. "It's her job to sell you so you'll sell her product. They're trying to make tea sexy." The tagline, "Awaken Your Sensual Side with the Sweetness of Milk and Honey," had Tansy smiling. There was a bulleted list of all the health benefits the tea provided. She paused on the last one. "Is womb wellness a thing?"

Astrid made a choking-laughing sound. "What? Really?"

"Well, I never." Aunt Camellia snatched the brochure away. "Here, Lord Byron. You don't have to steal this one. You can have it."

"You can have it," Lord Byron repeated, but made no move to take the brochure.

"See, even he knows it's nonsense." Aunt Mags laughed. "Here I thought you were a dumb bird."

Lord Byron squawked.

"Don't listen to her, sweet boy," Aunt Camellia crooned. "She's still angry that you stole her hairpins."

"I'll dispose of it," Astrid offered, taking the brochure.

"How do these look?" Tansy asked, holding out the tray of soap for inspection. She knew the missing hairpins was still a sore subject for Auntie Mags. Unlike Aunt Camellia, Auntie Mags wasn't an animal person. Then again, Auntie Mags was barely a *people* person.

"They're lovely," Astrid chimed in, nodding at the tray. "And they smell divine."

Aunt Camellia swore the fresh goat's milk made all the difference. Whatever it was, it was the only soap Tansy used. Not the fancy molded ones of course—those were merchandise. Once, when Aunt Camellia had pneumonia, they'd run out of soap and they'd been forced to use store-bought. Never again. The sisters had stayed up all weekend making batch after batch of soap, following Aunt Camellia's recipe to the letter. Of course, Aunt Camellia's always turned out better than anything they could make. Rosemary was convinced Camellia put a secret ingredient into the mixture when they weren't looking. Astrid defended their aunt, saying her years of practice had given her process a finish they had yet to master. Tansy suspected both of her sisters were right.

"Aunt Camellia?" Tansy asked, standing aside for Aunt Camellia's inspection.

Camellia Hill took her reputation for making moisture-rich honey-infused soap seriously. It followed that if a Honey Hill Farms embossed ribbon was on the soap, the soap had to meet her aunt's exacting standards. Standards that had been set and passed down from generation to generation—in the Hill Bee Log. The Bee Log was full of anecdotes and observations, gains and losses, farming techniques they'd used for over one hundred years, gardening and beekeeping secrets, and all the honey recipes the Hills lived and breathed by—and kept well guarded. Over the years, Poppa Tom's Bee Girls had referred to the Bee Log often and done the best they could to hold on to their family philosophy.

Aunt Camellia leaned forward to peer over Tansy's shoulder. "Perfect. And I like the new flower molds, too. Those details are lovely."

"Hopefully the shoppers will think so, too." Today she, Astrid and Nicole Svoboda—their part-time help—were taking the Honey Hill Farms van, chock-full of inventory, to San Antonio.

Behind her, the kitchen table was piled high with several stacks of packaged homemade Honey Hill Farms soap. This batch was all that was left.

Tansy surveyed the table. "I'd say we're good for the day." The farmer's market at the wildly trendy Pearl Brewery in San Antonio might be a drive, but they always came out ahead financially. Normally they sold out before noon. But this time, they'd pulled a near all-nighter and doubled their inventory. The lotions, candles, honey and honey butters were already packed up and ready to go.

"Even so, I bet we'll sell out." Nicole had arrived long before sunup with fresh doughnuts and pastries for their drive. "I love the smell of lavender." She breathed deeply, tucking a strand of bright pink hair up and into her sloppy bun. Nicole was all about self-expression. She said changing up her hair color or adding a new tattoo was part of her journey of self-discovery. It didn't hurt that the hair and tattoos really irritated her very traditional, very opinionated, very gossipy mother. She stretched, the tiger tattoo on the inside of her left arm stretching, too. "It's so soothing I could curl up right here and take a nap."

It was true. Lavender was one of the key ingredients in their best-selling soaps. The batches of lavender-honey and lemon, which had lemon zest on the surface, and the ever-popular lavender-honey and rosemary, with bits of fresh lavender and rosemary swirled in, were cut into tidy bars. The classic lavender-honey soap and the extra mild goat's milk and honey soap—which Tansy was currently packaging—were poured into molds, and sold in packs of three.

Amidst the cellophane wrap, wide-width Honey Hill Farms embossed ribbons, and rolls of biodegradable Honey Hill Farms stickers, Nicole kept up a steady stream of chatter. During the week, Nicole helped her mother out at Honey Hair on Main, the only beauty shop in town, which meant she had the inside scoop on anyone and anything happening in their community.

"You'll never guess what I heard about Silas and

Libby Baldwin," Nicole was saying, carefully stacking the soaps into a plastic tub.

"What?" Aunt Camellia turned. "They've been married, what, almost two years? Are they expecting?"

"Divorcing is more like it," Nicole said. "Poor Silas had the papers served to him yesterday while he was working at the bank. He's heartbroken."

Tansy and Astrid exchanged a knowing look. Libby had been a mean girl in high school—a mean girl who'd regularly targeted their little sister, Rosemary. Silas was a nice guy, too nice for someone like Libby. Still, Tansy hoped they'd both emerge relatively unscathed.

"Speaking of divorces." Nicole unwound more ribbon, then paused. "Libby's sister, Kate. And Harald Knudson."

"It's official? I'd heard rumors but…" Auntie Mags shuddered. "The man is monstrous but this last one seemed equally delightful so it appeared to be a match made in heaven." For all her indifference, she was studying Camellia with concern.

"She talked him into that fancy vacation house on the coast and that sports car, and now she's getting them both in the divorce." Nicole wrapped the ribbon around her finger and sighed. "She and Libby stopped at the salon on their way out of town to celebrate their freedom."

"How…classy." There was no missing Auntie Mags's sarcasm.

Nicole's voice lowered as she leaned forward. "You know I don't spill clients' secrets—"

Tansy was relieved to see she wasn't the only one that had set everything aside to listen to Nicole. She hated that she was this curious.

"Kate didn't paint a pretty picture about the Knudsons' homelife, let me put it that way. She mentioned all the trouble Leif's been in, suspended from school and all. And he's hanging out with those Dwyer boys." Nicole said "Dwyer boys" with outright disapproval. They were synonymous with trouble. From shoplifting to causing fights to selling marijuana. And while Nicole's mother, Willadeene Svoboda, had never been able to prove it, she blamed the Dwyer boys for the rock chucked through her salon's plate glass window. Tansy couldn't help but notice the timing of the incident. Willadeene, the worst gossip in the county, had made some unkind comments about the boys' mother taking off and then, two days later, the beauty salon's window was shattered. It'd cost an arm and a leg to replace.

Poor Leif. Tansy thought about the floppy-haired teenager she'd brushed past in the grocery store, his eyes glued to his phone. Being a teenager was hard enough. Being a teenager with Dane and Harald to guide him?

"Kate sort of hinted around about Harald, too. Drinking too much and getting into a temper and yelling at everyone." She shrugged.

Tansy glanced at her aunts. Auntie Mags remained aloof but Aunt Camellia looked angry.

"Kate even hinted that, maybe, she and Dane...you know." Nicole made a gagging sound. "Mom had a field day with that one."

Tansy's stomach clenched. What? And Willadeene Svoboda heard about this? This was bad.

"Kate and Dane?" Aunt Camellia asked. "What about them? Didn't they go to high school together?" She frowned.

"Kate was a year ahead of Tansy and Dane. Libby was in my class." Astrid shook her head. "You're not saying…"

"*I'm* not saying it. Kate is. To my mom. So, we all know how that's going to go." Nicole held up both her hands. "It caught—and spread—like wildfire."

Tansy was certain, of all the people on earth who disliked Dane Knudson, she was top on that list. But even she was having a hard time believing this. Yes, Kate Owens was beautiful and, probably, tempting, but she'd been married to Dane's *father*. She swallowed. Dane was a self-absorbed, attention-seeking, pretentious ass, no arguing that. But this? If this was true, it was unforgivable—and straight-up diabolical.

Aunt Camellia crossed her arms over her ample bosom, her cheeks going deep red. "You're telling me that Kate Owens is telling everyone Dane and she had a…a…dalliance?" She snorted. "She's a piece of work, isn't she?"

"Yes, ma'am." Nicole chewed on the end of a strand of bright pink hair. "Just awful. And my mother is no better."

"Those Owens girls just love stirring things up." Aunt Mags glanced at Astrid, then Tansy. "Libby was the one that made high school so unbearable for little Rosemary, wasn't she?"

Tansy nodded. Kate and Libby could be pictured in the dictionary next to the term *mean girl*.

Astrid spoke softly, giving Tansy an apologetic look. "Not to defend Dane here, but I have a hard time believing even he'd stoop this low."

Aunt Camellia shook her head. "He most certainly would not."

Tansy was surprised by how vehemently her aunt jumped to Dane's defense. Then again, Aunt Camellia always championed the underdog. Instead of saying something that might upset her aunt even more, she went neutral and said, "It sounds like Dane and Harald need to be spending less time trying to make money and more time repairing their family." But she had to add, "Leif is the one I'd worry about. That kind of talk? True or not? No one wants their family slandered that way."

"Believe me, I know." Nicole and her mother did not get along. They probably only saw each other because their grandmother had left the beauty salon to them as equal partners. Not long after her grandmother's passing, Willadeene had let everyone know how her mother and daughter had teamed up to rob her of her inheritance. It forever put a wedge between Nicole and her mother.

"It is shameful to know this is what people are talking about." Aunt Mags shook her head. "But this wouldn't be the first shameful thing associated with the Knudson family name. It likely won't be the last."

Tansy had to laugh. "Wow, Auntie Mags, tell us how you really feel."

That broke the tension. Even Astrid was giggling.

"I'm only saying what we're all thinking." Auntie Mags was smiling. "Now, you girls need to get on the road if you're going to get set up before nine."

"We'll do our best," Astrid said. "But it won't be the same without you, Aunt Camellia. You're the one with all the answers. And people love you."

"You be your charming self and you'll be just fine. Don't forget the honey ham stuffed biscuits I made for your lunch." Aunt Camellia handed her the plastic container full of biscuits and patted Astrid's cheek. "Dr. Abraham is giving me the whole morning."

"He's not giving you a thing," Auntie Mags argued. "It's not like he's coming to *give* your menagerie of animals their health checks for free. You do pay the man for his veterinary services. And well, I might add."

Aunt Camellia started her defense of her animals with the dogs—listing off an endearing trait for her one-eyed Chihuahua, Butters; Oatmeal the Saint Bernard; the shaggy mutt, Pudding; and the super-hyper red-and-white-patched pups, Ginger and Pepper. Before she moved on to the cats or livestock, Tansy called out a goodbye. She carried the tub of soap out to the waiting van, loaded it, then closed and locked the back doors. Nicole followed with the box of breakfast pastries and climbed in the back seat. Astrid pulled the back door around, the sound of the aunties' voices muffled, and shook her head.

"Still at it?" Tansy asked.

"Of course." Astrid giggled. "Poor Dr. Abraham."

It was a little after seven when they arrived, and parking was already a challenge. Then came the least fun part of the day: setup. Three women, three carts stacked high, rattling down the paver-lined walkway toward their designated canopy. Tansy led, the rattle of glass honey jars faint amidst the commotion of several hundred vendors setting up. It was a solid hour before the farmer's market opened, but the grounds were already packed. Nicole was right, they'd sell out in no time.

But her gaze caught, and held, on the booth directly opposite theirs. Texas Viking Honey's black-and-gold logo was impossible to miss. *Seriously?* She sighed.

Maybe he wouldn't be here. Maybe. Hopefully they'd sell out. *And fast.*

"Viking Knudson is looking exceptionally Viking-y this morning," Nicole said.

Of course, he's here. Tansy didn't look. If she ignored him, he couldn't ruin her day.

"Beekeeper by day. Weight lifter by night?" Nicole sighed. "I know we're not Knudson fans but it's sort of hard not to appreciate that view."

"He is handsome," Astrid murmured.

"And he knows it," Tansy reminded them—even as her gaze wandered to the Texas Viking Honey canopy. *Oh...dear.* He was looking *exceptionally* manly. And rather, well, Viking-like. His long blond hair was down, the sides pulled back and into a braid. But it wasn't the hair. It was the shirt. Rather, the *chest* stretching the shirt to its limits. "Should we keep an eye on him? Make sure he doesn't fall over from blood loss?"

Nicole was all but drooling. "Blood loss?"

"The shirt." Tansy nodded. "It's tight. Like cut-off-the-circulation tight."

Astrid frowned, eyeing Dane Knudson's especially impressive biceps. "Can that happen?"

"Maybe we'll find out today." Tansy allowed herself one minute to look at him. All of him. The shirt was a little—okay, a lot—tight. People would notice. That was the whole point. "He's just doing what he always does." She began unloading the carefully packed wooden crate—arranging each Honey Hill jar with care.

"Mesmerize shoppers with his Thor-like physique, glorious hair and pale blue eyes?" Astrid asked.

"Yes." Dane's ridiculous good looks were definitely a draw on days like today. The Pearl district was already a hot spot. Add this morning's city of tents and canopies full of produce, crafts, homemade and cottage-industry goods, and Texas Viking Honey—with Dane Knudson in his skintight Texas Viking Honey shirt—would have a long line. "Exactly."

"Is that his little brother? I haven't seen him in a while," Astrid asked, her brows high. "He looks like a mini-Dane."

"Poor kid." Even from here, Tansy could see how not-thrilled mini-Dane was to be here.

"Poor kid? I don't know about that." Nicole twirled a strand of hair around her finger. "From what Benji says, Leif more than looks like his big brother. He's just as insufferable as Dane was in high school, too." Benji was Nicole's teen son—who she'd had when she was barely a teen herself. They were super close and Nicole was prone to go all momma bear if she felt like her boy needed protecting. Benji was sweet, shy and awkward, the kind of kid mini-Dane would probably badger relentlessly.

"My vote?" Tansy turned her back on the Texas Viking Honey canopy and the Viking manning the tent. "Let's pretend they're not here—at all. Let's enjoy the day and sell things and have fun. Okay?"

Astrid worked her magic with the display, making everything look its best. They assembled the wooden beehive display, separating the jars onto shelves of wild-flower honey, cream-honey, home-churned honey butter, and mesquite honey. Astrid stood back and nodded with satisfaction. "That should catch the eye."

"And if the honey doesn't, you will," Nicole laughed. "Seriously, a guy just tripped over his own feet staring at you."

Tansy smiled. It was true. Dane Knudson might be an added draw for Texas Viking Honey but Astrid was just as attractive—in a sweet, non-cocky, welcoming sort of way. And unlike Dane, her sister had no idea how lovely she was. Astrid didn't need to resort to wearing skintight shirts for attention.

DANE HAD TO ADMIT, Tansy Hill was quite the salesperson. It was all in the smile. He'd never seen that smile directed his way. It was…distracting.

"Dane." Leif elbowed him. "They have questions."

They turned out to be a group of teens waiting for Dane's attention. "What can I help you with?"

"Can we get a selfie with you?" one of the girls asked.

Another one giggled, then said, "You totally look like the guy that plays Thor."

So I've heard. He smiled. It wasn't the first selfie request he'd received, not that he was complaining. The more selfies of him in a Texas Viking Honey & Riverside Cabins shirt out there, the better. "How can I refuse?"

All four of them giggled, making Leif groan—the patience limit for any teenage boy long exceeded. "Are you buying honey?" Leif asked.

The third girl reached for a jar of honey. "I'm totally buying some." She paused, smiling at Leif. "Which is your favorite?"

Dane watched his brother turn a dark shade of red. He waited, holding his breath, but Leif didn't say a word. Instead, his brother reached for a jar of clover honey and handed it to the girl.

"I'll take two of these." The girl said, still smiling at Leif. "Please."

Leif was staring, quiet and red-faced, at the girl. "'Kay." He grabbed another jar and sat it on the table in front of her. The long, lingering staring session between the two became increasingly awkward for Dane and the girls waiting for their selfie. But Leif and the girl were completely clueless.

It was sort of cute.

But when a line started to form behind the girl, it lost all cuteness.

"Okay, so let's take that picture," Dane said, smiling up at the camera, making change for the girl still moony-eyed over Leif, then steering his brother aside so the teen-hormone-fueled staring thing could continue while Dane conducted business.

Now was the time to really promo the event space and build interest. These were the people who would drive an hour for a unique experience with loads of ambience. That was what he was selling—an experience. He'd been hammering out the details on potential partners and distributors. One was a honey mead and whiskey vendor. His glossy brochures invited guests to "Come drink like a Viking. Enjoy honey mead and whiskey in a Viking hall." And, with luck and a substantial markup, people would buy a few bottles to take home.

As the sun moved across the sky, Dane handed out glossy pamphlets, sold honey and posed for far too many pictures.

"You should come dressed as Thor next time." Leif sat in the lawn chair sideways, his long legs draped over the arm.

"Why?" Dane asked, counting the remaining jars as he packed them away for the drive back.

"Did you not hear them? All of them?" Leif rolled his eyes. "How you look like Thor?"

"Does he?" The question and the voice were full of familiar disdain. "I don't see it."

Dane turned to Tansy Hill. "You here for a selfie?"

"I came to return your *trash*." She held out a stack of brochures. "Drink like a Viking?" She winced. "Really?"

Leif chuckled.

"I work with what I've got." He crossed his arms over his chest—noting her reaction as he did. She noticed. A lot. *Interesting.* Those mossy-green eyes of hers were currently glued to his torso.

And even more interesting? That she had no pithy comeback. Nope. Not a word.

"You feeling okay?" he asked, unable to help himself.

"I'm fine." She smoothed the wisps of hair sliding free of her ponytail as her gaze fell from his chest to the pamphlets in her hand. "Why?" There it was. The fight, sparking in her eyes.

"You just seem a little…dazed. Staring like that." He smiled. "Distracted?"

"What? No. I wasn't staring." The words were rushed, almost alarmed. She swallowed, hard, her gaze falling to the box he was packing. "You have honey left?"

"Just a few bottles." He smiled.

"Mighty Thor didn't sell out?" She laughed. "See what I did there? The double entendre?"

"Genius." He chuckled.

"Here." She held the pamphlets out. "It looks like you sunk a lot of money into printing these—it would be a shame to see them discarded and blowing all over the place."

His fingers brushed along the edge of her hand before clasping the stack of pamphlets. He jerked away but the unnerving hum, the slightest vibration, lingered on his fingertips. "Nice to know you care."

"I don't." She rubbed her palm along her thigh—the same palm he'd touched. "I do care about trash blowing all over." She shoved her hands into the pockets of her jeans, her shirtfront quivering with indignation. The quiver caught his attention, taking any sting out of her saying, "Believe it or not, everything isn't about you."

"I like your bee." He eyed the bee brooch pinned right over her heart. The pin was very definitely quivering. "It almost looks like it's buzzing, Tansy Hill. Did I get you all worked up? Is that what you're feeling? Because of me?"

She glared up at him, her lips pressed tight until the words spilled out. "If your little brother wasn't sitting right there, I'd tell you exactly how you make me feel, once and for all."

Dane had no doubt she had plenty to say. And that it would be interesting. "Go ahead. He's probably wearing earbuds—"

"I'm not," Leif interrupted.

"He's not listening." Dane sighed.

"I am," Leif argued.

"You're listening?" Dane faced his brother. "Now? After not listening all day long?"

"This is interesting." Leif shrugged.

"Interesting?" Dane considered the word as he turned back to Tansy.

But Tansy was walking away, back to her neatly packed carts and her waiting sister.

"She gets to you," Leif said.

"No." Dane went back to packing up, deciding to do a count when they got home. "I get to her."

"Whatever." Leif shook his head. "You don't think she's pretty? I mean, the bee thing is weird but she's still pretty."

"She is," Dane agreed. The bee thing was…Tansy. She'd always worn bees. Always. He couldn't remember a time when she hadn't had a bee somewhere on her person. Hair clips or socks. Shoes or backpacks. She'd taken her grandfather's Bee Girl label to heart. "She's also a pain in the ass."

Leif helped pack up the rest, eager to get on the road. He even helped carry the folding chairs—so they didn't have to make two trips. But once the truck was loaded up and ready to go, the engine wouldn't turn over. No click. No chug. No nothing.

"Great." Leif rested his head on the back of the headrest and closed his eyes. "Just great."

"You have a hot date or something?" Dane asked, popping the hood, sliding out of the truck cab, and peering into the engine compartment. He pulled the band from his pocket, twisted his hair into a tight knot and secured it before bending in to take a closer look.

His father had said he'd had the alternator replaced. He'd said it…but that didn't mean he'd done it.

He walked back to the open driver's side window. "Did Dad get the truck repaired?"

Leif shot him a look. "I would know that *why*?"

Their father only told them what he wanted to tell them—whether or not what he told them was true was another matter altogether. "Point taken." Dane sighed, propping his forearms on the window and leaning forward.

The parking lot was emptying, cars and trucks and motorcycles all passing without pausing to offer help. Until the pale yellow Honey Hill Farms van pulled along beside them.

"My sister is making me stop." Tansy Hill didn't look at him. She stared straight out the window. "My sister also wants me to ask if you need a ride home."

What he needed was a ride to an auto-parts shop but it was getting late and it'd be a struggle to see anything—let alone fix the alternator—without good lighting. No, he and Leif could come back tomorrow and take care of things then.

He studied Tansy's profile. "If you're sure it's no trouble?"

"I didn't say that." She sighed. "Let's get this over with." This was killing her, he could tell.

"You heard the lady," he said to Leif.

Leif rolled his eyes, taking his sweet time as he climbed out of the truck and slammed the door. Once Dane had the windows rolled up and the doors locked, he opened the back door of the van.

"Nicole." Dane smiled. "How's your day?"

"Better than yours." She shrugged and clutched her knitting needles and blue-green yarn to her chest.

"Wasn't your hair green last I saw you?"

"Yeah—last month." She smiled, waited for them to climb in and pulled the sliding door shut behind them.

He and Leif sat on the third-row bench seat, the tinny

crackle of the rear speaker reverberating with the strum of a mandolin. "What radio station are we listening to?" he asked his brother, moving aside a mostly empty box.

Leif didn't acknowledge him or his question.

He poked his brother—who pulled out an earbud. "*Now* you're listening to your earbuds."

Leif glared, plugged his earbud back in, and went back to staring out the window.

"What are we listening to?" Dane asked, louder this time.

"Whatever the driver wants to listen to," Tansy answered.

"Message received." He held up his hands, the bright beam of a passing truck illuminating the contents of the box at Dane's side. Namely, a glossy-slick brochure with a smiling woman in a bathtub on the cover.

Sensual Honey Tea? He glanced at the rearview mirror, feeling like a kid with his hand in the cookie jar as he skimmed the flyer's bulleted list of benefits of this "all organic and sensually rejuvenating" natural beverage.

This was definitely not a standard Honey Hill Farms sort of product. This was how they were thinking of branching out? With sensual tea?

Dane sat back, smiling. As tempting as it was to tease Tansy Hill about Sensual Honey Tea the whole seventy-odd miles back to Honey, there was the distinct possibility he'd wind up walking home the moment he tried it. It might be worth it.

But Leif wouldn't think so. And Leif was the one he had to live with so… Instead, he'd sit back, smile whenever she dared look in the rearview mirror and—since there was no other option available—keep the peace. For now. But next time they met, he and Tansy were going to have an in-depth and, hopefully, painfully detailed conversation about the Hill family's potential venture into sensual health. Maybe he should bring Leif along. The kid didn't laugh enough and that conversation was guaranteed to bring laughter. Well, he'd be laughing anyway. Tansy? Not so much.

CHAPTER FOUR

The drive from San Antonio back to Honey took at least four months, or that was how it felt to Tansy. Almost everyone else had fallen asleep, so she was left alone with her thoughts and Dane's smiling eyes each and every time she glanced in the rearview mirror. He didn't fall asleep. No, he sat in the very middle of the back seat, directly in her line of sight, with Leif slumped into his side and resting his head against Dane's broad shoulder. For a moment, she almost thought it was sweet. Until he opened his mouth.

"I'm surprised." Dane's gaze locked with hers. "You've got me cornered with no way out. I was expecting another anti-expansion lecture."

Tansy bit into her lower lip. She had half a mind to give him what he wanted. After an hour, maybe she'd wear him down a little. *Right*. She almost snorted. He'd never listen. String her along? *Yes*. Test her patience with snide comments? *Absolutely*. But listen? "I'm driving."

"Ah, right. Not great at multitasking?" He nodded. "Good to know."

Her fingers tightened around the steering wheel. *Don't say a word*. She swallowed. *Not one word*.

"I guess now isn't the time to talk about the Junior

Beekeepers meeting, either?" He barely paused. "Right, right. It can wait."

She pressed her lips together. Today had been a good day—Dane Knudson aside. She didn't want to end it on a low note. Otherwise she'd give in and pelt Dane with so many years' worth of verbal artillery that she'd wake everyone up and make the rest of the drive miserable. She managed to sound calm as she said, "I can't look at my phone and check my calendar—since I'm *driving* at the moment." She paused, adding, "But, as I told Everett, I can handle it on my own. There's no need for you to have to be there, too."

Dane was silent for a few seconds. "Leif wants to join."

Tansy didn't buy it. "You can drop him off, like all the other parents and guardians. No need to stick around."

"Maybe."

That was it—then silence. She kept waiting, her gaze darting to his reflection, thinking he'd say something more. After the fourth intercepted glance, Tansy gave up and vowed not to use the rearview mirror again. She had two perfectly good side mirrors, she'd make do. It was only ninety miles. How hard would it be to pretend he wasn't there? *Not hard at all.*

But rain started and a rapid succession of brake lights set Tansy's nerves on edge. Driving at night was always *fun*, add in the morons that insisted on going well over the seventy-five-mile-an-hour speed limit or the dare-devils that liked to weave in and out of traffic and the increasing deluge and her grip went white-knuckled.

"Looks like we're in for rain the whole way." Even whispering, Dane's voice carried in the quiet of the van.

Tansy turned her windshield wipers to high and edged into the right lane so the sports car coming up behind her could speed by. It did, without slowing a bit.

"Dumbass," Dane mumbled. "That's how you get into an accident."

Tansy didn't argue. First, she one hundred percent agreed with him—something she'd never admit to. Second, the rain was making it hard to see five feet in front of her. And lastly, she was too tense to say anything. By the time the rain slowed and they reached the sign that read "Welcome to Honey, the Sweetest Place in Texas," Tansy was all raw nerves and knots.

She'd never been so happy to drive under the ostentatious Texas Viking Honey archway. Now that the clouds had parted, the smooth white limestone and clay walls of the Knudson homestead stood out, almost glowing, in the light of the low-hanging full moon. The homestead was fashioned after some ancient Knudson kin's manor house in Denmark. Poppa Tom had admired the original Knudson settlers' efforts, often mentioning the true craftsmanship and exacting attention to tradition they'd put into their new home.

With its long dark windows peering out of the stark white facade, the large structure looked…sad. *Probably disappointed in the current Knudsons*. She was grinning when she pulled to a stop.

"Where are we?" Astrid asked around a yawn.

"Dropping off the Knudson brothers." Tansy managed to keep her tone neutral.

"I don't even remember falling asleep." Nicole's arm stretched forward between her and Astrid's seats. "Did we miss anything?"

Tansy shook her head.

"It was quite a ride." Dane sounded very pleased with himself. "Very eventful."

"It rained," Tansy offered up as explanation.

"It was a…a bonding experience." He was smiling, she could hear it in his voice.

Did he think he was funny? *What does that even mean?* Tansy didn't take the bait. She ignored the questioning look of her sister—and the feeling that Nicole, sitting directly behind her, was staring at the back of her head wearing a similarly curious expression—and turned on the dome light overhead.

"Hey, Leif," Dane said softly.

She had no plans to acknowledge Dane's existence *but* that was before he'd sounded like *that*. Loving and gentle. It was so unexpected, so lacking in his normal condescending tone, that Tansy found herself glancing into the rearview mirror.

"We're home," Dane murmured, giving his brother a little pat—and wearing the sweetest smile.

Tansy had seen that smile before but, this time, there was no doubting his sincerity. Dane was a self-absorbed, holier-than-thou ass but he did love his brother. *So, he had one redeeming quality.* One. And it was pretty big. Dane—being patient was heartwarming… She tore her gaze away. While it was tempting to honk and wake up the younger Knudson so she could end this whole ordeal that much quicker, she couldn't. Leif was a kid. A grumpy kid, but a kid. She had no quarrel with him. Waking him up like that would be mean and, no matter what Dane thought, she wasn't mean.

Dane chuckled at his bleary-eyed and groggy brother "Pretty sure you're too big for me to carry inside now."

Tansy did not linger over the adorable image his

words conjured. Dane, all big and strong and full of muscles, carrying his gawky teen brother inside like a sleeping baby. Why was she thinking about his muscles? When had the word *adorable* ever applied to Dane? Since high school anyway? And that was before he'd broken her heart with his public sham of a prom proposal. She sighed. *Enough.* No thoughts of Dane's muscles or smiles or adorableness or…or anything. She sighed again, her grip tightening on the steering wheel.

"Come on, Leif." Dane was sounding far more Dane-like now. "Tansy's getting impatient—she might end up booting us out and backing over us if we don't get a move on."

She glared at his smiling reflection.

"I'm awake," Leif grumbled, rubbing his eyes and yawning. "I'm up."

"Then we should let these ladies get home." Dane leaned forward, opened the van door and stepped out.

"Thanks for the ride." Leif climbed out, yawning and stretching as he headed straight for the door—without a backward glance.

"Yes, thanks for getting us a ride, Astrid." Dane ran a hand over his hair, his shirt pulling tight across his chest. "Pretty sure Leif and I would have been stranded if you hadn't pleaded our case."

"Tansy would have stopped." Astrid, good sister that she was, was quick to defend her.

I might have offered Leif a ride.

Dane chuckled, shooting Tansy an openly incredulous look.

"You're welcome." Tansy used a saccharine sweet tone of voice. "Go ahead and close the door now, Nicole."

"Um…" Nicole hesitated.

"On that note, I'll wish you ladies a lovely evening." His chuckle ended when he rolled the van door shut.

Tansy didn't wait, she pulled forward, turned around and headed back down the drive.

"He's waving," Nicole whispered.

"How nice for him." Tansy almost managed not to look. Almost. But, darn it, she glanced his way at just the right time and wound up making eye contact. *Did he just wink? At me?*

"For real, what did we miss?" Astrid asked.

"We totally missed something." Nicole leaned forward between their two seats.

"No, you didn't." Tansy shook her head. "He's just—"

"Superhot and—"

"*And* the most patronizing and narcissistic man on the face of the planet?" Tansy cut Nicole off, glancing over her shoulder at Nicole. "Yes, he is. You can do so much better."

"I didn't say I'd date him, ever." Nicole snorted. "I know he's the bad boy and I officially got over my bad boy stage about three years ago. *But* I have eyes you know? Wait, did you just agree he was superhot? You said 'and.'"

Tansy shrugged. She would neither confirm nor deny Dane's physical appeal.

"The hair. The shirt." Nicole sat back, sighing. "I bet he has tattoos, too. I have a weakness for tattoos." Nicole burst into laughter when Tansy glared at her in the rearview mirror.

"What was the whole bonding thing?" Astrid asked, using air quotes around *bonding*.

"Nothing. As usual. There was no bonding. Nor will there ever be bonding." Tansy heard the bite in her words and took a deep breath. It didn't help. "He was trying to…provoke me." A sound of frustration slipped out before she said, "He loves to get a rise out of me."

"And it worked." Nicole patted her shoulder.

"I know," she ground out. "I'm a perfectly well-adjusted, competent and functioning adult. Then he shows up and I'm falling all over my words and seeing red. There's something about him that just…just…"

"He's your Achilles' heel." Astrid put her hand on Tansy's arm. "It's not exactly a mystery, Tansy. After what he did. I shouldn't have left you alone with him."

Tansy took a deep breath. "No, no, Astrid. You were tired. It was a long day. And *none* of this is your fault. He and I are the problem." As far as she knew, most adults didn't need chaperoning or a moderator to conduct a civil conversation. She and Dane? *Maybe a referee is more appropriate?* "How about we stop talking about *him*." She glanced at Nicole. "Or his hair or his tight shirt or potential tattoos and find something more productive to talk about?"

"Good idea." Astrid patted her arm. "I think we need to repaint some of the boxes in the Wonderland." She sat up, crossing her legs in her seat. "I want to touch up the Cheshire cat, he's getting a little faded."

At Honey Hill Farms, each of the beeyards had a theme. Some were color based, like Lavender Blue. The yard was closest to the lavender fields so the boxes were done in blue and purple. Other yards showcased Poppa Tom and their ancestors' woodworking skills and sense of whimsy. Wonderland was an homage to Alice's Wonderland—mismatched patterns and whimsical painted details in vibrant colors. Cottage Square had each bee box painted up to resemble storybook cottages. Fairy-Tale Village yard had a castle- and carriage-shaped hive box. There was even a miniature version of the town that had a model city hall right in the middle. Tansy's personal favorite was the Impressionist yard. Each box was painted in the style of Monet or van Gogh.

"I still think that's another way to bring in some money," Nicole chimed in from the back seat. "People would love having custom painted bee boxes. I could help. Tap into my creative side."

Tansy wasn't so sure. As lovely as each unique bee-yard was, maintaining the boxes presented its own set of challenges—and that was on top of caring for the bees. Besides, they wouldn't be worrying over money for long. The Honey Festival was a month away and, once they'd won, all their worries would be over.

"THE FIGHT WAS with Clay Dwyer?" Dane sat opposite Mrs. Lopez, the high school principal, her large wooden desk between them. While there were more motivational posters and knickknacks on the shelves, the Honey High School principal's office hadn't changed much since he'd gone to school here. Back then, he'd come in to get accolades from the administration, not a talking-to for disciplinary issues. Leif didn't give a damn about his academics or what administration thought of him. Initially, Dane admired his little brother. It'd taken Dane years to stop looking for recognition—especially from his father. If Leif had figured that out already, he'd save himself a lot of second-guessing. Now Dane realized the truth was the opposite. Leif acted out the way he did to get attention. Instead of being mad at Leif, Dane was furious with their father. His little brother shouldn't have to resort to fighting to merit a few minutes of their father's attention.

"Do we know what happened? Leif is good friends with Clay's brother, Eddie." *Weren't they?* Clearly something had happened. Leif wasn't exactly the most lighthearted kid, but the idea of him throwing punches was hard to process.

"Neither boy will say who started the altercation or what the disagreement was over." Principal Lopez scanned over the paper on her desk. "Unfortunately, the boys bumped into one of the science teachers as he was wheeling a cart of slides and microscopes to the storage closet. Several boxes of the glass slides and two microscopes were broken."

"We'll make certain to pay for the damages."

"That would be appreciated." Principal Lopez nodded. "In addition to the fiscal reparations, we feel a week of in-school suspension plus after-school cleanup duty is in order." She leaned forward, folding her hands on her desktop. "He'll work in the cafeteria, help scrape gum off the underside of the tables and mop the floor— that sort of thing."

Dane nodded. "A little hard work never hurt anyone." Leif would hate every minute of it. But maybe, hopefully, this would make his little brother think *before* he acted. "Anything to prevent this sort of thing from happening again."

"I'm glad you agree." Principal Lopez took a deep breath, looking more uncomfortable than he'd ever seen the woman. "There is one more thing I'd like to discuss with—"

But she came to a halt as the door opened wide, startling them both, and his father walked in.

"What's happening here?" His father shot him a squinty-eyed look before scowling Principal Lopez's way. "Why is my *son* here?"

"He's listed as Leif's secondary guardian, Mr. Knudson." Mrs. Lopez didn't bat an eye. "This wasn't a situation that could wait."

"They tried to call you." Dane ran a hand along the back of his neck. "I tried to call you. I tried to find you. I went to the hunting cabin—"

"I was there." His father cut him off and sat in the chair beside him. He was still scowling as he spoke to the principal. "Leif's been beaten up? By that Dwyer boy out there? I won't stand by and do nothing. That sort of behavior isn't called for—not one bit."

Dane took a slow, deep breath. "Leif wasn't the victim here. It was a fight."

"Oh?" His father perked up. "He was fighting? I hope he gave as good as he got."

"That's why we're here, Dad." Dane nodded at Principal Lopez. "They broke some things, caused a ruckus. *Both* boys are in trouble."

His father crossed his arms over his chest. "Aren't there supposed to be teachers watching out for this sort of thing?"

"It started in the locker room, Mr. Knudson—right before the class bell rang. The coaches separated them and the boys assured them it was over. Once they were in the hallway, the fight resumed but it was broken up as soon as possible." If Principal Lopez was offended over his father's not-so-subtle accusation, she hid it well.

"Hmm." His father had gone back to scowling, only

this time it was at Dane. "You can go. Whatever decisions need to be made, they're mine to make."

Dane didn't want to be here. He didn't want to be Leif's secondary guardian—hell, he had no business being anyone's guardian. But his father's haphazard parenting gave him no choice.

It was Dane who had attended more parent nights, counselor meetings and principal meetings. Through their combined effort, Leif had been making progress with his schoolwork and his behavior issues. It was a sad fact that the principal and teachers knew he was the go-to reliable one not Harald Knudson. Even sadder? At the end of the day, their father could undo all the progress they'd made—it was his right.

And then I'll have to do damage control once Dad flakes out again anyway.

"Thank you for your time, Mrs. Lopez." He stood, giving her a nod.

She stood, offering Dane her hand. "I appreciate you coming in, Mr. Knudson."

Dane closed the principal's door behind him and surveyed the main office. The school secretary, Mrs. Corliss Ogden, was a tiny bulldog of a woman with white hair piled so high it added a good six inches to her height. An assortment of pens and pencils and neon highlighters protruded from her hair, one pencil on the verge of slipping free. Mrs. Ogden had been the school secretary back when he was a student here. She stopped munching on what looked like honey brittle long enough to give him a pinched smile. "Want some?" She held out her tin.

"I'm good, thank you." He recognized the Honey Hill Farms sticker on the lid.

"Suit yourself." She went back to clicking away on her keyboard at a glacial pace.

He grinned and turned.

There, below a large array of more motivational posters and a massive copy machine, was Leif. He sat on a bench, with a swollen bottom lip and cotton shoved up both nostrils. He slumped, staring at his backpack on the ground between his feet. On the opposite bench sat Clay Dwyer—who was sporting one hell of a puffy red right eye. The boy was a couple of years older than Leif, bigger and taller and, from the looks of it, ready to start throwing punches at the slightest provocation.

Which was probably why Leif was staring down at his backpack.

Since Mrs. Ogden wasn't physically equipped to break up any potential brawl that might commence, Dane sat beside his brother. He didn't like the side-eye the Dwyer kid was shooting Leif's way so he leaned back against the bench, stretched his long legs out in front of him and crossed his arms over his chest. Dane liked weight training and it showed. While he'd never been tempted to raise a hand to *anyone*—especially not some hotheaded kid—he had no problem staring down Clay Dwyer until the boy's head drooped forward and his clenched fists relaxed.

The minute Jed Dwyer stepped into the front office, Dane was reminded of where Clay's hostility and attitude came from. Jed was the best mechanic in town but there wasn't much else to commend the man. The single father was big and gruff and mean and made no bones about it. After a long string of not-so-discreet domestic disturbances, his wife had run off and never looked back. Now he and his three boys lived on the outskirts of town in an old pier and beam house that should be condemned.

"What now?" Jed barked, staring down at his son.

"Mrs. Lopez would like to speak with you, Mr. Dwyer." The ancient, diminutive Mrs. Ogden peered over the glasses on the tip of her nose. By all appearances, she wasn't the least bit intimidated by Jed's narrow-eyed glare or the tightness of his jaw. "She'll be with you in a minute, so have a seat." She nodded at the bench beside Clay.

Jed didn't move.

"Suit yourself." Mrs. Ogden went back to loudly munching brittle and click-clacking away on her keyboard.

There was something wrong with the office clock, Dane was sure of it. The second hand was dragging. One minute felt more like an hour. By the time Principal Lopez's door opened, the tension level in the room had Dane on edge and itching to leave—he could only imagine how Leif felt.

Dane stood. "Get your stuff," he murmured to Leif.

"I appreciate you coming in," Mrs. Lopez said as she shook his father's hand.

"Yes, well." His father spoke directly to Jed Dwyer, his tone razor-sharp. "It's not like I had much of a choice now, did I?"

Dane shot his father a look. Challenging a man twenty years his junior with a good fifty pounds of work-earned muscle made all the sense in the world. *Not exactly role-model behavior.* He got the whole protective thing—he felt the same way—but Leif didn't need his father causing a scene. Dane nudged his father, hard. "We appreciate your time, Mrs. Lopez."

His father's jaw was locked and it was clear he wasn't happy, but he stopped glaring at Jed Dwyer. "Let's go."

Dane led the way, holding the door wide for his father. Leif grabbed his backpack and hurried after them, almost tripping over his own feet in the process.

"Mr. Dwyer." Principal Lopez stepped aside so Jed Dwyer could come inside her office.

"Come on, boy." Jed took hold of his son's upper arm and pulled him to his feet, forcibly steering Clay into the principal's office.

A cold, hard knot formed in the pit of Dane's stomach as he watched the exchange. He'd been all too willing to blame the Dwyer boys for the trouble Leif had found himself in. But the reality wasn't that clear-cut. *Real life seldom is.*

He turned to find Leif, alone, waiting. "Where's Dad?"

Leif shrugged. "He got a phone call."

"He left?" Dane glanced down the long, empty hallway. Was he going to talk to Leif? Tell him what the plan was—*if* the plan was still what Dane and Mrs. Lopez had discussed? Why had their father bothered to show up if he wasn't going to stick around? He ran a hand along the back of his neck and sighed. "What is he, a ninja? I didn't know the old man could move that fast."

The corner of Leif's mouth kicked up for a split second before he winced.

"Hurt?" Dane asked, eyeing his brother's lower lip. It looked more swollen now. Painfully so. "Probably want to get some ice on that."

Leif nodded.

"Let's go." Dane led Leif outside. He spied his father in his truck in the parking lot, the engine idling. From the amount of hand gestures, his father was having quite a telephone conversation. *It'd better be damn important.* He'd dropped everything to get here for Leif—including the long-awaited teleconference with the green architect one of his former colleagues had recommended for the expansion. Dane got into his own truck and sped out of the lot.

"I need to make a quick stop." Dane pulled into the gas station on the edge of town, parked, and climbed out of the truck. He turned and asked, "You want anything from inside?"

"I'm good," Leif murmured.

Dane wracked his brain for something to say—something to comfort his brother. Leif wasn't okay, today had made that blatantly obvious. What if he said something that made it worse? *It's not like I have any idea what I'm doing.* "Be back, then." He closed the door, filled the gas tank, then walked across the parking lot and into the convenience store. Once he'd paid for the gas and a large paper cup full of ice, he stepped back outside.

His gaze caught on a woman, a toddler on her hip. She was vaguely familiar, tall and slim, with long red hair. Her green eyes met his. His smile of greeting vanished as she shot him a cold look and brushed past him, and into the shop. *Have a nice day.* Someone should. He shook the cup of ice and headed for his truck.

I can't seem to catch a break.

Tansy Hill, wearing a bright yellow attention-grabbing shirt with a honeycomb print, stood beside her clunker of a truck, filling the gas tank. He didn't say a word. Maybe if he was really quiet, and really lucky, she wouldn't see him.

Tansy turned, her mossy-green eyes scanning her surroundings.

Or not. He could feel her gaze but wasn't about to acknowledge her. There was no point. While he usually didn't shy away from a good bout of verbal sparring, he didn't have the energy to go toe-to-toe with her today.

He held his breath, keeping his attention on his truck, until he pulled open the driver's door, climbed in and held out the cup. "Here."

Leif took the cup and looked inside. His little brother's jaw clenched tight and he pressed a hand to the side of his face but Dane saw the quiver of his chin. For an instant, Leif wasn't some hostile, rebellious teenager, he was Dane's little brother. *And he's hurting.*

Dane reached out, resting a hand on Leif's shoulder. "I... If you need to talk, I'm here."

Leif nodded but kept his face covered.

"You ready?" Dane started the truck—but there was a knock on his window. All he saw was bright yellow, but it was enough. He closed his eyes and took a deep breath, dreading the inevitable. Without looking, he rolled his window down. "Miss Hill. What an unexpected treat." He glanced at her, shielding his eyes. "Hold on." He reached for his glove box, pulled out his sunglasses and put them on. "Better."

"Funny." She sighed. "As a decent human being, it is my *duty* to tell you that your right rear wheel looks extremely low." She walked away without giving him a chance to say a thing.

Well, damn. Dane glanced at Leif, who was sort of

smiling, and shrugged. "Too much?" He took off his sunglasses.

"I guess." Leif shrugged back. "It's kind of...your thing."

"Is it?" he asked, pulling alongside the air pump machine. "Guess I'll check the tire. You hold that ice to your face." He climbed down, squatted by the rear of the truck and surveyed the tire. *Well, damn again.* He was standing when Tansy's rattletrap of a truck rolled up to the parking lot exit alongside him. "Tansy?" He stepped forward and knocked on her passenger window.

She ignored him.

"Tansy." He knocked again, sighing. Of course, she was ignoring him. It was his own damn fault. "Thank you."

Tansy's head spun in his direction and her eyes went wide, then narrowed. She seemed to be waiting for something.

"Really," he added, sincere.

She blinked several times before she nodded and pulled out onto the road.

Was she smiling? Nah. The only time Tansy ever smiled at him was when she'd bested him. *That* made her happy. *Boy, did that make her happy.*

After the day he'd been having, a tire blowout on the highway would be the cherry on top. He glanced down the road, Tansy's highlighter-yellow shirt visible through the back window of her truck cab. If someone had told him Tansy Hill would save the day, he'd have laughed out loud. But she had. And Astrid hadn't been in the car to make her this time, either. He liked knowing that a little too much. *I'm a dumbass.*

DUMBASS. LEIF HELD the ice to his lip, watching his brother watch Tansy Hill's truck rattle down the county road. She'd totally just saved their butts even though Dane was a jerk to her. Then again, Dane had a lot going on. *Thanks to me.* He stared into the ice cup, his insides knotted. People sucked. Period. Like, all of them.

And Tansy must be trouble, too. Why else was Dane so…weird around her? Sure, she'd saved their asses twice now but there was something about her that made Dane act the way he did when she was around so… Leif shook his head.

His father drank too much and sucked at being a father. First his mom died and his dad flipped—at least, that's what Dane said. Dane said their dad hadn't always been the world's worst father. Leif had a hard time believing that. He didn't remember his mom. He did remember his father's wives two through four. They weren't all bad. Not until the end. Then his dad went to the hunting cabin, things got tense, people in town started talking and Dane was left to keep everything running smoothly. Or at least, Dane tried.

Kate had been the worst. Kate was the reason today had happened. Clay. Talking trash about his father, making Kate out to be some victim and Dane to be a real rat bastard. Hell yes, Leif had thrown the first punch—but Clay threw the last. The whole fight, Leif saw red. He wanted to shut Clay up. Then Kerrielynn Baldwin had stepped in. Nothing like seeing the most popular girl in school get pushed to the ground and knowing it was his fault. Leif had been making sure she was okay when Clay slammed his head into a locker. Their tussle broke that science equipment, too. Leif's lungs felt tight and his hands fisted just thinking about it. All of it.

"You ready?" Dane climbed into the truck.

Leif let out a slow, unsteady breath. "Sure," he murmured, turning the ice cup in his hands. Dane glanced his way and Leif braced himself. He didn't want to talk about it. How could he? He didn't believe Dane had hooked up with Kate, but a lot of people did. And they kept talking about it. Talking to him about it—like he had the inside scoop or something. Leif was sick of hearing about it.

"You want to drive home?" Dane asked, holding the keys out.

Leif stared. "I don't have my license."

"You have your learner's permit. I'm in the car." Dane jingled the keys. "The more practice the better."

Leif glanced at his brother, then the keys. "I'm grounded." And, if he wanted to drive, now probably wasn't the best time to remind Dane of that.

"Yeah." Dane sighed but didn't take the keys back.

"My lip hurts." He used his other hand to point at the ice cup he had pressed to his lip.

"Good thing you're not using your lip to steer." Dane frowned at him, crossing his arms over his chest. "You don't want to drive?"

"I do." If he ever got up the nerve to take off for good, it'd be easier if he could drive. Sometimes, that was all he thought about—going someplace where no one knew him or his father or brother or any of the crap about their family.

"Then take these." He tossed the keys.

Leif slid across the bench seat and put the key in the ignition.

"Watch your speed." Dane put on his seat belt. "Use your blinker. We should be good."

Leif buckled up and turned on the truck. Every once in a while, Dane was cool. Like now. If he wasn't always trying to be Leif's dad and brother, Leif would probably like him more. Then again, he was a better dad than their father was.

"Oh, and the brakes are stiff." Dane pointed at the floorboard.

"Right." Leif put the truck in gear and started forward slowly.

"Relax. You got this, Leif." Dane slumped back against the truck seat like he didn't have a care in the world.

Even after he'd snuck out, been suspended from school, failed pre-Cal and gotten into a fight at school, it was like Dane still believed in Leif—like Dane trusted him to get this right. It was like Dane didn't see Leif for the loser he was. Leif knew it. Their dad knew it. Everyone in school knew it. So why didn't Dane? *He's a dumbass.*

But the vise pressing the air from Leif's lungs let up a little. As Leif drove them down the country road toward Texas Viking Honey, he was smiling.

CHAPTER FIVE

"I'M LEAVING FOR the Madigans' in ten minutes." Tansy went through her backpack, making doubly sure she had everything she'd need. The tiny town of Rose Prairie, where the Madigan family farm and beeyard was, took a good thirty minutes to reach—too far to double back if something was forgotten.

When Texas had offered an agriculture exemption for keeping bees to help with the dwindling bee population, Honey Hill Farms jumped at the opportunity. There were plenty of landowners that wanted the exemption but none of the hands-on work of beekeeping. So they paid the Hills to maintain the hives and let the Hills keep the honey—a win for the bees and the Hills.

"I'm ready." Astrid patted the plastic hanging bag containing their beekeeping suits. "Full suits, gloves and tape."

"Lots of tape." Tansy nodded, smiling when Astrid dropped another roll of wide blue painter's tape into the pocket on the front of the bag.

While the Hills primarily raised the more gentle-natured Italian bees, the Rose Prairie bees were feral, and the majority of feral Texas bees were Africanized. The upside was how adaptive these bees were to the Texas heat, resistant to mites and pests, and productive honey makers. The downside was their aggressive nature. Amongst the Texas beekeeping community, these bees were called *hot*—referring to their temperament. Astrid said they were cranky but Tansy thought they were just plain mean. If one started stinging, the others followed suit and that's why proper beekeeping gear was so important for this visit. The tape kept a bee from trying to slip in between a boot and ankle cuff, the space at the end of the zipper, or any place a bee or two might sneak in. More tape was always a good idea.

"You're stopping by Lorna's?" Aunt Camellia was tucking several plastic containers full of food into a brown paper shopping bag.

"After we're done in Rose Prairie. She's handing off the Junior Beekeepers stuff for tomorrow night's meeting." Everett had assured her the meetings all but ran themselves, and if that was the case, she'd be able to handle them on her own in future—without Dane Knudson's help.

"Good. Van says Lorna's about to pop any day now so you make sure you give her this. Just let me repack this into a cooler bag."

"Pop?" Tansy winced. "That sounds just awful."

"Fine." Aunt Camellia opened the pantry and pulled out a large insulated shopping bag. "Lorna should be delivering baby Franks pretty quick." She started stacking food containers inside. "The last thing she and Bud need to worry over is cooking and cleaning—first babies can be a challenge."

"She must be so excited," Astrid cooed. "I can't wait to babysit." Astrid loved babies and animals and bees with equal enthusiasm.

Tansy didn't mind bees or animals but babies made her nervous. They were too small. And noisy. And fragile. "We'll make sure she gets it." Tansy shifted her backpack and took the packed-full insulated bag. "Don't worry."

She and Astrid finished loading the van and headed for the farm-to-market road that led them to the highway and Rose Prairie beyond.

"I want a baby," Astrid announced so suddenly that Tansy almost drove off the road.

"Where did that come from?" Tansy asked, steering the van between the lines once more.

"Not now, obviously." Astrid shook her head. "Eventually. I want lots of babies."

"Lots?" Tansy wrinkled up her nose. "How many is lots?"

"More than two." Astrid sighed, leaning back against her seat and hugging herself.

"Do you have someone in mind to help you make these babies?" Tansy laughed. "I guess I sort of figured you'd tell me when you found the guy you'd want to... impregnate you."

Astrid turned a deep red as she stared at her sister. "Tansy."

"What? It seems like a perfectly reasonable question." She was laughing harder now.

"Impregnate me? That sounds *so* romantic." But Astrid was laughing, too. "In answer to your question, no. I don't have someone in mind. It's not like there are a whole bunch of options in Honey. We know *everyone*."

Tansy didn't argue. The pool of single men in Honey was more like a puddle. A teeny-tiny puddle of men she knew too well to ever consider romantically. "I guess we're doomed to dating apps?"

It was Astrid's turn to wince. "Um, no. It's all about meeting to…well, you know."

"Hook up?" Tansy glanced at her sister. "Well, I guess you could consider it practice for when you do meet Mr. Tall, Dark and Baby-Daddy Material."

Astrid burst out laughing again, waving her hand dismissively. "Enough of that. How about some tunes?" She leaned forward and flipped on the radio to a classic rock station.

Peter Gabriel's "In Your Eyes" came spilling through the speakers, instantly transporting Tansy to *that* day.

"Oops." Astrid changed the station. "Sorry."

"Unless you're programming the radio playlist, you don't need to apologize." Besides, it was ridiculous for the song to still get to her. It was just a song. And, if she could ever disentangle said song from the look on Dane's face during one of the more humiliating experiences of her life, it would probably still be one of her favorite songs.

Astrid settled on a safe classical music station for the remainder of the drive, talking about Nicole's dating app life and the possibility of venturing into breeding queen bees as another income stream.

Finally, they were bouncing down the rough gravel road that led to the periphery of the Madigans' property line, then Tansy parked and gave Astrid a look.

Astrid gave her a thumbs-up.

"I'll get the smoker started." Tansy held out the garment bag to Astrid, then reached for the cylinder smoker. She opened the funnel-like top, added bits of burlap inside the metal canister, and lit the fabric on fire. It would take a few minutes before it was smoking well so she set the handheld smoker on a large flat rock to burn down.

"Good?" Astrid asked, securing the front zipper beneath the Velcro seal and holding out her arms for inspection.

Tansy turned Astrid around, double-checking for any potential points of entry and applying tape as necessary. "Good."

"Your turn." Astrid stood aside, tape at the ready, as Tansy pulled on her well-worn white keeper suit. In Texas, the vented suits were almost a requirement. Today offered a glorious May morning with spring-like temperatures and a light breeze but by noon, it would be inching into the nineties. In August, the heat was downright miserable. Without the ventilated suits, they'd be dripping sweat and soaked through, facing potential heat exhaustion before they'd finished inspecting the hives.

"Give me a slow spin." Astrid stepped back to watch, then knelt, taping Tansy's elasticized pant cuffs tight against her brown leather work boots. She stood, added a piece over the slight gap at the top of one of Tansy's zippers and nodded. "Clear."

Tansy gauged the slow burn inside the smoker, closed the funnel-topped lid and gave the bellows a few quick pumps. Clean white smoke billowed into the morning air.

"Good to go." Astrid gave her a glove-covered thumbs-up. "Who knows, maybe they'll be more cheerful this time?" She handed Tansy a J hive tool, shrugged, and stuck an L hive tool and frame grip into one of her oversize pockets. "Maybe?"

"Sure." She knew Astrid couldn't see her roll her

eyes, but there was no stopping it. In the two years they'd kept these bees, the bees had never—not once—been anywhere close to cheerful. "Anything's possible."

"That's the spirit." Astrid set off, giggling, smoker in hand, for the row of bright white boxes along the tree line.

"Let's do it." Tansy pulled their handy wooden wagon with an array of supplies along behind her.

With Hill bees, smoke wasn't always necessary, with the Madigan bees, smoke was required. They puffed smoke into and around the hive to intercept the bees' communication signals before they ever cracked the hive open. Then, after more puffs, the frame-by-frame inspection could begin. If the hive looked healthy and their honey stores abundant, the sisters would trade out a few honey-full frames with the empty ones in Tansy's wagon.

Astrid worked the lid loose and removed it carefully, using the tool to make just enough room to slide the frame perch into place. Her sister worked slowly, her movements calm and steady, easing the frames in the box apart. "Something tells me they're not happy to see us." She pulled one frame up for inspection.

"I'm getting that. The smoke isn't making a bit of difference." Tansy pressed the bellows a few more times, hoping to calm the bees swirling around them, stinging their gloves, landing on their suits and veils, and generally making their displeasure known.

"Not much." But Astrid kept working, pulling up another frame. "But they've been busy." There was a smile in her voice, completely calm as she finished inspecting each one.

Astrid gently brushed some bees aside. "Bingo." She

turned, placed the honey-laden frame into their extra box and replacing it inside the hive with a clean frame the bees would immediately set to work on. "Next."

Two hours later, they were driving back to Honey.

"One got you right there." Astrid pointed at her cheek.

"I know." She'd come out with only one sting, so she had no complaints—especially considering the amount of honey they'd managed to harvest.

Astrid leaned forward, directing the air-conditioning vent onto her face. "That feels so good." She twisted up her long strawberry blonde hair and clipped it up on top of her head. "Much better. Are we heading to Lorna's now?"

Tansy nodded, she and Astrid singing along to songs on the radio until they'd reached Honey. The Frankses lived in a cute cottage on one of the oak-lined streets a few blocks off Main Street. They parked the van, grabbed the still-cold insulated bag of food and knocked on the front door.

One look at Lorna and Tansy couldn't argue with Van's description. Poor Lorna did *look ready to pop.* It took effort not to stare at the woman's stomach. Lorna was tiny, not much taller than five feet, and *all* belly. If a strong wind hit her, she'd probably tip over.

"Camellia is so sweet." Lorna started moving the containers into the freezer. "Our freezer is so full I won't have to worry about either of us going hungry."

"Is he excited?" Astrid asked, handing her containers.

"He's all nerves." Lorna laughed. "He's not sleeping well. And all I have to do is make a funny face and he's running for the car keys. Poor thing."

Tansy found herself staring at Lorna's stomach, feeling all sorts of sympathy for Bud.

"He's going to be the best father." Astrid sounded almost dreamy.

"He's out installing the new clothes dryer in the garage." Lorna lowered her voice, glancing at the back door. "I'm happy the dryer arrived before the baby did." She ran a hand over her stomach. "But I'm also happy there's something to keep him busy—and not hovering."

Astrid laughed.

"I appreciate the food, especially when y'all have company staying with you." Lorna put the last container into the freezer and closed the door.

"Company?" Tansy took the empty insulation bag from the woman. "Nope. Just us Bee Girls. And, you know, Aunt Camellia's gazillion animals."

Lorna laughed, placing her hands on her stomach. "Bud saw a woman in town when he was picking up the dryer. He said, from her red hair, she had to be a Hill."

Astrid pulled a long strand of her hair over her shoulder. "It's a rare natural color but, to Aunt Mags's horror, you can almost get her exact shade from one of those at-home color kits."

Lorna chuckled and rested her hand on her back, her stomach sticking out even farther. Tansy tried not to stare. "I really appreciate you and Dane covering for me, Tansy. I can't help but feel a little guilty about this—Everett and his weird sense of humor. It's no secret how you two feel about each other." Lorna headed around the kitchen counter. "I've got everything all boxed up over here. I tried to color-code things and highlight what's most important."

"You didn't have to do all that, Lorna." Tansy hurried to take the banker's box before Lorna reach for it.

"Sure I did." Lorna shrugged. "The meeting is one thing—the barn painting is another thing altogether." She patted the box. "But don't worry, I made a copy of the binder for Dane and already had it delivered to him, too."

Great. Meaning it was unlikely he'd forget and leave her to do the Junior Beekeepers stuff herself—as she'd hoped.

"Tomorrow is just a regular meeting, but the barn painting is…more. I've already got all the permission slips signed and most of the supplies picked up and stored at the school. Dane can pick up the paint." Lorna rubbed her back, a slight furrow on her brow. "I think I've covered everything."

"I'm sure you have." Tansy offered the woman a smile.

Lorna nodded, smiling in return. "At least you two will be on the same page—for this."

"That would be a first." Tansy tried to joke but saw the concern on Lorna's face. "I'm teasing. We will be fine, Lorna, please don't worry. Dane and I can act like adults."

Astrid shot her a disbelieving look.

"He *has* grown up some." Lorna slowly lowered herself into a well-padded kitchen chair. "His little brother was in my biology class last year so I've been able to see the lengths he's gone to to help Leif. That kid can be a real…challenge." She took a slow breath and went on. "Dane has met with teachers, talked to the counselor and principal—you name it." She glanced at Tansy.

"I know I shouldn't like him but I sort of do. Dane, I mean." She held up her thumb and forefinger. "A little."

"That's so nice of him," Astrid murmured, using the pause in conversation to ask Lorna about her pregnancy and the baby and steer them away from the topic of Dane.

But Tansy pondered Lorna's words. Dane Knudson would always be an ever-present thorn in her side but she couldn't fault his brotherly devotion. Tansy had said she'd cover the next few months' Junior Beekeepers activities and she would. Since there was no way of removing Dane from the situation, she'd have to make the best of it. As long as Dane kept the hair and the tight shirts and goading in check, they *might* be able to pull it off. It was a stretch, no doubt about it. But Lorna, in her very poppable state, didn't need to worry about a thing. She and Dane were both adults. They could do this. They could. Maybe if she kept saying it, eventually she'd believe it.

DANE HAD READ through the color-coded binder Lorna's husband had delivered with wide-eyed appreciation. He'd love to have someone as detail-oriented and thorough as Lorna Franks to help out at Texas Viking Honey. She'd included a club roster, their calendar and meeting expectations—which Dane realized was code for "rules." All of the Junior Beekeepers Club members had signed a contract saying they understood and accepted these rules so he didn't think there would be any problems.

Except for Leif. "No phones," Dane said again. He'd explained no phones was one of the Junior Beekeepers rules, but Leif didn't give a crap. His little brother had made it clear he had no interest in attending or participating. Dane had made it equally clear Leif didn't have a choice.

For the last two hours, Leif had alternated between muttering under his breath and openly glaring at Dane. Like now, as he shoved his phone into his pocket. His sigh was long and loud and left no room for misunderstanding.

Yeah, I get it. You don't want to be here. We don't always get what we want, kiddo.

Dane walked along the path from the high school to the large metal barn in the back field. It had been replaced since his days at Honey High School. Now the building housed all the expanded agricultural programs offered at the school. In a ranching and farming community like Honey, there were plenty of options to choose from.

Leif sighed again and slowed, dropping back to trail after Dane.

Dane was at his wit's end, but there was no help for it. Since Leif's fight with the Dwyer boy earlier in the week, Dane was in full-on hover mode. After their enjoyable drive home from school the day of the fight, Leif had gone back to resenting him, big-time. And Dane didn't know what else to do. He had chalked up Leif's behavior as some sort of rebellious stage but... what if there was more to it? He'd dismissed the counselor's questions but what if Dane was wrong. *Was* Leif involved with drugs? Drinking? Keeping Leif close—like dragging him to the Junior Beekeepers meeting—was Dane's only option.

The whole situation sucked. Not just the Leif part, but the Tansy Hill part. If he was being honest with himself, he'd signed on to help out with the Junior Beekeepers in large part because he enjoyed tormenting Tansy. Juvenile or not, there was something truly rewarding about watching her go beet red and sputtering with fury. *Probably because she tried to act so damn superior all the time.*

But, as he sipped his morning coffee, he'd accepted that he couldn't pester or tease Tansy during the Junior Beekeepers meeting. He was an adult, a sort of role model, and he had to act like it. For Tansy and him that meant calling a truce. The idea was hard to swallow but he hadn't been able to come up with any other solution.

He turned, waiting for Leif to amble close to the door before pulling it wide. A wave of overlapping, excited voices and youthful laughter greeted them. With a final sigh and an extra-long death glare Dane's way, Leif stepped inside. Dane stared up at the fading sky, took a deep breath and followed him in.

Other than Leif, his only experience with teenagers was that he'd been one. It was a hell of a nice surprise to find that there wasn't a single sullen, eye-rolling, exasperated youth amongst the group.

Well, other than Leif.

According to the club roster, the club was made up of fourteen middle school and high school students. And, right now, all of them were inspecting Leif and him with wide-eyed curiosity.

"Mr. Knudson." Tansy stood behind a long table stacked high with cookies and tiny cakes and a large jug of what looked like lemonade. "I brought snacks." Her hazel-green eyes barely glanced his way. "Leif." She waved his brother forward, smiling brightly. "You have to try one of Aunt Camellia's honey-orange cupcakes."

Dane studied her, his stomach flooding with an odd

mix of dread and anticipation. That smile was…something. A good start, sort of. Not that it was for him, but still.

Leif glanced at him, then Tansy, then the snacks. With a shrug, Leif headed for the table. His brother never passed up food.

Dane headed to the table to survey the treats, too. If Camellia Hill had made them, they'd be too good to pass up. He picked up a napkin—resisting the urge to give Tansy grief over the fact that it had a honeycomb print—and reached for a cake.

"How are you? Excited about tonight's meeting?" Tansy sounded surprisingly enthusiastic.

It took effort to swallow back his usual sarcasm. "Well… I'm…" Dane glanced up in time to realize she wasn't talking to him, she was talking to Leif.

"Um…" Leif said around a bite of cookie. "Sure."

"Good." Tansy smiled, leaning forward to whisper. "I think we're going to need all the extra hands we can get when we paint the barn. The younger members outnumber us."

Leif shoved the rest of the cookie in his mouth and nodded, looking confused.

Dane knew the feeling. He brought out the worst in Tansy, so her soft tone of voice and seemingly sincere smile triggered all sorts of uneasiness. *Not that any of it's for me.*

"Tansy, I'm so glad you're here." A young girl stepped up, clipboard held against her chest. "When Mrs. Franks said you'd agreed to take over leading the club, um, I was so, so excited. I know how busy you are but there is no one who knows more about bees and beekeeping and honey than you." She smiled, showing a metal retainer and straight white teeth. "Oh, um, you, too, Mr. Knudson," she hurried to add as she turned to acknowledge him.

Dane chuckled, recognizing a case of hero worship when he saw it.

Leif made a weird gasping sound, then started to cough.

"I was happy to do it. Don't sell yourself short, Kerrielynn. You've worked out at the farm the last couple of honey flows—you know your way around a hive." Tansy, again with the warm, disconcerting smile of hers.

Kerrielynn lit up from Tansy's praise. "Thanks to you."

Leif cleared his throat.

"Oh, and I looked over your application and," Tansy sort-of whispered, "I'd say you're a strong contender for Texas Honey Queen next year."

Leif kept on coughing so Dane offered him a cup of lemonade.

The girl, Kerrielynn, turned pink and hugged the clipboard close. "Oh, I hope so. It would be…it would be *everything*, you know? It would be such an honor." She paused, turning to a still-coughing Leif. "Are you okay, Leif?"

Dane was beginning to wonder the same thing.

Leif nodded, but at the look of sheer panic on his face, Dane handed him another glass of lemonade. Leif shook his head, doing his best not to cough—and managing a shaky breath.

"Ohmygosh. Are you choking?" Kerrielynn hurriedly tossed her clipboard aside and came around the table. "I'm CPR certified."

Leif took a deep, ragged breath and moved back.

Dane wasn't sure what was wrong but his brother was breathing.

Kerrielynn wasn't convinced, stepping closer to Leif.

"No." Leif held his hand out. "No." He cleared his throat and swallowed, hard. "Fine," he managed, coughing again, and stepping farther away from Kerrielynn.

"Are you sure?" The girl was truly worried.

"Yes." The word sort of exploded out of Leif. "I… I…" He cleared his throat and swallowed down the glass of lemonade Tansy offered him. "I'm sure."

Kerrielynn stared at him.

Dane's stomach sank. His little brother's impatience with the girl was surprising. Leif was acting strange in a new, totally unfamiliar way. *Great.*

Leif set the empty cup down on the table. "Thank you," he murmured. His gaze darted to the girl.

"You're welcome, Leif." Kerrielynn smiled slowly.

Leif frowned.

Dane scratched the stubble along his jaw, beyond perplexed. His sullen, mopey, eye-rolling, angry brother had a nice girl smiling at him like that and what did he do? Scowl and frown and look…well, Leif looked pissed off.

"Are you thinking about joining the Junior Beekeepers?" Kerrielynn tucked a long strand of brown hair behind her ear, as if Leif wasn't acting like a jerk. "It makes sense since, you know, um, you sort of own Texas Viking Honey." She shrugged, smiling more broadly. "I mean, your family does." She nodded at Dane.

"It does make sense," Tansy said. "I honestly thought you were a member already, Leif."

Leif's one-shouldered shrug was his only answer.

"You...you want to come sit with us?" Kerrielynn collected her clipboard and nodded at the group of teens munching snacks around one brown folding table. "I think you know everyone."

"I'm good." Leif turned and headed to a chair in the back corner of the room, far removed from everyone else.

"Okay." Kerrielynn's smile faltered before she shrugged. "That's cool." She headed to the table and sat amidst the other Junior Beekeepers.

"Huh." Dane watched his brother, beyond confused. Did his little brother have something against this girl? Why was Leif so hell-bent and determined on closing himself off? His gaze shifted from Leif to Kerrielynn sitting at the table of teens—flipping through the papers on her clipboard and laughing at something one of the other kids said.

"That was...sort of odd?" Tansy asked.

Dane glanced at her, waiting for her to say something more. She tended to add a humdinger at the end—some final parting shot or final word. But she seemed engrossed, arms crossed over her chest, as her attention bounced between the table of awkward teens and his brother slumped in a folding chair in the corner. Until now, he hadn't taken the time to really look at her. Instead of her usual ponytail, her long, reddish-brown hair hung around her shoulders and down her back. He frowned. She looked...different.

He wasn't sure if it was the curve-hugging white T-shirt and jeans versus her usual shapeless coveralls or the long, silky hair or the slight sheen of gloss to her lips but... Definitely *different*. In a good way. Maybe *too* good. He'd always made an effort to avoid the word *sexy* when it came to his long-term nemesis but… He cleared his throat, hard, and tore his gaze from an undeniably sexy Tansy.

What the hell was wrong with him? This was just Tansy. But why the getup? The snug shirt—and her arms crossed—had some sort of magnetic hold on him. He was trying not to look or remember just how soft she'd felt pressed against him long, long ago. Trying, and failing.

He swallowed but the tightness of his throat didn't ease one bit. He preferred her sassy ponytail and baggy coveralls and biting comments. *That* Tansy, he knew how to handle.

Her head swiveled his way, eyebrows raised in question, making her earring sway. A little honeypot earring dangled from one ear and a honeybee dangled from the other.

His attention lingered on her throat, all his hard-fought memories dragging him back to a time when he'd run his nose along her neck. Her skin had been so soft.

She caught her bottom lip between her teeth.

Her glossy, full lip. *Dammit all.*

Those big mossy-green eyes studied him long enough to make his insides warm. "Dane?" she whispered.

"What?" He crumpled up the napkin he'd been gripping and tossed it into the trash can, fighting back a flare of irritation at himself. Those thoughts were best left in the past. He tried to focus on the red spot on her cheek, not the rest of her. "Did you get stung?"

Tansy ignored the question, her eyes narrowing. "I get the feeling Leif doesn't want to be here."

"That's very perceptive." *Way to play nice.* Dane

reached for another cookie and nodded toward the table. "Nice napkins. Your contribution?"

"Kerrielynn brought them. You know, if Leif doesn't want to be here and you have something else you need to do, I can handle this."

Dane swallowed his bite of cookie. "Are you offering to run these meetings yourself, Miss Hill?" If he was smart, he'd thank her and leave. He had enough to do as it was.

She seemed to ponder her reply. "It would be for the best, don't you think?"

Definitely. But if he accepted her offer, was he… admitting defeat? Or worse, would he *owe* Tansy Hill? "As much as I'd like to accept your *generous* offer, I can't." His sarcasm was anything but subtle.

"Why not?" Her disappointment was comical—and at the same time not funny at all.

He resisted the urge to remind her that he had just as much knowledge and experience as she did. There was no point. It wasn't about his beekeeping knowledge or whether or not he was of value to the club. It was entirely about her not wanting him here and him worrying over her motivation. "I gave my word to Everett and Lorna that I'd help out," Dane grumbled, glancing at his brother. "Besides, it'll be good for Leif." Leif would come around. "Whether he likes it or not."

Tansy's laugh was soft, and it caught him so off guard that he found himself staring at her. Most of her laughter was at his expense. At the moment, she looked and sounded…sympathetic. "Leif needs this. Something good. Like friends that don't cause trouble or get into fights." He sucked in a deep breath. Why was he sharing with Tansy, of all people?

Tansy looked as startled as he was, but she nodded. "It's hard being the oldest sibling. Watching them make mistakes instead of listening to your advice or asking for help? But you can't give up."

Dane forced his gaze from Tansy to Leif, mulling over her words. Leif didn't want to hear a thing he said, could barely tolerate him. *But I won't give up.*

She sounded almost pained as she added, "You're a good brother, Dane."

Dane went back to staring at her. As nice as it was, all sorts of mental red flags popped up.

"You're really going to stick around?" She turned, looking up at him. "Do this Junior Beekeepers thing with me?" Her eyes looked emerald green underneath the fluorescent lights of the barn.

He nodded, his throat too tight to answer. Try as he might, he was having a hell of a time ignoring the hair and the shirt and the lip gloss and her sparkly earrings swaying against the long curve of her neck. She wasn't *just* sexy. She was pretty—even prettier than she had been back in high school. Thankfully, he was older and a good deal wiser. He took a deep breath, preparing to say something he'd never, ever planned to say to her. "I think it would be in everyone's best interest if we— you and me—call a truce."

Tansy took a deep breath but, slowly, she began to nod. "I see."

"When it comes to anything Junior Beekeepers re- lated, of course." He couldn't help but grin.

"Of *course*." Her eyes flashed when they met his. "I know it will be a challenge…"

The fire in her eyes had his heart tripping over itself.

"Not really. *I* can behave, Miss Hill." Was he goading her? Yes. Was he enjoying it? Hell, yes.

Her eyes narrowed. "I'm glad to hear that, Mr. Knudson." She held her hand out. "Shall we shake on it?"

He was still grinning as he took her hand and gave it a solid shake. But once she'd let go and the Junior Beekeepers meeting was called to order, Dane was no longer grinning. Each time she smiled or laughed or spoke with her hands, she made the hollow ache in his stomach harder to ignore. Worse, his palm still tingled from their brief contact. No matter how hard he rubbed his hand against his jeans, he couldn't erase the feel of her touch.

CHAPTER SIX

THE ELGINSTON SPRING & FIDDLE FEST was always a fun event. Elginston was a tiny town twenty minutes down the road but still within Lewis County. The town had bragging rights as the birthplace of some 1930s genius bluegrass fiddler, and every May, fiddlers from far and wide came to play and compete in Fiddle Fest. It was one of Tansy's favorite festivals because it boasted not only a wide array of handcrafted items for sale and yummy food, but world-class music, too.

Another reason she was so partial to it? The organizer always made sure to put Honey Hill Farms booth far from Texas Viking Honey—if the Knudsons even participated.

"I doubt they'll be here," Nicole said again, handing the last of the beeswax candles to Astrid.

"It doesn't matter one way or the other." Tansy stowed the cash box in the large tote by her feet, refusing to make eye contact for fear Nicole and Astrid would call her on her outright lie. Was it so wrong to wish Dane Knudson wouldn't turn up so she wasn't distracted for most of the day? Lorna had said Dane had grown up some but Tansy hadn't believed it. And then the Junior Beekeepers meeting had happened. Not only had he proposed a truce, there was that moment of understanding between them. It had been one hundred percent unexpected and surprisingly nice. After all that, she needed...space.

"She and Dane have called a truce." Astrid stepped back. "How does it look?"

But Nicole wasn't looking at Astrid's artful display, she was staring—open-mouthed—at Tansy. "What? When?" She blinked her sparkly eyelids—she was playing with new makeup looks to complement her new purple streaks. "How?"

"It's the right thing to do." Even if she'd felt unsettled ever since. "For Junior Beekeepers meetings *only*."

"Oh." Nicole wrinkled up her nose. "Huh. How... mature of you both." She shrugged. "I meant to tell you, Benji had the best time. You two know I love my son more than anything, but I can't help worrying about him—he's all sorts of awkward. He gets it from his dad."

Nicole and her high school sweetheart had become parents when they were barely fourteen. Even though they'd outgrown their relationship, they'd remained friends and seemed to have figured out the whole co-parenting thing. Benji Svoboda was indeed awkward, but in the most endearing way. He was quiet but eager to help and all around sweet.

"He sure knows his honey." Tansy had a soft spot for anyone who shared her enthusiasm for bees and honey. And boy was Benji enthusiastic.

Nicole nodded. "I know. If you guys decide to hire some extra help this summer for the honey flow, Benji would probably do it for free."

Tansy and Astrid exchanged a look. At the moment, free was just about all they could afford.

"My oh my, look at this." Ida Popplewell inspected

Astrid's carefully arranged display. She and her husband, Waylon, owned and operated the local bakery. No matter the festival, their booth was always one of the first to sell out. Resisting one of their delectable pastries or breakfast confections was all but impossible. "It's prettier than a picture out of *Better Homes and Gardens* or *Southern Living*, that's for sure." She smoothed the front of her croissant-and-muffin-print apron. "I was telling Corliss Ogden just the other day that you'd be a wonderful interior decorator, Astrid—if Honey Hill Farms ever closed up, that is."

Tansy's heart tightened. None of the Bee Girls dared air their precarious financial situation with anyone. Gossip in a small town spread like wildfire and could be just as devastating.

"Not that that will ever happen." Ida chuckled. "You girls are just as devoted to those bees as your Poppa Tom was."

Astrid took Tansy's hand and gave it a gentle squeeze.

"I best get back to my own tent, quick-like, or Waylon will get all sorts of grumpy and chase away our customers." She paused. "If you see Willadeene or Corliss, you send them my way, won't you? They missed the last Honey Bee Ladies Society meeting—going to some concert—and I need to catch them all up."

"Yes, ma'am." Astrid nodded, holding out a jar of their creamed wildflower honey. "I know it's your favorite so I set a jar aside—in case."

"Oh, Astrid, you are a thoughtful one, aren't you?" Ida took the jar. "It is my absolute favorite. And I know there won't be a jar left if I come back later." She grinned, handed over a ten-dollar bill, tucked the creamed honey into the pocket of her apron and bustled down the aisle between the rows of vendor tents.

"Look at you making bank." Nicole gave Astrid a thumbs-up. "You're a natural-born salesperson, Astrid Hill."

Astrid grinned. "I knew she'd want a jar." She shrugged, turning to Nicole. "Your mom and Corliss went to a concert instead of the Honey Bee Ladies Society meeting?"

"Right?" Nicole shook her head, purple hair shaking, too. "Mom leaving Honey? Possibly missing out on the next big scandal? It's unheard of, I know."

Tansy and Astrid exchanged a look. Willadeene did love to gossip. Aunt Camellia said the woman had an uncanny ability to sniff out scandal wherever she went. Tansy thought it was more likely that Willadeene excelled at stirring things up and spreading the word. Either way, Tansy did her best to stay clear of the woman.

"But luckily, nothing big happened so she didn't resent Corliss forcing her to go to Austin." Nicole tucked a strand of purple hair back. "Somehow they scored tickets to some Pink Floyd laser show thing."

Tansy paused and glanced at her sister, who was staring at Nicole.

So I'm not hearing things. "What?" Tansy couldn't help but grin at the idea of Willadeene Svoboda and Corliss Ogden and her mile-high hair swaying in time to Pink Floyd.

"Oh, don't let that Corliss Ogden fool you. She might be all buttoned-up and stacked hairpieces but," Nicole whispered, "she's a handful." Nicole loved her mother but didn't approve of all the gossiping.

"Corliss Ogden?" Astrid shook her head. "The high school secretary?"

"The very same." Nicole grinned. "According to Mom, Corliss's got quite a handsome fellow in the city, too. Mom says he was downright dreamy. Almost like Robert Redford. And he's younger than Corliss."

"Corliss?" Astrid looked more stunned than ever. "Corliss Ogden?"

Tansy giggled, trying to imagine Corliss Ogden and her Robert Redford–like younger boyfriend out on the town. "I'm going to need a minute to process this new development." She shook her head, noting Astrid's nod. "I wonder who else is living a secret life?" Tansy peered around the growing sea of tents and canopies with narrowed eyes.

"Oh, and Mom said something about seeing your aunt Mags's doppelgänger at the gas station on the way out of town. Like she went on and on about how it was like looking at Magnolia twenty years ago or something. She was totally fixated on it. I mean, it's weird, but not life-altering, you know. Everyone has one. A doppelgänger, I mean. What's the big deal?" Nicole rolled her eyes. "But my mom is…my mom."

Tansy chuckled. Talking to Nicole was always an adventure.

"Back to the secret life thing. If anyone had one and I knew, I'd tell you—you know that. Y'all know everything I know." Nicole did overshare with Tansy and Astrid and the aunts from time to time, but she kept her circle of confidantes to *just* the Hill women. She said that, due to her mother and her mother's friends' constant need for drama, the only people she truly trusted lived on Honey Hill Farms. "Then again, I didn't know a thing about this truce between you and Dane so I guess there might be some secrets to learn yet."

"It's not a secret." Tansy didn't want to make this into a thing. It wasn't.

She hoped their handshake would prevent things from going horribly wrong during their Junior Bee-keepers leadership turn. And, after the handshake, he *had* behaved. Actually, he'd been…quiet and broody. More like Leif than the Dane she was used to. By the end of the night, she'd been on edge and jumpy and scrambling, unsuccessfully, for a new way to convince him to let her handle the meetings on her own.

Astrid draping an arm over her shoulders gave Tansy a start. "I'm proud of you. I can only imagine how difficult it is—between his expansion plans and the way he *lives* to press your buttons."

"Too bad he's pressing the wrong ones." Nicole twined a strand of hair around one finger. "Can you imagine? Pressing your buttons—the *right* buttons, that is—with those giant Viking hands. Oh, hmm, *or* being squished against that muscled-up wall of a chest?" Her exaggerated wink was overkill.

"Nicole!" Tansy squeaked. Not only had she imagined it, she'd experienced it. She'd tried to forget, tried to keep all the tender memories of Dane locked away, for self-preservation. It hadn't worked. His chest may not have been as wall-like back then, but she remembered being squished against him and how amazing it had felt to be held in his arms.

Thanks to Nicole, she was caught up in a tidal wave of heart-pounding Dane-memories. Like his large hands pressing her back or cradling her cheek. The tender look in his oh so blue eyes that had made her insides go soft and warm.

It was all too easy to imagine being held against him now, in all his brawny manliness. His touch. He'd smell good, he'd always smelled good… Considering how toe curling his kiss had been in the past, she didn't want to consider how she'd respond to one of his kisses today…

Stop. What was wrong with her? Astrid and Nicole were right there, watching her. Her cheeks were flaming—they'd notice and jump to all sorts of conclusions. *And they'd be right.* An unexpected giggle slipped out. Between the increasing pressure on her chest and her inability to get him—and those images—out of her head, her laughter was beginning to sound rather unhinged.

"He *is* hot." Nicole fanned herself, her grin full of mischief as she nudged Astrid. "Even you won't deny that."

So what? Hot or not, Dane was Dane. *Just no.*

The concern on Astrid's face helped Tansy snap out of it.

"Um, whatever. You are being…plain ridiculous." Tansy forced a smile. She didn't want anything to do with Dane—she certainly didn't want anything to do with his hands or his broad chest or any other part of him.

Nicole spoke quickly, "And he's—"

"Nicole," she sighed, picked up an empty wood crate and turned, plowing into the poor person who had the misfortune of being right behind her.

"Right there," Nicole murmured.

"Oh, I'm so…" Tansy sputtered to a stop. *No.* Couldn't she catch even the slightest break?

"Sorry?" Dane gripped her shoulders and frowned

down at her. "Yeah. Ow." He released her and rubbed the center of his chest, right where the corner of the wooden crate had slammed into him.

"Yes. I am." Tansy wasn't going to stare at him or his hands or his chest. "I didn't see you," she breathed, glancing at her sister and Nicole.

Nicole's mouthed *Sorry* might have helped—if she wasn't smiling.

"Glad to hear it wasn't on purpose." But the usual teasing wasn't there. If anything, Dane sounded snippy.

"Why would I..." She broke off. "Of course, it wasn't on purpose."

His dismissive snort was all kinds of infuriating.

She glared up at him, braced and ready—but he wasn't even looking at her. He was scanning the growing city of canopies for something or someone. "It might help if you watch where you're going."

His blue eyes locked with hers. "Something tells me you'd have found a way." Impatience rolled off him in waves.

She gripped the wooden crate so tightly there was a good chance she'd be using tweezers to pull out splinters later. "A way to what? Wound you?"

"Wound? No. Irritate and inconvenience?" He shrugged. "Something like that."

Dane was always hurling teasing, yet barbed, insults at Tansy but this was different. Mean and outright nasty. There was no sign of his condescending smile or gleeful sarcasm. In his eyes there was...anger. When his attention returned to scouring the crowd, Tansy took a deep breath.

"Um..." Astrid's flustered expression didn't help.

"What's up, Dane? You're not your usual charming self." Nicole smiled.

It was Dane's turn to take a long, deep breath. He rolled his neck, a long blond strand of hair falling along his face, before giving Nicole a pinched smile. "Not a thing."

Which is a bald-faced lie. "Perusing the competition before things get started?" Tansy set the wooden crate down. "I didn't see a Texas Viking Honey booth."

"You were looking for me?" Dane countered, a hint of amusement in his voice. "I'm flattered."

No. "Don't be. I wasn't looking for you." Tansy swallowed, her earlier thoughts resurfacing with vivid details. Her throat tightened but she managed, "More like scanning the tents and faces."

It was silly to blame Nicole but she *was* the one who'd brought Dane up and then, out of nowhere, he appeared. Now who was the ridiculous one? *I am.*

There was a definite smile in Dane's voice now. "But you did notice that mine was missing."

Really? Tansy shot him a look.

Dane's delight faded. "You're looking a little red there, Tansy. Everything okay?"

"Peachy keen." She'd be better if she could rein in her imagination. And if he'd take one big step back. He did, in fact, smell just as good as she remembered. *Not helping.*

"Glad to hear it. I don't suppose Leif has wandered by?" Dane studied her for a few seconds longer than necessary.

What was the look for? Why were his eyes so brilliantly blue this morning? It was harder to swallow this time. "Not so excited about working in the Texas Viking Honey booth?" Tansy crossed her arms over her chest.

"No booth today." He looked at Tansy and grinned. "You're welcome."

"For what?" She instantly regretted asking.

"Giving you some…space." He shrugged, rubbing his chest.

"Space?" She managed a smile. "It might come as a surprise, Mr. Knudson, but your involvement today doesn't make a bit of difference to me."

"Well, it sort of does." He nodded at Astrid's pretty display. "No real competition to speak of means the likelihood of selling all your honey is that much higher."

Tansy swallowed down a litany of unsavory words. "If you're saying you didn't come today so we could get more sales, save your breath."

"That's a strong accusation, Miss Hill." He kept on grinning. "*Did* I say that?"

"What are you trying to say, Mr. Knudson?" Tansy was definitely in need of space now. "Is there a point, because things are officially getting underway in—" she glanced at her watch "—seven minutes. Feel free to go visit another booth. Any other booth."

Dane's chuckle was deep and gravelly. "Are you trying to get rid of me?"

Yes. Go. Leave. Now. "*I* didn't say that, did I?" she mimicked, hands on her hips.

"You didn't have to." His gaze locked with hers.

For a minute, Tansy couldn't breathe. Not when he was looking at her like *that*. Intense and heavy and… and mesmerizing. It was irritating. *He* was irritating. "What does that mean?" she murmured, more than a little dazed. *Why am I asking?*

"Your eyes. They say what your mouth won't." His gaze darted to her lips then, the muscle in his jaw clenching tight.

The whole *right buttons* conversation scrolled through her brain—followed by the vivid imaginings of her being caught up against that chest by those hands. *Was it hot?* It felt hot. She ignored the urge to fan herself.

"I suppose I should be careful." He rubbed the likely-sore spot on his chest again. "I don't want to say or do something that'll make you *accidentally* dump a bucket of color on me at the barn painting." He eyed the wooden crate. "Like you *accidentally* gouged my chest."

"I didn't do that on purpose. It *was* a…" She stopped the moment she saw how much he was enjoying this. He was teasing. Fine. *Turnabout is fair play.* Eyebrows raised, smile in place, Tansy rubbed her hands together. "Now *that* is an idea." From the corner of her eye, she saw Astrid and Nicole watching them, Astrid with alarm and Nicole with interest.

But beyond them was a far more terrifying sight. Willadeene and Corliss and Ida and *so* many more. From the looks of it, the whole Honey Bee Ladies Society was watching with wide-eyed interest. It was one thing to see them whispering and giggling over potential gossip at someone else's expense but *these* whispers and giggles were about her. No, not just her. Coldness flooded her, setting the hair along the back of her neck on end.

Me and Dane. She took a deep breath and whispered, "Dane, please behave. Please." She wasn't just protecting herself here, she was protecting him, too. He was the topic of more than enough gossip as it was—she didn't want to get pulled into that. She swallowed and added, "I'll owe you one."

DANE'S MORNING HAD started off bad and showed no signs of improving. After his cup of black coffee, he'd gone out to inspect a beeyard that'd been left unsupervised for three weeks. Turned out his father had fired a beekeeper and Dane had only found out when no time sheets had been turned in by the employee. In three weeks' time, a handful of hives in one apiary were now under siege by hive beetles.

Bees were hearty, but so were their adversaries. It was the beekeepers' job to help protect the hive. The most common threats to a bee colony were parasitic varroa mites, honeycomb-devouring wax moths or, their current enemy, invasive small hive beetles. It took time for the hives to recover from the damage the tiny pests could cause.

Instead of getting worked up, Dane had decided it was a good learning opportunity for Leif. Hive beetles were a part of beekeeping and, like it or not, Leif was a beekeeper so...

Leif hadn't been in his room. In fact, he was nowhere to be found. And since his little brother wasn't answering his texts, Dane had no choice but to get worked up. It wasn't the first time Leif had run off to avoid work but, since Leif's fight, Dane couldn't shake the feeling that something more was going on.

After his phone calls had provided no leads and he and his father wound up in another pointless shouting match, Dane had climbed into his truck and started driving. It hadn't taken long to wind up in Elginston.

Nothing else was happening close by, so maybe Leif was here looking to get out of work and have some fun.

A quick in-and-out, grab Leif, then home. At least, that had been the plan.

Now he was face-to-face with Tansy and she was asking him for a favor.

But there was no way he'd heard that correctly. No way. He'd hit his chest, not his head, right? It was the only way this would make sense. He was running low on caffeine but, as far as explanations went, it seemed like a stretch. Worse, he seemed to be caught up in some alternative reality where Tansy Hill was almost being playful with him. And…tempting. At least, her very full, pink lips were. He tried to tear his gaze away and, ten seconds later, he was staring at her mouth again.

"Dane?" The sense of urgency to Tansy's whisper grabbed his attention. "Can you smile or something?"

He blinked. How long had he been standing here? How long had he been staring at her? He straightened, glancing around him. *Dammit.* Just like that, her request made sense. Not only was the whole Honey Bee Ladies Society ogling them like they were the best thing since sliced bread, but Honey's own Wicked Witch of the Hill Country, Willadeene Svoboda, was front and center. *Sonofabitch.*

His stomach was already in knots over Leif, now there was a trickle of dread—and sweat—running down his back. It took everything he had not to round on Willadeene Svoboda and her venomous tongue. He couldn't count the number of times he'd envisioned telling the woman off, but he knew better. She wasn't the sort of tiger to change her stripes. She was rotten to the core, and the best course of action was as little as possible and try not to draw attention.

Tansy let out a slow breath, her eyes going wide. "Oh. Dear. Umm… That's one *scary*-looking smile you're wearing, Dane," she whispered, more panicked than ever.

He hadn't meant to laugh but, for some reason, he did. "As far as mornings go, this one has been a steaming pile of—"

"I get it, I get it." She held up her hand. "Lovely imagery there."

"What can I say, I have a way with words." After all these years, he shouldn't still enjoy making her squirm this much.

Tansy tore her gaze from his and rolled her eyes but there was no easing of her posture. "At least that's a real smile."

The slight increase in the tittering and whispers from the blue-haired audience not-so-surreptitiously watching them was enough to turn Tansy's cheeks scarlet.

"Don't make any sudden movements or they're likely to attack." Dane nodded in the women's general direction.

Tansy covered her mouth but her laughter spilled out.

He leaned forward, keeping his voice low. "You know, we could have some fun and give them something to talk about."

"You're playing with fire." Just when he thought her eyes couldn't get any wider. "I don't want them to talk about me—at all. Even if I am passing up a chance to slap you." She looked entirely too pleased at the thought, though there was a twinkle of humor in her eyes.

He laughed again. "That would be one way to go."

How would she react if she knew what he was thinking? Less slapping and more…kissing. *What the hell am I thinking?* He wasn't smiling anymore.

"Dane." Astrid stepped up then, no hint of her always-serene expression in place. "We…we'll keep an eye out for Leif."

Right. Leif. "That'd be terrific." He pulled his phone from his pocket. No messages. He should get back to searching. Not standing here doing whatever *this* was. *Making an ass out of myself, that's what this is.* But, before he could take his first step, the Ladies Society swarmed in on them.

"We looked and there are no pigs flying." Willadeene stepped forward and Dane could almost hear the Wicked Witch theme from *The Wizard of Oz*.

Don't hum it. Do not hum it. He couldn't stop himself from laughing. "Good one."

Tansy shot him what could only be described as a warning look.

Willadeene glanced between them. "I was sure we'd see at least one, seeing as how you two aren't at each other's throats. Dane laughing and you smiling and the two of you whispering that way."

"*So* intently?" Corliss added, her oversize glasses so thick they magnified her eyes until they seemed to take up most of her face.

"Oh…no…well…" Tansy's cheeks went from pink to white.

As much as Dane liked to make Tansy sputter and panic, he didn't like Willadeene Svoboda rattling her this way, or making another false claim that Dane was having an affair with someone. "Bees." He shrugged. "We were talking about bees. And beekeeping." He cleared his throat. "I found some SHB in a couple of hives and figured Tansy might have new ideas on how to get rid of them."

Tansy nodded, her expression blank.

"SHB?" Ida asked.

"Small hive beetles," Astrid explained. "Nasty things."

Corliss, Ida, Willadeene and crew looked skeptical.

"Oh, they're horrible." Tansy was all business. "They lay eggs in the comb, ferment the honey and their larvae chew through *everything* in their way. Left unchecked, they can destroy a hive." She snapped her fingers. "That fast. They're a real problem for beekeepers and bees."

"My goodness." Corliss nodded.

Ida scrunched up her nose in distaste. "That sounds horrible. Can't you just spray them with chemicals and call it a day?"

"Most chemicals will kill the bees, too." Tansy shook her head. "It's not an easy fix, that's for sure. I...I was telling Dane to make sure his hives were in a sunny, well-ventilated location—"

"Which they are," Dane cut in, feeling the need to defend himself.

"Also, a good ground drench will help get to the larvae. And traps he can use and rotate, to help reduce them." Tansy went on as if he hadn't said a word.

Willadeene was watching them closely, her arms crossed over her chest. "You're telling me the two of you are talking about parasites?"

She even looked like the Wicked Witch. *Leave your flying monkeys at home?* Dane chuckled, earning him odd looks from everyone.

Willadeene shrugged, all innocence. "I guess we

should thank the bees for bringing you two…*together*." Willadeene was the queen of carefully placed pauses. With a pause, she managed to imply what she wanted without her actually outright saying a thing. She was good at that, saying just enough to make filling in the blanks glaringly obvious—that way she could deny she'd said a thing. "So nice to see you two…getting along, this way."

He was pretty sure Willadeene had it out for him because his father's ex, the one before Kate, was one of Willadeene's cronies. Apparently, the divorce was enough to make the Knudson family one of Willadeene's favorite topics of conversation. Now she was fishing for new Knudson-centered gossip.

"Getting along? Maybe? *Together* is a stretch. I'd say I'm flattered that our bee talk is so engrossing but—" he glanced at Tansy, the slight shake of her head enough to make him reconsider his words "—I get the feeling you were hoping for something more, Mrs. Svoboda?"

Willadeene's smile was tight and her eyes narrowed. "I'm sure I don't know what you mean, Dane Knudson."

"No?" His laugh was hard, all the words he wanted to say damn near choking him. "Well, that's…good."

"If you say it's all about the bees, Dane, I'm sure that's *all*." Willadeene's drawn-on eyebrows ascended almost into her hairline.

"Just bees." Tansy shot him an odd look, one he couldn't decipher. "And the Junior Beekeepers."

"That's right. *The two of you* did volunteer to fill in for Lorna Franks. For the *bees*. Of course. What else?"

Was she really going to push for this? The idea of Tansy and him together was laughable. Or it would be if he hadn't gotten all caught up in her at the Junior

Beekeepers meeting. In her eyes and her hair and her stupid bee earrings. When they'd touched...well, it'd been a jolt to the system. He didn't know what to do about Tansy but now wasn't the time to worry about it. All he needed to do was keep his mouth shut so the target on his back wouldn't quadruple in size. *Easier said than done.*

"I'm glad you two stepped up," Ida said, sounding sincere. "Lorna doesn't need to worry over an unruly group of teens *and* a new baby."

That wasn't how he'd describe the Junior Beekeepers. Listening to them carry on about bees like they were the coolest thing around had reminded Dane he was lucky to do something that made him happy.

"Benji mentioned Leif came to the meeting." Willadeene's *sympathetic* smile was a little too forced to be genuine. "Maybe getting involved with the Junior Beekeepers will help?" She lowered her voice. "*Everyone* knows he's been having...*problems.*"

Dane had to grit his teeth to prevent himself from responding. Leif was struggling, yes, but her spreading trash around about their father and Dane wasn't helping. If he had it his way, the woman wouldn't say Leif's name.

"Leif is a delight," Tansy gushed, smiling at him. "A perfect fit for the Junior Beekeepers. After all, beekeeping is in his blood. He left really looking forward to the next meeting, I think?"

He nodded. He'd never expected her to defend Leif, but he appreciated it. And, if "really looking forward to the next meeting" meant Leif had practically run from the barn when the last meeting ended, then sure. "He can't wait."

"Good. That's good. Violet Taggert and I volunteered to bring lunch out to you-all at the barn painting." Willadeene was delighted to share this news. "I'm bringing cowboy cookies. My specialty."

No shit? Awesome. Dane stared up at a white fluffy cloud sailing across the blue sky until he was confident his face wouldn't give him away.

"I'll look forward to it." Willadeene gave Nicole a slight wave. "Nicole."

"Mom." Nicole didn't wave back, she barely looked at her mother.

With a very loud, very affronted sigh, Willadeene headed off—the others trailing after her. "I don't know what's wrong with that girl…" Her voice trailed off.

"I take after my dad," Nicole muttered. "Thank goodness for that." She turned to them, shaking her head. "I'm so sorry. I just… I can't even…"

"Parents," Dane supplied. He wasn't going to hold Nicole accountable for her mother. "What's that saying? Following in their footsteps or making our own way?"

"Oh, option two. One hundred percent." Nicole shuddered. "One Willadeene is more than enough."

Dane caught the quick, pained look exchanged between Astrid and Tansy. *Dammit all.* He ran a hand over his face. *At least we have parents to complain about.* The Hill sisters only had their aunts. It might not be the same but anyone would be lucky to have Camellia and Magnolia Hill in their corner.

"Hey, Tansy!" Kerrielynn sort of bounced up to the booth, as bubbly as she'd been at the Junior Beekeepers meeting. "Hi, Mr. Knudson. Leif didn't say you were here, too."

Here, too? Meaning Leif *was* here. He took a deep

calming breath and did his best not to react. "I wasn't sure I was coming." He shrugged. "Where is he, again?"

"I put him to work at the FFA arts and crafts booth, over by the petting zoo." Kerrielynn pointed. "I didn't even know he'd signed up to help."

That makes two of us.

"I was all, 'Thank goodness you're here.' It was totally perfect timing since we were way shorthanded." Kerrielynn adjusted one of the jars of honey.

Astrid nodded her approval at the girl's handiwork. "That's so nice of him."

Dane sighed. *Yes. Yes, it was.* It was a hell of a lot better than what he'd been picturing—Leif doing something foolish or bad or illegal. But dammit, that didn't suddenly make Leif's disappearing act okay. His little brother was still grounded from his fight. That meant he was supposed to be working at the farm for the next month—*not* volunteering. Something he and Leif had talked about after Leif had driven them home. Dane had made his expectations perfectly clear. That way there was no confusion. Leif had done this deliberately. But why?

How had Leif even gotten here? He couldn't drive yet. As far as Dane knew, Clay Dwyer was the only one he knew with a car and license. He was pretty sure that wasn't an option anymore. One more question to add to his growing list.

"It's great he's lending a hand." Tansy slipped the neck loop of her apron over her head.

It's frigging wonderful. Dane frowned, eyeing the bright blue apron with white daisies and bees. *Tansy and her bees.*

"Maybe you can convince him to join the Junior

Beekeepers, too." Tansy reached around her waist to secure her apron but lost one tie and floundered for it, turning in a circle to reach for it.

Dane watched, shoving his hands into his pockets so he wouldn't tie her apron. He didn't need to—she had a sister and friend and young protégé all able and willing to do so. *Any second now.* He waited, his hands fisting.

"Oops, stop spinning." Astrid laughed, grabbing the ties and making a nice bow in the middle of Tansy's back. "There."

He blew out a slow breath, smiling as the two sisters laughed. Siblings. Getting along. *Imagine that.* It could happen. Before he could look away, Tansy's green eyes met his for a second. But, for that second, Dane wasn't sure which way was up. Tansy was smiling at him. A real smile, without a hint of teasing or hostility. She'd never been more beautiful.

He tore his gaze from hers and sucked in a ragged breath. He *needed* to grab Leif and leave—now—and deal with the damn hive beetles chewing through his hives.

"Well, I just wanted to say hi," Kerrielynn said. "And to thank you both, again, for helping out. It's, um, way cool. And thanks for letting Leif help out, too." She smiled up at Dane. "He's the GOAT. I don't know how we'd get everything done without him."

Great. "Sure." He nodded, sighing as the girl walked back the way she'd come. To Tansy, he said, "The GOAT?"

"Greatest of all time." She nudged him. "At least you know where he is now."

"Yeah." He glanced down at her. She was smiling up at him as if all his problems were solved. *I wish.* "I guess I'm supposed to forget he took off without telling me and I'm not supposed to drag his butt home, to do what he's supposed to be doing because he's grounded for fighting at school." Why did she have to look so damn beautiful when she smiled? His throat went tight.

"Oh, Dane." Tansy nibbled on the inside of her lower lip, her gaze searching his. "That's a tough call."

His name echoed in his ears. She'd said it, without sarcasm or heat, and he liked the sound of it. Everything was off. Watching her worry her lip with her teeth didn't help. The knot in his throat turned jagged and an uncomfortably heavy warmth pressed in on his chest. "Whatever." He ran a hand over his face but it didn't help. He could still see her mouth. More specifically, her teeth nibbling the swell of her pink lower lip... *Enough.*

"You owe me." He didn't know why he said it only that he needed to feel like he was in control in some small way. *What a joke.*

Tansy stared up at him, the slightest crease between her brows. "I...I know." And she didn't look happy about it.

Abrupt or not, he turned on his heel and walked back through the tent maze toward the parking lot. He had a lot weighing on him, he was tired and on edge and hadn't had near enough coffee for half of what he'd dealt with since he'd rolled out of bed. That was why he was out of sorts. A little space, some hard work, he'd get his head straight in no time. Then he'd see this whole thing between Tansy and him wasn't a thing at all. It was...nothing to worry about. He climbed into his truck, started the engine and turned on the radio.

Peter Gabriel's soulful voice flooded his truck cab. "Perfect." He ran a hand over his face and started laughing. He knew every word to the damn ballad "In Your Eyes." Why? Because it had been *her* favorite song. He'd wanted to take her to prom, put in a request so they could dance to the song, and sing it—for her ears alone. He'd been such a damn fool, too young and naive to realize his heart was about to be broken. "A lifetime ago," he murmured. He turned off the radio and made the long drive home in silence.

LEIF SAW KERRIELYNN round the end of the row of tents and canopies, headed his way. He swallowed against the tightness of his throat, doing his best to act normal— then knocking over a container of paintbrushes. He knelt, shoving the brushes back into the container.

"You need help?" Kerrielynn asked.

"I'm good," he murmured, not looking up. *I'm a moron.* He finished collecting the brushes and stood, putting the container on top of the folding table.

"I think Tansy Hill is, like, the coolest human being in all of Honey." Kerrielynn had a large to-go coffee cup in each hand. "It's hot chocolate." She offered Leif one.

"Thanks." It was already around eighty degrees but he wasn't going to say no.

"I mean, I've always known *who* she was. If you're into bees and live around here, you know who the Hills are." She glanced his way. "And Texas Viking Honey, too. Your brother and the whole Thor thing."

Leif didn't manage to hide his smile. "He really hates that."

"He does?" Kerrielynn faced him as she sipped her hot chocolate. "Why? It's a compliment, isn't it? And, you know, I'm betting it helps with sales."

"I think so." Leif remembered the long lines of customers waiting to get a selfie—and a jar of honey.

"Interesting." She sipped her hot chocolate. "Can I ask a question? About your brother and Tansy." Kerrielynn sat her cup aside and squirted red paint into a plastic cup. "What's that about?"

Like I know. He shrugged. "They don't like each other."

Kerrielynn looked at him and blinked. "They don't?"

He took a moment, choosing his words with care. "I think *they* think they don't like each other."

"Makes sense." Kerrielynn nodded. "But, really, they are so into each other. Am I right?"

"Maybe." As much as he'd like to think Kerrielynn was someone he could talk to…well, people were good at hiding who they really were. Or pretending to be someone they weren't. He didn't think Kerrielynn was like that but he wasn't about to let his guard down, not yet.

"You don't talk much, you know that?" Kerrielynn laughed. "But I guess I talk a lot. At least, my parents say I do. And my little brother, Ford. He says I never shut up. Brothers…" She glanced his way. "I just ran into yours at the Honey Hill Farms booth. I sort of got the impression Dane didn't know you were here."

"Just now?" Leif stopped screwing the lids back on the paint bottles. "Dane is here?" He was in so much trouble. His gaze scanned the crowd. Dane was easy to spot, as tall and big as he was.

"You two didn't come together?" Kerrielynn asked.

"No." He'd left before the sun was up and been lucky enough to hitch a ride or he'd probably still be walking. Leif glanced her way. He'd come here for one reason and, because he was too chicken to spit it out, he'd wound up cleaning paintbrushes and opening paint jars that were screwed on too tight.

"Are things...okay?" She adjusted the paintbrush beside the cup of paint. "I mean...in general. At home and stuff?" She was staring at him—he just knew it. "Well, you know."

He knew all right. He was a screwup. He'd done it to himself—wanted to keep everyone at arm's length. Hanging out with Eddie, meant hanging out with all the Dwyer brothers. They didn't give a crap about anything. He wanted to be like that, too. But he'd never meant for anyone else to get hurt. He felt like an ass, that she'd been caught in the middle of it. She hadn't been hurt, but she could have—and knowing that ate at him. *Now is as good a time as any.* "I've been meaning to say I'm sorry. The fight. I am, though." He had a hard time meeting her gaze. "I didn't mean for you to get pushed—"

"I know." Kerrielynn cut him off. "You didn't push me, Leif. Clay did. You...you stopped to make sure I was okay and then..." She winced.

Then I got my head slammed into a locker? He nodded.

"You can't let him get to you. Clay, I mean. He's a dick. Plain and simple. He makes up stuff about everyone. He even told people we'd dated." She glanced at him and shook her head. "We never dated or kissed or anything."

Leif *had* heard that rumor. Clay had gone on and on about it, saying Kerrielynn wasn't a good kisser. There was no way Kerrielynn would ever get involved with someone like Clay. *Or someone like me.* "I didn't believe that."

"You didn't?" Kerrielynn blew out a deep breath. "That's a relief. People don't ask, you know? They just believe what they hear, even when it's stupid." She glanced at him again. "Like the thing with Dane and Kate. I know that's so *not* true. None of it."

"How?" Leif waited. He didn't believe it, either. Mostly. But their dad treated Dane like crap. Dad barely talked to Dane but when he did, he was a smart-ass—talking down to him, belittling his ideas and treating Dane like an outsider instead of family. Leif didn't understand how the two of them wound up hating each other, but he knew they did. Even if Dane had wanted to get back at their father, he wouldn't have done it that way. He was curious to find out how Kerrielynn could be so certain.

"Easy. Kate—she used to babysit me and my brother. She was not a nice person, at all. She lied, all the time. She'd have boys over and friends, she even told my parents I broke a vase they got for their wedding. But some guy did it. Thankfully, my mom believed me. She said Kate had this look on her face when she lied. She did, too, because I saw it and knew—*Oops, there goes Kate lying again.* Anyway, she didn't babysit after that." She took a deep breath and went on. "My mom was at the beauty salon when Kate and her sister came in and told Mrs. Svoboda about her affair." She shook her head. "If Willadeene knows, everyone knows. Mom said Kate was really loud, too, like she wanted to be overheard. Plus, Mom said Kate was making the same face—her lying face—when she was telling the story. Mom says it's a lie, too. And that people need to mind their own business. I agree." She nudged him. "*And* why would your brother be interested in Kate when he has someone like Tansy? It doesn't make sense."

Leif didn't argue. He wasn't so sure about his brother and Tansy but he was relieved to hear that some folk didn't believe the BS Kate and that bitch, Willadeene Svoboda, were spreading.

"Ugh. I guess I do talk a lot." Kerrielynn's smile faded. "Sorry."

She did. But it was nice. She was talking, not lecturing or taunting or drilling him with questions. Just talking—like he was someone worth talking to. "I don't mind." Leif managed to look her in the eye then.

"You don't?" Kerrielynn's eyes went round. "Cool." She was smiling again.

Leif nodded, handing her more plastic cups to fill—in no hurry to leave. It was cool. *She* was cool. Dane would be mad at him, but Leif was pretty sure it would be worth it.

CHAPTER SEVEN

WHEN TANSY WAS growing up, she'd believed twilight on Honey Hill Farms was a magical time. Amidst the pollen heavy bee-friendly blooms of the esperanza, buttercups, verbena, purple coneflowers and sky blue asters, Granna Hazel had a hidden moonlight garden. She often teased Poppa Tom, saying the fairies needed their own flowers to tend and those bees wanting a midnight snack might be looking for something special—knowing full well bees stopped foraging after dark. Not that she'd ever needed to justify a thing when it came to Poppa Tom. She was his everything. If she wanted night-blooming flowers, she got them. Twilight teas and after-dinner coffees on the great wraparound porch were accompanied by the fragrant jasmine, the large white-and-purple datura trumpets, and vanilla-scented heliotrope. Tansy, Astrid and Rosemary had never found the fairies Granna Hazel mentioned, but they'd spent many an evening looking. Those were some memories Tansy treasured most—the nights of flashlight searches, giggles and fireflies beneath a star-crowded sky. Maybe that was why the porch of the great old house was a favored place.

Aunt Mags rarely missed her evening routine. She'd sit, rain or shine, on the wide wraparound porch sipping tea from a fine china teacup as the sun went down. This was her time to be quiet and center herself, she'd say.

While tonight's sunset was lovely, Tansy was restless. Still, her gaze trailed the fluffy pink-and-tangerine marshmallow fluff clouds as they drifted across the lavender sky—each one more lovely than the last.

"You're awful quiet this evening." Aunt Mags sipped her tea, her gaze fixed on the evening sky.

"Just…tired, I guess." Unsettled was more like it. She had been all day—jittery nervousness keeping her nerves pulled tight.

"Hmm," Auntie Mags murmured, glancing her way.

Tansy lifted her arms so her seatmates, Jammie and Beeswax the cats, could arrange themselves, wedged between her and the calico-print cushions. "Better?" she asked as they settled. Jammie yawned, and Beeswax went back to snoring softly. "I'll take that as a yes." She cradled her teacup with both hands, breathing in the calming chamomile. *Apparently, calm isn't in the cards for me.* She sighed, her mind turning over the morning's events again.

Dane's face. Those blue eyes fixed on her. *You owe me.* It wasn't just what Dane had said, it was the way he'd said it. The way he'd looked at her.

When *she'd* said it, she'd been joking, sort of. There was enough talk circulating about the Knudsons, so playing nice for Willadeene and the Honey Bee Ladies Society seemed logical. It was the right choice for both of them, surely he saw that? Or not. *Because now I owe him.*

"Nicole said it was an interesting morning." Aunt Mags glanced at Tansy over the teacup's rim. "Something about her mother stirring up trouble?"

Tansy shrugged.

"No matter how many times your aunt asks me to join the Honey Bee Ladies Society, my answer will remain the same." Mags sighed with feeling. "At least until *that* woman is gone. Willadeene Svoboda is the worst sort of gossip."

"Is there a good sort of gossip?" Tansy asked, scratching Jammie-cat's stomach as he stretched.

"No, I suppose not." Aunt Mags took another sip. "What was she after this time?"

Tansy shrugged again, remembering the gleeful look in the woman's eyes. It wasn't hard to figure out what the woman was thinking, but *why* Willadeene was so determined that she and Dane were a *thing* was the real mystery. It was too far-fetched—even for Willadeene Svoboda. Since no one would believe it, there was no need to worry. *So, stop worrying.*

Jammie-cat yawned and went back to sleep. "Life as a cat—one of Aunt Camellia's cats—has to be pretty awesome, don't you think?" Any of Aunt Camellia's pets, for that matter.

Aunt Mags's finely arched brows rose. "If the idea of bathing oneself with one's tongue, eating vile-smelling canned food and fending off the occasional flea or an overabundance of dog slobber is your idea of awesome, then I suppose."

"Poor Oatmeal." Whenever the massive Saint Bernard mix got stressed, he began to drool uncontrollably.

Tansy laughed. Honey Hill Farms' animal menagerie wasn't just cats, goats, a parrot and guard donkeys. There were also five dogs of varying age, size and personality. While they were all technically Aunt Camellia's, all the Bee Girls did their part to care for all the animals on the farm.

Curling around Jammie and Beeswax had an instant soothing effect on the dog but left the felines in a puddle that required a bath. Giving the cats a bath was *never* fun. "Fine. Maybe not."

Aunt Mags grinned and went back to studying the sky. "You know, Poppa loved this time of day."

Tansy nodded. She could remember sitting, in this very chair, on Poppa Tom's lap.

"He said he'd send all his worries and stresses with the sun—knowing they'd be there to greet him in the morning." Mags sat her teacup down, folded her hands in her lap and looked at Tansy. "But he did try to work through whatever was weighing on him first, talk it out, so he had one less worry."

Tansy stared into her tea and then sighed. "It's Dane. He's just… He's so… And I let him make me so… He picks and I react—every time." An impatient groan slipped out. "Willadeene showed up and it was like—" She broke off, searching for just the right words. "Almost like she'd caught us doing something wrong?"

Thankfully, Aunt Mags didn't say anything.

"We were arguing, as we do." Tansy glanced at her aunt. She didn't mention her deliciously inappropriate thoughts about Dane seconds before she'd collided with him. Or that she'd been red-cheeked and more rattled than she'd been…maybe, ever. "But I saw Willadeene and she was wearing a certain look." Maybe Tansy should have handled things differently? But how? "Dane doesn't like the woman—it was all over his face—but he managed to control his temper even when she kept on watching and smiling and saying how nice it is to see us *together* and *getting along*."

"He shouldn't like her. I have no doubt Kate started the rumor—but Willadeene was the one to make sure everyone heard it." She frowned. "If I were a gambler, which I'm not, I'd bet on it."

Even though it turned her stomach, she'd been thinking along the same lines.

"Why was Dane out and about instead of manning his booth—and staying out of trouble?" At the jingle of a tiny bell, Aunt Mags's green eyes scanned the porch.

"He didn't have a booth, he was looking for Leif. So distracted and worried that he plowed into me and wound up gouging his chest with the corner of a shipping crate." She rubbed her chest. "Which had to hurt."

"Nicole says Leif Knudson is nothing but trouble." Aunt Mags lifted one perfectly manicured hand so the newest porch companion, Butters the one-eyed Chihuahua mix with an extreme underbite and wild tufts of untamed fur, could jump up onto her lap. "But the poor boy didn't stand a chance, did he? With Harald as his father and Dane for a brother." Butters turned several circles before curling up into a tiny ball on Aunt Mags's lap.

For the second time that day, Tansy found herself defending a boy she barely knew. "I don't think Leif *wants* to be trouble." She ran a hand along Beeswax's back. "He came to the Junior Beekeepers meeting with Dane. Honestly, he seemed…sad." She kept on petting the cat until Beeswax's lion-worthy purr started. "So did—does—Dane. Seem sad, I mean."

"It's no secret that theirs is not a happy home, Tansy." Aunt Mags rested a hand on Butters's back. "Mostly from their own making, I might add." She shook her head, finishing her tea and setting her cup on the table. "It's also no secret that Willadeene has been targeting the Knudsons since Harald divorced Willadeene's pal, Beulah Zink—*before* this most recent fiasco of a divorce to Kate." She sighed. "You being nice to Dane—"

"I wasn't being *nice* to Dane. We were trying not to attract attention."

"And it backfired." Aunt Mags waited for Tansy's nod. "I'm sure she's already concocting reasons for this sudden change between you two—reasons that will likely cast you as the victim and Dane as the villain." She shrugged. "Really, dear, you have nothing to worry about."

Her aunt's attempts to comfort her weren't helping. She didn't give a fig about Dane but Dane wasn't the only one impacted by this sort of talk. *Poor Leif.* "No one will believe it. It's ridiculous."

"Is it?" Mags asked, stroking Butters's head. "After a lifetime of exchanging barbs and making each other miserable you're suddenly getting along. It's suspicious, and that's all it takes to plant a seed." She paused, smoothing Butters's wiry hair. "Willadeene Svoboda is very good at planting *those* sorts of seeds." Mags sighed. "I wouldn't worry. Any fallout will land on Dane Knudson's very square, very capable shoulders, which should make you happy."

The problem was, it didn't.

"What are we talking about?" Astrid backed out the screen door carrying a tray stacked high with cookies. "And are you hungry? Because these look remotely edible." She stooped and slid the tray on top of the wicker table.

Over Astrid's shoulder, Aunt Camellia shrugged.

Astrid might be the bee whisperer but she was a terrible cook. Like scorched-cobbler-to-the-point-that-there-was-no-saving-the-baking-pan terrible. Still, Aunt Camellia was an eternal encourager. If Astrid wanted to try again, Camellia would stay close with advice—and a fire extinguisher.

"Edible is always good." Tansy leaned forward to inspect her sister's latest baking endeavors. "They're pretty."

"Aunt Camellia might have helped with the glaze." Astrid smiled back, over her shoulder, at Aunt Camellia.

"It was a trifle too tart is all." Aunt Camellia slipped an arm around Astrid's waist. "A pinch or two of sugar set it all to rights."

"I figured this time, instead of trying a tea cake, I'd start small." Astrid watched as Tansy reached for one of the beehive-shaped cookies. "Honey sugar cookies." Her unsteady voice was all nerves. "Auntie Mags, are you going to try one?"

Aunt Mags was convinced that keeping her facial expressions to a minimum prevented wrinkles so she had one hell of a poker face. Reading Aunt Camellia was easy—her facial expressions were often overly animated to the point of melodrama. At the moment, the "Try one or else" glare she was sending her sister's way left no room for misunderstanding.

"Of course." Aunt Mags sat forward to select a cookie. "They do, indeed, look edible."

Astrid was a ball of apprehension so Tansy lifted the thin cookie and took a massive bite. It was hard not to choke as Astrid, Aunt Camellia and Auntie Mags all leaned forward, waiting.

"They're good." Tansy ate the rest of the cookie and reached for another one. "Light and crisp, with the perfect hint of honey and sweetness."

Aunt Magnolia took a tentative bite, chewing carefully, before nodding in agreement. "Well done."

The tires on gravel and approaching roar of a car engine drew all eyes to the long drive that led from the county road to the main house. Poppa Tom had installed old-fashioned streetlamps from the bend in the drive up to the flagstone path leading from the white picket gate to the wide porch steps. It was welcoming—and also gave the Hills a heads-up on who was coming to visit. Granna Hazel didn't mind surprise visitors, but she preferred a few seconds to get together refreshments and make the porch presentable.

Tansy smiled as Aunt Camellia stood, absentmindedly fluffing the pillows and straightening the tea tray just so. *Just like Granna Hazel.*

"Are we expecting someone?" Aunt Mags finished her cookie and set Butters on the porch. She stood, running her hands over her skirt and smoothing her hair.

"Maybe Abner found more mail?" Tansy leaned forward for another cookie. Abner Jones had been the mailman as far back as Tansy could remember.

"It wouldn't be the first time." Aunt Camellia sighed. "I can't imagine the gas he goes through, meandering back and forth with lost or misplaced mail instead of making one stop a day. If you ask me, it's time he started thinking about retirement."

Aunt Mags nodded, staring down the road. "You can't blame the poor man for staying busy." It was a gentle reprimand, just enough to remind them that Abner was widowed and on his own.

"No, no, of course not." Aunt Camellia chimed in. "If it is Abner, I'm sure he'd love to sample your cookies, too, Astrid." She patted the back of the porch swing pillow until she was satisfied with its appearance.

Astrid took one. "I've been too scared to try one because…well, you know." She lifted Jammie, squished into the chair beside Tansy and draped the cat across her lap. "At least nothing caught on fire this time."

Aunt Camellia snorted with laughter. "At least we have a fire extinguisher this time."

Finally, a car appeared around the bend in the drive.

"It's not Abner," Aunt Mags said, resting her hip on the porch railing. "Someone lost, maybe?"

Occasionally, a traveler would wind up here, needing directions. More than likely, that was the case. The small white car stopped at the gate but the engine didn't turn off and no one emerged. The four of them exchanged a long look.

"I'll go check." Tansy stood. "Come on, Butters, you can protect me." The tiny dog jumped up, his curly tail wagging. "Aunt Mags, you need to teach your dog how to be intimidating." She walked down the steps.

"He's not my dog," Aunt Mags argued.

"Sure he's not." Tansy stared down at the dog scampering around her in circles. "Butters and I know the truth."

Tansy had barely taken two steps when the driver's door opened and a woman stepped out. In the fading light, it was hard to get a good look at her. But she'd turned and was getting something from the back seat. A…baby? Finally, the woman straightened. "Hi."

"Hi." Tansy waved. "Can we help you? Are you lost? The back roads are a little confusing—"

"I don't think so." She took a deep breath, shifted the child to her hip and headed toward the house. "Is this Honey Hill Farms?"

Tansy nodded. "Yes."

She opened the gate and came in, her steps slowing as she reached Tansy. "Then I'm where I need to be."

Now that the woman was standing on the flagstone front path, the porch light and streetlamps provided enough light for Tansy to see the woman clearly. And what she saw… Tansy's heart stuttered to a stop. Glossy thick red hair. Bracing emerald green eyes. She was *so* familiar.

"Um…I'm looking for Magnolia Hill?" The woman scanned the porch then froze, her gaze fixed on Aunt Mags.

"And you are?" Aunt Mags didn't sound like Aunt Mags. She didn't sound intimidating or calm or in control—she sounded breathless and…*scared*.

"My name is Shelby. Shelby Dunholm." It was more of a whisper now. "I… I…"

Look exactly like my aunt Mags. Tansy couldn't stop staring at her. The red-haired woman. Both Nicole and Lorna had mentioned her. But, how could she have guessed?

"We're just having some tea. If you'd like to join us, Miss Dunholm?" There was a definite tremor in Aunt Mags's voice.

"Yes, please." Aunt Camellia was all charm. "We have honey sugar cookies, too."

Tansy glanced back at her family, unsure what to do or say. Astrid looked just as startled as Tansy felt. Aunt Camellia was doing her best to smile but there were tears in her eyes. It was seeing Aunt Mags leaning against the porch railing, shaking, that tore at Tansy's heart.

"Ma," the toddler announced, tugging on Shelby's shirtfront.

Tansy had been so blindsided by the newcomer's appearance that the toddler hadn't really registered. It was all chubby and smiling, with a wisp of red hair atop its round head. Tansy wasn't much for kids but this one was precious. It smiled at Tansy, waving.

"Hi." The baby waved. "Hi. Hi."

"Oh... Um..." Shelby swallowed, shifting the baby to her other hip. She drew in an unsteady breath and stepped back. "No. I... I should come back. I need... She's hungry."

"You're welcome." Auntie Mags was gripping the porch railing now, her tone a bit desperate. "Anytime. Please."

Shelby nodded, then shook her head. She hugged the baby close. "I should go." A mix of yearning and anger and sadness shifted across her features.

"Are you sure?" Tansy murmured.

"I... Yes." Shelby nodded, pulling herself upright. "This was a mistake." She turned on her heel, marched back to her car, put the baby in the back seat, then climbed inside and slammed the door behind her. Seconds later, the car had turned around and disappeared back around the bend.

Crickets and cicadas. Granna Hazel's collection of wind chimes stirred and sang in the evening breeze. Somewhere on the farm, an owl hooted and one of Aunt Camellia's dogs barked.

Tansy, however, was speechless. There wasn't a

peep of sound from the porch. Only absolute silence. She wasn't the only one struggling for the right words. *Where to begin when there was so much to say?*

Aunt Camellia broke the silence. "Mags—"

"I think I'll turn in for the night." Aunt Mags's words rushed out, the front screen door slamming behind her. Poor Butters trotted up the steps and began scratching and whimpering to be let in.

"You go on and give her some cuddles." Aunt Camellia opened the screen door and Butters ran inside, the tinkle of the bell on his collar jingling as he ran up the stairs to Aunt Mags's room.

Tansy squeezed back into the chair beside Astrid, a thousand questions running through her mind. "Should *we* check on her?" Tansy whispered, looking to Astrid, then Camellia for some sign as to what to do next.

"I don't know." Astrid rested her head on Tansy's shoulder.

"No, I don't think so. Not yet anyway." Aunt Camellia gave them both a gentle shoulder squeeze.

"The baby was precious," Astrid murmured.

"She was, indeed." Aunt Camellia stared out into the dark, a deep furrow on her brow.

Tansy couldn't stop replaying the exchange, over and over. Shelby. The baby. Aunt Mags. "The baby had red hair, too." They'd all seen her, they all knew. But it was significant. All of this was.

"This is a lot for us. Imagine how she's feeling." She came around and sat, facing them. "I know you two have questions." Her smile wavered. "It's up to her to answer them. Or not."

Tansy nodded. None of them would push—that wasn't their way.

"Until then, we're here for her." Astrid took Tansy's hand.

"Always." Tansy cradled her hand in both of hers, her heart squeezed so tight it hurt.

"Bee Girls, always," Astrid murmured. "Taking care of one another, no matter what."

Camellia smiled as Jammie and Beeswax curled together on her lap. "Just like Poppa Tom wanted."

Thinking of the big barrel-chested man that loved to laugh and spend time with his family led to more questions for Tansy. What had happened? What about Poppa Tom and Granna Hazel? Did they know about Shelby's existence? What had happened to Aunt Mags? Why had she kept this secret for so long?

There was only one thing that Tansy knew with absolute certainty. As hard as it was to wrap her mind around it, there was no denying it. One look and Tansy had known. Auntie Mags was Shelby Dunholm's mother.

"I THINK IT'LL WORK. Hell, I think it'll look great." Everett Taggert tipped his cowboy hat back on his head and surveyed the framing for the Viking Hall event space. "I mean, assuming you get the plans approved by city council."

Dane scratched his stubble-lined jaw. "Unless something's changed, they were looking at this as a win-win."

Everett shrugged.

"If you're trying to tell me something, spit it out." Dane ran a hand along the back of his neck, rubbing at the stiffness. "I'd rather stop now than waste time I don't have." He was tired of fighting for things no one else wanted. If he was the only one that saw the potential in all this, maybe he needed to step back and re-evaluate *everything*.

"As far as I know, everyone's still gung ho." Everett followed him around the stakes that marked out the hall's floor plan. "You are looking a little rough, though."

"Yeah, well…" Since chasing down Leif in Elginston last Saturday, Dane had been busting his ass. Not only was he trying to keep some sort of balance with Leif but he'd been trying to unravel his father's latest mess. Little things like sleep and regular meals and shaving had taken a back seat.

He glanced down, his eye catching on the walking path. His ancestors had fit the large, earthy and muted jewel-toned river rocks snugly together to form a series of paths that wound all over the property. As he got older, he'd come to respect the quality craftsmanship and backbreaking effort of the preceding Knudsons. They'd taken no shortcuts—this path reflected that. It was a deep red border stone that grabbed his attention. A vein-like crack ran across the large, smooth surface. Something about the imperfection put a knot in Dane's throat. He knelt, running his finger along the hairline fracture. *Hold it together.* He rolled his neck and stood, brushing his hands together. "One more thing to fix."

"I'm happy to lend a hand, Dane." Everett's brow furrowed. "I could use the exercise." He patted his flat stomach.

Dane shot his friend a warning look. "Be careful, I might take you up on your offer."

"Good. I meant it."

Dane didn't doubt it. But, even with Everett's help, it wouldn't make up for the two employees his father had let go—three if he counted last week.

He might be COO of Texas Viking Honey, but his father seemed determined to make sure that didn't mean a damn thing. Dane wanted copies of their past season harvesting supplies, his father couldn't find the file. Dane wanted to upgrade their software, but his father had canceled their subscription altogether. Dane wanted to set up access to their bank and accounts online, his father refused to sign off on the paperwork. His father wanted him to run the place, day in, day out, but he didn't want Dane's questions or interference. He preferred to keep Dane in the dark on most things—make sure he kept all the power.

"Your dad still holing up in the hunting cabin?" Everett scratched the back of his neck.

"If the pattern holds, he should be emerging soon." Dane was all too familiar with his father's post-divorce routine. Like a bear waking up from hibernation, Harald Knudson would emerge from his den—hunting cabin— and move back into the main house grouchy and irritable and raring for a fight.

Not that having his father back under the same roof would make the man communicate. It had gotten to the point where Dane was beginning to believe his father wanted him to fail. *But if I fail, Texas Viking Honey fails.* Didn't his father get it? An all too familiar flare of resentment had Dane clenching his jaw. "I'm hoping he'll take some time to get things squared away here *before* he starts looking for his next Mrs. Knudson."

Everett clapped him on the back. "Maybe he'll find

some middle-aged vixen that winters in Florida to sweep him off his feet and finally hand over Texas Viking Honey to you."

"I wish." Dane had to chuckle at the thought. His father? With an age-appropriate spouse? *Unlikely.* The older Harald Knudson got, the younger his wives seemed to be. And outright handing over Texas Viking Honey to Dane? It was impossible to picture.

"Until that happens, what are you going to do? You can't do it all. I know people keep saying you look like Thor but, I hate to tell you this, you're not." Everett laughed as Dane glared his way.

"Hilarious," Dane ground out, but he ended up smiling, too.

They'd been friends since grade school. From flag football to college graduation, Everett always had his back. He had a level head and a terrific sense of humor but he also had no problem calling Dane out when he needed it—or teasing the shit out of him, just because. Everett was one of the few people Dane could be completely candid with.

They wandered along the river path, winding through a cluster of black willows, then up and away from the river, to one of the apiaries. Soon enough, the sound of water was muffled by the hum of the bees. Dane handed Everett some gloves and a slip veil to use over his cowboy hat—Everett wasn't exactly at ease around the hives.

"Thanks." Everett tugged on the gloves and dropped the veil down over his hat to cover his face and neck.

Dane nodded in answer then walked farther into the beeyard. The air was vibrating, hundreds of honeybees flying back and forth from the hives to their chosen pollen source. Dane scanned the long rows of white hive boxes. The bees didn't care about the fading white paint or aging wood or that the weathered ground tarps beneath their hives weren't doing much in the way of protection, but Dane did. It wasn't about the appearance, it was about the bees' viability. Keeping the hives healthy and productive included strong hive boxes and solid ground cover—simple ways to keep pests at bay. Pests like small hive beetles, wax moths or the dreaded varroa mite. Every single one of the Texas Viking Honey beeyards needed some maintenance. It'd cost a pretty penny. Even though he was already exhausted and his father would probably push back, this was something that had to happen—soon.

Finding Leif and lead beekeeper, Birmingham, working over an open hive at the end of a row, instantly lifted Dane's spirits.

"Leif learning the ropes?" Everett adjusted the veil, his gaze fixed on the golden bee flying back and forth in front of his face.

"I guess so." Leif was here of his own accord, working the bees, doing something useful. This was progress, and Dane wasn't going to screw things up by interfering. Leif wouldn't want him hanging around and Birmingham wouldn't appreciate Dane's interruption, either.

Birmingham had been Texas Viking Honey's lead beekeeper for almost forty years and, in all that time, his way of doing things hadn't changed. The man didn't take too kindly to anyone—especially "young-uns" like Dane—getting in his way or telling him how to work the bees. Not that Dane would ever do such a thing. As far as he was concerned, this place was just as much

Birmingham's home as it was his or Leif's. "If anyone can handle Leif, it's Birmingham."

Everett chuckled. "Does the old man still thump you on the back of your head?"

"Only if you're not paying attention or being disrespectful. And if he heard you calling him the old man, he'd knock you but good." Dane grinned. "Leif might be a bit taller than Birmingham, but that won't stop the old man from keeping him in line." Dane hoped no head smacking would take place but, at this point… "It's good for Leif. Hell, it's good for both of them. Neither of them do too well with people."

Everett chuckled.

Dane grinned but waved Everett back. "I don't want either of them thinking I'm spying." He led Everett around the yard, taking a new path that led back to the house.

"I've got news you might not like hearing." Everett paused.

Dane stopped and turned, waiting. *Dammit all.* "About the permits?"

"No. Nothing like that." Everett pulled off his gloves and bee veil. "It's just that…well, Lorna might be out a little longer than we thought." He held up his hands. "Before you get worked up, hear me out. I admit, I might have been having some fun asking you and Tansy to oversee the Junior Beekeepers together—but I never imagined the two of you would *really* do it. Not with two of you the way you…are with each other. I should have considered how stubborn you both are."

"So, you're saying…"

"You're off the hook. Jenny is going to step in and take your place. She and Tansy get along and, let's face it, Jenny has more energy than the two of us combined." Everett shook his head. "My sister is the human embodiment of the Energizer bunny—with no off switch."

"Hold up." Dane frowned, sifting through Everett's words.

"Weren't you just telling me you've got more than you can handle here?" Everett gestured wide. "I figured you'd be relieved."

I should be. Everett *was* right, about everything. Dane shouldn't be taking on more if he didn't have to. So why was he feeling…*disappointed*? The answer wasn't as much a mystery as he'd hoped. "I guess Tansy's thrilled?"

"I haven't talked to her yet." Everett shrugged. "I wanted to clear it with you first, so I wasn't speaking out of turn."

"How about I tell her? We've got the barn painting tomorrow. It wouldn't be right to leave her in the lurch for that." After that? He had no idea. But finding Leif here today, with Birmingham, got Dane's hopes up. Maybe his little brother would join Junior Beekeepers and find some friends—*and* take an interest in his family's legacy.

And Tansy? It wasn't just about teasing her until her eye twitched or her face went red. It was about… It was probably best if he stopped himself there.

"Are you sure about that? Even with Willadeene Svoboda bringing out lunch tomorrow?" Everett started humming the Wicked Witch theme from *The Wizard of Oz*—he knew all about Dane's nickname and opinion of the woman. "As a thank-you for all your hard work."

"Another good reason for me to be there tomorrow." He was supposed to leave Tansy and Leif to fend for themselves against that woman? That wasn't going to happen. "I'd hate to disappoint her by not showing up." He smiled.

"Her, Tansy or her, Willadeene?" Everett shot him a narrow-eyed look.

"Both, I guess." Dane chuckled.

"What should I tell Jenny? Help out tomorrow? Or tell her to wait?" Everett paused. "She can be a lit-tle…outspoken at times and with you and Tansy *and* Willadeene—"

"A *little* outspoken?" Dane laughed. Jenny Taggert had grown up with four older brothers so she'd had no choice but to speak up for herself. As a result, she was a woman of strong opinions. But she was also a hard worker and, as Everett pointed out, had energy to spare. "We *are* painting the side of a big-ass barn so the more hands the better." He shrugged. "Your call."

After he gave Everett a quick tour of the honey house and Everett talked Dane into meeting him to play pool later that week, Everett took his leave—taking a jar of creamed clover honey with him.

Dane had a million things to do before the sun went down but first, he had to eat and hydrate. The later it got in May, the warmer the temperatures. The more he sweat out, the more water he put in. He pushed through the kitchen door and stopped, stunned to find his father sitting at the long wooden kitchen table.

"Dane." His father kept flipping through a stack of papers on the table before him, his reading glasses perched on the end of his nose.

"Dad." Dane headed for the refrigerator, pulling out a container of leftover roast. He'd followed Van's direc-tions and the results had been surprisingly delicious.

"Hungry?" He grabbed a water bottle and honey crisp apple and paused for his answer.

"Nuh-uh." His father didn't look up from the papers.

"Looks like some light afternoon reading." Dane scooped roast onto a plate, put the container back in the refrigerator and closed the door.

His father cleared his throat. "Something like that."

He grabbed some bread and deposited everything on the long kitchen table, earning a sigh from his father. He pulled out a chair and glanced at the pages his father was poring over.

"Where is Leif?" His father glanced at Dane's plate. "Looks good. Where'd you order that from?"

"I made it." Dane started stacking the slices of roast onto the bread. "Leif ate earlier. He's out in the willow apiary with Birmingham."

His father looked up at him then. "*Leif* is *working*?"

Dane nodded, grinning broadly.

"Huh." His father glanced at the door, not smiling. "That's a surprise." He set the page he'd been reading on top of the stack and leaned back in his chair.

Dane took a swig of water. "I figure Birmingham can handle it."

His father's brows arched. "Leif is... Well, this doesn't change a thing. Tomorrow he could up and take off again, get into more trouble." He sighed. "I've been pondering options."

What the hell does "options" mean? Dane set his sandwich down, his stomach twisting. "Like?"

"What Leif needs—what we can't give him." His father frowned. "We've done everything that damn school wants, but it hasn't made a bit of difference."

We? His father probably couldn't name a single one

of Leif's teachers. Dane stared down at his plate and took a slow, deep breath. "He is passing all of his classes now."

"Humph. Not by much." His father shook his head. "That fight destroyed school property. We don't know if or when it could happen again. At this point, there's only one option left for the boy." His father folded his hands on top of the papers, grimly determined.

Dane waited, the finality of his father's words had dread seeping into the marrow of his bones.

"There's a good military school in Virginia. You heard the principal. Mrs. Lopez said he needed structure, routine and discipline." His father shrugged. "I can't imagine a better place for all three."

Dane was staring, he couldn't help it. Was his father so out of touch with Leif that he honestly thought sending Leif away—spending less time with him—was for the best?

"Patrick says it's a decent place. He's not going to steer me wrong." He nodded.

Dane's skin went tight, flushing hot and brittle. His father had talked to his drinking buddy, Patrick Coffey, about *this*. The man was ancient and mean and had a terrible relationship with both of his children. *You'll listen to him, but not me?* He placed his hands on his lap, shaking with anger. He had to be smart about this. Fuming or getting defensive with his father was the surest way to have Leif packed off by the end of the week. He took a deep breath and did his best to keep his emotions in check. "Dad, I'm asking you, please, to reconsider."

"It's not like I haven't thought this through." His fa-

ther blustered, scowling Dane's way. "He'll go to summer school there, first. We'll see how that goes."

The *we* his father kept throwing out was rubbing
his nerves the wrong way. *What we? There's no we
here.* "Sending Leif away is the surest way to make him
hate you and me. He's acting out because he wants attention." Dane swallowed against the tightening of his
throat. "Besides, Leif needs to work *here* this summer.
We're so shorthanded now, he has to." It was a dig and
he knew it but this was all bullshit, plain and simple.
"We're down two full-time employees and three part-
time people and honey flow is coming soon." He waited
for his father to confirm or deny this. When his father
stayed silent, Dane continued. "Unless you've lined up
temporary workers—"

"I'm not asking you, Dane. I'm telling you." His
father straightened the papers. "Some things have to
change around here." He picked up a manila envelope
and placed it on top of the papers—a business card
slipped free and skidded across the tabletop to Dane.

Dane was searching for a way to ask what kind of
changes, exactly, his father was referring to, but the
business card caught his eye and the apprehension
gnawing at his gut intensified. "Silas Baldwin?" Dane
picked up the card, reading the neatly printed block
print. It took him a minute to steady himself. "From
the bank?"

"Do you know another Silas Baldwin?" His father
frowned at him. "I don't appreciate the tone, either."

Dane ignored his father's last comment, zeroing in on
the stack of papers instead. "What's this about, Dad?"
He nodded at the papers, bracing himself for what was
to come.

"He's bringing a friend out to appraise that piece of property on the other side of the creek." His father stood and walked to the counter. He poured himself a steaming cup of coffee, added three scoops of sugar and carried the mug back to the table to sit.

Where was all this coming from? Dane's chest was squeezed so tight it was hard to get the words out. "Once everything is up and running with the expansion, we will see a nice uptick in revenue."

"Maybe. Maybe not. It'll take time." His father paused, his gaze falling to the pages. Seconds later his jaw tightened and he straightened the stack. "I've been thinking about selling that property for a while. It's a seller's market." He stiffened, his chin thrust forward in defiance as he met Dane's gaze. "Now seems a good time."

Growing up, his father had waxed eloquent about family and holding on to one's heritage. This land, his father had said, was knitted into the very fiber of their being. In the three years since Dane had come home, he'd never once heard his father mention selling off *any* property. Why would he? Now an appraiser was coming out and Dane was supposed to be okay with it? He knew he should keep his mouth shut until he'd had time to calm down, but all the anger and frustration and shock bubbled up and out into the silence of the kitchen. "This is our home. You, me and Leif. We are a family, Dad. The *three* of us. Families talk about things, together—"

"Hold on, now." His father's brows rose, his eyes narrowing as he regarded Dane. "This is your home, yes, but until I'm dead and in the ground, this place and everything on it belongs to *me*." He shifted forward, tapping the stack of papers with his pointer finger. "You can disagree with me all you want, but I'll do what I think is best, son—about Leif and the farm. I don't need, or particularly want, your permission." He stood, his face going red. "I didn't ask you to give up your fancy job and come back. You don't like the way I do things, don't let the door hit you on the way out."

Dane stayed in his seat but couldn't keep the edge from his voice. "Then who would work this place? Who is going to keep Texas Viking Honey afloat? You're making choices that will impact us all, Dad." He took a deep breath. "Choices that can't be undone."

His father stared at him, long and hard. "The place hadn't fallen apart before you showed up, acting like you were here to save the day. Nothing needs saving. Texas Viking Honey will be fine, with or without you."

"You really believe that?" He held his breath. "You keep lying to yourself, lying to me and Leif, and we'll lose everything." He was sick just thinking about it. "Everything's not fine. You'd never sell off property if you didn't have to." He saw his father's jaw tighten and knew he'd struck a nerve. "But you're so damn proud that you'll sell off property—our home—instead of coming to me so we can figure things out. It might be easier to keep denying there are problems, but that won't make them disappear. What's going on, Dad?"

"What sort of problem are you talking about, Dane? How much it eats you up that you don't know everything? That you're not the one calling the shots? That's the only problem, here." His father's laugh was hard, the twisted smile on his face harder still. "I have a solution for you. If you're going to keep arguing with everything I do, maybe it would be best if you left." His father slammed his coffee cup onto the table and stomped out of the kitchen, slamming the door behind him.

Dane sat until his pulse had slowed and he could breathe again. One thing his father was right about, he'd never asked Dane to come home. Leif had. The chances of Leif admitting to that now were slim. More likely, his little brother would help him pack his bags and show him the door.

The truth was simple. He couldn't leave. Not because he'd sunk a good portion of his 401(k) into the expansion, but because something was wrong. Very wrong. If he left, who knew what would happen to Leif, his father, Texas Viking Honey or his home. He was fighting an uphill battle, but there was no way in hell he'd lose.

CHAPTER EIGHT

SATURDAY MORNING WAS clear and crisp, perfect weather for barn painting. At least, Tansy hoped that was the case. She'd painted many things in her time but this was a little different. At the intersections of Highways 290 and 16, sat an old red barn. According to the Junior Beekeepers website, the barn had become the unofficial welcome sign in the early 1900s. The bright, postcard-like mural covered the entire side of the highway-facing barn. While the design hadn't changed over the years, the cheerful greeting sign needed a complete repaint every two or three years due to sun exposure and weathering.

Tansy arrived with the sun, thankful to have some tranquility and time alone. Since Shelby Dunholm's appearance and quick exit last Saturday, there'd been underlying tension in every corner of her home. Not that Aunt Mags wanted to talk about it. The next morning, Tansy had helped Aunt Camellia and Astrid make Aunt Mags's favorite breakfast of vanilla honey French toast and gathered around the mosaic-topped kitchen table ready to listen. But Aunt Mags had come downstairs, thanked them for the food and picked up her newspaper as if it was any other morning—as if their worlds hadn't been forever altered. It had been the same every morning since then.

Something had to give. Tansy slipped her Honey Hill Farms cap on, pulling her ponytail over the fastener strap at the back of her head.

The only deviation from their weekly schedule had been when Lord Byron had stolen a mirror, an earring and a silver perfume stopper from Aunt Mags's room. If the bird hadn't taken up residence on one of the large wooden rafters overhead, Aunt Mags might have carried out her long-standing threat and sent him off to the taxidermist's. The earring was the only thing that had been recovered which had only added to Aunt Mags's foul mood.

None of them knew what to do or say about Shelby so they stayed quiet.

She set up a folding table beneath a nearby sprawling oak tree, stowed the ice chests full of ice and water bottles underneath, and unpacked the muffins, breakfast tacos and juice cartons Kettner's Family Grocery had donated. *No one will go hungry, that's for sure.*

The rumble of a truck announced the arrival of Dane and Leif, their truck bed loaded down with supplies.

You owe me. Tansy swallowed. Things had gotten so off track last time she'd seen him. His mood. Her memories and daydreams. All of it. Hopefully, without Nicole around to put ideas into her head *or* the Honey Bee Ladies Society breathing down their necks, today would be uneventful.

Dane stepped out of his truck and stretched. His long hair was pulled back into a loose knot at the back of his head and he had a slight stubble covering his strong jaw.

"Morning." The corner of his blue eyes crinkled as he smiled.

Tansy took a long, deep breath. *It's a smile.* People

smile. No need to feel alarmed or…dazzled or flustered. "Morning."

"Looks like they cleared out any debris for us." He slammed the truck door, taking in their surroundings. "Reduces the chance of running into critters that might not take too kindly to us being here." He headed to the rear of his truck and opened the tailgate. "I think we've got everything we need. And plenty of food. Van?" He waited for her nod. "I don't think there's a more generous man alive."

Good, something they could agree on. "He's a rare soul, that's what Aunt Camellia always says. I don't disagree."

Dane's smile changed—like he was holding something back. Almost like he had a secret? He looked at her, his head tilting to the side, before he scratched the stubble on his jaw and shook his head.

What was that look about? She wasn't about to ask. Knowing Dane, he was goading her. That was what he did, after all. *Whatever it is, I don't want to know.* And if she kept telling herself that, maybe she'd believe it. She sighed. Fine, as long as she didn't make direct eye contact, she might get through the day just fine.

The passenger door opened and Leif slid out to stand against the hood of the truck, looking every bit a human thundercloud. Tansy was pretty sure he'd melt before noon in his two sizes too big dark T-shirt, black jeans and scuffed combat boots but there was nothing to be done about it now.

"Hey, Leif." Tansy waved. "Thanks for coming today. What's that saying, many hands make light work?"

The teen ran his fingers through his overlong hair and glanced her way, shrugging.

"I think that's right. It doesn't matter." Tansy held out a breakfast taco. "Fuel for work."

Leif pushed off the truck and walked over. "Thanks."

"Guess we're the first ones here?" Dane came back, canvas tarps, bags of paintbrushes and plastic buckets in hand. He placed everything along the barn wall and turned, surveying the empty field. "Are we early?"

"I told you." Leif's snort was all irritation.

"A bit." Tansy winked at Leif. Leif's crooked grin was gone almost as quickly as it had appeared. "Everyone should be here in about ten minutes." She slid a muffin and another taco to Leif. "You get first pick."

"Cool." Leif stepped forward to take the food, his posture easing somewhat.

"I'll get started unloading." Dane glanced back and forth between the two of them, grabbed an orange juice and headed to the rear of the truck.

Tansy followed. "Need help?"

Dane swung himself up into the bed of the truck with ease. He'd always been fit—even back in high school. Tansy hadn't thought much of it until the hem of his T-shirt started riding up to reveal a bit of Dane's well-chiseled back. Her eyes were glued to him, watching as he turned and stretched—the glimpse of his sculpted stomach making her mouth dry.

Stop staring. She blinked, dragging her gaze from his torso to his… Don't look at his butt. Focus on something normal-ish. Like his…arms.

Dammit. There was nothing normal-ish about Dane's arms. She'd heard people comparing Dane to Thor, rather the Australian actor who played the role of Thor, more than once. With the hair and the eyes and his size, she understood why people might think that way. But, to her, Dane was...well, he was more. *Those* arms *are definitely more.*

Tansy was peeling her eyes off Dane Knudson's overtly masculine form when he turned to face her, a paint can in each hand.

"Here." He paused. "What?" He set the paint cans down. "What did I do now?"

Tansy shook her head, her lungs too empty to breathe.

"You're glaring at me." He frowned. "Already. Before eight in the morning. On a Saturday."

She fought back her smile. "Is *ten* in the morning on a Saturday a more appropriate time to glare at you?"

"No. Saturday is a no-glaring day." He shrugged, the corner of his mouth cocking up. "Everyone knows that."

"Oh, *everyone* does?" *Stop smiling.* "This is an official thing?"

"Yep." He nodded, reaching across to scratch his shoulder—the muscles in his arms taut and big and unavoidable.

Tansy swallowed hard. "I feel the need to check your sources."

"You should take my word for it. For today." He squatted in the truck bed, tucked a loose strand of wheaten hair behind his ear and smiled. "Truce, remember?"

There goes the whole no-eye-contact thing. She looked away, severing the connection before she could get all flustered and warm. There was no guarantee she'd feel that way, of course, but why chance it? Instead, she'd focus on his...hair. Harmless enough. Or not. Why didn't his man-bun look ridiculous? He has a *man-bun*. But, on Dane, it worked. More than worked. *Dammit, dammit*. Apparently, her only option was not to look at him. Period.

"Good." There was a hint of smugness to his tone.

No. This is so not good. If she was good, she wouldn't be fixating on every little thing about him. But she was. And if she didn't come up with a scathing comeback soon, he'd suspect something was up.

Thank goodness. She breathed a sigh of relief as two trucks and a minivan came bouncing across the field. "There they are." Tansy grabbed the paint cans and carried them to the barn.

The arrival of the Junior Beekeepers Club set things in motion. Kerrielynn had borrowed her mother's minivan and packed up all the middle school students inside. They erupted from the bottle green vehicle chattering and laughing and full of energy. They circled around the table to grab breakfast while the high school kids were still parking their trucks. Once the kids discovered the food, it disappeared at an alarming rate. *Maybe there won't be any leftovers*.

"We are so excited to get started this morning." Tansy meant it, too. All the enthusiasm was hard to resist. Overall, it was almost as potent as a cup of coffee. "Mr. Knudson and I are here to help, but your officers have worked very hard to come up with a plan of action that should get the mural and the side of the barn painted before the sun goes down."

"Not a problem." Dane rubbed his hands together.

There was a ripple of laughter.

"I agree with Mr. Knudson. Let's get to work." Kerrielynn scanned her clipboard. "First things first, let's get everything unloaded and sorted—matching paint colors, three paintbrushes, two rollers and roller pans each."

Tansy stood back and watched, amazed, as the group did exactly as Kerrielynn said.

"Huh." Dane, hands on hips, looked perplexed. He leaned over and whispered, "If I start carrying around a clipboard will I get results like this?"

Tansy scratched her temple. "I don't know, but I'm tempted to stop on the way home and get one myself." She smiled up at him.

Dane's face changed then, the muscle in his jaw clenching tight. His blue eyes swept over her face, lingering on her lips until her cheeks warmed. The smile he gave her shook her to her core.

This is bad. Dane was Dane. He wasn't an option. She needed to get out of her head. The best way to stop all the weirdness was to get to work. Lucky for her, there was plenty of work to do.

"Leif, can you get this open?" Kerrielynn held out a paint can opener to him.

Leif hopped to it, taking the tool and opening the gallon of paint without a word or a long-suffering sigh.

"I am definitely getting a clipboard." The level of awe in Dane's voice had Tansy laughing.

Between Kerrielynn, the planner, and Felix, the doer and Junior Beekeepers vice president, there wasn't much for the two of them to worry over. Kerrielynn named tasks and Felix delegated them to kids he thought could handle them.

The kids were brushing off the barn wall while she and Dane climbed up the ladders to tape off the work area. Once that was done, the work began.

The barn side mural was a sort of faux postcard, with a solid black background and white trim. It was the inside that held all the detailed work: the iconic profile of Honey's clock-tower-topped courthouse, a winding river and several old-fashioned skep basket beehives were depicted in bright, inviting colors. The massive words, "Welcome to Honey, Texas" covered most of the upper left corner, with the word "Honey" appearing on the label of a large jar of golden honey. The words "The Honey Capital of Texas" were underneath, smaller but readable. And, of course, there were bees. Bees flying around the courthouse, bees flying around the honey, and the bees tending to the row of wildflowers that edged the bottom of the postcard frame. None of the images were overly complicated but there was a substantial amount of work to do.

The younger kids went first, rolling black paint into the large taped-off rectangle until it was covered. Afterward, Benji and a few high school students got to work painting the white frame.

She'd almost convinced herself she'd imagined the whole Dane thing until he appeared beside her.

"Going pretty well, don't you think?" Dane's voice drew her eye, but the instant their gazes met, she shied away.

"Yep." She nodded, hating the way her pulse picked up. "They're amazing."

"It's the clipboard. I knew it." Dane chuckled.

"Right." She breathed a sigh of relief when Oren Diaz, Van's nephew, flagged down Dane. "You're needed."

But Dane was staring beyond her now, wearing such a hopeful expression Tansy followed his gaze.

Leif crouched low, painstakingly brushing white paint along the frame and laughing at something Benji Svoboda had said. Kerrielynn and Felix were laughing, too. From the outside looking in, it wasn't that big a deal. Just teens hanging out, being teens.

Tansy knew it was more than that. Lorna, Nicole, Willadeene—pretty much everyone in Honey used words like *troubled* or *a handful* or *struggling* alongside Leif's name. Seeing Leif this way had to be a relief for Dane.

Tansy frowned. *She was happy for Leif, not Dane.*

Oren called Dane again so Tansy took it upon herself to sidle just a bit closer to where Leif and Kerrielynn were working.

"That looks amazing." Kerrielynn stopped beside Leif, nodding as she inspected the work so far. "Thanks for coming today." She smiled down at him.

Leif smiled back. No glare or sullen pout or air of overall inconvenienced irritation. Nope. He was actually smiling.

Kerrielynn turned a brilliant shade of pink before staring at her clipboard.

Leif stood, putting a hand against the fresh black paint to brace himself. He didn't notice, he was staring down at Kerrielynn like... *Like the rest of the world doesn't exist.* His mouth opened, closed and opened again but nothing came out. When he pulled his hand off the barn, he stared down at it, frowning at his paint covered hand.

Tansy glanced at Dane. Was he seeing this? Did he know his little brother had a crush on Kerrielynn? A big one. It was sweet, really. Kerrielynn was a good girl. But she was nice to everyone—poor Leif could wind up with a broken heart. *On top of everything else.*

But Dane was talking to Oren and had missed the whole thing.

When Tansy looked back, Kerrielynn had discovered Leif's predicament.

"Oops, oh no. I guess it's not too bad since you're wearing black but..." Kerrielynn laughed, offering Leif a rag. "Here."

"Thanks." Leif was smiling again. "Kerrielynn."

Kerrielynn turned an even darker shade of pink—her big brown eyes as round as saucers as she stared up at Leif Knudson. "You're w-welcome Leif." She stumbled over the words.

Boy did I read that wrong. Maybe Leif wouldn't wind up with a broken heart, after all.

"Did he do something?" Dane whispered, so close to her ear that Tansy jumped.

"What?" She frowned at him.

"Leif." He sighed. "You're making that face again." He pointed at her face.

"I don't know what *that face* means." She sighed. "But Leif didn't do anything." She glanced at Leif, nodding in his direction. "Just look."

Dane looked. "What am I looking at?"

"Your brother." Tansy waited, crossing her arms over her chest.

"How did he get paint all over his hand?" Dane was frowning now.

"Not that." Tansy sighed. "Dane, come on. You don't see *what's going on*?"

Dane scratched his jaw, his brow furrowed in confusion as he stared at his little brother.

But Leif and Kerrielynn's charged staring session ended when one of the middle school kids called her name. Kerrielynn took a deep breath, smiled at Leif again, then headed to the other kid.

Leif, however, continued to stare after the girl as if he were trying to figure something out. Something important. The deep breath he took was both perplexed and…yearning.

"That." Tansy nudged him, hard.

Dane's entire demeanor changed. "Oh." He went from defensive to concerned in a flash—twice as perplexed as Leif. "Oh hell," he murmured, shaking his head.

Tansy was so surprised, she started laughing. "What sort of response is that anyway? Isn't having a crush part of adolescence? Kerrielynn is sweet and it looks like she might be crushing on Leif, too."

"Looks can be deceiving, now, can't they?" Dane's jaw tightened as he glanced her way. "And Leif can't afford to be disappointed right now."

Tansy was still reeling from the solid accusation in Dane's blue eyes. What did that even mean? And why was he looking at her like she'd done or said something wrong? He was worrying over Leif—that made more sense. "Kerrielynn wouldn't string him along, if that's what you're worried about. What you see is what you get."

His gaze remained locked with hers, searching. "I should take your word for that?" He shook his head. "That's a relief." He stalked off, moving one of the ladders around the side of the barn and putting a whole lot of space between them.

What had just happened? There was no way he…

No, he wasn't referring to what happened between them in high school. Besides, he'd been responsible for the whole mortifying *Say Anything* prom proposal. He'd been the one to lead her on and humiliate her—even if she had turned the tables on him at the last minute. He'd done that. *Not me.* So why did the snap in his words leave a sting? And why was she following him into the barn to find out?

DANE RESTED THE ladder on its side on the barn's packed-dirt floor. It was cooler inside, the scents of earth and dust and cedar filling the air. And quiet, the conversation and laughter of the Junior Beekeepers muffled. He wiped his hands on a handkerchief as he inspected the thick beams and sturdy frame of the solid old structure.

In a minute, he'd go back out there, be an adult and act like nothing happened. Nothing *had* happened. But he wanted it to. All morning he'd fought the hold Tansy had on him.

He knew better. He did. He'd tried to ignore it, ignore her, but he couldn't. The moment she'd smiled at him over the stupid clipboard comment, he knew he was in trouble.

Then, instead of being thankful she'd pointed out his little brother's puppy-dog eyes for Kerrielynn, he'd let his frustration with himself get the best of him. Why couldn't he get her out of his mind? Why couldn't he cut out whatever it was that kept him tethered to her?

"What did that mean?" Tansy's voice wasn't exactly a surprise.

He braced himself as he turned to face her. She'd pulled the barn door closed behind her and stood, arms crossed over her chest, head tilted defiantly. Even in her too-big overalls and rubber boots embossed with bees and flowers, she was beautiful. *Dammit*. He tore his gaze from her, his frustration mounting. "I need a minute." He tucked the rag back into his pocket. "Alone."

Tansy stared at him, open-mouthed. "You're telling me to leave?"

"Ideally, yes."

A furrow creased her brow and her lips pressed flat but she didn't move.

He stood there, doing his best to glare at her and wound up studying her mouth. She didn't want this. Hell, she'd probably laugh at him if she knew what he was thinking. He was the damn fool. Touching her, kissing her, holding her in his arms. None of that was going to happen. But that didn't stop a wave of pure, unfiltered want from slamming into him—so intense it damn near brought him to his knees.

"I was trying to help." Her voice was soft, not nearly sassy enough.

This was where he should say thank you. Instead, he blurted, "I don't need your help with my brother." Which was a damn lie. He needed all the help he could get when it came to Leif—but he didn't want it from her. Fighting was good—anything to pit a wedge between them.

"Fine." The word erupted from her. A frustrated murmur spilled out before she said, "You are the most…"

He looked at her, waiting. "Go on."

"Oh." Her groan was pure exasperation. "You make me so…so…"

"Infuriated?" He didn't remember moving closer to her. Had she closed the distance? "Frustrated?"

"Yes and yes." Her eyes were blazing now.

"Believe me, the feelings are mutual." His breath caught as she licked her lips.

"Then why are you staring at my mouth?" It was a whisper.

He was so stunned, he wasn't sure what to do. One minute, he was processing what she'd said, the next he was reeling from the shock of her body flush against his. Her lips, soft as silk, brushed across his in invitation.

He didn't pause to think. Fool or not, this was what he wanted. He twined his arms around her waist as her hands gripped the back of his neck. His hands slid up to cradle her face, to tilt her head back for more. And when her lips parted for him, he shuddered at the stroke of her tongue against his.

"Oh my." Violet Taggert, Everett's mother, stood in the now open door.

For a minute, he and Tansy were frozen. Dammit. Their ragged breathing echoed inside the barn. This was real. This had happened. Tansy had no-holds-barred kissed him. And it had been good. Better than good. But now, even though Tansy was still leaning on him, he had to let her go. *Dammit all to hell.*

"Oh my?" Willadeene Svoboda came inside as he and Tansy jumped apart. "What's happening here?"

He had nothing, nothing. No words would come. He was acutely aware of how empty his arms felt—and how rapidly his heart was thumping.

"They were putting the ladder away." Violet shot him a look. "For a minute, I thought Tansy might fall over." The next time she had him alone, Violet was going to give him an earful about this, he could tell.

Willadeene looked downright gleeful as she said, "It

looked to me like Dane caught her." Her smile grew. "No wonder you're both so red-faced. That's one heavy ladder."

Well, shit. Had she seen them or was she guessing? He didn't dare look Tansy's way.

"We have food." Violet waved them out. "The kids are getting everything set up."

"It's so nice that they don't need constant…supervision, isn't it?" Willadeene glanced back and forth between them. Whether or not she'd actually seen a thing, the eager sparkle in her beady eyes suggested she was already concocting shareable scenarios to take with her. Nothing she came up with could come close to the truth.

That kiss… He could still taste her on his lips. He should be cursing himself instead of wanting more. He did, though. He wanted more.

But next time, they'd have to be more careful. *Next time.* He risked a glance Tansy's way and grinned. It was a relief to see she was as rattled as he was, her answering smile quick, nervous—and gone. "They're a great group of kids." Tansy's eyes locked with his.

There was no need to ask what she was thinking. It was there on her face—in her hazel-green eyes. The same look she'd worn that day at Elginston when Willadeene had shown up. *Don't worry, I'll behave.* He gave her a slight nod.

Blankets and quilts were collected from trunks and truck beds, the work area was straightened up so everyone could sit, and, using a little elbow grease, Dane managed to pry open the old spigot alongside the barn so everyone could wash their hands.

Violet popped the hatch on her vehicle. "We saw the sign driving down the highway." She smiled. "Dane and

Tansy, it's good of you to step in so this project could get done in time for the Honey Festival."

"Of course. Especially with the influx of out-of-towners they're expecting." Tansy glanced at him, nibbling on the inside of her lip.

It took everything he had not to stare at her mouth. "They've done most of the work." Dane carried two large insulated bags to the table under the tree.

Violet followed, sliding the handles of another insulated bag onto her shoulder. "Ah, youth. I remember those days."

Dane grinned. Violet was more alert and sprier than most women half her age. She and her husband, Leland, owned and operated a dairy goat farm—they both worked hard all day, every day, and Dane respected the hell out of them. All five of the Taggert children had the same work ethic and zest for life, Everett included.

Dane watched as the kids lined up, took turns getting their food and water bottles, and found places to sprawl on the blankets spread out in the shade of the oak tree. They were tired and hot but their spirits were high.

"Nice weather for it today." Violet shielded her eyes and stared up at the powder blue sky. "I'm thinking it'll be a scorcher before you're all done, though."

"Not a cloud in the sky." Willadeene nodded.

"It's already on the warm side." Dane plucked his damp T-shirt from his chest. "Someone needs to complain to management. I think the air-conditioning is out."

Violet laughed, shoving a bottle of water at him. "You big goof. Stay hydrated."

Tansy laughed then, her brows raised.

Willadeene instantly perked up at the sound, her head swiveling so she could study Tansy's face.

"Oh, and, Tansy, Van asked that you thank Camellia for the honey cake recipe. He said he ate the whole thing." Violet smiled.

Van and Camellia. Dane took a bite of his barbecue sandwich to hide his smile.

"That man." Willadeene took one of the chocolate candy cookies from the plastic food container and shook her head.

Dane, Violet and Tansy all waited. There was nothing bad to say about Van Kettner. Dane had never met a more generous, bighearted gentleman in his life. If this woman tried, he'd set her straight—the consequences be damned.

"He's more interested in recipes than finding a perfectly acceptable woman to take care of him." Willadeene took a bite of her cookie.

Dane was pretty sure Van had found himself a more than acceptable woman—if he ever chose to act on it. He wondered how Camellia Hill would respond. He couldn't imagine a better suited couple alive. Dane glanced at Tansy. She'd picked up on Leif and Kerrielynn. Did she know about Van's feeling for her aunt? Maybe he should give her the heads-up, like she'd done about Leif and Kerrielynn? *Maybe I should mind my own business.*

"I don't think Van minds being single," Violet was saying. "It's not like he hasn't had the opportunity to settle down with someone." She shrugged. "Back in the day, he could have picked anyone he wanted."

"He still could," Willadeene asserted.

Tansy shot him a wide-eyed look.

He was pretty sure they were thinking along the same lines. *Willadeene* thought that *Willadeene* was the perfectly acceptable woman. Dane suppressed a shudder. Poor Van. In a way, poor Willadeene. After seeing the way Van Kettner had looked at Camellia Hill in the grocery store a couple weeks back, Dane knew where Van's heart lay.

"Some people are happier single." Tansy came back, taking a cookie from the container Willadeene offered. "Van strikes me as content."

Willadeene snorted. "More like people fool themselves into believing they're happier single. But I suppose I'd rather that than see a marriage cut short because they rushed into it or picked the wrong person."

Dane didn't miss the side-eyed glance the woman shot his way. *Yeah, yeah*. She was talking about his father. He got it. The thing was Dane could remember when his father had been a happily married man. He'd loved Dane's mother and had been a doting, if gruff, father and a savvy businessman, wheeling and dealing and always looking for opportunities to increase their income. But after Dane's mother had died his father stopped being present, and he'd lost the drive to carry on business as usual. The only exception to that was the signature Viking Clover Honey. The last recipe his father had concocted had hit the shelves eighteen months after his mother's death and become their most successful honey to date. Dane considered the clover honey a sort of last love letter from his father to his mother.

Today's Harald Knudson was an entirely different man than the one Dane remembered from his childhood. That man wouldn't have divorced three times, allowed his relationships with his sons to deteriorate or stood by while his family business fell into a precarious situation. While Dane acknowledged the man as his father, it was hard to respect him.

"These are delicious cookies." Tansy took another.

"It's so nice to see you two are still…getting along." Willadeene pointed between he and Tansy.

Tansy almost choked on her cookie.

"Since we're in charge of all these kids, I can't pour a bucket of paint over her." Dane took a cookie. "It'd set a bad example." He shrugged.

Violet laughed. "I appreciate you two behaving." She sent him another one of those meaningful looks, then added, "For the kids."

"For the…*kids*." Willadeene was wearing that delighted expression again—the one that triggered a dozen mental red flags.

"You-all get enough?" Violet called to the teens chatting and resting in the shade.

An overwhelming chorus of yeses echoed but the older boys jumped up for more food—Leif included.

"How's it going, Leif?" Violet asked. "Having fun?"

Leif shrugged. "Thanks for the food." He stepped aside so Kerrielynn and Crissy Abraham, Felix's sister, could get what they wanted.

"We're here to help clean up." Kerrielynn's shy smile was for Leif and Leif alone.

Dane glanced at Tansy at the same time she looked his way. She crossed her arms over her chest, self-satisfied. He had to smile.

"Such nice young people." Willadeene gave them each two more cookies. "Good to see you-all working hard and making good choices…even you, Leif. After all that business with the Dwyer boys and all, it's such a nice...*surprise*."

Dane's hand fisted, crumbling his cookie to bits. What was wrong with the woman? Who decided singling out a fifteen-year-old was good for a morning's entertainment?

Tansy stared at the woman, open-mouthed. Violet's cheeks were going a deep red. Even the kids looked uncomfortable.

"Oh." Leif shrugged, smoothing his shaggy hair back from his face. "Surprise." He took a bite of cookie.

Kerrielynn giggled.

Leif smiled.

And the tension evaporated.

"Let's pack everything up and get out of your hair," Violet said.

Uh-oh. Dane knew that voice—that was Violet's "you've got a scolding coming" voice. *Oh, to be a fly in the car for the drive home.* He'd love to hear Violet light into Willadeene.

"Yes, ma'am." Kerrielynn was instantly in clipboard mode. "I need some volunteers to help pack up."

Leif shoved the rest of his cookie into his mouth and stepped closer to Kerrielynn. He didn't say a thing, but his blue eyes swept over the girl's profile and he took another one of those full-body deep breaths.

Well, hell. Dane swallowed hard. He wasn't equipped for this.

"I'll leave the cowboy cookies," Willadeene said, dumping them all into one large container. "There should be enough for everyone's afternoon snack." Willadeene finished packing up her canvas bag.

"I'll get it." Leif took the bag and followed Felix to finish loading up.

Willadeene's eyebrows rose as she leaned forward to whisper, "He's doing so well. No one would ever suspect him of all that trouble." She sighed. "We can hope it's a phase he'll grow out of."

That was it. Dane had tried to play nice, tried to let her comments roll off his back, but no more. "I don't really care what you—"

"He's really enjoying himself." Tansy cut in. "And he's super talented. He did all the detail along the trim there." She waved Willadeene to the barn. "See?"

"She just saved your rear end, you big goof," Violet whispered to him, shaking her head. "Believe me, I'll set Willadeene Svoboda straight on the ride home. I don't tolerate that sort of nonsense and you know it." She patted his arm. "But you'd best be careful. Don't give her what she wants."

Dane gave her a one-armed hug. "Easier said than done."

"'Cause you're as stubborn as a goat." Violet patted him again. "I would ask if you and Tansy are *really* getting along but, after what I saw in the barn, I'm thinking I don't need to worry about you dumping paint on her?"

His gaze wandered to Tansy, over by the barn to show Willadeene their progress so far. "No need to worry. Not too much anyway."

"Glad to hear it." Violet shook her head. "But, it might be best to find a better setting before you two start canoodling again?"

He heard the slight reprimand in her voice. "Yes, ma'am."

It took quick reflexes, but he managed to dodge Wil-

ladeene Svoboda for the remainder of their visit. By
the time the silver SUV was bouncing away down the
well-rutted road, he rolled his neck to ease the tension
knotting his muscles. He turned to find Tansy staring
at him—and she wasn't happy.

"That woman," she murmured. "She's…she's…"

"The Wicked Witch of the Hill Country?" He started
humming the theme song.

Tansy froze, her eyes round as saucers. Then she
burst into laughter. "That's mean." She kept laughing.
"You're horrible." The laughter didn't stop. "But you're
so right."

For so long, Dane hadn't wanted to look at Tansy
Hill and feel something—feel anything—but what he
wanted didn't appear to matter. First the kiss. Now how
fired up she was over protecting Leif. He was feeling
things all right, things he'd never felt before, and it was
disconcerting as hell. All the while he was laughing
along with her, a tiny thread wrapped itself around his
lungs and pulled tight, cutting his laughter off.

She wiped at the corners of her eyes. "At least the
cookies were good."

Dane nodded, struggling to get his bearings. Or
make sense of *this*. He liked the sound of her carefree
laughter. He liked her smile. He liked the way her eyes
flashed green in the sunlight. At the moment, there
wasn't a thing about Tansy Hill he didn't like. And
considering how that had turned out last time, he was
pretty damn scared.

"But, having to endure that woman? Well, no cookie
is *that* good." Tansy pointed over her shoulder at the
retreating car. "I should have thought to ask Aunt Camellia to make something." Her gaze caught on his

and held, her smile fading as her attention wandered to his mouth.

A dozen kids were talking and laughing and scurrying all over the place, but all of that was hazy. Tansy, on the other hand, was crystal clear and painfully beautiful. *This can't be real.* He took a deep breath and spoke, needing something—anything—to ground him again. "Tansy." He ran a hand over his hair, his throat tight.

"I shouldn't have done that… In the barn." She took a deep breath. "I'm sorry."

"Don't be." He stepped closer.

She smiled up at him then. "I'm not—really." Her gaze lingered on his mouth so long, he damn near reached for her. But then, she shook her head and stepped back. "Let's get to work. This mural won't paint itself."

She'd done it again, astonished him. And even though a part of him worried this couldn't end well, he'd deal with that later. For now, he could hardly wait to see what sort of surprise she had in store next.

CHAPTER NINE

"I SHOULD HAVE bought another cup of coffee. I think I'm going to need it."

"I told you." Astrid laughed. "You could have stayed home today, you know. I could handle the booth alone. It's always slower on Sundays and I know you're tired. I heard you up and around—and that was after painting all day in the hot sun while managing a herd of unruly teenagers. And Dane."

Dane... She drew in a steadying breath. She'd had all sorts of thoughts about him. "Sorry." Tansy smothered a yawn. "My brain wouldn't turn off, you know?" She hadn't told Astrid what had happened. *What I did.* If she hadn't thrown herself at Dane, that kiss wouldn't have happened. It had been spontaneous and reckless and bone-meltingly wonderful.

"I know your brain." Astrid smiled. "I wasn't aware it ever turned off. What were you pondering at two in the morning?"

Mostly Dane. And kissing him. It was pathetic, really. One kiss and she seemed to have forgotten who Dane really was. Tansy stood and stretched, searching the row of canopies and tents for familiar faces. "Where do I start... The Honey Festival is a couple of weeks off. Healthy & Wholesome Markets contract. Keeping our home. Beating Dane—the Knudsons..." After yesterday, she wasn't sure how she felt about that part. Not just the knee-weakening kiss, but how sweet he'd been to her for the rest of the day. Not the sarcastic thing where he said one thing but his snarky delivery and superior expression guaranteed he meant something else. No, he seemed sincere. *Seemed.*

"Oh, so nothing big." Astrid shook her head.

"Exactly." She took a sip of coffee, eager to change the subject. "I wasn't the only one up, you know. Aunt Mags was cleaning out the pantry. Everything, and I mean everything, was out and lined up on the counters."

"Oh dear." Astrid frowned. "That's a bad sign."

"I offered to help but she said it was therapeutic for her." Tansy held her Honey Hill Farms travel mug to her temple, soothing the slight ache there. "I asked if she wanted company and she said she was *just fine.*" Aunt Mags wasn't fine—they all knew that. But none of them had any ideas on how to make it better.

A customer interrupted their conversation with a question. Astrid explained the different varieties of honey they had and listed off the benefits of their homemade soaps and lotions. In the end, Tansy loaded up one of their logoed canvas shopping bags with three jars of honey, four gift packs of soap and two bottles of Honey Silk Lotion.

"Nicole's right," Tansy said, waving after their customer. "You are a born salesperson."

"I suppose that's a good thing, since we do have to sell stuff." She stooped, lifting the table cover and rifling through a wooden crate. "We're going to need to make more Honey Silk Lotion. We're getting low."

"I think that was on Aunt Camellia's to-do list." Tansy opened her phone. "But I'll send her a quick text."

Astrid laughed. "You know you'll get a novel in return."

It was true. Aunt Camellia's texts were more like a rambling train of thought. While amusing, it took at least two reads to figure out what she might be after. "Fair. I'll make a note to tell her when she gets here." She glanced at Astrid. "I wonder if Aunt Mags will come, too."

The aunts always attended the Alpine Springs Arts and Wine Festival. They both loved art, a good bottle of wine and the opportunity to dine at one of the eccentric bistros scattered between the galleries and shops. No trip was complete without a stop at the Alpine Springs Chocolatier. Aunt Mags, after several glasses of wine, would say this was the only festival that had any sense of culture, which always made Aunt Camellia smile and say, *You mean chocolate. It has chocolate.* And they'd both laugh.

They could use some laughter. Wine and chocolate, too.

The morning clipped along, a steady flow of customers buying out all the Honey Silk Lotion, and every jar of mesquite honey and wildflower honey they'd brought with them. Tansy happily tucked away the profits and finished off her coffee. "I'm out." She tipped her mug upside down.

"Oh, that face." Astrid laughed. "I did pack lunch. No coffee but it's something." She pulled the small cooler from under the table. "I brought some of the bread Aunt Mags baked, peanut butter, some of last year's creamed lavender honey, some grapes and…a lemon-honey cupcake."

"One?" Tansy ignored the rumble of her tummy and flopped into her camp chair. "I'm not sure I'll make it."

"One each." Astrid pointed into the cooler. "I know better." She crossed her arms over her chest. "Do you need me to go on a coffee hunt?"

"No. But I love you even more for offering." Tansy grinned.

"You go." Astrid pulled her up. "It'll perk you up to move around *and* I'll make the sandwiches so they'll be ready when you get back."

Tansy's groan was for Astrid's sake. "Fine."

"Yeah, yeah. Life is so hard." Astrid shooed her out of the booth. "If you're going to make that grumpy face, maybe you should leave the 'Honey Hill Farms Means Happiness' apron here with me?"

"Rude." But Tansy handed over the apron. "Extra peanut butter on mine, please."

"Like I don't know that." Astrid took the apron and blew her a kiss. "Have fun. Get an extra espresso shot or two."

Tansy stuck her tongue out and headed down the row, scanning the banners and signs for anything with the word coffee or latte or espresso. A Latte Coffee was the last booth on the last row. Tansy was so happy, she almost sprinted to it. She ordered a large latte with an extra shot of espresso and headed back to the Honey Hill Farms booth, more fortified.

"Help me, p-please." It was a wail, high-pitched and frantic. "I—I can't find th-them."

Tansy's heart picked up, turning in the direction of a little girl crying.

A big sniffle, followed by, "H-help me, Thor, p-please…"

Tansy came to a stop, her beloved coffee all but forgotten at the image that greeted her.

Dane was kneeling in the grass, holding the sobbing little girl's hand. "Hey, hey, now. We'll find them." The thing was, he looked almost as terrified as the little girl. His blue eyes searched the crowd—and landed on Tansy. Some of the tension eased from his rigid shoulders and tight jaw.

Tansy was already heading that way but the plea on Dane's face cinched it. *Like I have any idea how to help.* She hurried, offering him a reassuring smile. "Hey, Thor." She couldn't resist. "What's up?"

He ignored her teasing and glanced at the girl. "Annie here is looking for her folks."

"Oh." Tansy smiled at the little girl. "Well, Annie, we can help you."

"Thor is the b-best h-hero." Annie wiped her nose with her forearm. "Will says so." She sucked in a wavering breath, more tears welling up.

Poor Annie. "Who is Will?" Tansy asked, glancing at Dane.

"M-my b-big b-brother." Annie dissolved into tears, leaning into Dane and wrapping her arms around his neck.

Dane stared at Tansy and mouthed, *What do I do?*

I don't know, she mouthed back. Annie was terrified, she needed comfort, so Tansy mimicked hugging Annie.

He hugged the little girl—more awkward than she'd ever seen him. "Okay." He patted her back. "Let's go find your folks, Annie."

"It'll be okay now." Tansy chimed in, offering up a smile. Inside she knew this had disaster written all over it. She was pretty sure they were the two least qualified people to handle this situation.

Annie sniffled, but her little head nodded. When Dane tried to hold her hand, she burrowed closer against him.

"Do you want Thor to carry you?" Tansy asked. He shot her a heavy-lidded glare—which she ignored.

Annie nodded. "P-please."

Dane sighed and scooped Annie up.

Tansy smiled up at the girl. "You can see better up here, too."

"Yes. Thor is tall." Annie wiped the tears from her eyes and looked up at Dane. "'Cause y-you're a s-strong superhero. You can save the day."

There was such certainty in her little voice that Tansy melted inside a little. "I know he will." She patted the little girl's back.

The look on Dane's face as he stared down at Annie said it all. He was no longer awkward or uncertain. This little girl believed in him and, now, he looked every bit the protective and capable superhero Annie thought he was.

That's quite a picture. Tansy took an unsteady breath. *Very superhero-y.* "All you need is a cape," she murmured.

Dane didn't miss a beat. "It's in the wash." He winked at her. "Any ideas where to start?"

"Um…" Tansy nibbled on the inside of her lip. "There is an information booth somewhere… And a medical booth? People there will know what to do." She glanced at Dane for confirmation. But his eyes were pressed shut and his jaw was clenched so tight Tansy worried for his teeth. "Dane? Um, Thor?"

His eyes popped open. "Sounds good." He set off quickly, his long legs covering a lot of ground in a few steps.

Tansy hurried to catch up, sloshing coffee onto her hand. She took a long sip, needing it now more than ever. *Even if it is tepid.*

Annie rested her head on Dane's shoulder, her breathing deep and even.

Oh, my heart. There was something about the giantness of Dane holding little Annie that did, in fact, cause Tansy's heart to stumble over itself for a few beats. It would have been the same reaction if it was another giant man being sweet—not that she personally knew any man as giant or handsome or as incredible a kisser as Dane. *Am I going to think about that kiss every time I see him?* Tansy frowned and took another sip of her coffee.

After ten minutes of asking around, they were directed to the lost and found center on the edge of the park. The woman working there took one look at Annie and frowned.

"I'm on my own today—my partner called in sick. I can handle purses and phones and that sort of thing but I've got a bum knee and I'm not all that quick on my feet." The woman frowned. "I don't suppose you two could help me out?"

Tansy glanced at Dane at the same time he glanced at her.

"There's a children's area." The woman pointed. "Why don't you-all take her there and I'll radio our security officer to be on the lookout. He can bring her folks to you."

It wasn't the answer Tansy was hoping for but it made

sense. Leaving Annie here would probably upset her all over again. At the moment, she was dry-eyed—and hanging on to Dane for dear life. Even if they wanted to leave her here, it'd take a lot of effort to pry Annie off of Thor. "That one?" Tansy nodded at the oversize fenced-off booth.

"Yes." The woman smiled. "They have arts and crafts and cookie decorating and all sorts of fun." She patted Annie's back. "Doesn't that sound nice."

Annie nodded. "I like cookies."

"Me, too." Dane shifted her to the other arm.

Tansy took that to mean they'd stay with Annie. *It is the right thing to do.*

The woman pulled out her walkie-talkie. "Bert? Over? It's Glenda over at the lost and found."

After a few seconds static: "Bert, here. What can I do for you, Glenda?"

"I've got some nice folks here that found a lost little girl. I need you to call your friends over at the station, pronto, so we can find her folks."

"I could use a cookie to go with my coffee." Tansy nudged Dane into motion as Glenda relayed the details over the walkie-talkie.

He sighed but followed her. "I could use some coffee to go with our cookies." The closer they got to the children's booth, the louder the noise. Most of it was happy—but it was still a lot.

"I'm definitely going to need coffee." Dane winced at an especially shrill squeal.

"My daddy likes coffee, too." Annie leaned back and peered up at him. "My mommy likes tea."

"My aunts drink tea. I'll drink coffee or tea." Tansy

pointed out an empty table along the edge of the partitioned off space. "Someplace visible."

"Tea." Dane's grin was sly. "Weren't you-all considering some sort of new tea line for your shop?"

"I don't think so." Tansy had no idea what he was talking about. "How about I go get us cookies to decorate?"

Dane sat, smiling as Annie sat close enough to almost be in his lap.

Tansy leaned forward. "Should I get extra cookies, Annie? I bet Thor eats more than one at a time?"

Dane's eyes narrowed.

Annie glanced up at him, then nodded. "I bet he eats at least three." She shrugged. "Maybe ten."

"Three sounds good. With extra sprinkles." Dane nodded at Annie.

"Maybe my momma will be here to share some?" Annie asked, her eyes welling up again.

"Maybe we should make one for her?" Dane sounded so gentle as he spoke to the little girl.

Annie's lower lip wobbled but she nodded.

"Okay." Tansy headed to the table with the large Cookie Station sign overhead. She grabbed three cookie kits, paid and carried them back to the table. "They're huge, more like cookie cakes."

Annie sat up on her knees, fully invested in watching Tansy open the cellophane-wrapped box. One large cookie, three small tubes of colored frosting, one large tube of white frosting and sprinkles. "There are *sprinkles*." She smiled up at Dane.

"One of my superpowers is cookie decorating." Dane opened his cookie box, his expression grave. "Don't feel too bad if mine looks and tastes the best."

"How can yours taste better?" Tansy rolled her eyes.

"Because it's mine." Dane pointed at his chest.

Annie turned to Tansy, adding simply, "And Thor is the best."

Tansy laughed. "You're right, Annie. I think *Thor* is the best." She studied Dane, cocking her head to one side. "The real Thor, that is. None of those wannabe Thors. They're the worst." She popped the seal off the frosting tubes and handed them to Annie as she spoke. "Acting important all the time. Wanting attention. Having to be right. Being condescending. Teasing all the time. Wearing too-tight shirts—"

"Don't you mean 'shirts that fit well'?" Dane interrupted. "Interesting that that's one of the things that bothers you." He smoothed his snug-fit T-shirt into place.

She'd actually said all of that out loud. While she scrambled to come up with some sort of excuse or comeback, she opened Annie's sprinkles container.

"Annie!" A woman's voice. "Annie, baby!"

Tansy turned, searching out the woman.

"Momma?" Annie stood in her seat. The moment she saw her mother, she was jumping up and down and waving. "Momma, look! Look who saved me. It's Thor."

Dane groaned and covered his face.

"It's sweet." Tansy pushed against his shoulder. "And now you can say you are, in fact, a hero."

Annie's mother scooped her up. "Baby girl. I'm so sorry. I'm sorry."

Tansy couldn't move, held in thrall by the scene playing out in front of her, by Annie's mom. The way her face crumpled as she turned into Annie's hair, the fierce hold she had on her daughter—as if she couldn't bear the thought of letting go for fear of losing her little girl again. The pure, all-consuming love of a mother for her child.

Dane's touch was the anchor she needed. She didn't remember putting her hand on his shoulder or gripping the fabric of his shirt. His hand, covering hers, wrapped her in such warmth that she didn't immediately pull away.

"This nice couple has been keeping an eye on her." Glenda, from the lost and found, nodded at the two of them.

But we're not a couple. They were the opposite of a couple. She let go of Dane and shoved her hands into her pockets.

"Thank you, so much." Annie's mother was sobbing, but smiling. "She went with her brother and then decided not to go with him but never made it back to me. We've been looking."

"I was safe with Thor, Momma." Annie pointed at Dane. "Will!" she shrieked. "Will, come meet him!"

Dane was an adorable shade of red. "I'm not—"

"Whoa." The moment the boy saw Dane, he froze. "He's… You're… Whoa."

Tansy laughed, she had to.

Dane's blue eyes darted her way, not in the least amused.

"Thank you, both of you." The mother nudged Will forward. "Say hello, Will. I'm sure Mr. Thor would be happy to meet you."

Dane sighed.

As amusing as it was to watch Dane squirm, a flash of red beyond Dane and Annie snagged her gaze. *Was that? Yes, it was.*

Shelby Dunholm.

"If you'll excuse me." Tansy couldn't let Shelby leave—not without trying to talk to her. "I have to do something."

Dane frowned at her. "Everything okay?"

"A-okay here." She smiled at Annie. "Don't forget your cookie, Annie. You can give my cookie box to Will."

She was out of the children's area before anyone could say a word. A half a dozen scenarios played through her head before she reached Shelby's side. But once Shelby turned her way, and those green eyes met hers, all that came out was, "Shelby? Hi."

Shelby's smile was timid. "Hi."

"Hi. Hi." The baby, buckled into a stroller, waved up at Tansy.

"Well, hello." Tansy smiled at the baby. "You're adorable."

"Her name is Beatrix," Shelby said. "I call her Bea."

Bea? As in Bee? "My name is Tansy." She held her hand out.

Shelby paused, then shook her hand. "Shelby. But you know that."

Tansy nodded. "Would you like to get a cup of coffee, maybe?" She held her breath, waiting for Shelby's response.

DANE'S GAZE TRAILED after Tansy. She was a woman on a mission, briskly heading toward something that had captured her attention. Before he could figure out what she was after, Annie's brother, Will, stepped directly into his line of sight.

"I have a question about Minotaur." Will was wearing a T-shirt emblazoned with Thor's hammer. If this kid started asking Dane questions about Thor, Will would realize Dane wasn't Thor.

"He wins, Will." Annie sighed. "He always wins. He's Thor."

Will frowned but nodded. "True."

Annie pushed her oversize flower cookie toward Dane. "This is for you. With lots of sprinkles, too. Taste good?"

She'd used the whole container. And, from the looks of it, most of her frosting, too. He broke off a piece and ate it. "Delicious." *So much sugar.* But he smiled, eyeing the coffee Tansy had left behind. It was probably cold and gross—but it was caffeinated. *And my only option.*

"It's a thank-you present." Annie beamed.

"We should let you get back to your day." Annie's mom took Will's hand and reached for Annie.

The little girl gave him a quick hug. "Bye, Thor."

"Bye, Annie." He patted her back. "Bye, Will. Next time—maybe we talk about the Minotaur." He shouldn't have said that. If, by some miracle, he did run into them, the boy would have questions and expect answers.

Will perked up at that. "Cool."

"Thank you, again. Please tell your lovely girl-friend...wife thank you, too?" Annie's mom was ready to leave, it was all over her face.

Dane didn't correct her—it would only slow her down. "I will."

The woman nodded, steering her kids out of the children's area.

He slipped the band from his hair, smoothed it back tight, and pulled his hair through for a loose knot at the back of his head. *That was something.* He ate the cookie, finished off Tansy's cold coffee with a grimace and took in the dwindling crowd. He'd sold out and was in the midst of packing up when Annie came running his way, so there was no need to hurry back.

Now that Annie was safe and sound, he found himself wondering where Tansy had gone off to and why. Chances were she was mad at him—which was the norm.

If he'd stopped and thought through what he was doing, he never would have held her hand. They were in a public place, where anyone could see. Unlike yesterday. But he'd seen the yearning on her face and he'd... acted. She'd been missing her mother. He and Tansy had that in common—it was a wound that never fully healed. He'd meant to comfort her, and himself. But then she'd leaned into him and he'd been too caught up in the way she fit against his side to move at all.

She hadn't seemed angry when she'd run off. But she *had* run off.

Without realizing it, he was searching the crowd. Magnolia's deep red hair was unique enough that she was easy to spot. And where one Bee Girl was, another was sure to be close. Tansy was there, ponytail swinging and hands gesturing as she talked. Even at this distance, he couldn't ignore the pull between them.

He'd spent the better part of last night making a long list of all the reasons this was a bad idea. They didn't like each other, they were industry rivals and, of course, she had broken his heart into a million pieces. And yet, one look, one touch and some damn electrified current snapped between them.

She'd probably deny it. Tansy was Tansy. But...she

had kissed him. And she didn't seem sorry about it. Neither was he.

Still, one kiss shouldn't have him making lists or reading into anything. She wanted him. He wanted her. That was all there was to it.

He blew out a slow breath and stared up at the blue sky overhead. *Moving on.*

He was done here. After a quick cleanup, he could head back to Honey and the mile-long list of things he had to do there. He wasn't even supposed to be here. But when his part-time employee had called in sick, a rare event, Dane had no choice but to step in. It hadn't been all bad. Business had been good and if he hadn't been here, Annie and Will wouldn't have met Thor but Dane shook his head. Tansy got a big kick out of that. *Yeah, right.* He dumped his trash and glanced at Tansy again. Annie's mom *had* wanted him to thank her... He'd best get to it.

He was almost at her side when he realized Tansy wasn't talking to her aunt. This woman was too young, maybe a few years older than Tansy—and she was pushing a baby stroller. But she must be family, since her resemblance to Magnolia Hill was uncanny.

"Dane Knudson." The voice was loud and so close he jumped—almost tripping over his own feet.

He turned to find sisters Ida Popplewell and Uma Bumgartner, and their friend Corliss Ogden. "Ladies. Good afternoon."

"It is, it is, indeed." Ida nodded.

"Couldn't ask for nicer weather." Uma Bumgartner shielded her eyes. "How were sales?"

"All sold out." He rubbed his hands together. "About to pack up and head home."

"I'm glad we caught you, then." Corliss stepped forward, her mile-high hair listing slightly to the left. "You know Willadeene and Violet brought lunch out to you-all yesterday? At the barn painting."

Dane nodded. "The cookies were good."

"It's my recipe." Corliss grinned. "Of course, they were."

Dane chuckled.

"But, to the point, we were wondering if you saw something..." Uma broke off and glanced at Ida.

"Were Violet and Willadeene snapping at one another?" Corliss pushed her thick-rimmed glasses up her nose. "Willadeene's madder than a wet cat and Violet's not speaking to her."

"Corliss," Ida hissed.

"What?" Corliss shrugged. "It's true. What did I say?"

Dane chuckled again. "They were fine when they got there and, as far as I could tell, they were fine when they left." Which, according to the extreme disappointment on their faces, wasn't what they wanted to hear.

"I told you we should ask Tansy." Corliss sighed.

"Have you seen her?" Ida asked. "Tansy, I mean."

"I did." He nodded. "Earlier." Something about Tansy's interaction with the red-haired woman said they wouldn't appreciate any interruption. Or, given the audience, speculation. Knowing this group, there'd be all sorts of speculation. Tansy had helped him with Annie, he'd try to steer these lovely ladies as far from Tansy as possible. *We can call today even.*

"Oh." Uma smiled. "How nice." She elbowed Ida.

Ida nodded. "Isn't it, though?"

That's not helping, either.

Suddenly, Corliss Ogden pitched forward. Her arms pinwheeled but Dane stepped in and caught her before she face-planted in the dirt path at their feet.

"Oh, I'm sorry. I'm so sorry." It was the red-haired woman, her stroller the cause of Corliss's near fall. "I didn't see you."

"It's fine, child." Corliss assured her. "I don't mind being scooped up by a big, strong man once in a while."

The red-haired woman smiled, slightly, but her gaze darted beyond them. "I am sorry. If you'll excuse me." She moved on.

"*Who* was that?" Ida asked.

"Was it just me, or did she look *exactly* like Magnolia Hill?" Uma whispered.

It isn't just you.

Corliss patted his arm as he set her on the ground. "Land sakes, Dane Knudson. You have the muscles of a Viking, that's for certain." She fanned herself. "I'll have to swoon more often when you're around. Now, where is Tansy?"

He'd managed to shift the ladies so that their backs were to Tansy—which was good since Tansy was completely oblivious to anything but the red-haired mystery woman. Even now, she was hurrying after the woman.

From the look on both women's faces, this wasn't a conversation Tansy would want overheard. Whatever was happening, it was important and private. If he didn't do something, and fast, everyone would learn the Hills' personal business. After being stuck in that public hell for the last few months, he wouldn't wish it on his worst enemy. Which, technically, was Tansy.

"Ladies, I need your advice." They were the first words that came to mind. What he'd say next, he had no idea. The women weren't the least bit interested. Right. Something bigger, juicier. He sighed. "Your... romantic advice," he declared, rewarded by all three women's round-eyed stare.

"Romantic?" Ida stepped forward, lowering her voice. "You know we'll help, Dane."

Great. He had their full attention, so now what?

"Who is the lucky girl?" Uma's hands were pressed to her chest. "Does she know how you feel?"

Dane opened his mouth, but nothing came out. He'd set the trap and caught himself. A quick glance told him Tansy was still talking to the woman. Dammit. "I'm not sure she's interested."

"Not interested? In you?" Corliss pushed her glasses up. "I can trip her so you can catch her, if you'd like. I guarantee that'll do the trick."

Dane was so surprised he was laughing. "Thank you. I think?"

"Sometimes, these things call for desperate measures, Dane." Uma nodded. "I don't think my late Charles would have ever noticed me if I hadn't driven into his car in the grocery parking lot. Rest his sweet soul."

All Dane could do was stare. The woman was absolutely serious.

"And Ida would never have caught her Waylon if she hadn't faked spraining her ankle falling down the stairs of city hall." Uma patted her sister's arm.

"He was there to renew his registration. I remember it like it was yesterday." Ida smiled.

Dane wasn't sure if he was amused or horrified. He had so many questions. Did either Charles or Waylon know about this? The fake sprained ankle was bad, but driving into a man's car? That was concerning.

"Hush now, you two. Dane is asking for advice. You keep telling him these things and he's liable to run the other way." Corliss's tone was disapproving. "Now, then, Dane. You're not sure the girl you're interested in returns the…interest?"

Sure, why not. Dane nodded. He chanced another look at Tansy. She was giving the red-haired woman a business card.

"Have you properly wooed this girl?" Uma glanced at her sister.

"You know, made your intentions known?" Ida went on to say, "What *are* your intentions?"

He ignored the last question. "No, I guess I haven't." He could hardly wait to hear what these women considered wooing. Honestly, he was a little afraid.

"Then you start there. Flowers." Uma sighed. "My sweet Charles always brought me armloads of flowers."

"Poems and chocolate, too." Ida was ticking things off on her fingers. "Or wine."

Beyond Ida, he saw the red-haired woman walk away. Tansy watched her go, her shoulders drooping. She looked defeated and it gutted him.

No, this was Tansy. She was strong. She was fine.

But the minute Tansy reached up to wipe the tear from her cheek, Dane was cursing himself. He wasn't going anywhere. *Because I'm a damn fool.* He stepped around the women, to Tansy. He stepped close enough to shield her from prying eyes. "Tansy," he whispered.

She sniffed, her attempt to glare pathetic. "What?"

"You have an audience. Behind me," he murmured. "Take a minute."

"Oh no." She blinked again, a tear rolling down her cheek.

That tear almost had him pulling her close, audience be damned.

"Who? It doesn't matter." She took a shaky breath. "Shit."

He stared at her. She never swore. "I think I misheard that."

She managed an actual glare.

He shrugged. "I figure since you gave us a ride home from San Antonio, saved us from being stranded on the side of the road with a flat tire, prevented me from committing possible bodily harm to the Wicked Witch of the Hill Country on several occasions and assisted Thor with today's rescue, I'd shield you from prying eyes since I owe you."

Her green eyes searched his. "Right. Wouldn't want me to get confused over your motivation." She sighed. "Who says chivalry is dead."

"Tansy…" He stopped himself before he said something he shouldn't. He'd made the mistake of opening himself up to her before and it'd taken years to get over it. *You either learn from your mistakes or you're destined to relive them.* That was a bit of wisdom from Camellia Hill. Wisdom he needed to remember when it came to Tansy. "You know me." He smiled.

Her eye roll didn't meet her usual fully exasperated standards. "I do. You keep popping up. Like every time I turn around, there—here you are."

"Is that a bad thing? Are you making an observation? Filing a complaint?" He resisted the urge to wipe away another tear. *Dammit all.* He scratched his jaw and grinned. "Hold up." He knew just how to lighten the mood. He waited for her to look at him. "Maybe I *am* Thor."

The sound of her laughter bubbled up and out to wash over him and flood him with happiness. *Damn. It. All.* It was official. He wanted to kiss her, yes, but there was more to it. It terrified him to admit it, but Tansy's laugh was the sweetest thing...ever.

CHAPTER TEN

"This is a great opportunity for the older Junior Beekeepers—getting to help with a hive removal." Tansy had her phone wedged between her shoulder and her ear, scribbling down the details. "The kids will be so excited, Daisy. Thank you."

"No, thank you for removing them from the feed barn. Daddy, and his babies, will be happy to see them go." Daisy Granger's sigh was edged with amusement. "And, believe me, those miniature horses are his babies."

"Um, hello. Aunt Camellia is up to…ten animals now." Tansy counted on her fingers. "I think? Yes, that's right. A variety, too."

"On second thought, I think I'll let Daddy keep his mini horses." Daisy laughed. "I'll see you this weekend."

"Thanks again." Tansy ended the call and sent an immediate text to the high school Junior Beekeepers text chain. As enthusiastic as the younger members were, the liability was too high to chance.

Beehive removal. Grangers' place. Meet at Honey Hill Farms, 7am, Saturday. Reply with a yes or no, please.

She hit Send and set her phone on the kitchen counter. "That will be fun." The bees, the kids, the mini horses. *Dane*. She couldn't remember a more eventful Alpine Springs Arts and Wine Festival than the one she'd had today. Shelby. *And Dane*. "Lots of fun."

"What?" Astrid glanced at Tansy's phone screen. "Oh. That will be a fun Saturday."

"What what?" Camellia asked, stirring the beginnings of a new batch of Honey Silk Lotion. "Don't forget the Honey Festival is weekend after next."

As if there was even the remote chance of this happening. Tansy hurried to Camellia, slipping her arms around her aunt's waist to hug her from behind. "I won't." She kissed her aunt's cheek. "You know I won't. *Nothing* is more important than that." Everything was riding on it—*everything*. They would win. They had to. If they didn't… She couldn't think about it without feeling sick.

Camellia patted her arm.

"We've got the blue ribbon in the bag." Tansy gave her another squeeze and stepped back.

"That's right. Don't put any negative energy out there." Astrid was a big proponent of visualization. She said you had to see your goal to be able to reach it.

"You're right." Camellia smiled at Astrid. "And I appreciate the reminder."

"Daisy Granger needs a hive removed in one of the pastures—inside one of the mini-horse shelters. The Junior Beekeepers will help with that on Saturday." Tansy checked the forecast for next Saturday on her phone. "It's supposed to be clear and sunny. It won't take the whole day, I promise."

"I imagine they'll learn a whole lot." Camellia went back to stirring the beginnings of her lotion.

The kitchen door flew open and Auntie Mags

stormed in. She was *fuming*. "Where is *he*?" Each word was delivered with clipped, sharp precision and threat.

Tansy and Astrid exchanged a look but stayed silent. They'd heard that *he* before. They knew exactly who the *he* was. Lord Byron was at it again.

Camellia tapped her wooden spoon against the side of the ten-gallon bucket and glanced at her sister. "Goodness, Mags, what's wrong?"

"What do you think? Your *parrot*." Her green eyes were narrowed to slits. "That's it. I don't know how he's getting in, Camellia, but enough is enough. He has to go—"

"Lord Byron was in your room again?" Camellia handed the spoon to Astrid. "I've made sure to keep him here and in the sunroom. At night, he's been in his cage."

"Then there's two of them because he's left me a lovely bird-poo surprise right in the middle of my vanity." She crossed her arms over her chest, eyes flashing.

"Oh dear." Camellia swallowed.

"Oh dear, is right." Aunt Mags's voice wavered as she leaned heavily against the kitchen counter. "And he took a photo." She breathed deeply. "*The* photo." Her voice broke then.

"Magnolia." Camellia stepped forward to take her sister's hands. "I'm so sorry, sweetheart."

"Don't be sorry, get it back." Aunt Mags's anger gave way to anguish. "It's all I have."

"I will. I am," Camellia assured her. "Girls, watch the lotion." She hurried into the sunroom, closing the door behind her.

Aunt Mags stayed propped against the kitchen counter, her arms wrapped around her waist and her green eyes fixed on the sunroom door. Aunt Mags might appear as aloof and impeccably put together as ever, but Tansy knew better. On the inside, her Auntie Mags was lost and broken.

Like Shelby. She was in exactly the same state. Lost and scattered.

"I'll make chamomile tea." Tansy filled the kettle and turned on the gas stove top.

The loud crash from inside the sunroom had them all jumping. Lord Byron squawked, followed by the sounds of his wings flapping. He was agitated, his voice loud and clear. "Little thief. Little thief."

If Aunt Mags's lips hadn't pressed tight, Tansy might have laughed. Aunt Camellia rarely chastised him so, when she did, the poor bird went out of his way to make it up to her. He'd follow her around and bring her things and use a baby voice until Aunt Camellia would forgive and forget the bird's latest offense. Until the next time Lord Byron figured out a new way into Aunt Mags's room and stole more shiny things.

After a bit, the sunroom door opened and Camellia came out. She'd turned her apron into a makeshift pouch—a pouch that was clearly full. "I have it." She hurried to the table and upended her apron onto it. "And a few other things, as well. He keeps finding new places to hide things."

Aunt Mags pushed off the counter and crossed to the table. She took the silver picture frame Camellia offered her and held it against her chest. "Thank you," she whispered.

Aunt Camellia came around the table to hug her sister. Camellia gave the best hugs. Big and strong and warm and reassuring. All things Aunt Mags desperately needed. "I'll go clean up the mess he left." Aunt Camellia collected disinfecting wipes, some paper towels and bleach spray. "Please turn off the burner, Astrid." She nodded at the stove and left.

Tansy filled the teapot and carried it to the kitchen table, then brought cups and saucers. "Tea?"

Aunt Mags sat, staring down at the picture frame. She ran a finger along the edge, sighed and placed it facedown in her lap. "Thank you."

Tansy dropped a tea bag into each cup and filled them with steaming water before sitting at the table.

Astrid set a plate of honey sugar cookies and tangerine honey tarts in the middle of the table and sat, too. "Thanks for the tea." She raised her cup at Tansy.

"Thanks for the treats." Tansy reached for a cookie.

It was quiet until Aunt Camellia returned. She stowed all the cleaning items away, washed her hands and joined them at the table.

It fell silent again.

"We sold out today." Astrid drew her legs up into her seat. "And most of our new travel mugs, too."

"Really?" Aunt Camellia's brows rose. "That's good, then."

Aunt Mags took a cookie and tart, asking half-heartedly, "Anything eventful?"

"Not really." Astrid shrugged. "Not for *me*. Tansy had a little adventure."

"It wasn't an adventure. A little girl got lost so we helped her find her mother." Tansy shrugged. "You know I'm not much of a kid person, but she was so sweet. And she called Dane Thor and said he had to help her because he was a superhero." And he'd been sweet and gorgeous and better than Thor could ever be.

"Dane?" Aunt Camellia frowned. "How was Dane involved?"

"Annie, the little girl, saw Thor—" Tansy used air quotes "—and ran to him. He panicked and asked me for help." She took in their shock, then suspicion. "I know. He was surprisingly…" Handsome. Warm. Gentle. "Well-behaved and pleasant." She paused, glancing at Auntie Mags. She had to tell her. "He also gave me a heads-up when Ida, Uma and Corliss showed up."

Aunt Mags's green eyes searched hers, one dark red eyebrow rising in question.

"And…" Tansy took a sip of tea. "Shelby was there."

Aunt Mags set her teacup down. She rested her forearms on the table, hands clasped. "How was she? Did she see you? Did you talk to her?"

"Tell us everything." Aunt Camellia nodded. "Don't spare a single detail."

Tansy nodded. "We said hi. I said something boring about nice weather. She said it was perfect festival weather and that she enjoyed festivals and small towns. I told her to come to Honey during the Honey Festival since it's the best one all spring. She said she'd think about it."

"Really?" Aunt Mags's smile was small. "Did you… Was there anything else?"

"I asked if she was traveling alone and she said it was just her and Beatrix. That's her daughter's name. She goes by Bea."

They all exchanged a smile over that.

"Her mother died two years ago and her father didn't approve of her coming here to look for…for you. And she didn't want to bring friends because she wasn't sure what to expect." Tansy replayed the afternoon. "I gave her my card and told her she was welcome to call or visit anytime. Then Dane showed up." And she'd been happy to see him. She'd tried to convince herself that was a result of her scrambled-up emotions but she wasn't buying it. *Focus*. "I hope that's okay—giving her my card and all?"

"Yes. Thank you." Aunt Mags leaned back and turned over the photo in her lap. She stared down at it for a long time before handing it to Astrid. "This is Shelby when she was a few hours old." There was a sort of reverence on her face. "She is my daughter."

It wasn't a surprise. They'd all known. Still, Aunt Mags confirming it made it *real*. Aunt Mags was a mother. And a grandmother.

Astrid stared down at the small photo, her smile sad. "She was beautiful. She *is* beautiful."

"She looks exactly like you." Camellia covered one of Mags's hands with hers.

"I appreciate you giving me time but now I... I..." Mags sniffed and sat up straight. "I was seventeen years old, young and in love and so naive. *He* was beautiful." She shook her head. "Beautiful and sweet-talking and, as it turned out, *horrible*. He was big and strong... He *took* what *he* wanted and left." She took a sip of her tea and went on. "He'd enlisted and was gone before Poppa got to him." She glanced at Tansy, then Astrid. "Your father was off at college already. I'm thankful for that. I think Poppa or your father would have killed him if they'd gotten their hands on him."

Tansy took the photo from Astrid, listening as Aunt Mags shared. It was hard to hear, hard to know what her beloved auntie had endured. And this baby—Shelby... Tansy studied the picture. She was so tiny and helpless. *She was perfect*. Tansy's heart twisted so sharply it hurt to breathe.

"Anyway. It…it was done and she was coming." Her gaze darted to Camellia. "Times were so hard then. Poppa was talking about taking out a second mortgage on the farm and worrying over feeding us. Momma was just starting to struggle with her memory. I couldn't bear adding to it all." She smoothed her hair again. "Poppa tried, he did, but I could tell it was hard for him to look at me. No one outside the family knew about… what happened to me or that I was expecting. I wanted to keep it that way. I spent the last part of that summer with our aunt Gertrude and came back home after the birth. Shelby had a new family and good life and I came home to mine." She reached for her teacup, turning it in its saucer. "But every day since, I wake up and wonder where she is—hoping she's happy and well."

Tansy's tears blurred the image so she handed the photo back to Aunt Mags. From the corner of her eye, she could see Astrid crying softly and reached for her hand.

Aunt Camellia patted her sister's arm. "And now she's here."

"Perhaps. But she's still a million miles away." Auntie Mags picked up the photo and pressed it against her chest.

"She is still here, Aunt Mags." Tansy was pretty sure Shelby sticking around was a good sign. She hadn't just stayed because of her love of festivals and small towns. "Maybe…maybe she needs a little more time."

"Did she say that?" Aunt Mags's green eyes fixed on her face.

"No. We didn't have that sort of talk." She nibbled

on the inside of her lip. "It was a public place and it was all very superficial. She was nervous in the beginning. When she mentioned her mother had passed two years before, she almost left. I don't think she'd intended to share that." Tansy remembered the look on Shelby's face. Guarded—but yearning. "I managed to get in a few more words and, when we parted, she wasn't running or hurrying away."

"That's something, I suppose." Aunt Mags frowned. "Poor darling girl. To lose her mother."

All four of them understood that pain.

"And that's when Dane warned you?" Aunt Camellia set her teacup down. "Did the ladies see Shelby?"

All eyes swiveled Tansy's way. "Yes. Shelby left and he stepped in and blocked me from their view—I admit I was rattled." Rattled, as in near crying. "He told me to take a minute for myself." *Because he owed me.* He'd made sure she understood that. But for all his clarifications, Tansy couldn't shake the feeling there was *more* to it. Not that his explanation wasn't plausible, it was. Still, there'd been something about him, something in his eyes. *He probably had something in his eye.*

All three of them were staring at her.

"I barely had time to exchange polite hellos with anyone before Dane said there was some urgent Junior Beekeepers information we needed to discuss." And he'd taken a hold of her arm to steer her away. "I waved goodbye and he walked me back to our booth before anyone asked any questions." *Almost* like a rescue mission.

"We are talking about Dane Knudson?" Aunt Mags sounded incredulous. "Why would he do that?"

"Maybe he was being nice?" Astrid, ever the optimist, took a cookie and glanced up to find their aunts eyeing her with open disbelief. "Okay, okay. I'm sure he's planning something devious." She took a bite, her brows rising. "There? Better?"

It's not like he hasn't done that before. Tansy forced a laugh.

"I know he's been a right toot in the past but—" Camellia shrugged "—it's not impossible he was trying to do something nice for Tansy."

Tansy felt ridiculously buoyed by her aunt's comment but said, "I think it was his way of paying me back for helping out with Annie."

"I suppose that makes sense." Aunt Mags shook her head. "Be that as it may, I... I suppose I'm grateful."

"Me, too." Aunt Camellia lifted her hands so Beeswax could jump into her lap. "Come on, sweetie." Jammie, who was older and insisted on being next to Beeswax 24/7, sat beside the chair and yowled. "There's room, Jammie-kins." She patted her chair until the cat was up and curling around his sibling.

"You two need to spend less time in laps and more time being cats." Aunt Mags glared at the felines. "There's a lovely, juicy parrot living right under this very roof. Aren't you supposed to keep the house vermin-free? Bring your owners tokens of your prowess? I'd love a dead-as-a-doornail parrot delivered right at my feet."

"Uma, Ida and Corliss don't always gossip." Camellia went on as if Mags hadn't said a thing. "We'll have to hope they won't."

"That's not being hopeful, that's being delusional." Aunt Mags shot her sister a look. "You know better, Camellia. Those women will tell Willadeene everything.

Wanting to believe a person can do better doesn't mean they will—or that they would want to. All you're doing is setting yourself up for disappointment." She pointed at Tansy. "Tansy, for example, would never trust Dane Knudson. She knows him too well and knows to keep him at arm's length and protect herself."

It was a solid reminder. Keeping Dane at arm's length was always the best option. Yes, the air was extra charged between them and her insides sort of melted when he smiled and his kiss had her clinging and breathless. But...

How had she let this happen? When had she let her guard down? Somehow, she'd conveniently set aside their past. *Probably around the time I threw my arms around his neck.* And she couldn't be mad at him. She'd started it and she sort of hoped there'd be more kissing in their future.

This was a problem. A big one. *One I created.*

"I'll get back to the lotion." Astrid stood, brushing crumbs from her lap.

"I'll help. Maybe we can check in on the south yards before the sun goes down?" Tansy cleared her and Astrid's teacups from the table. "If you're game?"

"Always." Astrid never said no to time with the bees.

"Good." Amidst the buzz of the bees working diligently toward one common goal, life was simple. She needed simple right now. Bees and family and honey and knowing, in her heart, what she wanted—what was right. Simple, as in Dane was an untrustworthy and prodding rival not an appealingly tempting and supremely kissable hottie. Because he was oh so appealing.

Simple was good. Simple was predictable and easy. The question was, would things ever be simple between her and Dane again?

THE MINUTE DANE'S alarm went off, his nerves kicked in. He'd given himself a week of no Tansy. After he'd rushed her back to the Honey Hill Farms booth at the Alpine Springs Arts and Wine Festival, he'd decided the best thing to get his head straight was space.

And it hadn't worked one damn bit.

No matter how hard he pored over old order sheets, negotiated prices on pest strips for the hive or did a sugar shake test to check for mites, he couldn't stop the flashes of memory or sensation that only Tansy stirred. Things between them were getting dangerous. Too tangled up in each other's business—and emotions. He was headed for trouble, he knew that, and he wasn't doing a damn thing to stop it. But, fool that he was, he was looking forward to spending time with her today.

"Leif!" He thumped on the wall that separated their rooms. "Rise and shine." He listened as he tugged on some loose-fit carpenter jeans and a thin gray Texas Viking Honey T-shirt. *Nothing.* He knocked on the wall again. "Leif, wheels up in five minutes." Once he'd stepped into his well-worn leather boots, and slicked his hair back into a tight ponytail, he left his room and headed to Leif's. He knocked. "Coming in." He waited five seconds before pushing the door wide.

It looked like everything Leif owned had been dumped on the floor so it took a minute to realize Leif wasn't there. He eyed the empty bed. "Damn."

All this week, Leif had come home and pulled on his bee suit to work with Birmingham. After the sun went down, Leif washed up, did his homework and went to bed. Whatever the reason for Leif's turnaround, Dane was going to have a much easier time showing their father Leif was right where he needed to be.

Now he's gone.

Dane hurried down the back stairs into the kitchen. "Dammit." He checked his phone—no messages—and flipped on the coffeepot. "Dammit all." He pulled a mug from the cabinet and set it on the counter, waiting as the coffeepot boiled and gurgled.

There was a crunching sound. Dane paused. A scrape and more crunching. He turned slowly. It was Leif, chowing down on Fruity O's cereal. Dane was grinning like an idiot. "Morning."

Leif didn't respond. He was entirely engrossed in the book he was reading.

"Morning," Dane said, a little louder. Still nothing. Dane stepped forward, tapping on the top of the pages.

Leif looked up, pulling his earbud from his right ear. "Hey." He nodded.

"Morning."

"What's wrong with you?" Leif frowned, using his spoon to point at him. "Seriously. That smile? That's not normal."

"Coffee." He tried to rein in the grinning. "Coffee makes me happy."

"Uh-huh." Leif's brows rose. "You've *never* been that happy about coffee before."

Dane chuckled. "What are you reading?" Leif shifted the book so Dane could see the title. *"Practical Bee-keeping, A Field Guide."*

"It's recommended on the National Beekeepers website." Leif shrugged.

"Haven't read that one." He headed back to the counter and poured himself some coffee. "I remember Birmingham made me read something? He swore by it. I can't remember the name and it was dry as dirt, but it taught me a whole hell of a lot. So did he."

"I'll ask him." Leif closed his book. "He might be old, but he knows everything about bees."

"Some people speak bee." Dane poured himself a cup of coffee. "That's what Mr. Hill used to say. That man would know, too, he spoke bee more fluently than anyone I've ever met. Don't tell Birmingham I said that or he'll smack me on the back of the head."

Leif smiled. "I'm telling him the next time I see him."

Dane almost choked on his coffee.

Leif started laughing.

"He'll do the same to you if I tell him you called him old."

Leif was laughing even harder. "I'd like to see him try it. He'd need a step stool."

"That's two." Dane was laughing now, so relieved. "Age and height." He poured his coffee into an oversize travel mug. "Ready?" He'd called Jenny midweek to tell her he was going to stick it out for a while—for Leif. She'd told him to call if something came up.

So, he had a way out. Call Jenny and he'd be done with Junior Beekeepers and this mess with Tansy and life would go back to normal. But… Leif would be disappointed. That was the explanation he was allowing himself to consider.

The scenery along the drive to Honey Hill Farms was enough to remind Dane why he loved his home so much. In the years he'd been gone, he'd traveled. But nothing and nowhere touched his soul the way this region did. And this year there'd been plenty of rain so the grass was green and the blooming wildflowers rippled in waves of color.

They drove the white river rock road—near sparkling in the early-morning sun—leading to the Hills' family home. It wound around a cluster of live oak and trailed alongside a honeysuckle-laden fence. As a boy, Dane had been convinced this place was magical. It had been the only place his father smiled after his mother died—that made it special.

Leif leaned out the window of the truck. "That's some house."

Dane nodded. "It's something."

The house was pale mint green with bright white trim. A tall turret window stuck out on the left side as if it had been added as an afterthought. The wide wraparound porch had decorative finials—he remembered finding bees carved into some of the woodwork. Like the Knudsons, beekeeping was in the Hills' blood.

That's why Dane had held on to such hope about his father and Camellia Hill. Not only had she made him happy, she'd understood his world—she was already a part of it. Whatever ended their relationship had caused the sort of rift that couldn't be healed. His father wouldn't talk about it, and the older he got, the more Dane was afraid to find out. One thing he knew, losing Camellia was one of his father's biggest regrets. First his mother, then Camellia…his father was never the same.

Dane surveyed the vehicles already parked out front of the house. "This group believes in being on time."

Teens of all ages were gathered around Tansy's old truck.

Leif was out and jogging toward them the moment Dane had the truck in Park.

Dane shook his head, watching his little brother. Leif ran his fingers through his shaggy hair, smoothed his shirt and headed straight for Kerrielynn. Kerrielynn was smiling ear to ear when she saw Leif. *Off to a good start.*

Tansy appeared, carrying a massive basket overflowing with muffins. She placed it on the tailgate and stepped aside, waving the kids forward. She was so beautiful he couldn't take his eyes off her. *Dammit all.* Seeing her made him happy. He probably looked just as lovesick as Leif. His hands tightened on the steering wheel as she laughed at something Benji said. Losing Camellia might be one of his dad's biggest regrets. He was looking at one of his.

He took a fortifying breath and made his way to Tansy. "A very good morning to you, Miss Hill." He leaned against the truck, giving her a smile. "Ready for some beekeeping adventures? Today is likely to be a little more…hands-on for us than our painting expedition."

Tansy's cheeks seemed awful pink when she stared up at him. "You think so?" Her smile was slow and sweet. "You never know. Today could be downright uneventful."

He shook his head, tossing subtlety aside. "I suppose we'll just have to wait and see." He cleared his throat. "You're in charge—I'm here to keep things interesting."

"Interesting." Tansy studied him, still smiling. "Muffin?"

So far, so good. "Thank you, Miss Hill. I think I will."

Tansy rolled her eyes—but she was laughing as she turned back to the Junior Beekeepers milling around. "I hear there's a big end-of-the-year school dance tonight," she called out. "If we work hard, we will be back here before lunch—with plenty of time to spare."

A dance? Dane glanced at Leif, who was staring at Kerrielynn, who was counting heads. *Was Leif going?*

"We're all here." Kerrielynn held out her clipboard.

"Let's load up. My van or Kerrielynn's. Seat belts on." Tansy opened the doors on her van. "We've got bees to rescue."

No surprise, Leif was climbing into the front passenger seat with Kerrielynn. Dane knew better than to ride with them—he didn't want to cramp his little brother's style. But, by the time he'd made his way back to the Honey Hill Farms van, it was full, too.

"I guess I'll take my truck? Unless you want me to ride up top." Dane shrugged, backing up to inspect the top of her van.

"You did say you were going to keep things interesting." She stood beside him, her head cocked to the side as she assessed the van's roof. She grinned at him. "If that's what you want to do. By all means."

The drive to the Granger place was a little longer but Dane didn't mind the quiet. He listened to a podcast on a new development in varroa resistant queen rearing. It was interesting stuff. He'd be curious to know what Tansy's take would be. Knowing her, she'd have a whole slew of opinions.

As soon as they'd unloaded and gathered, Tansy held up her bee suit. "I know there are lots of folk on social media that handle bees without protective gear but I don't know these bees so I'm going to suit up." She paused. "Something you should know. *Every* beekeeper has their own way of doing things. Whatever works for them and their bees."

Watching Tansy was torture. She was cute and animated when she was talking bees, and the way she stretched and twisted to dress, well. Her Bee Kind T-shirt hadn't seemed all that snug, but watching her wiggle into her suit had an instant effect on him. Breathless, heart thumping, head spinning. He had to tear his gaze away so he wouldn't stare at the soft fabric clinging, just right, to the swell of Tansy's breasts.

Her gaze met his and she stopped talking. It was a second, no more, but that second was so charged the air between them seemed to vibrate.

Or it's the bees.

He blew out a slow breath. *Why am I standing here?* Like he didn't know how to put on a damn bee suit. He yanked on his jacket and jerked up the zipper, leaving back the hood. If he didn't get himself together, even the Junior Beekeepers would pick up on his feelings for Tansy.

That brought him up short. *Feelings.* For Tansy. He took a deep breath.

"If you brought a suit, put it on." Tansy was talking, oblivious. "If not, Mr. Knudson and I will let you borrow from the extras in the van. And tape—to help keep things sealed up."

Thankfully, that ordeal took a while—long enough that he couldn't worry over the revelation that was twisting his gut. There was time to figure that out later, when he wasn't chaperoning a bunch of kids around a hive of bees.

"I know some of you are getting ready for your level-one beekeepers apprentice test. Who wants to get the smokers ready?" Tansy let Kerrielynn pick a student for the task.

"That's how they realized there was a problem." Tansy pointed at the water trough next to the shelter. "Lots of dead bees floating in the water. Anyone know why?"

Oren Diaz nodded and said, "Bees can't swim."

"That's right." Tansy nodded. "If you want to keep bees, not only do you need to make sure they have access to a water source, you have to keep them from drowning. Anyone have ideas to help this?"

"Corks," one kid yelled out. Another said, "Chicken wire." Lastly, "A stick."

Dane listened to their answers, impressed. Her question-and-answer session had the kids fully engaged by the time they reached the feed shed. "While Mr. Knudson and I see what we're dealing with, everyone stay put." The kids made a half circle several feet back while he and Tansy stepped in to scan the space.

Pretty or not, the space between the functional roof and the aesthetic arch they'd added for the mini-barn look was an ideal place for bees to settle in. Dane's eyes caught on a quarter-size hole along the seam of the wall and roof. "There?"

"That's it." Tansy nodded. "Good eye."

"A compliment? I knew it was going to be an interesting day." Her soft laugh triggered a surge of warmth in his stomach. A few aggressive puffs of smoke later and he was cutting into the ceiling planking. He climbed up the heavy-duty three-step stool and peered inside the hole to better assess the situation. "I know bees are master architects but I still marvel at what they're capable of."

"Careful, Dane. You almost sound like you *care* about the bees." Tansy stood beside the ladder, smiling up at him.

"Wouldn't that be something?" He carefully cut the honeycomb into large pieces, gave it a once-over, and handed it to Tansy. Tansy took the comb, used rubber bands to secure it in an empty frame and slid the frame into the nuc box that would keep them safe to transport the bees to their new home. She'd pause now and then, waving the kids closer to point things out or ask them if they saw anything special on a certain frame.

"No queen?" Dane handed down another piece of comb.

"Not yet." Tansy peered up into the hole. "I'll find it."

"You'll find it?" Dane chuckled. "Not if I find her first."

"Oh please." Tansy sighed, her features blurred by the veils they both wore but Dane would have bet money she'd rolled her eyes at him. "We'll see."

"Is that a challenge, Ms. Hill?"

"Well, it is sort of unfair since you're up there and I'm down here, but sure." Tansy's gloved hands were on her hips.

"You're the only person I know who can look sassy in a bee suit." He shook his head.

Tansy giggled. "I'll take that as a compliment."

He was glad she couldn't see how big he was smiling.

The kids were far too excited over the queen competition. Luckily, the bees didn't seem all that upset over the occasional squeal or laugh when either he or Tansy thought they'd found her.

"Found her! Found the queen." Tansy banded the loose honeycomb into the empty frame and knelt. "Guess I was wrong about your eyes." She sounded so gleeful, he had to smile.

Tansy carefully scooped up the queen into a queen clip. The clip's slats were wide enough for smaller worker bees to get in and tend to the queen, but too narrow for the queen to escape. Tansy held the clip up and, one by one, the kids came up to see her. "Now the bees will follow. She's sort of like the pied piper— where she goes all the other bees follow." She placed the clip inside the nuc box. "Once they're all settled in their new home, we will let the queen out."

It took a couple of hours to get the comb out of the roof space, banded into frames, stored into the nuc boxes and answer all the kids' questions but Dane considered it a successful extraction.

Leif had told him he was getting a ride home with Kerrielynn so Dane started packing his tools into the back of his truck when Tansy walked by. Her hood was back and her cheeks were flushed from the weight of her bee suit. She looked content. Instead of being smart and letting her walk by, he said, "I have a question."

Tansy stopped, spun on her heel and cocked her head to one side. "Oh?"

"You told Benji the hive is going to Honey Hill Farms. Why not my apiary?" He didn't want the damn bees, he was teasing. But Tansy was closing in on him, her expression all over the place, and she looked so beautiful he could barely breathe.

"I'd prefer they went to a good home. One where

the beekeepers value the *bees*, as more than a revenue stream." Now that there were no veils in the way, he got the full-force throat punch her fiery green eyes delivered. "By the way, how is your expansion going, Dane?" There it was. Nobody did sass like Tansy.

"Today was good. We work well together." It was a dodge, he didn't want to fight with her. *Two revelations in one day.* "You're a good beekeeper."

"Oh…" She blew out a slow breath. "Thank you?"

"You're welcome." She had every right to question his sincerity but… He wanted things to change. He'd enjoyed today, working with her—being with her. That's what he wanted. He wanted her. "You're beautiful, Tansy Hill." Well… *Shit.* He sure as hell hadn't planned to say that.

Tansy's mouth fell open and her eyes went as round as saucers.

Yeah, surprise. He shook his head. *For me, too.* "Don't read anything into that." He forced a chuckle. "We'll come back, right? Around dusk, for the hive?" She seemed closer now—so close he could run his fingers along her jaw. He wanted to. More than anything, he wanted to touch her. This was all too much, too fast.

She nodded, her features a mix of confusion and wariness.

Not exactly the reaction he was hoping for. "I'll get going." He moved quickly, climbing into his truck, to grip the steering wheel with both hands. This wasn't a big deal. He'd surprised her, sure, but he hadn't said anything that wasn't true. She was a good beekeeper. She was beautiful. Those were facts. It wasn't like he'd said something he'd regret.

He hadn't said he loved her.

Where the hell had that come from? He shook his head. *No. No.* He'd never say that. He didn't know if he *could* ever love her. But deep inside, he suspected loving her had somehow, someway, become another fact of life. Dane Knudson loved Tansy Hill. Once again, his poor fool heart was hers to break.

LEIF TOOK A SIP from his water bottle, thankful for the shade Kerrielynn's van provided. He was hot and tired but happy. Today had been freaking awesome. Kerrielynn was…awesome. They were going to the dance tonight. She'd asked him. He grinned, watching as she dug through the ice chest for something. He wasn't sure why she'd asked him but he was glad she had.

So far, today had been good. Really good. And not just because of Kerrielynn, either—though that was most of it.

Dane had been upbeat—and kind of obnoxious— all morning. His brother was being funny and having a good time, and they were doing something together without Dane hovering or telling him what to do. He'd even let Leif ride with Kerrielynn alone, even though there was room for him. Leif got it. Dane was trying.

But his phone started ringing and Leif knew it had to be his father. He was the only person that called anyone. Normal people texted. He stood, bracing himself, as he carried his phone around the end of the van. "Hello?"

"Where are you?" That was something else about his dad—he didn't believe in hellos or goodbyes.

"Junior Beekeepers thing." He sat on the van fender, staring around the field.

Dane was talking to Tansy. More like, they were

staring at each other. Kerrielynn was right, they did that a lot.

"And who said you could go to this Junior Beekeepers thing?" his father snapped.

Great. His dad was pissed. Not that it was unusual—he was always pissed about something. Leif knew his answer wasn't going to help. "Dane." He sighed. "I joined the group. It'll look good on college applications."

His father's snort rubbed Leif all the wrong way. "How about you pass this year before we start thinking about college."

Leif rubbed a hand over his face. "Sure." At least Dane saw how hard Leif was working. Did his dad know about his grades or that he'd been working with Birmingham? Did he care?

"Dane talk to you yet?" This time, he sounded concerned.

Which put a knot in Leif's stomach. "About what?"

His father sighed. "School." He cleared his throat. "Summer school."

What the hell? "I'm passing everything. I don't have to take summer school." He propped his elbow on his knee and stared down at the brittle brown grass at his feet. By now, it shouldn't hurt that his father didn't give a rat's ass about him. It shouldn't, but it did.

"Well, now…" He sighed again. "We'll talk about it tonight."

"I have plans for tonight." And there was no way he was breaking his date with Kerrielynn.

"Have you forgotten you're grounded? I don't know where Dane gets off thinking he can bend the rules like this, but I don't like it."

No shit. If Dane did something, no matter what, his father didn't like it. But their dad expected Dane to break the summer school news to him? So Dane could be the bad guy? *Whatever.* His dad was an asshole. Period. But it did irritate him that Dane was keeping a secret like this from him. And Leif was sick and tired of being caught between them. Leif ground his teeth together so hard, his jaw hurt. "My battery is almost out."

"Now you're going to lie to me? You don't want to hear what I have to say? Tough. I pay for that damn phone, remember." He was all fired up now. "You get yourself home."

Leif shook his head. He wasn't going home. He wasn't going to get sucked into whatever bull-crap problems his dad was caught up in. He saw how hard Dane worked to cover for their dad. Dane was the one keeping Texas Viking Honey on track. The office light was on when Leif went down for his 2 a.m. snack, every night. Dane was the one filling in when someone called in sick, or taking Birmingham's suggestions to fix up the apiaries, or putting together plans to make Texas Viking Honey into something bigger and better. Dane was doing everything—including taking care of Leif. Leif didn't give his brother enough credit. It'd be hard to handle all that. And Leif knew he wasn't making things any easier.

"You hear me?" His father's voice was so loud Leif held his phone away from his ear.

"Yeah." Leif ground out the word.

"Good." And the phone disconnected.

"Hey." Kerrielynn was leaning against the rear of the van. "Hungry?" She held out an apple. "I think we're about ready to go."

He stood, tucked his phone into his pocket and took the apple. "Thanks."

"Did you see that?" Kerrielynn nodded at Dane's truck driving away.

Looks like I lost my way home. Leif couldn't help but smile then. "See what?"

"Um, for a minute there, I totally thought your brother and Tansy were going to kiss." She sighed. "Wouldn't that be so romantic?"

Tansy was staring after Dane's truck, her hands fisted at her sides. He didn't know if that was a good thing or a bad thing. But it was something. Dane needed something good in his life, something that was just his—that made him happy. Watching the two of them today, he couldn't help but think Tansy might be that something.

"Leif?" Kerrielynn nudged him, standing close by his side. "You don't want them to get together?"

"No, I do." Leif glanced at her, feeling more awkward than ever. When she got this close, he worried she'd hear how hard his heart was beating.

She rested her head on his shoulder. "Everyone deserves a little happiness, don't you think?"

It was hard to breathe, but he managed. "Definitely." He took a risk and reached for her hand. Her fingers threaded with his. *Yes.* He didn't even care if she did hear his crazy-fast heartbeat. *Everyone deserves this sort of happiness.*

CHAPTER ELEVEN

TANSY WASN'T OKAY. She was... Confused, certainly. Suspicious, too. But, mostly, she was hopeful. And happy.

You're beautiful, Tansy Hill. Those words had ensnared her. Add in the heat in his blue-blue eyes, the husky rasp of his voice, and she'd been speechless. She'd waited for some whip-smart sarcastic comment to break the hold he had on her. He was teasing. He had to be.

Or not.

When he'd stepped closer, Tansy's whole body had tightened with anticipation. She'd stared up into his eyes as he leaned into her—so caught off guard she'd almost reached out to steady herself on his truck.

Like Dane had been doing. His white-knuckled grip on the side of his truck bed had sent a thrill along her spine. She'd been aching for him ever since.

Even now, driving a van full of teenagers back home. *Get it together, Tansy.*

Her gaze darted around the road. She couldn't see his truck. She needed to stop fixating on the way his jaw had clenched tight and how his gaze had fixed on her lips. If she did that, she'd think about the barn and how exhilarated she'd felt wrapped up in his arms. He was so strong, so warm. Tansy swallowed, her heart pounding in her ears. She wanted to be back there, his hands on her, his lips clinging to hers…

"You okay, Miss Hill?" Benji, sitting in the front passenger seat, asked.

"I'm great." She forced a smile. "Just thinking about this morning. Things to do, that sort of thing." Like Dane. *Wait. No.* Not do Dane. *Kissing* Dane. Her cheeks were burning.

"Like what?" Benji asked, digging through one of the bags of trail mix Aunt Camellia had made for a snack.

Nothing suitable for your young ears. She shrugged as she said, "Where to begin?"

"I can make a list." Benji tossed a candy-covered chocolate piece into his mouth. "I make lists for my mom all the time."

"Really?" The first item on her list was no more thoughts of kisses, Dane *or* kissing Dane. *Time to check off item one on my list and change the subject.* "Your mom mentioned you might be interested in helping out at Honey Hill Farms?"

"Hey, wait." Felix leaned forward, grabbing the bag of trail mix from Benji. "I am, too. Kerrielynn said you guys are cool to work for and that she learns something new all the time."

"That's nice to hear." Tansy would have to look at the numbers but the likelihood of being able to pay both of them was pretty slim.

Still, now Felix and Benji were talking bees and Tansy was happily distracted the rest of the drive. She could talk bees all day. But when she got home and they were unloading supplies, she realized she was searching for Dane. He wasn't here.

It's a good thing. Which would have been a lot easier to believe if she wasn't so disappointed.

"Can we come back tomorrow and help get the bees moved into an apiary?" Kerrielynn asked. She turned, including the other high school students.

"Unless that would be weird." Leif shot Tansy an apologetic smile. "I mean." He lowered his voice. "You and my brother…" He shrugged, as if that was explanation enough.

For Tansy, it was more than enough.

"You and Mr. Knudson, what?" Felix asked. "You two are dating?" His eyes went round.

Tansy winced. This was not something she wanted to talk about with them. With anyone.

"Ha!" His sister, Crissy, smiled. "I told you." She smacked Felix on the shoulder. "They were all teasing and flirting and stuff."

Wait, we were? Tansy opened her mouth, ready to protest.

"Yeah, yeah, whatever." Felix shrugged. "More like, you heard Mom talking to Mrs. Popplewell about them last night." He batted his eyes. "How Dane was asking for help to woo someone." He snorted. "Who uses the word *woo*? Besides, she never said he was talking about Tansy."

"Or maybe Leif was talking about how Texas Viking Honey and Honey Hill Farms *are* rival bee farms. Not them *dating*," Benji pointed out. "Maybe Mr. Knudson doesn't want Leif hanging out here." He rubbed his hands together and grinned. "*Unless* Leif is a spy for his family's business. Is that why you're joining the club now?"

Tansy had a pretty good idea why Leif was here—and the boy's quick glance at Kerrielynn said it all.

"Leif, you're welcome here," Tansy cut in. "The bees and I need all the help we can get. The more the merrier." Except for this very moment. As delightful as the morning had been, she was ready for them all to go. Especially with this new Dane-wooing-someone news. "And Mr. Knudson and I—"

Kerrielynn's phone started vibrating. "Oops, it's my mom." She took the call and Felix called everyone into action before Tansy ever had a chance to clarify how things were between her and Dane. *It's probably a good thing because I have no idea how things are between us.*

Kerrielynn hung up. "Mom has tables reserved for us at Delaney's."

Meaning, more people. Tansy hadn't realized how exhausting all the people-ing was until today.

"She and a lot of the other parents want to take you to lunch—to thank you for today," Kerrielynn went on. "You have to go."

"Sure. Of course." *Peachy keen.* She forced a smile. "I've worked up an appetite." That much was true. "I'll need to freshen up a bit." If she'd been heading out to the fields, she'd have cleaned up after. Going into town for lunch was another matter.

"Mom's calling Mr. Knudson, too. In case he wants to come—since he's helping out too."

Even better. But she managed to keep on smiling, glancing down at her sweat-stained clothes.

"We can handle things out here, if you want to change?" Kerrielynn offered. The kids were as focused as worker bees—cleaning and putting things away without arguing.

"I'll be quick." Tansy dashed inside.

"Tansy's home. Tansy's home," Lord Byron called out from his perch in the front foyer.

"Yes. I am. Are you supposed to be out here?" Tansy didn't want a repeat performance of Lord Byron's latest heist. "I hope you're being a good boy."

"Good boy." The parrot made a cooing sound. "Good boy."

"We'll see." Tansy gave him a gentle rub. "Please, please be a good boy for Tansy. I'll give you extra crackers when I get home."

She twisted her hair up in a sloppy bun, washed her face, put on a clean T-shirt and jeans and some of her favorite dangly bee-and-flower earrings. *Better.* She'd enjoy Delaney's amazing chicken fried steak salad, come back and find a good place for the new bees, and still get back to the Granger place before sunset.

Saturday lunch hour saw the place packed to the gills with families fresh from sporting events or family outings. Somehow, Kerrielynn's mom, Olivia, had managed to secure enough space for the Junior Beekeepers and some family members. No Dane. She wasn't sure how to feel about that.

"We're so happy the kids have you. Kerrielynn says you know more about bees than anyone." Olivia Baldwin leaned forward to whisper, "I thought I'd mention that Lorna and I are friends. She's told me she might not be up to coming back and running the club."

Tansy frowned, her gaze scanning the faces of the kids who had such enthusiasm for bees. "Really?" This was bad news. Bees needed beekeepers. Whether these kids kept a backyard hive, a small apiary, or aimed big and went commercial—they were the beekeepers of tomorrow.

"But then, she just had her baby so who knows." Olivia smiled. "The first few weeks can be exhausting. Likely, she's not thinking all that straight."

"Let's hope so." Tansy immediately texted Astrid the news about Lorna and the baby.

"I wanted you to know that the parents would love it, if she doesn't come back, for you or you and Dane to take over." Olivia pointed at the table. "Something to think about. Now you go on and eat. I'm sure working out in that hot sun took a lot of energy. We saved you a spot with the parents, over there."

Tansy ate every bite of salad and enjoyed learning more about the kids she was so fond of. And got to know their parents—who were all very interested in Tansy's idea to develop a youth beekeeping apprenticeship program. Poppa Tom had always said, *The best way to make a beekeeper was to work under an experienced one.* Tansy agreed. While she loved the idea, it was up to Lorna, as the Junior Beekeepers Club's sponsor, to approve such a program. If Lorna stayed with the club, that is.

By the time Tansy said her goodbyes, she headed home to restock supplies and prep for her return to the Granger place. After she fixed the landing board Astrid had mentioned on one of the Alice's Wonderland hives, the sun was low in the sky. Time to head out. If everything went according to plan, she'd have plenty of time to load up the nuc box, take it home and place it next to the hive box she'd move them into tomorrow.

After a quick inspection of the nuc box, Tansy took her gloves but left her suit. There were a handful of bees circling the nuc's entrance but the rest were inside. She hefted the box into the custom transport rack she'd made for the back of the van, closed everything back up and headed home. After such a bizarre morning, she appreciated how seamlessly the pickup went.

Until she was driving around the bend to her own house and spied Dane Knudson leaning against his truck. He waved as she parked.

She stared at him, fighting back a smile. *Calm down.* "Him being here doesn't mean a thing." *Act normal.* She climbed out of the van. "This is a surprise." She sounded way too happy.

His brows lifted. "Oh?"

She headed around to the rear of the van, needing to occupy herself until there was no fear of her turning into some giggling idiot. Space, between her and those baby blues, was necessary. "You missed lunch." She pulled open the rear van doors. "I took that to mean you were done for the day."

"It meant something came up. We said we'd do this together so here I am." He shrugged, watching as she set up her collapsible wagon. "Besides, I realized I hadn't popped up on you in a while and figured—"

"A bee transport was the ideal time to do it?" Tansy straightened, wiping her hands on her jeans. *And now I'm smiling at him.*

"Why not?" He shrugged, glancing her way as the corner of his mouth kicked up. "Trying to keep you on your toes."

That crooked grin was bone melting. "Mission accomplished. I guess." There was no guessing about it. Dane Knudson was definitely keeping her on her toes.

She reached inside for the nuc. "Like I said, I didn't think you were coming."

"You already went?" Dane chuckled, looking more good-looking than any single person had the right to be. "That worried I was going to beat you to it and take them home with me?"

"No." *Stop looking at him.* She did, carefully placing the nuc in her wagon. "I thought I'd made myself pretty clear this morning."

"Did you? I don't remember much about this morning." Dane scratched his jaw. "I was preoccupied."

"Oh? Well, it was pretty uneventful." *I wish.* She blinked, her throat tightening. "Is Leif going to the dance?" She placed the empty wooden hive box in the wagon, too.

"I didn't know there was a dance till you mentioned it."

Poor Leif. "I know it's none of my business but I hope he is. I think he's really making friends here and, if they're all going, it would be good for him to go too." She held up her hands. "Now I'll go back to minding my own business."

"You?" He crossed his arms over his chest. "You're always in my business."

She glanced at him, ready to argue—

"But he's there—or he will be soon. At the dance. With his new friends." Dane studied her for a minute, then pointed at the nuc. "Need help with that?"

"No." She strapped the nuc into the wagon, added a battery powered lantern and grabbed her gloves.

He paused, surveying the rack inside. "That's custom."

"I made it." She patted the rack. "Keeps them from sliding around."

He crouched. "You could sell these, you know." He ran his hand along the wood, tilting it this way and that, to get a view from all angles.

"I guess." She shouldn't be so pleased with the interest he was taking, but she was.

"No, really." He stood, resting his hand along the top. "You could make them custom, to fit different vehicles."

"If I had the time and supplies, maybe." She shooed him back and closed the van doors. "Or the manpower. But the bees come first."

"I think you've mentioned that a time or two before." He took the handle of the wagon, grinning down at her.

That grin sent her pulse into overdrive. "Really, I don't need your help. Go…take care of whatever it was that had you so distracted." She reached for the handle of the wagon.

"I am." He stepped closer, his gaze sweeping over her face before locking with hers. "That's why I'm here."

The sheer intensity in his blue eyes knocked the air from her lungs. *Breathe.* It took effort. "Because I… I distract you?" Was that a good thing or a bad thing?

"You do." He stepped closer. "There's something I want from you."

"And that would be?" She blinked, beyond rattled now. "I swear, Dane Knudson, if you say you want to take this nuc I'll—"

"You'll what?" He grinned, stepping so close—too close.

"Something…unpleasant." She swallowed.

"Sounds ominous." His eyes swept over her face.

"You can keep it. I had something else in mind." His hand rested against her cheek.

His touch was so warm. "Like what?" Tansy whispered.

"What I've been thinking about doing all day." He swallowed. "I'm hoping, since there's no one around, we could try this again."

She was leaning into him then, aching. "You came here—"

"To kiss you?" His other hand came up to cradle her face. "Yeah, I did." He ran his thumb along her jaw. "If that's okay with you?"

She knew she should argue or laugh or think about all the reasons this was a very *very* bad idea... But that's not what she wanted. This was. All she managed was one word. "Yes."

DANE'S HEART HAD been pounding since he'd gotten out of his truck, now it felt like a wrecking ball trying to bash its way out of his chest. As soon as he'd heard the *y* sound, he pulled Tansy close. He'd tried to convince himself that he'd imagined how good their kiss in the barn had been. But the moment his mouth touched hers he knew that wasn't the case.

The cling of her lips sent a wave of raw hunger over him. He'd been aching for her, for this, and it was everything and more than he'd expected. With a sigh, she pressed herself against him, her arms twining around his neck and her fingers sliding into his hair. Soft. Firm. Her touch making him burn all the more. For her. One kiss ran into another. Where the urgency came from, he didn't know. He wanted this. More of this. More of her. When her mouth parted and his tongue trailed her lower lip, she swayed into him with a startled—delighted—moan.

Dane was rocked to the core. Tansy was in his arms. That little moan was for him. She was kissing him with the same hunger he felt burning through him. From her sweet sunshine-and-flower scent tickling his nose to the silk of her cheek beneath his hand, he was all too happy to lose himself in her.

The slam of a distant screen door startled them both.

Tansy jumped back. Her hands flew up to cover her mouth.

He'd spent years pestering Tansy, so he'd become pretty adept at reading her. He'd never, ever seen her like this. Which made him wonder: Was this good or bad?

Did he need to brace himself for what was to come? He wasn't expecting her to take a running leap into his arms—not that he was averse to the idea. But he'd be lying if he said he wasn't worried she'd start pushing him away.

But, dammit all, she was just as shaken up over it as he was. He'd felt her shiver in his arms and heard the hitch in her breath. *And that moan.* That moan had set him on fire.

He didn't know what would happen now but he wanted to find out—just the two of them. And since the van blocked them from view of the house, that was a possibility.

Tansy's hands lifted to reveal one hell of a smile. "Aunt Camellia," she whispered. "Refilling the hummingbird feeders. Every night."

That smile made it okay for him to breathe. It also

250 THE SWEETEST THING

made it hard not to pull her back into his arms to pick up where they left off. "Oh."

She drew in a wavering breath and reached for the wagon's handle. He didn't miss that her hand was shaking.

Dane was feeling more optimistic by the minute.

"You can help me get them settled." She glanced up at the sky. "Before it gets too dark."

"Good idea. Everyone knows bees *are* afraid of the dark." If she wasn't chasing him off, he wasn't going anywhere.

Her laugh was soft. "Exactly. Just like no-glaring Saturday."

"Have you found something that says it doesn't exist?" He raised his brows in question. "I bet you haven't."

"I haven't had time to look." She started pulling the wagon along the fence line and away from the house. "But, you're right, I imagine it would be hard to find something that says no-glare Saturday doesn't exist… Since it *doesn't* exist."

"Suit yourself." Dane scratched his jaw.

"I will, thank you." Tansy glanced up at him, her eye roll and smile visible in the fading light.

Twilight might just be his favorite time of day. As long as Tansy was staring up at him with those big eyes of hers, he was content to stand here taking in the view.

"The bees." She tugged the wagon along, a little faster than before.

Dane followed her past the main house, down a gently rolling hill and around a cluster of mesquite trees. Even though neither of them said a word, Dane felt the pull between them. That thread was back, twining around his heart and lungs.

Tansy glanced back, her smile shy. "I figured they'd like being by the mesquite trees? Since there were some at the Grangers' place."

"That's very thoughtful of you." Dane appreciated the neatly kept apiary. Five long rows, each containing between six and eight hive boxes, all painted with mesquite tree blossoms in varying shades. "You'll have to break out the paintbrush so they don't feel like outsiders." Dane nodded at the plain white hive box in the wagon. "Who knows, maybe the other hives won't mind. They might even throw the new bees a welcome party. You know, flowers, foodstuffs, that sort of thing."

Tansy laughed again. "Foodstuffs?" She stopped at the end of a row with fewer hive boxes. "I have to tell you, your bee *knowledge* is very different than mine."

He chuckled. "Viking stuff."

"Right." She brushed off the hive stand as she spoke. "Well, that explains it."

He lifted the empty wood hive box and put it on the stand, several feet away from the established hives. "Here?"

"Perfect. Thank you." She nodded, unstrapping the nuc box and placing it next to the hive. "We'll get you all switched over and settled in the morning." She patted the nuc box, as if all the bees inside were listening then froze. "Go ahead. Fire away." Hands on hips, she faced him.

"What?" he asked, knowing good and well what she was waiting for. But he didn't want to tease her about this. Reassuring the bees that everything was okay had been instinctual—something she'd likely done a million times without thought. It had been real and honest and the sweetest thing.

"I was talking to the bees." She pointed at the box. "I'm sure you have plenty to say about that."

"I was going to add that they might want to watch out for their neighbors." He nodded at the adjacent hive. "Something tells me *this* hive is *trouble*." Tansy's laugh made his heart happy.

Her green eyes locked with his and her smile slowly faded away. "What's happening here?"

"We're getting the bees settled."

"Dane…" She sighed. "This. Me and You." She pointed between them.

His fingertips ran along the side of her face. "I never imagined this."

"No." She shook her head, her breath husky as she said, "Me neither." A crease settled between her brows and she stepped back. "You don't think this is weird?"

"Weird?" He ran a hand along the back of his neck. "Might be a bit of an understatement."

"Exactly." She stood there, staring at him—her features shifting like waves on the ocean. It was a struggle for her to get out what she said next. "I keep expecting a boom box and a Peter Gabriel CD to appear. Are you waiting for—"

"You to laugh at me and walk off?" There was a slight snap to his words. "Yeah, I am."

Tansy went rigid, her eyes narrowing. "What did you expect me to do?" Her voice was shaking again— but this time it was all anger. "You tried to humiliate *me*."

That brought him up short. "How?" He stepped forward. "By going full John Cusack to ask you to prom? In case you didn't notice I made an ass of myself in front of a whole hell of a lot of people at that pep rally—"

"People who'd all have front row seats for your prank." She stepped forward, holding up her hand. "You know what—this is stupid."

"What prank?" She wasn't making any sense. He was the one who'd had his pride hurt and his heart broken, not her.

"Dane, don't." She looked—and sounded—disappointed. "Leave it alone. Let's drop it."

"No." She had no right to look at him like that. "You think I wronged you somehow. I have a right to know what I did. Supposedly."

"Supposedly?" Her right eye twitched. "You know."

Like hell I do. "Humor me." He took a deep breath and added, "Please."

She stared at the new hive box for a long time, her lips pressed tight and her jaw clenched. "I was tipped off. You'd planned a big surprise to humiliate me. The when and where were unknown but they didn't want me to get hurt. They said it would be a big production." Tansy's tone was clipped and aloof. "And then you asked me to prom and I had visions of *Carrie* and pig's blood and things went downhill from there."

"I'd have used honey. No pigs." It was a poor attempt at a joke, and Tansy wasn't amused. "Who told you this?" It was hard to keep the edge out of his voice.

"Frances Yanez and some of her friends." The look on her face gutted him.

"That group included Kate Owens. My father's most recent ex? That Kate? The woman that started a rumor that she and I were sleeping together while they were married? That Leif's on drugs? And Dad's an alcoholic?" He took a deep breath. "That Kate?"

She frowned. "That's Kate now, not Kate ten years ago."

"She wasn't as obvious, maybe." Kate had always been bad news. That's why he avoided her—then and now.

Tansy stared at him. "Frances said it—"

"Frances didn't want to get on Kate's bad side—hell, she's still scared of Kate." All this time, this is what Tansy thought? "Why did you believe them?"

"I-it made sense." She sniffed, wrapping her arms around her waist. "Why else would you ask me to prom? In the middle of a pep rally? In front of everyone?"

"I thought things were changing between us." *Might as well get it all out there.* "*Say Anything* was your favorite movie. I knew it was special to you. I saw the look on your face when we watched it instead of working on our economics presentation. Both times." He cleared his throat. "I wanted you to look at me that way."

She didn't blink or move—was she breathing?

"I didn't do any of that because I wanted to hurt you or uphold some stupid family grudge, Tansy." He broke off, swallowing hard. "I did it because I wanted you. To impress you. Go to prom with you."

She stayed quiet for so long, he began to worry. "You did?" It was the softest whisper.

"I did." He nodded. "Now that we've got that straight…" He wasn't sure how to feel. On the one hand, she hadn't flat-out rejected him. On the other hand, she'd believed him capable of something pretty damn heartless. "It's getting pretty dark."

"Okay," she mumbled, heading back the way they'd come.

Five minutes ago, his heart was Tansy's. Now he was feeling too bruised and vulnerable to know what to do. Where did this leave them?

The house came into view and they slowed. She stole a glance his way but didn't say anything. Dane was no better. After he collapsed the wagon and slid it into the back of the van, he turned toward her. The streetlamp she'd parked by cast just enough light to make out the features of her face. *Dammit*. Her lower lip wobbled and she wiped at her cheek. She was crying and, dammit all, he couldn't bear it. "Hey. It's okay."

"No, it's not." Tansy stared up at him, she swiped at another tear. "It's horrible. All this time—" She broke off. "I'm sorry." She gripped his forearm.

"Me, too." His hand covered hers.

"No, I mean it." Tansy closed the gap between them and slid her arms around his waist. "You're a condescending know-it-all who gets far too much enjoyment getting under my skin but you're not evil."

"Thank you?" He pulled her closer against him.

Her laugh was muffled against his chest. "You were trying to do something wonderful."

"Yeah, I was." He was content to stand there holding her. "What happens now?"

She stared up at him. "I don't know."

"That makes two of us." He smoothed the hair from her forehead.

"But I'm willing to find out." She nibbled on her lower lip. "I mean, if you—"

He tipped her chin up and brushed his lips across hers.

"I'll take that as a yes," she murmured against his mouth.

He pressed a kiss at the corner of her mouth, along the swell of her lower lip, and then the other corner. "Yes."

She mumbled something as she twined her fingers in his hair and tugged his face down to her. Dane was all too happy to comply. He met her, kiss for kiss, his hands sliding down her sides then up her back to hold her close. The way she wriggled and sighed against him had him leaning against the van to keep them upright.

There was a deep bark. Then another one.

"Shh, Oatmeal," Tansy said between kisses. "Go to the house, Pudding."

Another bark, high-pitched and squeaky.

"Butters…" Tansy sighed and let him go. "What on earth are you doing out here? Auntie Mags will be missing you."

Dane assessed the motley crew of dogs. One massive Saint Bernard, two patchy red-and-white terriers, a scruffy-haired one-eyed Chihuahua and some midsize canine with thick brown fur and cockeyed ears. "Are all your animals named after food?"

Tansy shook her head, then stopped. "Actually, yes. Except for Beeswax the cat and Lord Byron."

"That parrot's still alive?" Dane hooked his thumbs into her belt loops. "He never liked me. Took a snap at my earlobe once. Left a scar, too." He let go of one belt loop and touched the scar.

"Really?" Tansy reached up, too, rubbing his earlobe. "He did that? Ouch." She cocked her head to one side. "Was this when your dad was dating Aunt Camellia?"

He nodded. "The good old days."

"Interesting." Her smile was all sass. And he loved it. "Animals are supposed to be a great judge of character."

"Dogs. The saying is about dogs." He could get used to her smiling at him that way. "I'm not sure that applies to mean old parrots."

"Maybe... You'd better cover your ears, then. Lord Byron is alive and well and will probably stay that way for years—as long as he steers clear of Aunt Mags. They have a love-hate relationship. Meaning they both love hating one another." She took his hand. "Want some lemonade or something?"

"In there?" He nodded at the house.

She made a production of patting her jeans pockets. "I don't have any on me so, yes, in the house."

"Sassy." And he liked it. "You think it's a good idea?"

Tansy seemed to mull over his words. "I'm game for living on the edge. You?"

"If you're trying to challenge me, it's working." Dane laughed, letting her take the lead.

She led him up the back garden path, peaking in windows as she went, before climbing up the porch steps. "They're all in the back parlor so we should be fine." She opened the front door. "Up the stairs, last door on the left." She pointed.

"Where are you going?" he whispered.

"Lemonade." She smiled. "Maybe a snack. Now, shh." She shooed him to the stairs.

Dane winced with every creak and squeak of the stairs and wooden planks of the hall. It was a relief to reach the safety of Tansy's room. He closed the door and stooped to tug off his boots. *Which I should have done before I ever stepped foot in the house.* He set them beside the door and straightened.

Her curtains were drawn back so the room was flooded with moonlight. He tiptoed across the floor to the low bookshelf beneath the windows. The top was covered with an odd assortment of things. A blackened smoker, an old queen bee cage, a pair of gloves, a decorative box and two framed photos.

"You could have turned on a light." Tansy flipped on her bedside lamp. "Here." She handed him the massive glass of lemonade. "I thought we'd share." She tossed a bag of cookies onto her bed and joined him in front of the bookcase. "Those are my parents." She picked up the frame, smiling at the photo. "I'm sure you can identify those awkward little girls."

"I think I can." Little Tansy, Astrid and Rosemary looked like a handful. "Good-looking couple."

"They were obnoxiously in love with each other." She glanced up at him. "I grew up thinking that was normal." She rolled her eyes. "Sad that it's not."

"It is sad," Dane agreed. They looked young and fit—too young to have died. "What happened to them?" He froze. "You don't have to talk about it—"

"Mom drowned when Rosemary was a baby. My sisters and I took swimming lessons for years—we are all like Olympic-level swimmers." She shrugged, hurrying on. "When Mom died, Dad became superdad. Involved and active—our biggest cheerleader." She set the photo down. "Dad had a car accident years later. When he passed, the aunts and Poppa Tom and Granna Hazel stepped in to take care of us."

He wasn't sure what to say so he took her hand.

"Anyway." She smiled up at him. "Enough of the

serious stuff." She took a deep breath. "I hope Honey Hill Farms winning the blue ribbon next weekend won't upset you too much. It's important. Winning, I mean. Really important. I don't know how Honey Hill Farms will make it, otherwise."

Things hadn't been easy the last few years. He'd never stopped to think about the Hills' situation. His hand tightened on hers. "I had no idea, Tansy." He couldn't imagine losing his home. It would crush him.

"No, it's not exactly common knowledge." She nibbled on her lower lip. "So, if you can keep that to yourself."

"My lips are sealed." Dane was in shock. She was trusting him.

"Not that I'm looking for pity, Mr. Knudson." Tansy rolled her eyes, all sass.

"May the best honey win." He grinned at her. "And so *you* know, I won't let who wins interfere with you and me, in case you were worried." He wasn't sure why he'd added that but it was too late to take it back.

"Which will be us." She patted his chest, her smile growing when he laughed. "So, what do you want to do now?"

He pulled her into a loose embrace. "I was thinking we should do more of the kissing and maybe watch a movie or something?"

"I'm on board for both." She stood on tiptoe to kiss him. "Movie recommendations?" Her arms slid up his chest and around his neck.

He rubbed his nose against hers. "How about a little John Cusack, Diane Court, questionable stalking-like behavior and Peter Gabriel?"

She blinked up at him. "Are you serious?"

"About the stalking-like behavior? Or watching the movie?" He waited. "Either way, it's a yes."

"I always thought it was a grand romantic gesture." Tansy frowned, pushing against his chest. "But I haven't watched it in years."

"What do you think he was thinking, while he was holding that boom box over his head?" He paused, smoothing a long strand of auburn hair from her shoulder.

She stared at his chest, her hands running over the fabric as she spoke. "He was thinking how much he loved her and that he knew she loved him, too. She was scared of trusting him, but he was going to stand there to show her he would always be there for her. He loved her, with everything he had." Her gaze met his then.

He could get lost in those eyes. "All that? You've thought about this a lot." Dane had to admit there was something captivating in her certainty. Who wouldn't want someone to love them like that? "So he was waiting for Diane to scream out the window or something?"

"What? No." She laughed. "He was waiting for her to come down, throw her arms around him and kiss him. Then he'd know it would all be okay." She said it as if it was the most obvious thing in the world. "If I was Diane Court, you can bet that's what I would have done." Her eyes were glued to his mouth and her arms slid around his waist.

"I bet you would have." Dane was done talking about fictional characters. There were more pressing matters to attend to. "How about we start with some kissing?"

She nodded, her hands twisting in his shirt as she leaned into him.

He ran his nose along her temple, down the side of

her face, to nuzzle the spot beneath her ear. He breathed her in, letting her scent flood him. He felt her shudder, felt her hands slip beneath the hem of his shirt and pressed his lips to hers.

She tasted of lemonade. He couldn't get enough of the taste. Her mouth opened for him and things went from slow and sweet to white-hot and all-consuming.

He let go of her long enough for her to tug his shirt up and over his head. Once it was off, he caught her close. The slide of her hands on his stomach and the hitch in her breath had him twining his fingers in her hair.

"Dane," she whispered, tugging him back to the bed.

He braced himself over her, groaning aloud when she wriggled out of her shirt and pressed her lace-covered breasts to his chest. She felt so damn good.

Her hands trailed along his sides, up his shoulders, and down his arms—and all the while her lips explored his. Soft and hot. Greedy and giving. She wrapped herself around him and left him aching and breathless.

He gave in, tracing the contour of her neck and shoulder, side and waist. The feel of her lace-clad breast filling his hand made him groan, and she moaned, too, as he cupped her. She arched into him, reaching around to unhook her bra. He watched, her green eyes ablaze as she tossed it aside.

He stared down at her. Her want, for him, left him shaking. And damn did he want her, too. All of her. But when she hooked one leg around his hip, he buried his face against her neck. He had a choice to make. He wanted her, so bad it hurt but... It was too much, too fast.

He rolled off her, his hands gripping the quilt beneath him. *Dammit*. This was the right thing to do.

Tansy lay beside him, panting. "So…movie time?"

He closed his eyes and nodded. Looking at her would be a bad idea.

"Dane?"

"I'm trying to do the right thing here, Tansy." He ground out. "Maybe, put a shirt on."

She giggled and the bed shifted. "Done."

He opened his eyes. "That's mine." He propped himself up on his elbows. Tansy in his Texas Viking Honey shirt was almost as tempting as Tansy out of his Texas Viking Honey shirt.

"I'll give it back." Her gaze traveled over his chest and down. "Oh." Her eyes went round, locked on the very prominent evidence of his arousal pressing against his jeans. "Oh." She nibbled on her lower lip.

She wasn't going to make this easy for him. She never did. "Tansy." He flopped back onto the bed and threw an arm over his face.

"Right. Movie." She blew out a shaky breath.

Dane lay there until he heard the television come on. "It's safe." She was smiling. "What streaming service do you think the movie's on?"

Dane tossed the pillows on the floor and lay back, pulling her against his side.

Hours later, after the movie and lots and lots of kissing, Dane was dozing on the pile of pillows on Tansy's floor while she snored softly against his chest. The wooden floor was sprinkled in cookie crumbs and nowhere near comfortable but he was where he wanted to be. And that scared the hell out of him.

At two, he forced himself up. He scooped her up

and onto her bed, accepted the fact he was going home shirtless, and tucked a quilt over her. He leaned forward and pressed a kiss to her forehead. She smiled but didn't open her eyes.

There it was again. That thread—tugging at his heart. *Yeah, yeah.* He grabbed his boots, turned off her lamp and tiptoed down the stairs with his phone's flashlight on. The last thing he needed to do was trip over a dog or have a run-in with Lord Byron and wake the whole house. He pulled the front door open, slow and careful, then pulled it closed behind him. *Free and clear and no one was the wiser.*

It was when he was pulling away that one of the curtains in an upstairs window moved. He stopped, peering out into the dark. *More like my eyes are playing tricks on me.* It was after two in the morning, he was tired. The sooner he was home and sleeping in his own bed, the sooner he could dream of having Tansy back in his arms. He smiled all the way home.

CHAPTER TWELVE

"YOU'RE AWFUL CHIPPER this morning." Aunt Mags peered at her over her newspaper.

"Oh?" Tansy made herself a cup of tea. "I slept well." After all the cuddling and kissing and being tangled up in Dane, it made sense that her dreams were full of him. Waking up, on her bed wearing his shirt, had ended all that deliciousness and left her full of uncertainty.

It had been a wonderful night, there was no denying it. But would all the soft-spoken words and gentle touches continue now that the sun was out and there were other people in the mix? She didn't know what to expect from Dane, so it was probably best to keep what had happened between them a secret for now.

"I'm glad one of us is." Aunt Camellia was digging through boxes. "I don't think I'll sleep much until after this weekend is behind us." She sighed, wiped her hands on her apron and turned—her gaze searching. "And that's only if we win."

"There is no if, Aunt Camellia." Astrid sat, cocooned in cats, sipping tea.

Aunt Camellia made a noncommittal grumble.

"What's wrong?" Tansy paused, watching her aunt closely. She was upset. "What are you looking for, Aunt Camellia?"

"Nothing." Aunt Camellia straightened, her forehead

smoothing. Tansy didn't miss the way her gaze darted Aunt Mags's way. "Nothing at all."

Now Tansy was genuinely concerned. Aunt Camellia's cheeks were flaming and she couldn't make eye contact with any of them. She was hiding something. "Are you certain?"

"Absolutely." Aunt Camellia patted her curly hair. "I was... I was craving some of that prickly pear honey for my tea."

"Camellia Ann." Aunt Mags set her newspaper aside. "You are lying."

Leave it to Aunt Mags to call her out. Tansy had to sip her tea to hide her smile.

"I am not." Aunt Camellia turned away, washing the few dishes in the sink. "And don't you start throwing around middle names at me, Magnolia Grace. I'm your sister. You don't intimidate me. You shouldn't try to."

Aunt Mags stood, dropped her newspaper on the table and crossed the room. "I'm sorry." She wrapped her arms around Camellia. "I've no right to be snippy with you. My nerves..."

Aunt Camellia immediately forgot the dishes to hug her sister. "I know, Mags, I know. It's all right. Nothing to forgive." She hugged her sister tight. "We're all on edge, I suppose."

A knot formed in Tansy's throat. A big one. Aunt Mags wasn't one for hugs—let alone the long, clingy type.

Aunt Mags nodded but didn't let go of her sister. "You're too good to me."

"I know I am," Aunt Camellia said, giggling, as she patted Aunt Mag's back.

Aunt Mags started laughing, too, easing out of her sister's arms. "Let's find this honey."

They all pitched in to find the elusive jar of prickly pear honey but their search turned up empty so Aunt Camellia had to settle for wildflower honey instead.

"What's on the agenda today?" Astrid asked, washing teacups and placing them on the dish rack beside the oversize farm sink. "Settling in the new hive?"

Tansy nodded. "Eight full frames—it shouldn't take too long."

"Is your club coming back?" Aunt Camellia asked. "Should I make snacks?"

"I don't know who's coming." Tansy knew who she hoped was coming. "But they'll be in and out—no need for snacks. But thank you for offering, Aunt Camellia." She glanced at the clock on the wall. "I should probably head out and suit up. They're nice enough bees but I don't want to take chances with the kids." She shrugged. As soon as she opened the mudroom door, the dogs came barreling inside. She stepped back to avoid tripping, and waved.

"Have fun." Astrid waved back. "Careful, you almost look like you're enjoying yourself."

She closed the door right as her phone pinged.

Good morning. You'll never guess what I dreamed about last night. Can't wait to tell you. Finally getting to talk to my green architect about the expansion this morning so I won't be there today. I know you'll miss me.

Tansy stared at the text, all the warm fuzzies fizzling out. *The expansion*. She put her phone in her pocket, pulled her bee suit off the hook and opened the back door.

She took a deep breath. Bees could pick up on a person's mood—they were all about the pheromones. She took another deep breath. The sky overhead was a cloudless powder blue. The air was cool and crisp, fragrant with the many flowers blooming in the flower beds and window boxes all around the house. It was a beautiful day and she had work to do. Work she loved. She should focus on that.

Kerrielynn had already texted to say they were on the way, so she decided to get everything ready for them.

Still, Dane and the expansion kept gnawing at her insides. Rationally, there was no point in being mad at him—madder, that is. It's not like she didn't know about the expansion. She'd gone to him and voiced her protests and concerns. Had it made a difference then? *No.* Had she thought that had changed? The answer stuck in her throat.

Last night had been…lovely. She swallowed, shutting down the barrage of images and sensations that slammed into her to remind her of just how lovely it had been. All the little things. Like his big hands and the way he'd smiled against her lips… Her chest grew tight.

But, she hadn't been thinking clearly. She'd been under the influence of mega-charming Dane, his exceptional kissing skills and her all-time favorite eighties teen romance.

Dane had said the honey competition wouldn't impact what was happening with them. Tansy should do the same about the expansion. At least, she should talk to him about it. Not storm onto his property and confront him, but more of a sit-down-and-talk sort of thing. Not via text or over the phone, but in person.

She pulled out her phone and opened his texts. I hope your meeting goes well. Save the bees. She hit Send. She took a deep breath, typed out, We need to talk, and hit Send.

MONDAY, DANE TEXTED HER. He didn't respond to her initial request to talk. Instead, he'd typed, When do bees get married? Tansy didn't have a chance to respond before he replied. When they've found their honey.

Tansy replied with, Dork.

That night, her dreams were full of Dane—smiling at her, laughing with her. Holding her.

Tuesday, Dane was on a roll. He sent her a handful of bad bee jokes and a picture of Leif suited up and working with the bees. Tansy sent him a pic of the lavender fields at sunset. He sent her a Sweet Dreams text after dark—and all of Tansy's dreams were about Dane.

Wednesday—nothing. Tansy turned her phone off and on and checked the volume several times. She tried to tell herself that it had nothing to do with Dane's lack of texts but what was the point. It wasn't just that she missed his stupid bee jokes, it was the lingering concerns she had over the expansion. Finally, she texted, Dane, we really need to talk. She wound up tossing and turning most of the night, anxious and on edge and, dammit, missing Dane.

Thursday, he started texting in the wee hours of the morning and proceeded to text her every thirty minutes or so—all day long. Nothing serious, just a stream of bees being bees working.

Tansy rolled her eyes and texted, If you're too busy

to talk, why are you sending me texts? But she was smiling all the same.

"Who is that?" Astrid asked, clearing the dinner table.

"No one." Tansy rinsed and loaded the dishes into the dishwasher. She turned her notifications off and looked up to find Astrid staring at her phone.

She took a quick look around the kitchen before asking, "What is going on between you two?"

"Nothing." Tansy shook her head. "Nothing at all."

"Nothing?" Astrid wasn't buying it. "But he's been texting you all day."

She nodded.

"And the reason you've been on edge all week?" Astrid stepped closer to her.

"Have I?" Tansy frowned. "Worrying about the honey contest—"

"And Dane." Astrid shook her head. "Tansy, you know you can tell me. Something is going on. You've never snuck a boy into your room before."

"You knew?" She froze, then leaned forward to whisper, "Do the aunts know?"

"His truck was parked out front." Astrid wrinkled up her nose and shrugged. "They haven't said anything but…" She paused. "Did something happen between you two?"

It all came out then. The kiss in the barn. The weirdness between them. More kissing and clearing up the past. Even more kissing. And the wake-up call expansion text.

"Maybe he'll listen to you now? He knows it's important to you and, if things have changed between you, then maybe it will be more important to him." Astrid covered Tansy's hand with her own. "I think you're right to talk to him in person. Read his body language and facial expressions, that sort of thing."

"I guess so but… I'm scared." She clasped her sister's hand. "I want to trust him, Astrid. I want to, but there's a part of me that can't. It's like some self-defense mechanism. What if he still doesn't care? I can't be with someone that doesn't understand this plan is bad for the bees."

"But, if he did get it, you'd want to be with him?" Astrid was staring at her. "If you could trust him?"

"One hundred percent." She felt sick to her stomach. "What is wrong with me? Aunt Mags is right—I know better." She ran a hand over her face. "And right now is the absolute worst time to deal with this. Tomorrow is the first day of the Honey Festival." She squeezed Astrid's hand. "That's all that should matter right now."

Astrid squeezed her hand back. "I have faith in you, Aunt Camellia, the honey and our bees."

Astrid seemed so confident, Tansy couldn't help but feel better. About the Honey Festival. About Dane? Not so much.

That night, Tansy was more restless than ever, picturing everything that could go wrong with the honey judging. She felt miserable when she stumbled downstairs for her coffee the next morning. Aunt Camellia was in a panic—though she insisted she was fine—and Aunt Mags had taken the dogs for a walk. So she and Astrid made sure they had everything they needed and drove the Honey Hill Farms van into town.

"Good morning. Happy Friday—and the first day of the Honey Festival." Astrid was all enthusiasm, scanning her phone. "Nicole said she's heading to the fairgrounds now to help me get set up. I guess Benji is one of the helpers in the Bee Education Station?"

"Oh good." She'd seen how great Benji was with the younger Junior Beekeepers—he'd be a huge help today. "What do you think of starting a young beekeeper apprenticeship? Felix and Benji and Kerrielynn, of course. They want experience and these hours would count toward their certification tests."

"I say yes. I mean, we could use the help and they could use the hours. Seems like a win-win, to me." Astrid smiled. "See, this whole Junior Beekeepers thing wasn't such a mess, after all."

Except for the whole Dane part. But Tansy didn't argue with Astrid. At least Dane wouldn't be helping out today. The two of them were at different stations—Tansy's focus needed to be on the bees and honey. Their talk would wait. For now.

Her luck held out until one. Dane showed up—in what looked like his tightest shirt ever—to stand and watch her with Leif and the teachers along the edge of the tent. Even though she was determined to pretend he didn't exist, he seemed to take up a whole lot of her field of vision. Big and muscle-y, with his man-bun and his crooked smile and… *Oh, stop it.* She stared, blindly, at the graph projected on the screen behind her.

"As you can see, even if we don't harvest the honey the bees are still working for us." She pointed at the colorful slide on the screen. "Bees are the ones flying around pollinating things we need to keep healthy. Things like apples, cranberries and melons. Even *broccoli*." She wrinkled her nose. "Anyone here like broccoli?" A few hands shot up. "That's good. It's good for you. My aunts would be proud of you." Before she'd outgrown her aversion to the stuff, she'd stayed late at the dinner table until she'd eaten her greens. That's what Poppa Tom had called them. She'd called them "gross alien trees." The memory made her smile. "All of those foods rely on the bees. Cherries and blueberries are 90 percent pollinized by bees." She paused, using her laser pointer to circle food items. "Can any of you guess the one thing we eat that relies entirely on bees?"

Dane raised his hand but Tansy ignored him.

"Anyone?" she asked, looking everywhere but him.

Dane crouched next to a little girl and whispered in her ear. Seconds later, the little girl's hand flew up.

Tansy scanned the crowd again but no one else was raising their hand. "Yes?" Tansy asked, pretending she didn't see Dane's ear-to-ear grin while he continued to crouch by the girl.

"Almonds?" The little girl smiled up at Dane.

"That's correct." Tansy nodded.

The little girl gave Dane a high five and Tansy smiled before she could catch herself.

"Great job. You're the first student to get that right." She stepped back. "Now, Benji and Felix, who are Junior Beekeepers, will show you how to make honey butter." She did a quick scan of the pavilion but there was no place to hide.

Dane casually sauntered up to her—but there was nothing casual about the intensity of his gaze. "Miss Hill."

"Mr. Knudson." She stepped away from him and crossed her arms over her chest, watching as the students crowded around the table where Benji and Felix were setting up.

"That was an exceptionally informative presentation." He crossed his arms over his chest, mimicking her.

"Thank you," she murmured, impressed that his shirtsleeves hadn't split at the seams.

There was a pause.

"So…" He didn't sound nearly as jovial now. "You said you wanted to talk?" He sounded worried.

Tansy glanced at him. "You did see those messages?"

"Yeah. 'We need to talk' isn't something a man likes to hear. Or read. I guess I was delaying the inevitable." He uncrossed his arms, his brow creasing. "Woke up and saw things differently?"

"Dane." She glanced around them, lowering her voice as two teachers came forward to help the students. "What happened between us was…nice but it's a—a waste of time." She hadn't meant to sound so harsh but it was true. "We want very different things."

"I want you." He shrugged, as loud and confident as ever. "I'm pretty sure you want me too."

One of the teachers heard Dane, gave him a head-to-toe once-over and looked at Tansy. *Lucky you*, the woman mouthed out—giving Tansy two thumbs-up.

Tansy's cheeks were on fire. "There are people around. Keep your voice down," she whispered.

"I hadn't noticed." His voice was deep and husky, demanding her complete attention. The way he was studying her made it hard to breathe. It did seem like he was uncaring of anyone or anything happening around him.

"We want different things in business," she murmured.

"That has nothing to do with us." He was frowning now, those blue eyes of his locked with hers. "It shouldn't anyway."

Don't let your guard down. But she could remember the way his arms felt around her and the fire in his kiss. It would be one thing if this was about physical attraction. But it wasn't. Tansy had to face the hard truth that, somewhere along the line, her heart had made its choice.

"I scare you, don't I?" He stepped closer. "You're scared of what's happening between us."

Bingo. She shook her head. *Don't stare at his mouth. Or his eyes.* "You're hilarious."

"When I left, I thought we were in a good place. Something changed. I'd like to know what." He moved closer and, just like that, every bit of Tansy was flooded with anticipation.

We were in a good place. We... She swallowed. *Focus.* "Your text the next morning." She glanced away for a moment, needing to breathe. "It was a reminder that we...we can't work."

"What, specifically, made you upset? The good morning part? That I backed out of helping? Or the appointment with the architect. The *green* architect." He paused. "You did read the *green* architect part?" His gaze searched hers.

"I read it." It was barely audible.

"Here, I thought that would show you..." He broke off, his attention fixing on the demonstration. He wasn't watching, she could tell. His jaw was clenching and his lips were pressed tight.

Show her what? That he was still putting their homes and livelihood at unnecessary risk and didn't seem to care? Done.

But the more she sifted through his words, the more she remembered. Originally, he'd scoffed at the idea and expense of going green—even though she'd asked him to. *No.* He wasn't doing this for her. Her throat pinched so tight it was hard to ask, "What changed your mind?"

As he glanced her way, the corner of his mouth cocked up but he didn't say a word. And the longer he didn't say anything, the harder it was for Tansy to pretend she didn't understand what he *wasn't* saying. He *had* listened to her. And her heart was pounding away with happiness.

"It's been five days since I saw you. Five days of busting my ass and dealing with…a lot." He shoved his hands into his pockets. "Five long days thinking of you, kissing you, holding you. Aren't you a little glad to see me?" he whispered, those eyes of his blazing.

Her cheeks were flaming as she shook her head but said, "Yes."

He looked so happy, Tansy couldn't hold back her smile. It wasn't fair. He was so big and manly and adorable all at the same time. As much as she loved being the reason for that incredible, knee-weakening grin, she realized he was right. She was scared—of him and this and that her heart cared more about Dane than his expansion plans.

DANE WAS IN DEEP, deep trouble. He'd known it was coming. But he'd been a dumbass and acted like it was no big deal. And now there wasn't a damn thing he could do. If he could choose, Tansy Hill would be the last person he'd fall for. It was…*inconvenient*—on so many levels. And every meaningful relationship he already had was complicated. His father. His brother. Now Tansy…

Relationship? That implied she felt something for him, too. He wasn't so sure she did. He'd spent the week trying to get her to engage. Stupid texts, really. Bee jokes and GIFs that would make her smile. Because, dammit, he loved it when she smiled.

"Dane," Leif said, nudging him. "Stop staring at Tansy, and listen. We have a big problem."

Dane took a deep breath and turned toward his brother. "What's wrong?"

"I guess there was something in the breakfast tacos because both Crissy and Oren are puking." He nodded at the kids lining up. "Without them, we're short-handed."

"What's going on?" Tansy was looking back and forth between them.

"Oren and Crissy are sick." Leif frowned. "We've got one more group coming through."

"This was the last one." Tansy waved Benji and Felix forward. "Can you two help out Leif and Mr. Knudson? I can clean up here."

"On it." Felix nodded.

"If it gets me out of cleaning up." Benji grinned. "Not that I mind cleaning up. I'll clean up when I'm working out at Honey Hill Farms, don't you worry."

Felix elbowed in front of Benji. "Yeah, me, too, Miss Hill."

Tansy shook her head, but she was smiling. "Guys, I can't promise anything yet."

"Hey, we know." Felix nodded. "I just need the hours. You don't have to pay me."

"Me neither." Benji shoved against Felix.

"Guys," Leif groaned, waving them back to the booth.

"Nice." Dane glanced at her. "You've got people begging to work for you—for free. You're going to have to teach me your secret."

"Why would I do that?" She headed to the workstation and started loading things into a wooden crate. "If you're not careful, I'll lure Leif over, too."

If Kerrielynn was at her place, it wouldn't take much luring. But he wasn't going to offer that up. Instead, Dane grinned. "Good luck with that."

Tansy looked up at him. "Don't tempt me." The hint of mischief on her face was just enough to make him wonder what she was thinking. "Power tools and unsupervised teenagers. Not a good idea." She pointed toward his station.

"I don't know. Learning a little first aid and how to build a beehive would be twice as educational." He shrugged, then sprinted down to the pavilion he'd been assigned to—her laughter ringing out.

Dane jumped right into the presentation. It was simple. He let the boys do most of the presenting, but he took apart the hive box, pulled out and held up a frame from inside, then passed around a plexiglass-encased piece of honeycomb for them to see up close.

"Each cell in that honeycomb has a purpose. Bees store honey, pollen and babies in their combs," Leif said.

A little boy raised his hand. "My daddy said bees are mean and sting you."

"They don't sting unless they are protecting the hive." Leif smiled. "They're not mean, either. Maybe the one your dad was talking about was having a bad day." That caused a ripple of laughter.

Dane was impressed. His little brother was working the crowd and he didn't even know it.

"Leif, do you know what a bee uses to style their hair?" Felix asked Leif.

"No, Felix, I don't." Leif was smiling.

"A honeycomb, of course." Felix held up the honeycomb and pointed at it.

Dane wasn't the only one that groaned over the joke. A few people were laughing—but he recognized one laugh in particular. He scanned the crowd, spotting Kerrielynn standing with Tansy a little way back. They were laughing like it was the funniest thing they'd ever heard. And even though it was an old joke he'd heard a million times, he laughed, too.

He had it bad all right. Thinking about her, sound asleep on his chest, didn't help.

After the school buses were gone and everything was packed up, Dane went to set up the Texas Viking Honey booth. It went a lot faster when three eager teenagers were on hand to help. Leif was in deep conversation with Kerrielynn so Dane used that as an excuse to find the Honey Hill Farms booth.

"Looks like you're ready for tomorrow." Dane eyed their always-impressive display. With the honeycomb wooden shelves, blue-flower-and-bee-print tablecloth, and delicate lace-trimmed burlap tags on every item— everything about it was eye-catching.

"Ready." Astrid nodded. "What about you?"

"Nothing this fancy." He scratched his jaw. He had a black tablecloth with the Texas Viking Honey logo on it, the same as the black labels on his honey jars. That was it.

"It's all Astrid." Nicole came around the table to look at it from his perspective. "She has a good eye."

"New hair?" Dane gave Nicole's messy bun a look.

"Nope. It's been purple for a while." She held out her wrist. "New ink, though." It was an infinity sign.

"Nice." He nodded, glancing at Tansy.

Tansy was scribbling notes on a beat-up steno pad, her lips twisted to one side and her brow furrowed in concentration.

"She's got an idea," Astrid murmured.

"I can see that." Dane watched Tansy's pencil race across the page over and over. "Must be something important."

"No clue." Astrid shrugged. "She'll tell us once she's got it all down."

He nodded. "I guess I'll see you ladies this evening?"

"Wouldn't miss it," Nicole said.

"You wouldn't get all the good stuff out of the Honey Festival if you skipped the Honey Flow Dance." Astrid glanced at Tansy, then back at him. "We will be there. All of us."

"I'll see you then." He waved and headed back to his truck. Leif was inside, grinning. "You good?"

"Yep." Leif nodded. "We're coming back for the dance, right?"

"Yep." Dane chuckled, instantly understanding his brother's mood. For all his worries over things going south between Leif and Kerrielynn, it wasn't like he could snap his fingers and end it. Besides, he wanted Leif to live and love and be young—even if it meant risking heartache.

Like him and Tansy. He was running toward her, full speed without any road map to guide him. He'd skipped the dance the last year or two but there was no way he'd miss tonight. Dancing with Tansy meant having her back in his arms.

Thankfully, their father was nowhere to be found when they got home, so he couldn't ruin their good mood.

Dane showered, shaved and spent too long staring at the contents of his closet. Something other than his usual Texas Viking Honey shirt was in order. A blue button-down, some new jeans and his polished boots. He brushed out his hair, twisted it back and tugged it through a hair tie. "That's as good as it's going to get."

He headed next door and knocked on Leif's bedroom door. "Leif?"

No answer.

He knocked and opened the door, bracing himself for the disaster inside—the room was spotless. No clothes on the floor. No trash. Even his bed was made. He smiled, pulling the door shut behind him, and headed downstairs. There was a note propped on the kitchen table.

"Went on ahead. You were in the shower."

Dane didn't have to guess who'd picked him up. He didn't blame his little brother for wanting to spend more time with Kerrielynn.

Twenty minutes later, Dane was parked and walking across the fairway of booths and carnival games to the back of the fairgrounds. He smiled and waved at familiar faces but didn't pause long enough for a full-blown conversation.

"Hey. Who are we looking for?" Everett asked, clapping him on the shoulder. "Leif?"

If he told Everett he was looking for Tansy, he'd never hear the end of it. He nodded.

"I haven't seen him." Everett sighed. "Things any better?"

"We're getting there." Dane hoped his father realized how hard Leif was trying. This whole military school nonsense might disappear. And if it didn't, then

Dane and his father were going to have one hell of an argument.

"Looks nice, doesn't it?" Everett pointed at the dance floor.

Strings of painted paper lanterns and strands of gold-and-white lights zigzagged over the concrete slab. Wooden picnic tables skirted three sides, offering plenty of seating for the people gathered. On the far side, the band was playing something lively and carefree. Only a few couples were dancing but it was early yet.

"I'd say it looks more than nice." Van Kettner shook both their hands. "Evening, boys."

"You're looking all spruced up." Dane glanced at the older man. Starched slacks, a crisply ironed white shirt and his hair done just so. Dane only hoped Camellia Hill appreciated the man's effort. However... "Is that a bolo tie?"

Van reached up to adjust the oversize decorative turquoise clasp, then smoothed the two braided leather cords hanging down his chest. "Why, yes, it is."

Dane and Everett exchanged a look. Dane never considered a bolo tie a good idea. But this bolo was especially bad. The turquoise ornament was massive and the end of each braided leather cord was capped with a large ball.

"That's a...*statement* piece." Everett eyed the bolo.

"Sure is." Dane wasn't sure this was the sort of statement Van wanted to make. Still, if Van felt good wearing it, that was what mattered.

"You got your dancing shoes on?" Everett asked. "Watch out, my father tires out pretty quick and my mom's not the shy sort. She loves to dance and won't hesitate to drag a partner out on the floor."

Van chuckled. "Your mother is light on her feet. I've always enjoyed dancing with her."

"Good, she's coming up behind you."

Sure enough, Violet Taggert was headed their way. She was with Ida Popplewell and Camellia Hill. Dane smiled at the adoration all over Van's face.

"Miss Camellia looks nice," Dane murmured.

"Pretty as a picture," Van agreed. "But then, she always does."

Dane and Everett exchanged another look.

"Three handsome gentlemen," Violet said. "And three charming ladies. You know what this means?" She paused. "A dance."

"Where's Dad?" Everett asked, laughing.

"Getting some lemonade or something. He won't mind."

"Camellia?" Van held his hand out.

"I'd love to." Camellia blushed prettily. "I consider a man in a bolo tie rather dashing."

Everett and Dane exchanged another look and laughed.

"Have fun, you two." Violet smiled at Dane. "Shall we?"

He was breathless and laughing by the time they finished dancing—and that was when he spied Tansy. She was talking to Lorna and Bud Franks, laughing—and beautiful. Her long hair was down and her dress, a swirl of blue and green, would almost match her eyes.

"Good thing we're not still on the dance floor." Violet laughed.

"Why is that?" he asked, his gaze returning to Tansy.

"One look at her and you'd have stomped on my

toes." Violet patted his arm. "She looks lovely, doesn't she?"

"Always." He nodded.

"Then go tell her." Violet gave him another pat.

"That's all there is to it?"

"It's certainly a good place to start." Violet gave him a little shove. "Go on."

Bud smiled as Dane approached then shook his hand. "Good to see you, Dane. Things going well out at your place, I hear. How's the expansion going?"

Well, shit. Not the opening he was hoping for. "Good." He might as well use this as an opportunity to try to smooth Tansy's ruffled feathers. "I'm spending twice as much as originally planned for a thorough environmental study and I've hired one of the best green architects around." He met Tansy's gaze. "The Viking Hall is framed out but we're taking it slow and being *careful.*" It would be worth it. At least, that's what he kept telling himself.

"Always good to diversify your income streams." Tansy glanced up at him, her smile tight.

He nodded. "Don't want to put all your eggs in one basket. Or, bees in one hive?" It was a sad attempt at a joke and he knew it.

Tansy rolled her eyes but he thought the corner of her mouth kicked up a tad.

Time to change the subject. "First night out since Fiona was born?"

"Yes!" Lorna nodded. "It's amazing. But I keep checking my phone. Bud, too."

"My mom is with her so we know she's fine." Bud shrugged, slipping his arm around Lorna. "Since I know we won't stay out long, you'll have to excuse me while

I dance with my wife." Bud led Lorna onto the dance floor.

"Lorna's thinking about giving up the Junior Bee-keepers." Tansy started nibbling the inside of her lip.

Dane didn't care about the Junior Beekeepers at the moment. All he could think about was how pretty she was. And how bad he wanted to run his fingers through her hair.

"Did you hear me?" she asked, glancing up at him.

"I did. But then I looked at you and remembered what I'd come over here to say." It was true. Those green eyes had caught a hold of him and the rest faded away. "Maybe it's the dress?" Her blue-green dress covered in golden bees. *Beautiful*. His heart was pounding away, so loud she had to hear it. He took a deep breath.

"Oh?" Tansy fiddled with a strand of her hair.

"You look beautiful." He smiled.

"You, too."

"Dance with me." He held his hand out. "Or we can skip straight to the kissing part." His eyes swept over her lips. "I'm fine with that. More than fine."

Tansy was laughing when she grabbed his hand and tugged him onto the dance floor. "Dancing is fine. Kissing, here, not so much."

He let his hand slide around her side to rest low on her back. "Whatever the lady wants."

She rested one hand on his chest. "I didn't say I didn't want to kiss you."

"No?" he asked, taking her other hand in his. "That's good to know." He ran his thumb along the back of her hand. Having her in his arms was the sweetest torture but there was no way he was letting her go. He liked her right here, close enough to breath her in and feel her every breath. "I needed to touch you."

Tansy took a shaky breath. "If you keep looking at me that way, people will talk."

"People will talk no matter what." He smiled. "I'm not going to let that stop me from holding you." He lowered his head, his mouth at her ear. "I might have to dance with you all night, just so we can stay this way."

"But if we stay this way, does that mean there will be no kissing?" She looked crestfallen.

Dane laughed, pulling her a little closer. "That's not going to happen, Tansy. I promise you that."

CHAPTER THIRTEEN

"We should wait until tomorrow." Astrid pointed at the clock on the dashboard. "It's almost one in the morning."

Tansy followed Dane's truck through the Texas Viking Honey gate and down a gravel lane. They turned the opposite direction of the family homestead to reach a large clearing. "Astrid, this was your idea." There were still things to work out but knowing Dane had a green architect involved had set her mind at ease— somewhat. For now, she'd rather move on to the kissing part. She'd spent most of the evening dancing with or staring at Dane Knudson and enjoying the odd bee's knees cocktail. A little kissing was in order. Even better, a *lot* of kissing.

"Why are you smiling like that?" Astrid was staring at her.

"No reason." Tansy kept on smiling.

"Uh-huh. I saw you two, steaming up the dance floor." She giggled, fanning herself. "Just admit it, *he's* why you're smiling like that."

"I don't have to admit anything of the sort." She wrinkled her nose at her sister. "I think we are going to need flashlights—" The whole yard lit up. Dane emerged from the partially constructed Viking Hall and stood there, looking oh so proud of himself. She drew in an unsteady breath. *It's not fair how gorgeous he is.*

"Tansy, I watched him tonight. The way he watched you, the way he was around you. He *likes* you." Astrid glanced at her. "And then the *dancing*. I think you should give him a chance."

"I am." Tansy took a deep breath. Cautiously, sure, but a chance nonetheless. "We're here, in the middle of the night, aren't we? To see what he's so excited about. At your urging, remember?" Not that Astrid had to push all that hard. Because, somehow, she wanted to find a way to be accepting—if not excited—about Dane's expansion. He'd given with this green architect, she could do the same. "It—it would be so much easier if this didn't have to be an issue between us."

Astrid nodded. "Let's hope for the best."

Tansy walked around the front of the van. "It's huge." The clearing was covered with lumber and insulation, long wooden beams, boxes of building supplies, a tractor and other tools. Next, she inspected the Viking Hall. Even in its unfinished state, the structure was impressive. "You're going all out."

He rolled up his sleeves and stepped back, staring up at the building. "I wanted it to look like the Viking Hall built close to the Borre burial mounds—the ancient cemetery in Norway? There are no actual Viking halls standing, since they were made out of wood. But archeological research has allowed us to piece together how those halls were made and how they looked." He glanced at them. "Since I can't go there, why not bring a little of my heritage here?"

"A little?" Astrid stared up at the apex of the hall.

"Figuratively." His enthusiasm was so contagious

that it was impossible for Tansy not to jump on board. She followed him inside, listening as he explained the finished project. There was still so much to be done it was hard to visualize what he had in mind.

"Mead tasting and parties. Weddings." He rested his hands on his hips. "There's no venue like this in Texas."

"So, people will flock from all over?" Astrid sighed.

"That's the goal." He nodded, his gaze darting her way.

"What about the cabins?" Tansy asked. "Between the event hall and the cabins, you're talking about a lot of traffic." As much as she loved seeing him so excited, there were so many practical concerns to be addressed—for both their honey farms. She glanced his way, nibbling on the inside of her lip.

Dane nodded, his gaze fixed on her mouth.

"Dane?"

He clapped his hands together. "I have a plan for that. Don't you worry." He waved them forward. "The cabins will be this way. Hold on." He scanned the area, sighed and ran back out the front.

"I bet we'll be able to see the roof from our place." Astrid turned in a circle. "I think it'll be pretty cool when it's done, though."

"Maybe." Tansy could appreciate the idea but the reality was a different story.

Dane came back with a bright white flashlight. "No lights out there—careful." He sighed, the beam of the flashlight landing on a pile of fertilizer bags stacked right in their path. "Those were supposed to have been stored in the shed." He helped them over the bags and headed down a rock path.

"Have you started building the cabins yet?" Astrid asked, following close behind him.

"No. Phase one is the hall. Phase two, the cabins." Dane shrugged. "I'm still taking construction bids so I don't think they'll be done before next spring." He paused. "Over there is the closest apiary." He flashed the beam at the rows of bee boxes—stark white in the flashlight. "So far, there's been no issues with the bees or the construction team."

"Good to know you've talked to the bees about it." Tansy sighed.

Dane chuckled. "My bee isn't as fluent as yours or Astrid's but I didn't hear any complaints or pick up on any resistance."

Tansy sighed again.

They walked on in silence for a few minutes, following the beam of the flashlight. Overhead, the sky was clear enough to see a million stars but the farther into the trees they got, the more reliant they were on their single flashlight. He led them through a grove of oak trees and around the remnant of a stone wall.

"You said you had a plan for traffic?" Tansy reminded him. "Why do we not need to worry?"

"A shuttle. I'll have a lot on the edge of the street. An electric shuttle, meaning environmentally friendly, will pick up guests and deliver them back to their cars." He glanced at her. "What? No argument?"

Tansy laughed, she couldn't help it. "I'm working on it." But, really, it was a great idea. He really had thought this through.

Astrid giggled. "You two are…fun."

"You sure you want to do this?" Dane shined his

flashlight at their heels. "I don't have any lights strung up down there so there's not much to see."

"We're fine." Tansy paused to pull off her heels. "See?" He was making a valid point. Why was she pushing back? *Because he's Dane and that's what I do.* She'd need to work on that.

Dane shook his head. "It wasn't a challenge." He turned his flashlight beam.

"We're already out here." Astrid, love her, was trying to be supportive of Tansy.

"Less than halfway there." Dane paused.

"It is late." Tansy grabbed Astrid's hand and gave her a squeeze. "I guess we can come back."

"After the Honey Festival." Astrid squeezed back. "Things will be too chaotic until it's all done and over."

By then, the honey contest would be over. If they lost, Dane's expansion wouldn't matter so much to Tansy's family. Honey Hill Farms would be no more.

"Monday morning sound good?" He turned, the three of them walking back along the path. "I can make some coffee. Not good coffee, but fortifying." His laugh cut short. "Do you see…" Dane swung the flashlight down, the beam hitting the ground at their feet.

For a second, Tansy thought he'd spotted a snake or skunk or some other night critter. But there was a movement out of the corner of her eye and she turned, her heart stuttering to a stop.

"Is that…" Astrid's voice broke. "Fire? It's a fire."

Dane was already running, the flashlight beam swinging in time with his long stride as he sprinted toward the rising flames.

Tansy had her phone out and dialed 911. "There's a fire at Viking Honey. You'll see it from the road. Please hurry." She disconnected, turned on the phone's flashlight, and she and Astrid started running, too.

Fire was never a good thing. And in the country it could be cataclysmic. It would take precious minutes before their volunteer fire department rallied. If there was a way to contain the fire, they had to try.

When she and Astrid reached the clearing, the Viking Hall was a roaring blaze and the smoke billowing up was choking out the stars overhead. Tansy didn't stop, she ran to the van and opened the back doors, rifling through their gear. She grabbed their rubber boots, a shovel and a metal-lined hive roof.

"Here." Tansy handed Astrid her boots and the shovel, tugged on her own boots and tucked the hive roof under her arm.

Dane had started soaking the ground between the building and the construction material so she and Astrid went to the other side. Astrid started digging while Tansy used the hive roof to break up the ground cover—forming a bit of a firebreak. If there was no fuel to burn, maybe they could slow or stop the spread.

Tansy wasn't sure how long they worked. She was dripping sweat and coughing ash and her eyes were dry and raw, but stopping wasn't an option. All they could do was focus on the task at hand. The fire kept growing, snapping and crackling and devouring everything in its path.

The dent she and Astrid managed to make didn't do much. The fire singed the grass black and sent sparks flying—to land and catch and burn in an ever-widening radius.

"Tansy." Astrid grabbed her arm and pulled her back. "They're coming."

The deafening roar of the sirens was such a relief.

"Dane?" Tansy wanted to cry. "Dane!" She turned, taking her sister's hand and skirting the blaze.

The fire truck came bouncing across the open field and slammed to a stop. And behind it came half the citizens of Honey. It would be okay now, it had to be. But the more she searched the sea of faces, the less okay she felt.

She swallowed—wandering—searching. "Dane?" she called out.

Leif was there, covered in soot. "Tansy—"

"Where did you come from?" It didn't matter. He was here. Safe. She hugged Leif close. "You're okay?" She held him away, giving him a quick once-over. "You're not hurt?"

"No." But tears were tracking through the ash and soot on his face. "Where is he?"

"I'll find him, Leif. Don't worry. I'll find him and I'll bring him to you. He's fine." She hugged him again. *He has to be all right. He has to be.* "Okay?"

"I'll help." His arms were tight around her and he was shaking.

"Then stay here." She whispered against his temple. "All Dane cares about is keeping you safe. You have to do that, Leif, you hear me? Stay right here and stay safe for him, okay?"

Astrid put her arm around the boy's shoulders. "Come on, Leif." She grabbed Tansy's hand for a quick squeeze. "Be careful."

Tansy nodded before heading into the fray, searching for broad shoulders and a gorgeous man-bun. *Where are you?* She blinked against the falling ash. *Dane. Please,*

please be okay. Panicking wouldn't help but there was no way to stop it. *Not until I find you.*

There was constant motion all around her. The fire truck hoses were making short work of the main fire, but sparks had drifted and fires were cropping up all over. People were using blankets to beat out the sparks, treated sheets of plywood to smother them, or shoveling dirt onto live flames. She kept moving, horrified by how fast the fire was growing. It felt hopeless—more so because she couldn't find Dane.

"Dane?" she called out, her voice shaking. "Dane Knudson!" She spun.

There were more flames, rising up and devouring a line of Spanish oak, incinerating the cedar and brush beneath their sprawling branches. The crack and snap had Tansy jumping—and moving closer. People were there, running back and forth… Voices rose, calling to one another.

There were hives directly in the path of the flames. "The bees." Tansy hurried forward. Sure enough, a group of people were working to move the hives as quickly as they could.

"That way. Over there." Tansy almost burst into tears. *Dane*. He was there. *He was okay.* Single-handedly carrying a hive out of harm's way.

Tansy rushed to another hive, taking one side while someone—maybe Everett's dad—grabbed the other side. It wasn't light. Since honey flow was still a good month away, the hive had to weigh at least a hundred and forty pounds. *A year's worth of hard work.* Together, they set the hive next to the others. She sprinted back to the apiary.

"Tansy Hill, what are you doing?" Dane grabbed her

arm, his scowl illuminated by the leaping flames. "You need to get to safety."

"I'm just as safe as you are." She smiled up at him, doing her best to be sassy. "And…I can see you here."

He crushed her against him. "Dammit, woman…"

She bit back a sob, determined to stay strong for him. "Leif is here."

"What?"

"He's safe, he's with Astrid." She gently pushed out of his hold. "There's no time for this."

"Thank you." He grabbed her hand. "Tansy, I—"

"You can thank me later." She squeezed his hand.

He nodded and let her go.

When it came time to harvest honey, working hives and extracting honey could be backbreaking work. It was working box by box, frame by frame, taking things nice and slow. This was nothing like that. They were carrying full hives weighted down with bees, honey and brood, and rushing to find shelter for them. It had to be done this way—all at once, with scorching heat creeping steadily closer.

There were probably still a good thirty boxes in the apiary but the fire didn't care.

"Get back!" someone called. "Watch it!"

With a final snap and roar, one of the Spanish oaks split and fell—landing on a row of hives and knocking more to the ground. The hive boxes were older, dry and quick kindling. One lit and it was like dominoes. There was no saving them.

Tansy didn't know she was crying, she was in shock. Her sobs were covered by the hiss and roar of the fire.

"Tansy." Dane wrapped his arms around her and pulled her back. "Come on." The defeat in his voice almost broke her. "I need more help back here or I'll lose them all."

She gripped his hand in hers and hurried along at his side. "What about Mr. Taggert? Doesn't he have a water trailer?"

Dane pulled his phone from his pocket, keeping hold of her with one hand. "Everett." There was a long pause. "Yeah. Tansy said you... Thank you." He slid his phone back in his pocket. "His brother Hoyt is already on the way." He pulled them along until they'd reached the fire trucks and the blackened remains of the hall. "Sonofa-bitch." He crouched, his voice wavered. "It's gone." He shook his head and stood, walking blindly forward—until he saw Leif. "Leif." He let go of her then, dragging his little brother into a tight embrace. "What are you doing here? This is no place for you."

"I saw the fire..." Leif's words were muffled against Dane's chest. "You're okay?"

"I'm okay." He patted Leif's back. "Do me a favor and keep an eye on Tansy for me? Don't let her out of your sight." He looked at Tansy then. "I can't worry about either of you and fight this." He wasn't teasing, he meant it. "Both of you, stay put."

Leif nodded.

Why did he have to help? He was exhausted. He needed to rest. She *needed* him to be safe. "Dane—"

"Tansy...please." He pressed a hand to her cheek. "I can't stand here and do nothing—" He broke off, shaking his head.

"No, of course. Go." If their roles were reversed, she couldn't stand by and watch Honey Hill Farms go up in flames. She understood, even if the idea of him putting himself in danger made her sick. She stood on tiptoe and pressed a kiss to his cheek. "Be safe. Please. You have to or I'll be really, really mad at you."

He nodded and headed back to the apiary, disappearing in darkness and smoke. Several flood lamps had been set up, making it easier for the firefighters and volunteers to do their job. Once the hall was a sizzling heap of charred wood, the fire truck repositioned closer to the still-blazing apiary. Eventually, Hoyt Taggert arrived with the water trailer and not too soon after that, there were no more flames to be seen.

Tansy and Astrid stood, Leif between them, with their arms linked. Her throat hurt, her eyes burned, and she was shaking with exhaustion. It was over. The fire was out. It was horrible, there was no denying that. But no one had been hurt. Leif was here with them and Dane would be careful—that was what mattered most.

Through the smoke, she saw Dane. He was coughing and moving slowly, everything about him beaten down. She wanted to run to him but tightened her hold on Leif instead. He'd asked her to stay with his little brother, so she would. If something had happened to Dane... *No. Don't go there.* He was fine. They had plenty of time for her to get up the nerve to tell him how she felt. Because she knew. His blue eyes swiveled her way and Tansy smiled at him. *I'm so in love with you, Dane Knudson.*

DANE'S THROAT HURT, his head was killing him, and he had a nasty burn across his palm. The fire was out, but it was hard to feel victorious when he looked around him. The devastation was substantial. He'd lost two apiaries—the flames caught up to the few hives they'd managed to move. But, according to Van Kettner, while they'd been fighting the fire here, a yard on the opposite side of the hall had also been wiped out. Likely an additional three hundred hives or more.

Acres of pollen-heavy blooms and plants were gone. Meaning the surviving bees would have to work twice as hard for pollen. Chances were, he'd have a lot of bees swarming away—to find a healthier place to call home.

And the Viking Hall—and almost half of his 401(k) money—had literally gone up in flames. That was money he'd never get back. It'd been his dream and his investment, not his father's. Now that the hall was a smoking heap of lumber, he was thankful the investment had been his alone. Losing the hall gutted him, but he could try again—later. What mattered most now was rebuilding their home.

He'd figure this out later. He was too dazed to see tomorrow, let alone a long-term plan. For now, he wanted to hug his little brother, hug Tansy, for as long as he wanted. He sloshed through the mud and ash and circled the skeletal remains of the hall to where he'd left them.

People were gathering in the clearing, taking inventory of the mess, and talking together. Someone had brought food and water, which were being passed out—with towels and wet wipes, too. This was Honey at its best, rallying to support and help in the darkest of times.

"Dane? Leif?" His father was yelling, his shirt rumpled and his hair standing on end. "Boys?"

"Here, Dad. We're here." Dane waved at Leif to follow him.

"What the hell happened?" His father pointed. "I want to know what happened and I want to know, now."

"Calm down," Dane croaked, coughing against the painful grate of his throat.

His father turned and his anger cleared. "What the

hell happened to you?" He was staring at them both, seeing them—and panicking.

"I was putting out a fire." Dane cleared his throat, which made him wince. *That hurt like hell.* "It'll take some time for them to sort out the whys and hows, Dad." But knowing those things wouldn't undo these results.

"Well, give me something. I wake up to the smell of smoke and sirens and come over to find my boys looking like hell, half of my property burned and the whole town here." He stared around him with wide, disbelieving eyes.

His father had played the victim so often, Dane rarely felt much sympathy for him. But this time was different. His father wasn't acting. This was real. His father was in shock—exactly the way Dane was feeling. "I know. It's a nightmare."

His father nodded. "But you boys are okay?" He looked between Dane and Leif again.

Leif nodded but he kept himself at arm's length when their father tried to pull him close.

"We're fine." Dane placed a hand on his father's shoulder and gave it a gentle squeeze. "We're good."

"Good. Good." His father nodded and went around, shaking hands, saying thank-yous—trying to process what had happened.

Leif frowned after their father.

"He's in shock. Come on." Dane headed straight back to Tansy. He ran a hand along the back of his neck and winced again.

"Are you hurt?" Tansy grabbed his hand and stared down at the rising blister. "Ouch." Her hair was a mess of tangles and her pretty bee-print dress was black with soot, but she was safe and sound and worrying over him. "You need some burn ointment." Her eyes met his.

If there'd been even the slightest question of how much he cared for Tansy, it was gone. "All things considered I think I'm pretty damn lucky. Everyone is safe." He stared down at her. *You're safe.* He'd feel even better once she was in his arms.

"Let's see what kind of snacks they've got over there." Astrid hooked arms with Leif.

"You should get your hand looked at, Dane." Leif pulled his arm free. "There's a medic over there." He pointed at the fire truck.

"Leif, I'm really fine." But Dane saw the anxiety on his little brother's face. "If you're that worried, I'll have him look at it."

Leif nodded.

He winked at Tansy, the motion scraping his dry eye and making him regret it. "Okay." Dane headed for the fire truck, Leif at his side.

"He hurt his hand," Leif announced before Dane could say anything.

"Let's take a look." The man inspected Dane's hand. "I'm really sorry about all this."

"Me, too." Dane nodded, his gaze drifting back to the still-smoking timbers of his would-be Viking Hall. "I can't figure out how it started."

"Accidents happen." The man shrugged. "Maybe a faulty cord. Looks like there was some sort of fertilizer along the back? That feeds a fire, every time."

"The fertilizer did that?" Leif swallowed. "Made it worse?"

Dane hadn't wanted to mention that in front of Leif. Yes, it had been Leif's job to store the fertilizer, but

Dane didn't want Leif blaming himself for the fire. That was a hell of a lot for a kid to shoulder.

"Maybe." Dane nudged him. "Maybe not." Leif didn't believe him—it was written all over his face.

"What the hell are you doing on my property?" Their father's voice echoed across the clearing like a gunshot, drawing all eyes. "You two have no right to be here. None."

"Who is he…" Dane stood, holding the gauze in his hand. "Dammit." His father was yelling at Tansy and Astrid. He was up and moving but Leif beat him.

"Dad, there was a fire." Leif's voice was shaking. "They were helping."

"Is that so?" His father's fury was obvious. "I'm having a hard time believing either of these Hills would care if our place burned to the ground. Unless you came to watch, roast some marshmallows."

Dane faltered then. Had his father actually said that? *What the hell is wrong with you?* He remembered Tansy working alongside him in the flames all too well. It still scared the shit out of him just thinking about it. He took a deep breath—it hurt.

"Dad." Now Leif was angry.

"It's okay, Leif. He's upset. He has every right to be upset." Astrid's attempt to soothe Leif didn't go over too well with his father.

"Thank you for giving me permission, Miss Hill," his father snapped.

"I invited them here." Dane stepped between his father and the sisters. "I was giving them a tour—"

"Excuse me?" His father cut in, his nostrils quivering. "Before the fire started?" His father smiled. "Isn't that convenient."

Dane froze. "What?"

"You don't find it odd that they come out for a tour and the whole damn place goes up in smoke?" His father's eyes narrowed. "I'm guessing you had your eyes on them the whole time?"

Dane swallowed, so disgusted by his father's implications that he was speechless.

"It couldn't be them? All sweet and innocent." His father snorted. "You're a blind fool. They came out here to do exactly what happened—see your dreams go up in smoke."

Astrid's voice was shaking. "Are you accusing us—"

"You bet I am." His father pointed at Astrid, then Tansy. "Now the both of you get out of here."

"Dad." Leif grabbed his father's arm. "Astrid kept me safe. Tansy was out there, with Dane, trying to save the bees."

"Well, they're not going to stand back and laugh, now, are they?" His father crossed his arms over his chest and waited. "You're young, Leif. You want to give everyone the benefit of the doubt. Don't. That's how you get hurt—sometimes by the people you love." He glared at Dane now.

"Maybe you should go." Dane glanced at Tansy. After everything she'd been through, she didn't need to stand there and listen to his father's ranting.

Tansy stared at him in surprise. "But, Dane—"

"He doesn't want you here any more than I do," his father bit out.

Tansy flinched like she'd been slapped.

"No," Dane hurried to explain. "You don't—"

"You don't belong here." His father nodded. "Go on."

Tansy steered Astrid to their van.

"Dad, you're being an asshole." Leif damn near exploded. "You *are* an asshole."

Dane froze. He couldn't chase down Tansy and stop Leif from saying or doing something he'd regret. He'd never heard his little brother so full of rage.

"What did you say to me?" His father was livid.

"You heard me." Leif bowed up at his father. "You don't care about anyone but yourself." Leif put both hands against their father's chest and pushed, hard.

"Whoa, Leif." Dane stepped between them and put a hand on his little brother's shoulder. "Breathe. You don't want to do this."

"Damn right I do," Leif ground out, his face twisted and his eyes full of tears. "I hate him."

"You…" Their father glanced at Leif, then Dane. "You did this. You fix it."

Dane didn't answer. His little brother was angry, yes, but he was also heartbroken. It wasn't all that long ago, Dane had been in Leif's shoes. Only there'd been no one to stop Dane from hauling off and punching his father in the stomach. No matter what he said or did, he'd had to accept that his father wouldn't forgive him. And no matter what his father did or said, Dane had to accept he was responsible for reacting like that. Not his father.

Without another word, Dane pulled Leif aside, leading him farther away from their father and the devastation of the fire. He didn't stop until they sat along the riverbank, in the dark, listening to the crickets, without saying a word.

"Did you know he's sending me to some military school?" Leif choked out. "Even though I've been busting my ass to do better."

"You think I'd let that happen?" Dane shook his head, wishing there was enough light to see Leif's face.

"What can you do?" Leif stood and started pacing. "You're not my guardian."

"We will figure it out. I promise." He didn't know how but he wouldn't let Leif down. *Somehow.*

Dane stared up at the stars overhead—the weight of the day pressing in on his chest until he could hardly breathe. His lungs were already aching from smoke inhalation so he stood and stretched, willing the knots in his neck and shoulders to ease even the tiniest bit.

The fire, Leif, his father and Tansy... Tomorrow, he'd face the fallout. As long as Leif was talking to him, Dane could work with that.

He knew he could work with Leif, since he was mad at their dad, not at Dane. But Tansy... Could he go to bed this way? Worried his father had chased her away—worried that she'd think he agreed. And worrying she wouldn't give him a chance to explain he was trying to protect her not blame her. Never in a million years.

"The fire." Leif's voice was low. "Dane, it was an accident."

Dane nodded. "I know."

"I was pissed off." He stopped pacing. "We were drinking and smoking in the loft."

We? He had a hard time imagining Kerrielynn or any of the other Junior Beekeepers in that scenario. *Wait.* The loft, in the Viking Hall?

"Dad told me about military school. I lost it—didn't go to the dance." Leif rubbed his hands against one another. "I called Eddie and him and his brothers stole their dad's whiskey—and came over."

Dane felt like an ass. He'd been so caught up dancing with Tansy he hadn't even noticed that Leif wasn't there. Some big brother.

"We heard you guys and panicked—we were all buzzing pretty bad. I dropped the bottle. I guess one of the cigarettes wasn't out…" He ran his hands over his hair. "We tried to put it out but it spread and we just…we ran. It must have been the fertilizer, like the guy said." Leif stopped beside him. "I know saying I'm sorry doesn't make this better but I am. Sorry. I'll work, clean up—all of it. I am sorry, Dane. I'm grounded, right?"

He was furious and disappointed and so damn relieved that Leif hadn't been hurt it was a struggle not to react.

"Dane?" Leif's voice softened. "I know I screwed up and it was stupid. I'm not just saying that. You can ground me—"

"I am going to, believe me." He sighed. "I'll need your help with all of it. It's going to be a hell of a lot of work." Dane didn't even know where they'd start but he had a good idea of how. Not with expansions or event venues, that could wait. He'd start again, with what mattered most—family and the bees. "I appreciate you telling me the truth, Leif."

"I didn't want to," he murmured. "But I knew I had to. Plus, I didn't want you thinking anything Dad said was true about Tansy."

"I don't." Dane ran a hand along the back of his neck. "Tansy would never do anything like that. She'd never put the bees in danger." He chuckled.

"She likes you more than the bees." Leif sighed, irritated. "Why didn't you stand up for her? She probably thinks you sided with Dad. That's how it looked. Dumbass."

Yeah, yeah. Tell me something I don't know. He'd seen her face—how she flinched away. It'd gutted him then, it gutted him now to think about it. "I gotta tell you, you need to work on your motivational techniques." He shook his head. "I couldn't go after her when you and Dad were..." Dane blew out a long, slow breath. "I'll go see her tomorrow morning, before anything else. And I'll explain." Hell, he'd beg. He'd tell her he loved her and do whatever he could to make her love him, too.

CHAPTER FOURTEEN

THE DRIVE HOME was a blur for Tansy. She was exhausted, body and soul. And her heart... She swallowed, turning the van down their drive.

"Why are all the lights on?" Astrid sat forward.

Tansy peered out the front windshield and frowned. "Maybe the sirens woke them?"

"Maybe." Astrid smothered a yawn. "You know Dane doesn't believe what his dad said, don't you?"

Tansy glanced at her sister. "I know." But leaving had been hard. Harald Knudson had taken great joy in blaming the fire on them—in front of people she loved and admired. And Dane hadn't defended her, he'd told her to go. She got out of the van and walked to the front steps with her sister. "We look awful."

"You should see your hair." Astrid laughed. "Umm..." She stepped forward and pulled out a long branch topped with a ball of moss. "I don't think this belongs there."

Tansy shook out her hair. "You've got a smudge or two." She pointed at her sister's chin and cheek. "And there." Her cheek. "And there." Her forehead. She pulled the front door wide.

"I don't know," Aunt Camellia was crying. "I'm telling you, Mags, I've looked. Everywhere."

Tansy and Astrid ran into the kitchen to find the

room in absolute chaos. The tile-topped table was stacked high with books, recipe boxes, binders and a variety of spiral notebooks.

"What's going on?" Tansy asked. This was bad—Tansy had never seen them in such a state.

Neither aunt moved.

"Aunt Camellia?" Astrid stepped forward. "Aunt Mags? Is Rosemary okay?"

"She's fine, darling girl," Aunt Mags said, her green eyes widening. "What happened?"

"Oh, heavens to Betsy!" Aunt Camellia hurried around the table. "What on earth?" She hugged them each. "You smell like smoke."

"Is your skirt singed?" Aunt Mags didn't bother trying to hide her distress. "Are you all right, girls?"

"You didn't hear the sirens?" Tansy ran a hand over her knotted hair. "There was a fire." A real-life nightmare. The images were too fresh to blot out.

"A fire?" Aunt Mags pressed a hand to her chest. "No. Oh no. Where?"

"The Knudsons'." Astrid glanced her way. "It spread so quickly. It was terrifying."

More than terrifying. Tansy hugged herself.

"But no one was hurt?" Aunt Camellia grabbed her hand. "Everyone made out just fine?"

Tansy nodded. "I think smoke inhalation was the worst of it." She hadn't liked Dane's blisters, the way he had coughed or how raspy and thick his voice had sounded. She knew he was okay, but it didn't stop her from worrying about Dane. She didn't have a choice. He was there, in her mind and her heart—he always would be.

"Do they suspect foul play?" Aunt Mags asked. "Fire doesn't spontaneously occur."

Tansy felt Astrid's eyes on her but didn't acknowledge it. "It's too early to say." It was a far safer answer than sharing Harald Knudson's accusations. "At least two beeyards were lost—several hundred hives."

"Such a shame." Aunt Camellia shook her head. "How is Leif?"

"He was upset." Tansy eyed the tabletop. "Like you two were when we came in. What's going on?"

Aunt Camellia burst into tears. "I've lost it." She used the corner of her apron to wipe her face. "After all our hard work, I've lost it. With *everything* resting on it. I can't believe it."

"Lost what?" Astrid asked.

Aunt Mags pinched the bridge of her nose—never a good sign.

But Tansy knew. Deep in her stomach, she knew before Aunt Camellia said, "The recipe for the Honey Hill Farms Blue-Ribbon Honey." She drew in a deep breath, sputtering. "And without the recipe, we can't enter the contest. Every jar has to have an accompanying original recipe." She sobbed.

"It can't be lost." Astrid gave Aunt Camellia's hand a pat. "I'm sure it's here—"

"I've looked." Aunt Camellia shook her head. "I've looked in every book, every drawer, every one of Lord Byron's hidey-holes."

"How long has it been missing?" Tansy reached up, smoothed her hair back and tied it into a knot. "We will retrace your steps." Giving up wasn't an option.

"Sunday." Camellia wiped away more tears. "It was there." She pointed to the corkboard on the far wall.

"Saturday it was there." She walked over to it, patted the cork matting and turned. "But Sunday morning I went to check it—remember the last-minute changes we made—and it was gone."

"From the corkboard?" Tansy tried not to panic. "We didn't use a shiny tack." Lord Byron couldn't resist shiny tacks.

"I'm telling you, it wasn't *him*." Aunt Camellia's back stiffened. "I've ransacked every one of his hiding places—and then some. Look around you, the house is a disaster."

"There is another possibility." Aunt Mags began sorting through the stacks on the table, like with like. "We had company Saturday."

The Junior Beekeepers? "Those are good kids." Tansy shook her head. Had any of them come into the house? "None of them would do such a thing."

"I wasn't referring to the students, Tansy." Aunt Mags wasn't angry or accusing. If anything, she sounded apologetic. "You had a guest stay over."

Dane? Tansy glanced at Astrid, her lungs deflating. "He—"

"He was in your room for quite some time," Aunt Mags went on. "And when he left, I didn't hear you creeping back upstairs so I'm assuming you didn't walk him out?"

Tansy shook her head. "I was asleep." She sank into one of the kitchen chairs. Dane wouldn't have taken it.

"He was in an awfully good mood when he left." Aunt Mags glanced at her.

"That doesn't mean he stole it." Aunt Camellia patted Tansy's back. "It means he and Tansy enjoyed one another's company."

Tansy's cheeks were burning. "Watching a movie… and cuddling. That's all."

"You don't have to tell us a thing." Aunt Camellia waved her hand dismissively. "This is your home. What activities you choose to do in your room—"

Tansy covered her face with her hands. "We watched a movie. *Say Anything*—"

"Say Anything?" The aunts spoke in unison.

Tansy's hands slid from her face.

"The movie your parents saw on their first date," Aunt Camellia said, exchanging a smile with Aunt Mags.

"I know," Tansy whispered, nodding.

"It's always been one of Tansy's favorites." Astrid glanced her way. "I think it's sweet that you two watched it."

Tansy had, too, but now… Her head was as tangled and achy as her heart. Dane wouldn't have done this. "I can't believe he'd do this."

"It wouldn't be the first time a Knudson has stolen a recipe from our family, Tansy. It happened before you girls had come to live here." Aunt Mags pinched her nose again.

"What?" Astrid glanced between her aunts.

Tansy was too shocked to say a thing.

"Harald's first wife, Evelyn—Dane and Leif's mother. Well, she was a dear friend. Tall and blonde— Dane has the same presence she did. Warm and playful. When she passed, Harald was…well, the man broke. And your Aunt Camellia stepped in to help, as she always does." Aunt Mags spoke with true affection. "If it wasn't for you, I don't know how he would have managed."

"I loved those boys." Aunt Camellia shook her head. "Dane was such a joy, so bright and funny. He worked so hard to cheer his father. Baby Leif was a pudding, all smiles and giggles."

"He was a rather adorable baby." Aunt Mags shrugged. "As far as babies go."

"And I loved Harald. It just happened. He was here most every day, talking to Poppa and laughing. They'd always gotten along so having him here made sense."

Astrid sat in the chair beside Tansy. "What went wrong?"

"One day, Harald showed up and said all sorts of things that I didn't understand—then. How he had to put his children and his home first. That sometimes, as a father, sacrifices had to be made to meet his responsibilities. That beekeeping was hard and times were especially hard then." She shrugged. "He said he wished things were different, that I wasn't so clingy and needy and wouldn't pressure him for more."

All this time, she'd had no idea. "You are none of those things." Tansy's dislike for Harald Knudson continued to grow.

"That was it. No more Harald or Dane or baby Leif." There was so much pain on Aunt Camellia's face.

"The man's a bastard," Aunt Mags snapped. "He said all that to soothe his conscience. While your sweet aunt was envisioning wedding dresses, he'd snuck into the Hill Bee Log and tore out the family clover recipe." She paused. "He knew we used it as a special edition honey and that it was popular. Poppa Tom thought Granna Hazel knew it and Granna Hazel thought Poppa Tom knew it—I suppose we all just took it for granted that it was safe in the Hill Family Bee Log."

"But it wasn't," Aunt Camellia continued. "I didn't realize the recipe was missing until Viking Clover Honey hit the shelf. They were offering samples at Kettner's and the minute I tasted it, I knew. I came home, opened the Bee Log and it was gone."

Tansy was in shock. It explained so much. "I'm so sorry, Aunt Camellia."

"He's not a nice person. I figured he said those awful things tonight because he was so distraught—which I'd understand." Astrid shook her head. "Really, he's just mean. I don't blame Leif for being so angry with him."

Neither did Tansy. But it made her so sad to see such hostility between a father and son. Not just Leif and Harald—but Dane and Harald. No wonder Dane was so involved in Leif's life. Who else did they have, besides each other?

"What awful things did he say?" Aunt Mags's eyes narrowed to emerald slits.

"It doesn't matter." Tansy stood and hugged her aunt Camellia. "There's enough stress without adding to it."

"Dane Knudson is not his father." Aunt Camellia hugged her back.

Tansy wanted to believe that but she was suffering from a case of whiplash—thanks to Dane. One minute he was telling her he needed her to be safe, the next that she had to go.

"This is not history repeating itself." Aunt Camellia released Tansy.

"Can you remember the recipe?" Astrid asked.

"Mostly, yes." Aunt Camellia nodded. "It's just the last bit I'm uncertain about. We can tackle it tonight or start early in the morning?"

"It is early in the morning." Aunt Mags nodded at the clock. "It's four thirteen to be exact."

Astrid smothered another yawn.

Tansy had been exhausted before she'd learned about the missing recipe and how much of an ass Harald Knudson really was. "I say we reconvene at six thirty?" Tansy suggested. "We could all use a few hours' sleep before we get to work re-creating the honey recipe."

Tansy headed upstairs for a long shower. Even if she didn't sleep, she could use some time to digest the day's events. She washed her hair twice and used a loofah to get all the grime and soot off her skin. When she was clean, she moisturized with some spearmint eucalyptus lotion and towel dried her hair.

Astrid was waiting for her in Tansy's bedroom, sitting on the edge of her bed with Jammie on one side and Beeswax on the other. Astrid was stirring a cup of tea, and Tansy could smell the fragrant blueberry lavender honey syrup from where she stood.

Tansy smiled and sat on the bed beside Jammie. "Tonight was a lot."

"*All* of it." Astrid turned to face her. "That Harald stole the clover recipe? What a…a horrible twisted little man." She took a deep breath. "You can't believe Dane would do the same thing. You can't, Tansy."

"I don't want to. That's the truth." Tansy picked up Jammie and stared into the cat's golden eyes. "Just like I don't want Dane to believe we'd set fire to his property."

Astrid giggled.

Tansy looked at her. "What's funny?"

"Can you see us trying to start a fire?" Astrid shook her head, still giggling. "The way Harald Knudson said it was so dramatic." She pointed at Tansy. "Anyone who knows us would know we could never do such a thing. Even if we wanted to, we'd have had to rescue all the bees first. That would certainly have slowed things down."

Tansy grinned. "Good point. We would be the worst arsonists ever because of the bees. We'd also worry about burning any pollen sources or that the bees would get disoriented from the smoke. Burning down Texas Viking Honey sounds like way too much work. And not worth the risk to the bees."

"He knows you'd never." Astrid nodded.

"Does he? We've been back and forth so much, Astrid. But I need him to know I'd never hurt him." It was suddenly very hard to breathe.

Astrid draped her arms around her shoulders. "I don't think the words *safe* and *love* necessarily go hand in hand. But the way he looks at you…well, if a man ever looked at me that way—made my insides all fuzzy and tingly—I'd totally go for it."

"Fuzzy and tingly?" Tansy stared at Jammie. "It sounds like Astrid needs an antacid, doesn't it, Jammie? Poor Astrid."

Astrid rolled her eyes and flopped back onto the bed. "You can pretend to misunderstand me all you want, but you know *exactly* what I mean."

Tansy lay down, too, watching as both cats made the difficult decision of which way to lie down. "Good?" she asked, neither cat responded so she pulled up the covers.

Tansy turned off the bedside lamp and stared up at the ceiling.

When Astrid said it out loud, it sounded silly. But

when she thought about her reaction each and every time she saw Dane… "Fine. 'Fuzzy and tingly' works."

"I know." Astrid lay facing her but her eyes were closed.

She smiled and closed her eyes, but her brain wouldn't cooperate. Her first thoughts were of the recipe. The contest. On Sunday, the contest would be over. They had to find the recipe, or re-create it, so they could enter. There was no other choice. If they had to live over the Hill Honey Boutique on Main Street, they'd make it work but without the bees, it would never, ever, feel like home.

Then, of course, Dane popped into her mind. Soot-covered and coughing and fearless—working to save the bees. If she thought too long about the danger he'd been in, her chest felt tighter and tighter. Hopefully he was sleeping. Hopefully, he'd wake up and not suffer any ill-effects from the fire so they could straighten out this nonsense once and for all.

DANE WOKE UP feeling rough. His head hurt, an extra ten pounds of pressure compressed his lungs, his throat was sandpaper dry and he looked like he'd walked out of a boxing ring. But the sun was shining, coffee was brewing and he was going to see Tansy. He'd no doubt she'd want an explanation and, even then, she wouldn't make it easy on him. He wouldn't expect it any other way. After last night… He shook his head.

He couldn't see a path forward without her being a part of it. All he had to do was convince her their path was one and the same. *Easy*. He snorted and took a long sip of coffee. The heat felt good against his throat. He rubbed his eyes and peered out the kitchen window over the sink where he spied his father talking to Silas Baldwin.

Dane felt that cold hollowness eating at the pit of his stomach. No more. He carried his cup of coffee to the front door, so he could hear.

"We *have* insurance," his father said. "I don't have the check in hand, but it's coming."

"I understand, Mr. Knudson. But it will take time for the insurance claim to be investigated and even more time for a payment to be processed." Silas Baldwin braced himself. "As I mentioned, even with your insurance coverage, it's not enough to cover the damages and the *second* mortgage." His voice was sympathetic but firm. "While I realize you've experienced a substantial trauma, I can't move the payment dates back again. I'm already under fire for giving you this much extra time."

"You might lose your *job* over this?" His father's voice was deceptively low. "I'm sorry to hear that, Silas." Then he shook his head. "I *will* lose my home— my family's heritage, hundreds of years of blood, sweat and tears down the tubes because of a cash flow problem."

"Mr. Knudson, you agreed to all the terms when we went over the paperwork—"

"I can't believe what I'm hearing." When his father got angry, he got mean. "Here I thought you were my friend. Really, you're just an unreasonable, coldhearted, moneygrubbing used-car salesman, aren't you? What kind of man shows up the day after a fire wiped out acres and killed thousands of bees, to give me my eviction date?"

Dane had suspected something was off with the farm's finances but that was one aspect he'd never been given full access to. Eviction date? Dane set his coffee on the counter and headed out to meet them. "Morning, Silas."

"Dane." Silas was wound up so tight, Dane could see the vein popping out of his forehead.

"Coffee?" Dane offered.

"He's not staying," his father answered.

"I'm sorry to disturb you this morning, Dane." Silas offered him a tight smile. "I heard about last night. I'm so glad everyone is okay."

"I appreciate that. We were all damn lucky." Dane glanced at his father. "What's this all about?"

His father glared at him, thrusting his chin out like a belligerent toddler. If he hadn't overhead the meat of their argument, he might have laughed. As it was, Dane couldn't bring himself to laugh.

"Silas?" Dane shook his head. "I'm completely in the dark here so feel free to start at the beginning."

"I've been trying to reach someone for a week now so I figured I'd drop by on my way into town—as a courtesy. Then I heard about the fire and—"

Dane's father snorted. "You're here sniffing around, aren't you?"

"What's going on?" Dane didn't want to lose his patience, he wanted answers.

"The farm is behind on its loan payments." Silas paused. "I negotiated the best terms I could, lowest interest rates and all. But I can't give another month's forgiveness—I've already given two."

"You haven't given me a damn thing." Dane's father was red-faced.

"Loan?" Dane cut in. "What loan?"

There was dead silence then. Silas started sweating and his father's face immediately paled.

"A second mortgage was taken out on the home." Silas cleared his throat. "If we don't get some form of payment this month, I'm afraid we're looking at fore-closure."

"What?" Dane almost dropped his coffee. "Fore-close on...?"

"Everything." Silas's gaze darted from him to his father. "The property and everything on it."

"Well, hell, Dad. Don't you think that's the sort of thing you should share with Leif and me? Or were we going to come in from the apiaries one day with the locks changed and a For Sale sign in the front yard?" He knew he wasn't helping but Dane couldn't wrap his head around what he'd just heard.

"I'm taking care of it," his father snapped.

"Dad, you're not. You can't. This isn't something you can take care of on your own. Stop acting like it's not a big deal, dammit. You've already wasted time we don't have, from the sounds of it. Leif and I have a stake in this. We had a right to know what you were doing."

"Now you can have your moment and save the day." His father scowled. "You don't want to hear what I say, boy. You want to throw your money away on that hall and those cabins. You think I want those things here?"

Dane paused, anger rolling over him. "*You* told me to go ahead with them. You said the bottom line looked good."

"We needed the money. I didn't think it'd take a year and a half to get the damn ball rolling." His father's disappointed expression was the straw that broke the camel's back.

"You're telling me I sank part of my 401(k) into an expansion so you could use the profits to pay off a loan—when we could have used part of my 401(k) to pay off the loan directly?" Dane could only stare, his anger all but choking him. "What sort of sense does that make?"

His father was red-faced all over again. "You think I'd ask you for money and have to endure that? Hell, no. I'd never have heard the end of it."

"Instead, you'll risk our home for it?" He shook his head. "What was the loan even for? Not for any improvements around here, that's for damn sure."

"My personal life is none of your damn business. I don't need you judging me or looking down your nose at me more than you already do."

"It stops being your personal life when the consequences affect all of our livelihoods." Dane couldn't stop the words. "You and your damn pride. I hope it can keep you warm and fed because that's all you're going to have left when this is over."

"If you think you can hurt me, son, you're fooling yourself." Harald shook his head. "I cut you out of my heart the minute you knocked me to the dirt."

Dane reeled. He'd been a kid, about Leif's age. His mother was dead, Camellia and the Hills were no longer part of his life, and his father wasn't around much. Dane had made the mistake of going to his father for comfort—never again.

"What sort of son hits his father?" His father's tone was razor-sharp.

"What sort of father lets his son struggle with grief on his own? What sort of father shames him for his tears? What sort of father tells his son his dead mother would be ashamed of him?" That was when Dane had hit him. "I was a kid. I made a mistake. God knows I tried to apologize. I am sorry. Every damn day, I regret it." He took a deep breath. "I wanted my father back." He swallowed so hard, it hurt. "I still do."

His father's transformation wasn't something Dane had been prepared for. For years, his father was either raging against the world or chasing after a woman. He was proud and defiant or proud and charming. Now... now he was none of those things. His father was shaken—as if his whole world had been turned upside down.

"What is wrong with you?" Leif's voice sliced through the tension.

Sonofabitch. Dane didn't know when Leif had come down for breakfast or how much he'd heard, but none of it was good. His little brother didn't need to be dragged into this.

"You two suck at this," Leif yelled. "We aren't a family, we're a bunch of assholes."

"I'm going to go..." Silas murmured, and moments later, the low rumble of his truck signaled his departure.

Dane, Leif and their father faced each other in a standoff.

"A family would talk all this crap out. Instead, *you're* sending me away." Leif was shaking, his gaze fixed on their father. "You don't care that I've been working to make things better. Do you know what my grades are? That they want me to be the Junior Beekeepers vice president next year? That's a big deal. Does that matter? Any of that?" He swallowed. "Do you care?... About *me*?"

Dane bit his tongue. His father should answer for himself—even if it hurt Dane to see Leif struggling.

"You know what? You suck, Dad." He rubbed his nose with the back of his forearm. "And you suck for covering for him." Leif glared at Dane. "If you hadn't tried to smooth everything over, maybe he'd have had to be a dad. Maybe he'd have given a shit about me."

Dane's lungs folded in on themselves as Leif stormed into the house, stomped up the stairs and slammed his bedroom door.

His father headed across the yard to his truck, climbed in and drove off. Dane had no doubt he was headed toward his hunting cabin.

Dane wanted to yell. Or throw something. He was sick and tired of being the one left to handle things. His father didn't want him here. Leif didn't want him here. What the hell was he doing? Wasting his time and his money—on what?

He blinked, hating the sting in his eyes. Slowly, the blood stopped roaring in his ears and the knot in his chest eased enough for him to breathe evenly.

He could feel sorry for himself later. There were things that had to be done. Important things. See Tansy, for one. The sooner, the better. Seeing her would make everything better.

But first he needed to get Birmingham and Leif to the Honey Festival. They, along with Felix and Crissy, had volunteered to run the booth for the day. Now, more than ever, Dane was thankful for that arrangement. All he had to do was drop them off at the booth and submit the Texas Viking Honey entry for the honey judging contest. He'd called Julian, their insurance guy, and he'd promised to come do an assessment of the damage around noon.

Between dropping off Birmingham and Leif and Julian's visit, he'd go see Tansy.

The drive into town was unbearable. Birmingham wasn't a talker—unless it was about bees. Leif was more sullen than ever, and Dane's headache had reached colossal proportions. Not a word was said all the way to the booth.

"Leif!" Kerrielynn was a flash of brown hair as she launched herself into Leif's arms. "I'm so glad you're here."

Leif clung to the girl, eyes closed, arms tight. "I'm fine."

"I know." But she wasn't letting go. "I was worried."

Leif's eyes were still closed, but he was smiling.

"I needed to see you for myself." Kerrielynn let go of Leif, flushed and happy.

His little brother's mood didn't stand a chance against the sunshine Kerrielynn brought with her. *Sunshine is what he needs.* "I'll come back with lunch?" Dane offered, eager to check in his honey and go see Tansy. He needed to see her. "For now, I've got to get back out to the farm."

"You don't have to worry about a thing, Mr. Knudson." Felix gave him a thumbs-up. "We'll sell everything."

Birmingham nodded and sat in the camping chair in the corner of the booth. "I'll keep them in line."

"I know you will." Dane managed a smile. "I appreciate the help."

"I'm so sorry about the fire. Was it bad? Is there anything we can do?" Crissy asked.

"You're doing it." Dane nodded at his brother. "I'll let Leif fill you in on the details."

"Is it okay if I help out, too?" Kerrielynn asked, taking Leif's hand.

Leif's expression was conflicted. He was mad at Dane and he wanted Dane to know it. But he really wanted Kerrielynn to stay—which was up to Dane.

"More hands are always welcome." Dane smiled. "I appreciate it."

Leif gave Dane a grudging smile, then forgot all about him as Kerrielynn rested her head against Leif's shoulder.

At least things were looking up for Leif. Dane waved and headed for the honey contest registration.

Instead of the usual no-frills folding table and clipboards setup, there were green and white balloons, speakers playing "Sugar, Sugar" by the Archies and a whole group of people wearing green-and-white Healthy & Wholesome Markets shirts and caps.

"Lots of competition this year." Camellia Hill stepped in line behind him. "Entering anything special?"

"Clover honey. Same as always."

"It's an exceptional honey and recipe," Camellia huffed, hugging the basket close.

"Dad's pretty proud of it." Dane shrugged.

Camellia studied his face, a sad smile forming as she rested a hand on his arm. "Dane, I am so sorry about the fire last night."

He nodded, his throat tightening. She'd always been so kind to him. After the insults and hostility of this morning, her kindness meant more than he could say. "Thank you."

"Is there anything I can do?" Camellia patted his arm.

"I'm still figuring that out." Dane shook his head. "Is Tansy here? I really need to talk to her."

Camellia looked concerned. "She's a mite upset with you, Dane."

"She has every right to be." Dane faced the older woman. Once upon a time, he'd thought this woman would be his stepmother. She had a big heart and a level head and he could use her guidance right about now. "I messed up."

Camellia instantly softened. "I'm sure, whatever it is, you can straighten it out."

"I'm hoping so." He ran a hand along the back of his neck.

"You look tired. And a bit worse for wear." She shook her head. "Didn't get much sleep, I'll wager? So much weighing on you."

"More than I bargained for." He shook his head. In the last twenty-four hours, his whole world had been flipped upside down. Nothing he'd planned for still existed. Since he'd set eyes on Tansy, carrying hives in the fire, he'd struggled to hold it together. But now, he was so close to the edge, he feared he'd go over.

"You need to take care of yourself, Dane. I know it's not easy to carry the weight of the world on your shoulders. I want you to know I see what you're doing. For Leif and your father and your home. And so does Tansy." Camellia paused, as if she wasn't sure she should say what she said next. "Tansy's home taking a nap. Said her head was hurting."

Without thinking, he hugged her close. "You're an amazing woman, Camellia Hill." She'd always given the best hugs—and it turned out, that hadn't changed.

"Next." A woman in a green-and-white shirt waved him forward, took his honey entry and the recipe card, and had him sign off on his entry form. "Good luck."

"I'm going to need it." He winked at Camellia and ran for his truck.

The whole drive to Honey Hill Farms, he was working through what he should say. When he parked, every idea he'd come up with evaporated at the sight of Tansy, Magnolia and the red-haired mystery woman sitting on the porch.

He took the steps two at a time and paused as all three women, still seated, turned to look at him.

"Good morning." He smiled and held out his hand, swallowing around the lump in his throat. "Dane Knudson."

"Shelby Dunholm." She shook his hand.

"Good morning." Magnolia darted a look at Tansy.

Tansy didn't say a word. She sat staring up at him with red-rimmed puffy eyes.

"How are you feeling?" he asked, sitting on the stool in front of her. As much as he wanted to touch her, he didn't.

Tansy blinked again. "I'm a mess." Her voice was brittle.

His heart twisted sharply. Dane nodded, clenching his hands to keep from reaching for her. "I know the feeling."

"Oh, do you?" Tansy set her teacup down and pressed her fingers to her temples. "One minute, I know what's right. I can see it and feel it and everything is crystal clear. And then, a tiny thread of doubt slips in and I'm wondering what's real and why I'm such a fool where you're concerned."

"You're not a fool. You're...you're pretty damn perfect. I'm the fool." He tried to smile. "You've got a good head on your shoulders, Tansy. Whatever it's telling you, it's right."

"Not my heart?" Her eyes flashed his way. "I can't listen to b-both—they're telling me different things."

"Talk to me, Tansy." He swallowed. "Please."

She stared at him for a long time before she asked, "What would you do to protect your home or people you love?"

"Anything I had to." He frowned. "You'd do the same."

"Not if it meant sabotaging—hurting—someone else." She broke off, then said, "I wouldn't burn down your apiaries or hall any more than you'd steal the recipe Aunt Camellia and I have worked on for months."

"What?" Dane was lost.

"It's for the honey contest. If we don't win, we will lose everything, Dane. Honey Hill Farms will be no more..." She shook her head. "But the recipe is missing and that thread of doubt won't let go. Any more than you can say, with absolute certainty, that Astrid and I didn't have anything to do with that fire."

Dane was confused now. "I *can* say it, with absolute certainty. You'd never do that." He sifted through her words again, the ache in his stomach spreading up and into his heart.

"You know how the fire started?" Magnolia cut in.

Dane didn't look at the woman. "Wait. You think I did this? I took this recipe? Why?"

"It wouldn't be the first time a Knudson did." Magnolia's tone was brusque. "Your Viking Clover Honey is from our family Bee Log."

Dane sat back, gripping the stool to stay upright. "Oh my God. He wouldn't…" He stopped himself. He might not want to admit it but his father would do something this heinous. "I'm so sorry." He stood, running a hand along the back of his neck. "It's not enough, I know that. I don't know how to ever make up for what he stole." He ran a hand over his face, the anger and loss and grief pushing their way up until he couldn't stay quiet.

"You asked me if I would do anything for the people I loved and I said yes. You're first in that category, Tansy. I'd never hurt you intentionally. Last night feels like a bad dream." He cleared his throat. "I didn't want you to go, I didn't want to let you out of my sight. But he started and Leif…" He shook his head. "He's come so far but last night…" He swallowed. "I couldn't leave him. And I knew, if my father kept talking to you like that, I'd have to stop him. That's why I asked you to go." He drew in a deep breath, his heart cut wide. "I'm not my father. I never will be. I'd never take something from you or your family." He shook his head. "If you're doubting that, then maybe I'm the fool for listening to my heart and not my head. If you can't trust me, trust us, then how can we have anything?" He headed for the steps, hating the burn in his eyes and the vise squeezing his chest. "I've got to get home—insurance…" Which didn't make a bit of sense, but he didn't care.

He kept his eyes away from the porch as he backed the truck down the drive and out onto the road. It didn't matter how exhausted he was or how much his lungs ached, he had to keep going—keep doing—so losing Tansy, on top of everything else, didn't bring him to his knees.

CHAPTER FIFTEEN

TANSY TOSSED HER wadded-up tissue on top of the pile she'd already used. The box was empty, so she tossed it across the room and hugged her pillow to her chest. She'd pleaded a headache after Dane had left and been crying off and on ever since.

Dane. Oh, Dane.

A new sob rose up so she smothered it into her pillow. He loved her. He was worried about her. And she'd accused him of terrible things.

Her head ached, her eyes itched and her heart was obliterated.

First, she needed a pain reliever. She sat up, kicked off her blankets and went downstairs for some tea. In the kitchen, the radio was on low, big band tunes playing softly as Mags hummed along. She leaned over a puzzle, assembling what appeared to be the Eiffel Tower. Shelby sat at the end of the table, sorting through pieces and laying them along the edge. Baby Bea slept in the bouncy seat, Jammie and Beeswax lying on either side like dozing feline sentries.

Aunt Camellia sat, the dogs piled around her feet, in one of the large wicker chairs, knitting.

"I thought he was in trouble." Tansy pointed at Lord Byron, sleeping on the perch behind Aunt Camellia's chair.

"If he takes one more of my puzzle pieces, I'm making him into a stew." But there was none of the usual bite to Aunt Mags's threat.

"I'll make corn bread to go with it." Aunt Camellia grinned at Tansy.

"I'm more of a gingerbread person myself." Tansy managed a small smile.

"You're not serious?" Shelby asked, turning to look at Lord Byron.

"It's a vicious cycle. Lord Byron torments Aunt Mags and takes her things. Aunt Mags threatens to taxidermy or cook him, and Aunt Camellia comes to his rescue and feeds him crackers." Astrid sat on the opposite end of the table, putting puzzle pieces together.

Shelby didn't seem exactly comforted by this explanation so Tansy added, "It's okay. He's been around for as long as I can remember so, for all the threats, I'm thinking Lord Byron is safe."

Aunt Mags humphed but let it go—winking at Shelby.

One good thing had come out of the last few weeks of upheaval. Shelby and Bea had shown up to have tea with Aunt Mags this afternoon and, despite the scene with Dane, she'd yet to leave. She was sweet and thoughtful and, likely, totally overwhelmed by her new family but she seemed eager to get to know them all. Not as eager as Aunt Mags, of course, but close.

"I have the champagne flute done." She pushed the pieces toward Aunt Mags.

"Bravo." Aunt Mags smiled.

Tansy sank into the overstuffed chair opposite Camellia.

Aunt Camellia's knitting needles didn't pause. "Can't sleep, darling?"

Tansy shook her head.

"Would you like some tea?" Aunt Camellia asked, setting her knitting aside.

"Stay put." Tansy pointed at the pile of pups at her feet. "They're all so happy, I don't want to wake them."

"Why not some wine?" Aunt Mags interrupted, jumping up from the table.

"Why not." She yawned. "If it will help me sleep."

Aunt Mags pulled glasses from the cabinet. "You disappeared as soon as Dane left, I was hoping you'd gone off for a nap." She opened the bottle of wine.

All eyes turned Tansy's way. She'd gone upstairs to cry, shower, cry some more and realized she'd been horrible to Dane. *Again.* "No nap."

"Then again, I imagine sleep would be elusive after something so…so impassioned." Aunt Mags poured a healthy amount of wine into each glass.

"He is very overwhelming." Shelby took one of the glasses. "In a good way."

"I agree." Astrid took a glass from Aunt Mags.

"I admit, I was a little dazzled, too." Aunt Mags pressed a hand to her chest. "It's shocking, I know."

Aunt Camellia stopped knitting and pointed at her sister with a needle. "Don't belittle him, Mags. That boy has a good heart. Now that we know *all* he's been dealing with, I'd say he needs a bit of compassion."

That grabbed Tansy's attention. "What did I miss?"

"Nicole called. She and Benji ran the booth today, remember?" Astrid waited for Tansy's nod and stood. "Are you sure you want to know?"

Tansy shook her head. "No." But then she nodded. "Yes. I do." *Of course, I do*.

By the time Astrid had finished, Tansy took a large gulp from her glass of wine. His home, like hers, was in jeopardy. Not just from the fire but by the bank. And poor Leif. He'd told Kerrielynn, Benji and Felix all about military school. Dane would never send his brother away so... And then she'd pushed him away. *Oh, Dane*. Her heart couldn't take any more.

She knew they were all waiting for her to say something, but there were no words. *I'm a horrible person*.

"I've convinced Shelby to stay with us for a bit." Aunt Mags clinked her glass with Shelby.

Even hurting, Tansy saw what a gift this was—for all of them.

"Yay!" Astrid clapped her hands. "You have to stay through the honey flow. It's so much fun."

"Honey flow?" Shelby asked. "Remember, my bee knowledge is...well, I have none."

"If you want to learn, you're in the right place." Astrid set her wine aside to sift through puzzle pieces. "Honey flow, honey harvest, same thing. It's quite the production."

"But it's not until July." Aunt Mags glanced Shelby's way.

"The beauty of graphic design is I can work wherever there is Wi-Fi." Shelby set her wineglass aside. "As long as you're sure it's not an imposition? Bea is a good baby but she's still a baby."

A baby Mags and Camellia were outright smitten with. There was an overlapping chorus of protests.

"You're both welcome to stay with us as long as

you'd like." There was so much love in Aunt Mags's eyes. "This is your home now, too."

As long as we win the honey contest. If they didn't... Tansy took another sip, refusing to consider that this might be their last honey harvest.

"Don't make that face." Aunt Camellia used a knitting needle to point at her. "I know what you're thinking."

"What?" Astrid asked, looking up.

"This will not be the last honey harvest for us." Tansy took a deep breath. "There, is that better?"

Aunt Camellia nodded but she didn't look happy.

"I'm sorry." Tansy reached over to squeeze her aunt's arm. "I'm trying to only think good things." But she kept circling back to Dane. And the not-so-good things he'd been dealing with all on his own.

"We're all worrying over it." Astrid sipped her wine. "But worrying won't do anything except give you wrinkles." She smiled up at Aunt Mags.

"It's the truth." Aunt Mags patted Astrid's hand. "I think I'll put Shelby in the guest room. It's big enough for Bea's portable crib."

"If you need help settling in, let me know." Tansy hoped Shelby would stay long enough to really connect with them all—especially Aunt Mags.

"Thanks." Shelby tucked a long strand of red hair behind her ear. "A lot."

"Don't forget about the backward knob in the bathroom." Aunt Camellia's knitting needles were clicking along.

"And make sure to pull your door closed all the way so Lord Byron can't run amok in your room." Aunt Mags shot the parrot a narrow-eyed glare.

"He only runs amok with you," Aunt Camellia pointed out.

"We do look alike." Shelby leaned forward to put two puzzle pieces together. "I'll make sure to close my door—just in case."

Aunt Mags swallowed hard. "And when Rosemary comes home, everyone will still have their privacy." She smiled. "I can't wait to have all you girls under one roof."

"Me, too. It's been way too long since Rosemary's last visit." Tansy sipped her wine. "Maybe we should head to California and drag her home for a while."

Aunt Camellia put her knitting down, glanced at each of them, and frowned at Mags. "Why don't I get to have any wine?"

"It gives you a headache. Remember?" Aunt Mags held out the bottle of wine.

"Oh right." Aunt Camellia went back to her knitting. "I want to be clearheaded and sharp for tomorrow."

"I have a feeling it will be a good day." Aunt Mags raised her cup in a silent toast.

"I hope you're right." Not just for the honey competition, but for her and Dane. She couldn't leave it like this. She took a sip of wine and the words spilled out. "I have all of you and Nicole—who does he have?" *Me. He has me.* Not that he knew that. "He's dealing with so much and I… I let him down. How can I love him and be so quick to believe the worst thing about him?"

The entire kitchen came to a screeching halt. No sound. No movement. Nothing.

Tansy took a deep breath, mortified that she'd tossed it all out there like that. She eyed her wine. "Boy, this stuff is strong."

"Tansy, dear, you love, who, exactly?" Aunt Mags asked, at the same time Aunt Camellia said, "Of course you do, Tansy. And he loves you, too."

Tansy peered into her wine. "He didn't say that exactly."

Aunt Mags made another humph sound. "Not in three words, no. I believe it was more like, you're the first person in his 'people that I love' category, Tansy." Aunt Mags glanced at Shelby. "Or something along those lines."

Shelby sat back in her chair. "Only he said it in a much more manly way."

"Everything he does is manly," Astrid added. "This is good."

"Is it?"

"You're finally admitting you care about him."

Tansy finished off her glass of wine. "Then answer my question. Why do I keep trying to find a flaw? Some reason to keep him at arm's length."

"It's normal to be scared, I think? Opening yourself up to another person, giving them absolute trust. I'd be terrified." Aunt Camellia smiled sadly. "I'm afraid your aunt Mags and I aren't much help in the romantic department, being spinsters—"

"Speak for yourself, Camellia Ann. I hardly think being fifty-four makes me a spinster." Aunt Mags crossed her arms over her chest. "And since you're two years younger than me, you're not allowed to use that term, either."

Aunt Camellia waved off her sister's interruption. "You and Dane have a rather complicated history...that would make things even harder."

"But it's never too late to choose a new path." Aunt

Mags paused. "If you truly love him, you'll have to move forward—not back. Make new memories, together. That will give you a fresh start and strong foundation to build from."

Shelby glanced at Mags then and nodded. "Moving forward sounds like a good plan."

Watching her aunt and Shelby tore at Tansy's heart and gave her hope. Forgiveness was a gift. Could Dane forgive her for being so blind? *Please, please let him forgive me.*

Aunt Mags took a deep breath. "Plus, he is on the intimidating side, being so…"

"Big and manly," Shelby jumped in.

"Intense and handsome." Astrid kept working on the puzzle.

"All of that." Camellia nodded. "And letting go of the promposal incident…"

"One more huge misunderstanding." She eyed her empty glass. *Thanks for that, Kate Owens-Knudson.* "We don't communicate well."

"On the contrary, he seemed to have no problem communicating," Aunt Mags pointed out.

Tansy stopped then, mulling over each and every one of their conversations. She sat forward. "You're right. *I'm* the bad communicator. I see him and I get so…so rattled I stumble all over my words. He puts it out there, straightforward and then I get in my head and I start second-guessing everything." She nibbled her lip. "The only thing he knows, without a doubt, is that I want him. *So* much. All he has to do is smile at me and I melt. His kiss or touch…" She shivered. "But wanting someone isn't the same thing as loving someone."

By the time she finished, Aunt Camellia and Aunt Mags resembled owls, wide-eyed and blinking.

"Too much." Tansy winced. "Sorry."

"Maybe you should write it down?" Shelby suggested. "Decide what you want to say and write it all down."

"Good idea." Astrid nodded. She handed another puzzle piece to Mags. "Here."

"Keep it simple, Tansy." Aunt Mags nodded at her. "The poor boy was distraught when he left."

"I have an idea." Tansy nibbled on the inside of her lip. "It's not exactly simple…"

Astrid forgot the puzzle and came around to squeeze into the chair beside her. "You've got my attention."

"It's probably stupid." Tansy shook her head but she was smiling at her sister.

"So?" Astrid waited.

"So, Aunt Camellia, you're right. I am scared. I want to do this because I think it will mean something special. I don't want there to be any misunderstanding about how I feel or what I want from him." She leaned against Astrid. "I want him to know, without a doubt, that I love him so that it's safe for him to love me. If I don't chicken out, that is."

"I won't let you." Astrid patted her back.

"None of you will disown me if I make a spectacle of myself?" Tansy was pretty sure that's what this would turn into. But, if it worked, it would be so worth it.

"Cheers." Aunt Mags laughed. "It's time Willadeene Svoboda has something real to carry on about."

If Tansy could get all the pieces together and if she could get up the nerve to do what she was thinking, Dane Knudson would never doubt how much she loved him.

DANE WALKED INTO the kitchen, sweat-soaked and covered in ash. As far as he knew, Leif was with Kerrielynn and their friends. And his father was at the hunting cabin so he had the place to himself.

"I made dinner."

Or not. His father was at the stove, onions and garlic scenting the air. "I'm not saying it's good. But I made it."

Dane glanced at the table. It was set for three. "Is Leif home?"

His father glanced at the table. "I don't know what the boy's schedule is."

Dane didn't argue. He didn't have the energy—or interest. "I should shower."

"Fine." His father nodded. "It'll be a few minutes longer anyway."

But he couldn't head upstairs if his father had something up his sleeve. "Is something going on, Dad?" He didn't have the patience for any more revelations about his father. He'd been disillusioned enough for one day.

"No." His father glanced back at him. "Just dinner."

Dane nodded. "Give me a sec." He was so exhausted he used the handrail to pull himself up the stairs, left his dirty clothes on the bathroom floor and leaned against the wall under a bracingly cold shower until he was shivering. With any luck, it would revive him enough not to fall asleep, face-first, in his dinner.

He tugged on a Texas Viking Honey shirt and some worn sweatpants and headed back down the stairs.

"Better?" his father asked, sliding a plate of partially singed dinner rolls onto the table. "You look dead on your feet."

After the day he'd had, he needed to be too tired to

think or feel. "That was the goal." Dane sat at the table hoping this was just dinner and not the start of another yelling match.

Beyond the charred rolls, there was a bowl full of undercooked spaghetti noodles and another bowl of something that resembled marinara sauce—with several large chunks of hamburger.

"Spaghetti." His father sat opposite Dane and served them both. "I did my best with the meat. It was frozen through so I cut it into smaller pieces."

Dane tapped the meat with his spoon. It was hard as a rock.

"Don't eat the meat, then." His father scooped out the still-frozen beef onto the third dinner plate. "There. Vegetarian spaghetti."

Dane managed to choke down a few bites before his father grabbed his plate and pulled it away from him. He sorted through the rolls, salvaging three for Dane and two for him. "Here." His father slid the butter across the table to him. "I didn't make it so it should taste just fine."

Dane slathered butter on a roll, and took a big bite— into stone.

"Dammit all." His father threw the roll back onto the table. "How the hell did I burn the outside and leave it rock-hard in the middle?"

"I'm not all that hungry anyway." Dane shrugged. "I'm tired."

"It's barely eight." His father frowned.

"Well, Dad, it's been a hell of a day." Dane carried his plate to the counter, scraped his food into the compost bin, and rinsed and loaded his plate into the dishwasher.

"I was hoping we could talk about that." His father pushed his plate aside.

Talk? That was the last thing he wanted to do. "Which part?" He ran a hand over his face. "To be honest, I'm not sure I'm up for talking. But I appreciate the food."

"Five minutes." His father glanced at him. "All I'm asking for is five minutes."

Dane started making coffee. "Fire away." He pulled two mugs from the cabinet.

"I have some ideas on how to save our home." His father folded his hands on the tabletop. "I screwed everything up, I know it. But I'm going to need your help fixing it."

Dane rested his head against the kitchen cabinet door and sighed. "This isn't going to be a five-minute conversation." He opened the cabinet and pulled out some pain reliever.

"You started making coffee so I figured you weren't in any hurry." He pointed at the percolating coffeepot and mugs Dane had put on the counter.

"Fine. But you have to answer a question first." He waited for his father to nod, then asked, "Did you steal our clover honey recipe from the Hills?"

His father's eyes narrowed and his jaw clenched tight.

It was answer enough but he wasn't about to let his father off that easy. "I don't want reasons or justifications. I want a yes or no." Dane poured the coffee and carried both mugs to the table.

"Yes." His father growled the word. "But—"

"No. The why doesn't matter. You did it." Dane didn't understand his father. Who could do something like this, live and profit off of it, and not own what he'd done?

He didn't like his father. He certainly didn't respect him. But saying any of that, out loud, would only perpetuate their screwed-up relationship. Instead, he sipped his coffee. "We're not the only ones looking at losing our home and business. They're all in on this honey contest. If they don't win, they'll lose everything." He took another sip. "Honey Hill Farms will be gone. And Texas Viking Honey will, too. That's on you, Dad."

His father's jaw clenched tight. "I'd rather talk about what we can do to save our home."

"Fair." Dane rolled his neck and took a deep breath. "If you sell the piece on the other side of the river, what sort of dent does that make?"

"A third of what we need." His father propped his elbows on the table. "Waterfront property is desirable."

"I know. It's why I thought the cabins were a good idea." He glanced at his father. "I don't know what you want anymore, Dad. I'm not sure you know. And figuring it out is important, moving forward." He spun his coffee mug slowly. "I know what I want. This place, my home to be safe. Texas Viking Honey to stay afloat. And…I want to be a partner now. No more secrets or hiding stuff. We need to get back to our roots—focus on honey. Everything else will wait. I'm willing to do what needs to be done to hold on to it. Are you?"

"Of course, I am." His father stared at him for a long time. "I was thinking…" He cleared his throat. "What if I gave you 51 percent of the business—put you in charge? Let you do whatever it is you want to do?"

"Dad." Dane frowned. "Are you sure about this? You

make those sorts of legal changes, it's not the sort of thing that can be undone."

"I am." He sat back in his chair. "Between selling off the land and the insurance money, we've got a start. And I was thinking we could parcel off the hunting cabin, too. It's on ten acres—away from the bees and the house. If we sell it, we should break even." He pressed his hands flat on the tabletop.

"That's what you *want*?" Dane pushed.

"Yessir. I want you to take over. I want you and Leif to have this place. I want Texas Viking Honey to go on—better than ever. But I don't want to manage it." He tapped one hand on the table. "I've got plenty of work to do here at home. I can't lose you and Leif. You two are the only things that matter. I'm a fool for forgetting that."

Dane didn't say a word. His heart wanted to believe every word his father said but, until his father had made a real effort, he'd be wise to keep his guard up.

"Ever since your mother died a part of me has been missing. I kept looking for it in all the wrong places— women, mostly. The last one cost me. Cost all of us. Our divorce settlement wasn't pretty."

"And she said some things that could really have damaged Leif on her way out."

His father shook his head. "She's gone, the money's gone and you called me out on it. All of it." He tapped his fingers on the tabletop. "But you're right. I don't want to be some bitter old man who dies alone. I don't want my sons to hate me. I've been hard on you, said some things I'd no right to say. Your mother would be ashamed of me." His father's chin crumpled. "But she would be so proud of you."

Dane swallowed.

"I've made a mess of everything, Dane. I know it. I see it. I don't know how to fix it, but I want to try." His father was staring at him. "Or am I too late?"

"It'll take time to forge trust, Dad. Especially with Leif. But I don't think it's ever too late to try again. At least, I hope not." Dane smiled at his father, hoping like hell he wouldn't let them down again. He took a deep breath. "I have some of my 401(k) left—"

"No, no." His father shook his head. "I want to sell the cabin. It's the right thing to do."

He and his father talked for another hour. There was no guarantee it would all work out, but it felt good to know he wasn't taking this on alone. He was wary, this was his father, but he wasn't ready to give up on him altogether. His father was a stubborn bear of a man—if he wanted to change, he would.

Leif came in and stared between them, instantly on the defensive. "Who died?"

"No one." Dane shook his head. "Did you eat? I hope so because Dad cooked and it's not edible."

"Ha ha." His father stood. "I can make a mean peanut butter and jelly sandwich."

"I'm good." Leif stopped him. "Seriously, what's happening?"

"Well, I'm hungry." Their father started making sandwiches.

"We're trying to figure out how to fix things with our finances." Dane didn't see any point in sugarcoating it. "*We*—as in, you have a say-so. Have a seat."

Leif sat, wary. "Okay." He didn't look any more at ease after Dane and his father had filled him in on their plans.

Their father set a plate of peanut butter and jelly sandwiches on the table and sat. "Who knows, maybe we'll win the honey contest." His father chuckled. "Wouldn't that be a hoot?"

Dane shook his head. "No, sir. Honey Hill Farms needs this win. Even if we won, it'd still be their win."

His father stopped chewing to ask, "When did you start caring so much about the Hills?"

"When I fell in love with Tansy." Dane grabbed a sandwich. "Not that she'll have anything to do with me."

"You didn't help." Leif scowled at his father. "Tansy would never have started a fire. Or Astrid."

"I had no idea." His father looked truly stunned.

"Even if Dane wasn't crushing on Tansy, you yelling accusations at them like that wasn't cool. People were listening." Leif took a sandwich.

"I know." Their father stared at Leif. "What makes you so sure they didn't start the fire?"

"Because I trust them." Leif swallowed. "And because I did it."

Dane waited, bracing for his father's likely explosion.

"I was with the Dwyer boys, getting drunk because you want to send me to military school. And smoking." Leif watched his father the whole time he was talking. "It was an accident but I was so mad… I still am. I'm sorry about the fire, though."

His father studied Leif for a long time, then ran a hand over his face. "I don't want you drinking, you hear? But if you do, you do it right here so Dane or I can keep an eye on you. That fire… Seeing you two took a good ten years off my life." He took a sandwich. "I guess I owe those young ladies an apology."

They ate the entire plate of peanut butter and jelly sandwiches in silence.

"I appreciate the meal and the company." Their father cleaned up and headed up the stairs.

Leif leaned back, looking up the stairs in the direction their father had gone. "What the hell was that?"

"Our dad." Dane ruffled Leif's hair. "I guess some kid said something that made him realize he was being an asshole." He smiled at his little brother. "It gave him the kick in the pants to want to be better."

"Huh." Leif shrugged, glancing Dane's way. "You're not going to give up on her? Tansy, I mean?"

Dane stood, stretching. "No. I'm not. Like I'm not going to give up on you. But I'm too tired to think, so I'm going to bed. I'll figure something out." Tomorrow was the honey contest and the Hills had a lot riding on it. He'd wait until that was over and done with before talking to her. Assuming she would talk to him. He'd keep trying, what else could he do?

"I won't give up." He loved her, that wasn't ever going to change.

CHAPTER SIXTEEN

TANSY WAS A ball of nerves. Aunt Camellia, who was clinging to her hand, was no better. It wasn't just the contest, it was Dane. Would he be here? Would she be able to do this? She swallowed, but the knot in her throat didn't budge.

"It's so crowded." Astrid shaded her eyes as she took in the group gathered around the stage.

"There's a lot on the line." Tansy watched as the judges filed onto the stage, her gaze sweeping the crowd. No Dane. *Not yet.*

"People have come from all over for this one." Aunt Mags pushed her sunglasses up and went back to fanning herself with a bright green Healthy & Wholesome Markets paper fan. "Everyone wants a shot at that kind of money."

Meaning the competition would be stiffer than ever.

"Positive thoughts," Astrid whispered in her ear. "There's nothing else we can do."

Tansy was pretty sure there was something else she could do—namely, throw up. But she appreciated Astrid's determination.

"Ladies." Van Kettner walked up to the group, a small bag of honey chocolate fudge in his hand. "You-all must be excited," he said with a warm smile.

"You have no idea." Aunt Mags waved her fan, her long red hair stirring.

"I have confidence in you." Van nodded. "I've never tasted a honey so smooth and delicious."

"Dear, sweet man." Aunt Camellia patted his arm. "Oh my goodness, it's time. I feel faint."

"I forbid you from fainting," Aunt Mags whispered.

"You can take my arm, Camellia," Van offered, smiling when she did so. "I won't let you fall."

Aunt Mags glanced up at Van. "Well, if you must faint, then faint in his direction."

Aunt Camellia's hold tightened so hard, Tansy winced. "I'm so sorry." She let go of Tansy's hand, clinging to Van with both hands.

"It's okay." Tansy gave her a quick hug. "Breathe, Aunt Camellia." She pressed a kiss to her aunt's cheek.

Van patted her hand. "You'll win. I know you will."

"He's here," Astrid whispered, grabbing her hand. "I see him."

Tansy's heart stopped then picked up again, thundering in her chest. She took a deep breath. Even if they lost, there was a chance at things turning out all right—between her and Dane anyway.

Tansy stared in the direction her sister was pointing. Of course, Dane was staring right back at her. He wore a skintight black Texas Viking Honey shirt but his hair was down. *Oh dear.* Her nausea gave way to something far more invigorating and molten. She gave him a nervous wave.

Dane smiled and held up his hands. He had his fingers crossed. Then he pointed at her.

"He's wishing us luck," Tansy whispered, smiling back at him.

A petite woman with short black hair and wearing a bright green Healthy & Wholesome Markets shirt walked across the stage to tap on the mic. The sound echoed, silencing the crowd. "I'm Blanca Hinojosa, from Healthy & Wholesome Markets, and I'm so excited to be here today. We had a tough time narrowing the choices but we have our final three."

Tansy nibbled at her lower lip, her eyes burning. Without realizing, she sought Dane out.

Dane nodded her way. *It's okay*, he mouthed.

"Without further ado, let's announce our winners. Third place and a $20,000 cash prize goes to Texas Viking Clover Honey." Miss Hinojosa was clapping. "Where is our Texas Viking Honey representative?"

Dane made his way to the stage, but he wasn't happy. His jaw was locked and he avoided her gaze. He barely smiled when the woman handed him his check.

Van whispered, "Guess he was hoping for first place?"

But Tansy knew that wasn't it. He felt bad for winning now that he'd learned it wasn't his family's recipe. The shock on his face when he'd heard the truth had been real and gut-wrenching. Poor Dane. It wasn't fair. He'd been through so much the last few days.

"Second place and a $50,000 cash prize."

Tansy couldn't breathe. $50,000 would be enough. It would be close, but they could make it work—

"Our second-place winner is Wild Fire Honey."

Tansy took a shaky breath. *Oh no. This was it.* Tansy couldn't look at her aunts or her sister or Dane. She stared down at the ground, the air whooshing out of her lungs and her heart slamming against her ribs as the woman said, "We are so excited about our first-place winner. The first-place winner, who receives a cash prize of $100,000 and a multiyear exclusive distribution deal with Healthy & Wholesome Markets, is…"

The woman's drawn-out pause almost had Tansy herself fainting into Van.

"Honey Hill Farms Blue-Ribbon Honey."

She wasn't sure if it was Astrid or Aunt Mags or Aunt Camellia that screamed—maybe it was all of them. They'd done it. They'd won.

"Go on, Tansy, Aunt Camellia," Astrid whispered, her hand pushing her forward.

"I can't." Aunt Camellia waved aside the hand she offered. "You go on. Make us proud."

Her legs were so wobbly, she didn't know how she made it to the stage. But she did. She made it and she was smiling and hyperventilating all at the same time. *This is really happening.*

"Congratulations." Miss Hinojosa got her to hold an oversize ceremonial check, turn and take a picture. "We're so excited to be working with you. Not only did we love the flavor of your honey, I'm excited to be working with an all-female-owned honey farm."

"Thank you," Tansy managed, shaking the woman's hand.

"Congratulations." The woman from Wild Fire Honey was trying to not look too disappointed as she shook Tansy's hand.

"You did it." Dane's hands were warm around hers. "Congratulations, Tansy."

"I can't breathe." But the words were a garbled mess. She'd hoped, sure, but she hadn't believed it would happen. And yet… "I can't believe it."

Dane let go of her hands to clap. "You've earned it."

And just like that, it was over. Tansy forced the family onstage to pose for what felt like a million pictures before she answered questions from a local paper and a beekeeping magazine, but she had no idea if she'd made any sense. She and Miss Hinojosa exchanged numbers and emails and parted ways.

"Let me look at it." Aunt Camellia held the check up and kissed it before passing it to Aunt Mags.

"Don't smudge it." Aunt Mags stared at it, cradling the check in both hands. "One tiny slip of paper and all the world is right again."

"Isn't it wonderful?" Astrid asked, tears streaming down her face. "I can't stop crying."

"Happy tears are okay." Tansy hugged her close, her heart picking up when she saw Dane, Leif, Shelby and a few others coming their way.

"This is so exciting." Shelby hugged Aunt Mags, Bea balanced on one hip. "I'm so proud of you-all."

"It affects you, too." Aunt Mags touched the tip of Bea's nose. "You're both Bee Girls now."

"That's quite an honor." Van nodded, still holding on to Camellia's hand—Tansy noticed.

"We wanted to congratulate you." Dane stepped aside for his father.

"Oh." She swallowed. "Hello, Mr. Knudson."

"We want to give you this." Dane held out the Texas Viking Honey check. "It likely doesn't cover the income you lost as a result of…"

"My actions." Harald Knudson finally spoke up. "But, please, take it." He spoke directly to Camellia.

Tansy blinked, staring at Dane. *What was happening?*

He shrugged, a crooked grin suddenly creasing his handsome face.

All Tansy could do was watch. Poor Aunt Camellia stared at the man, expressionless. Harald Knudson, on the other hand, was a little too expressive for Tansy's liking. He could pine over Aunt Camellia all he wanted, but he'd missed his chance with her.

She glanced back at Dane and frowned—who laughed.

"You have my word that your recipe will never be used again," Harald added. "Please accept my deepest and most sincere apologies."

"I hope she doesn't." Aunt Mags took the check. "But we will accept this."

It took considerable effort for the man to stop staring at Aunt Camellia. When he did, he turned to her and Astrid. "Tansy, Astrid. I am sorry for accusing you the night of the fire."

"You did what?" Aunt Mags's eyes narrowed to emerald slits. "You spineless weasel of a man."

"My behavior was uncalled-for. I have no excuse, only regrets." Harald did look shamefaced.

"Of course, we forgive you." Astrid was Astrid. "You were distraught. It was horrible—just horrible. I can't imagine how you were feeling."

"See, I told you Astrid was cool, Dad." Leif stepped forward, holding on to Kerrielynn's hand. "Congrats on the win."

"Thank you," Astrid said. "For calling me cool."

Leif looked at Tansy, then stared meaningfully at Dane. "Tansy, did you still need help with that *thing*?"

This was it. Time for the *thing*. She nodded. "Yes." *No.* She definitely wanted to throw up now.

"Cool." Leif pushed her bee cart forward.

Tansy was shaking. *This is so stupid.* She glanced

down at the top of her Bluetooth speaker. *What am I doing?* But then she looked at Dane. She knew exactly what she was doing and why. She loved him—everything about him. *So much I'm going to make an absolute ass out of myself in front of everyone.*

She bent, pressed Play on her phone and lifted the speaker over her head, looking at him. Then the first few notes of "In Your Eyes" by Peter Gabriel reverberated across the fairgrounds.

Dane's blue eyes widened, but the corner of his mouth cocked up.

A good sign? Her face felt hot.

"What's happening?" Harald Knudson whispered.

"It's a thing… Between Tansy and Dane," Astrid whispered back. "It's supposed to be romantic."

Tansy's laugh was all nerves, about Dane and the crowd gathering. But mostly about Dane.

Dane crossed his arms over his chest. "Where's your trench coat?"

"Oh. Right." She set the Bluetooth speaker down and grabbed the trench coat. "It was underneath. Here." She pulled it on and picked up the speaker. "Should I start the song over?"

"No." He stayed where he was, his blue eyes searching.

Tansy went back to standing, the speaker over her head, the music blaring and the crowd growing until she was starting to lose confidence. For all the fire she saw in his eyes, he didn't make a move toward her. Had she lost her chance? Was this the worst idea ever? She nibbled at the inside of her lower lip—

And, Dane pulled her tight against him.

"Dane—"

But he was kissing her. Not some gentle brush of the lips, either. He was kissing her and she was kissing him back. She must have dropped the speaker because her hands were tangling in his hair... She didn't care if it was broken. She didn't care about anything else.

He rested his forehead against hers. "I get what you're doing here."

"I was hoping you would." She smiled. "I figured you'd either kiss me or yell at me—I believe those were the choices?"

"I'll always pick kissing you." He cradled her face. "Anytime. Anyplace."

"You know this won't be easy." She kissed his cheek.

"With you? Nothing ever is."

"You know we're going to have to learn to communicate a little better." She kissed his other cheek. "Okay, I'm going to have to."

"I'd say this is working so far." His arms tightened around her.

"You know that I love you." She stared up at him, holding her breath.

"Now I do." His blue eyes were full of such promise and warmth. He caught her hand in his and pressed a kiss against her palm. "I'll make sure you never regret it."

"As long as we have plenty of kissing time, I'm sure I won't."

"You've got yourself a deal, Miss Hill." At his grin, she dug her fingers into his Texas Viking Honey shirt.

"You know." She smiled, knowing he loved her sass. "It's okay for you to tell me you love me, too."

He chuckled, smoothing the hair from her cheek. "I

love you." He ran his fingers along her jaw. "I always have." He pressed a light kiss against her lips. "And I always will."

One month later...

DANE LAY HIS head in Tansy's lap, watching her talk about her day. It had become their routine. They'd meet along the fence line between their farms. He'd bring a blanket, she'd bring a snack and they'd share their day. Or sit, quiet, and be happy to be near each other.

"The aunts are making another apology dessert." Tansy smiled down at him as she ran her fingers through his long hair.

"I'm going to get fat." Dane patted his stomach.

Tansy lifted his shirt and ran her fingers across his stomach. "Hardly."

He stared up at her, happy to stay right where they were. "Would you mind?" He reached up to play with one of her dangling honeybee earrings.

"Nope." Tansy rested her hand on his chest. "I think I'm doomed to love you no matter what."

"Doomed?" He chuckled. "Not *lucky*? Or even *destined*? But *doomed*?"

"You're right, *lucky* is better." Tansy smoothed his hair back. "Oh, I wanted to tell you. Rosemary is going to send us a few queens from her lab in California. They're a new hybrid. More hygienic and pest resistant—"

He pressed his fingers against her lips. "Is this bee talk or Rosemary talk?"

Tansy shrugged. "A little of both."

"Tell me about Rosemary—save the bee talk for

later." Dane smiled up at her. "Please. Is she still coming home for the holidays?"

"All right, all right. Yes, she is. Supposedly."

Dane saw Tansy's frown. "I know you miss her."

"I do." She sighed. "But I want her to be happy—even if that means she's not here."

"You're a good sister." He smiled. "I think you're pretty awesome across the board."

"Because you love me."

"Yep." He nodded. "That makes me awesome, too."

"And lucky." She ran her fingers through his hair again.

"No man alive is luckier." He caught her hand and pressed a kiss to each fingertip. "You're mine."

"Yes I am." She rolled her eyes but she was smiling from ear to ear. "But there is one thing she told me about the bees—"

He pulled her head down for a kiss. Long and lingering and leaving them both a little breathless. That was one of the things he loved most—getting to touch and kiss her whenever he wanted. Which was pretty much all the damn time. So far, Tansy seemed to be on the same page.

"You've made your point." She sighed. "It's Dane-time, not bee-time."

"I like that. Dane-time." He chuckled. "We can talk about the Junior Beekeepers calendar, the apprenticeships, Rosemary's queens and this new observation deck you dreamed up during regularly scheduled business hours."

An observation deck so people can visit beeyards without getting stung. "I'm excited about that. I think it will be—"

He laughed. "You're going to make me do something drastic to distract you. Or was that the plan all along?" He sat up and pulled her into his lap.

"I'll never tell." She rested her head on his shoulder and sighed. "But this is comfortable."

He leaned forward, pressing a string of kisses along her neck.

Tansy's phone pinged. "It's Aunt Camellia. Aunt Mags wants to know if you like caramel or chocolate better."

"Tell them I'm on a new diet." Dane sighed, pushing aside the collar of her shirt to nibble her shoulder. "Tell them I'm allergic to sugar."

Tansy's breath hitched and she arched back so he could continue what he was doing. "They're going to continue to bake off their guilt so you might as well tell her what you prefer." She held her phone, ready to text.

"Will you tell her, again, that I accept their apology? I didn't even know they'd accused me of taking the recipe. I had no idea. Baking is no longer required." Dane knew it was pointless. The aunts would do what the aunts wanted to. Kind of like Tansy.

"It's just that they felt so bad it just sort of came out."

"I know, I was there." He shook his head, smiling at her. "It was awkward as hell." He took her phone and tossed it aside. Which earned him another eye roll.

"It was the first time I'd ever seen Aunt Camellia side with Aunt Mags. When they found the recipe and his other treasure in the top of Aunt Mags's closet, well, for a minute there, I thought Lord Byron was off to the taxidermist. Silly bird. I wonder if there's a term for a bird kleptomaniac?" But Tansy was laughing.

"Did I ever tell you how much I like your laugh?" He wrapped his arms around her and pulled her close.

"No," she whispered, cradling his face in her hands. "You realize, there's nothing I can do if you don't like it."

"I do like it." He traced her cheek with his fingertips. "I love the sound of it almost as much as I love you."

She smiled. "You do?"

"I do." He kissed her again, letting his lips cling just enough. "To me, Tansy Hill, you are the sweetest thing."

* * * * *

Hill Family Recipes

CHAPTER ONE:
LAVENDER-HONEY LEMON POPPY SEED MUFFINS

1 stick (¼ pound) salted butter, softened
¾ cup granulated sugar
2 eggs
1½ teaspoons vanilla extract
2 cups all-purpose flour
2 teaspoons baking powder
½ teaspoon kosher salt
½ cup whole milk
1 tablespoon lemon zest
3 tablespoons fresh lemon juice
2 tablespoons poppy seeds
1 cup lavender honey (½ cup honey, ½ cup water,
½ teaspoon dried lavender)*

1. Preheat the oven to 375°F. Line a muffin tin with parchment liners or grease each muffin cup.

2. In a mixer, cream butter and sugar in a bowl until smooth and fluffy, about 3 minutes. Add the eggs one at a time, mixing until incorporated. Mix in the vanilla.

3. In a different bowl, whisk together the flour, baking powder and salt.

4. On medium speed, slowly add dry ingredients and milk to egg mixture until well blended.

5. Scrape down the bowl and mix in the lemon zest, lemon juice and poppy seeds.

6. Fill each muffin cup ⅔ up.

7. Bake the muffins for 25 minutes, or until set and golden.

Serve warm with salted butter and a drizzle of *lavender honey.

*Lavender Honey:

1. Combine the honey, water and dried lavender in a small saucepan.

2. Bring to a boil over medium-high heat, allowing the honey to dissolve.

3. Reduce the heat to low and simmer for about 15 minutes.

4. Turn off the heat and let the honey sit to infuse for 10 more minutes.

5. Strain out the lavender before using.

CHAPTER TWO:
RUSTIC HONEY CAKE

½ cup unsalted butter, softened
1 cup honey
2 large eggs, room temperature
½ cup plain yogurt
1 teaspoon vanilla extract
2 cups flour
2 teaspoons baking powder
½ teaspoon salt

1. Preheat the oven to 350°F. Grease a 9-inch cast-iron skillet.

2. In a large bowl, beat butter and honey until blended. Add eggs, one at a time, beating well after each addition. Beat in yogurt and vanilla.

3. In another bowl, whisk flour, baking powder and salt; add to butter mixture.

4. Transfer batter to prepared skillet.

5. Bake until a toothpick inserted in the center comes out clean, 30–35 minutes.

6. Cool completely in pan on a wire rack. Serve with fruit, cream cheese frosting or additional honey.

CHAPTER THREE:
HONEY HAM STUFFED BISCUITS

6 large eggs
3 tablespoons milk or cream
salt and pepper
3 cups self-rising flour
2 cups heavy cream
12 slices of cheddar or Swiss or
Colby-jack, halved
4 ounces cubed or julienned ham
1 tablespoon melted butter

(Honey Butter: 1½ tablespoons honey
& 3 tablespoons melted butter)

1. Preheat the oven to 375°F. Brush sides and bottom of a 12-inch cast-iron skillet with melted butter and set aside.

2. Beat eggs and 3 tablespoons milk or cream together, season with salt and pepper. Soft scramble eggs, set aside.

3. Make dough: combine self-rising flour and cream with fork until flour is crumbly but will hold together pinched between your fingers. Knead until dough is formed.

4. Roll dough to ¼-inch thickness on a lightly floured surface. Cut into 6-inch rounds. Use scraps to form and make 12 rounds total.

5. Place ½ cheese slice, 2 tablespoons scrambled egg, 1 tablespoon ham and the remaining ½ cheese slice in center of round.

6. Pinch dough around the filling. Put pocket seam-side down in skillet. Repeat with each round until skillet is full.

7. Lightly brush the tops with melted butter, and bake for 15–18 minutes. Increase to 425°F for 5 minutes or until golden brown on top.

8. Remove from oven, brush with honey butter and serve.

CHAPTER FOUR:
HONEY BRITTLE
(AKA HONEYCOMB CANDY)

¼ cup honey
1½ cups granulated sugar
¼ cup water
1 tablespoon baking soda

*A candy thermometer is needed for this recipe.

1. Combine honey, sugar and water in a medium-sized, thick-bottomed saucepan. Bring to a boil over high heat. Stir occasionally.

2. Reduce heat and continue cooking and stirring until color darkens and temperature is 300°F.

3. Remove from heat and immediately add baking soda. Whisk quickly. Be careful, the candy mixture will triple in size and will be extremely hot! Don't get burned!

4. Pour candy onto prepared baking sheet (large baking sheet sprayed with vegetable oil) and let sit. Do not spread or touch.

5. Once cool, break into pieces.

(Can be stored at room temperature in airtight container for up to a week.)

CHAPTER FIVE:
HONEY-ORANGE CUPCAKES

1¼ cups all-purpose flour
1 teaspoon baking powder
¼ teaspoon baking soda
⅓ cup coconut oil
½ cup granulated sugar
3 tablespoons light brown sugar
1 egg
1 teaspoon vanilla extract
½ cup orange juice
⅛ teaspoon ground cloves
⅓ cup honey (plus 2 teaspoons for topping)

1. Preheat oven to 350°F and grease muffin tin.

2. Combine flour, baking powder and baking soda in a large mixing bowl.

3. Add the coconut oil, sugar, brown sugar, egg, vanilla, orange juice, ground cloves, and—of course—honey. Don't overmix!

4. Fill muffin cups halfway.

5. Bake until toothpick inserted into the center of each cupcake comes out clean.

6. Remove from oven, cool slightly, then transfer from tin to cooling rack to cool completely.

Optional Orange Frosting:

4 tablespoons butter, softened
1 tablespoon heavy whipping cream
½ teaspoon orange extract
2 cups powdered sugar (add more or less sugar for preferred thickness)

Blend together with mixer on low and pipe or spread onto cupcakes.

Top with honey drizzle.

CHAPTER SIX:
COWBOY COOKIES

2 cups all-purpose flour
2 teaspoons baking powder
2 teaspoons baking soda
1 teaspoon cinnamon
¾ teaspoon salt
1 cup butter, softened
1 cup packed light brown sugar
¾ cup granulated sugar
2 eggs
2 teaspoons vanilla extract
2 cups rolled oats
2 cups semisweet or milk chocolate chips
1½ cups shredded unsweetened coconut
1 cup chopped pecans
1 cup candy-coated chocolates

1. With the rack in the center of the oven, preheat to 350°F.

2. Whisk flour, baking powder, baking soda, cinnamon and salt in medium bowl.

3. Using a mixer, cream butter and sugars on high speed until light and fluffy. Scrape down sides. At medium speed blend in each egg and vanilla until well blended.

4. On low speed, add in the flour mixture until combined.

5. Stir in oats, chocolate chips, coconut, pecans and candy-coated chocolates.

6. Scoop heaping tablespoonfuls of dough onto a parchment-lined cookie sheet. Space 2–3 inches apart for spreading.

7. Bake 10–14 minutes or until cookies are set and lightly golden brown.

8. Remove from pan and let cool on rack.

CHAPTER SEVEN:
HONEY SUGAR COOKIES

2½ cups all-purpose flour
¾ teaspoon baking powder
¼ teaspoon salt
2 sticks unsalted butter, softened
¾ cup granulated sugar
¼ cup honey
1 large egg
1 teaspoon vanilla

1. Whisk flour, baking powder and salt.

2. In a mixer, beat butter and granulated sugar on medium high until light and fluffy. Add in honey, egg and vanilla and mix until smooth.

3. Reduce speed to low and blend in flour mixture.

4. Divide dough into halves, wrap in plastic wrap and refrigerate at least 4 hours.

5. Preheat oven to 350°F and line 2 baking sheets with parchment paper.

6. Using one half at a time, roll out dough to 1/8-inch thick and cut with cookie cutters. Reroll scraps until dough is used.

7. Place on sheets, leaving 1 inch of space between cookies.

8. Bake 15–18 minutes or until lightly browned. *Consider turning the pan halfway through baking time to ensure even baking.

9. Once transferred to rack and completely cooled, decorate with icing.

Cookie Icing:

2 tablespoons meringue powder
1 1-pound bag of powdered sugar
4–5 tablespoons water

1. Whisk together meringue powder and sugar.

2. Beat in water with mixer on medium speed until peaks form.

3. Beat in one more tablespoon of water if needed, depending on desired consistency

4. Spread or pipe onto cookies.

CHAPTER EIGHT:
VANILLA HONEY FRENCH TOAST

3 eggs
¾ cup milk
¼ cup heavy whipping cream
1 teaspoon vanilla
1 teaspoon honey
1 teaspoon ground cinnamon
2 teaspoons salted butter
8 slices thick bread (French, challah or country)

1. Preheat oven to 250°F (to keep slices warm).

2. Beat the eggs together with milk and cream.

3. Add vanilla, honey and cinnamon, and whisk together thoroughly.

4. Melt half the butter in a large skillet (medium-high heat). While butter is melting, soak each slice of bread in egg mixture for 10 seconds. When butter begins to simmer, place bread in skillet. *Leave space between bread slices. Cook approximately 3 minutes on each side until golden brown.

5. Place toast on cookie sheet in the oven to stay warm while cooking all the toast.

6. Serve with warm honey butter, butter, syrup, jam or fruit.

CHAPTER NINE:
HONEY SOAP

1½ cups goat's milk soap base*
3½ teaspoons oatmeal
3½ teaspoons honey
Optional: 2 teaspoons essential oils for scent

1. Cut goat's milk soap base into cubes and melt for 30 seconds—stir occasionally.

2. Stir in oatmeal and honey and essential oil (if using).

3. Fill soap molds (watch out for bubbles).

4. Set 2–3 hours or until set and pop out of molds.

*Goat's Milk Soap Base:

15 ounces coconut oil
30 ounces olive oil
6.4 ounces lye
16 ounces goat's milk (frozen is easier to work with)
¼ cup oats ground into fine powder

1. Melt coconut, olive oil and lye together—let cool but do not let set.

2. Add goat's milk and stir or use emulsion mixer to blend until smooth.

3. Add oat powder and mix in well.

4. Put in refrigerator until firm.

CHAPTER TEN:
WHIPPED HONEY HAND CREAM

16 ounces extra-virgin olive oil
16 ounces unrefined shea butter
¾ cup raw honey
3 tablespoons vanilla extract

1. Combine all ingredients except vanilla in a double boiler until melted together.

2. After melted, put in refrigerator to firm—approximately 5 hours.

3. Once firm, scoop mixture into a mixing bowl, add vanilla and whip until desired consistency.

4. Store in airtight containers.

CHAPTER ELEVEN:
HONEY TRAIL MIX

5 cups Chex cereal
l3 cups small pretzels
2 cups pecan halves
½ cup butter
½ cup honey

1. Preheat oven to 300°F.

2. Mix cereal, pretzels and pecans in a bowl.

3. Melt and blend butter and honey together.

4. Pour honey mixture over the cereal and coat well.

5. Pour onto parchment-lined cookie sheet, spread evenly and place in oven for at least 15 minutes.

6. Cool thoroughly and store in airtight container.

CHAPTER TWELVE:
HONEY BUTTER

1 cup unsalted butter, softened
⅓ cup honey

1. Beat butter until it is light and fluffy.

2. Mix in honey until smooth.

3. Scrape down sides and move honey butter into container.

CHAPTER THIRTEEN:
BEE'S KNEES COCKTAIL

½ cup honey
½ cup water
2 ounces gin
¾ ounce freshly squeezed lemon juice

1. Warm and blend the honey and water together to make a honey syrup.

2. Add honey syrup, gin and lemon juice to cocktail shaker. Shake to combine.

3. Strain into chilled cocktail glass, garnish with lemon and serve.

CHAPTER FOURTEEN:
BLUEBERRY LAVENDER HONEY SYRUP

½ cup water
2 cups blueberries
1 cup honey
2 teaspoons dried lavender (or 8 fresh whole
lavender blooms)

1. Combine water and blueberries in blender.

2. Place mixture plus honey and lavender in heavy saucepan.

3. Simmer for five minutes.

4. Remove from heat, strain and store. Keep refrigerated and use within 10 days.

CHAPTER FIFTEEN:
HONEY GINGERBREAD

3 eggs
1 cup sugar
½ teaspoon cinnamon
½ teaspoon cloves
½ teaspoon ginger
1 cup honey
1 cup sour cream
4 cups flour
2 teaspoons baking soda
½ teaspoon salt

1. Preheat oven to 350°F. Grease and flour a 13 x 9–inch baking dish.

2. Beat eggs, sugar and spices in a mixing bowl, then add honey and sour cream.

3. Add dry ingredients slowly, until blended.

4. Pour into pan and bake for 25–30 minutes or until a toothpick inserted in the middle of loaf comes out clean.

5. Remove from pan and cool on rack.

CHAPTER SIXTEEN:
HONEY CHOCOLATE FUDGE

3 tablespoons water
¾ cup honey
¼ cup peanut butter
¼ teaspoon vanilla extract
1 cup powdered milk
2 tablespoons cocoa powder

1. Combine water and honey in a quart-sized pot, warming to a gentle boil for 5 minutes and stirring continuously.

2. Dip fingers in cold water and touch the mixture—honey should pull threadlike.

3. Remove from heat and beat in peanut butter, add vanilla.

4. Sift in powdered milk and cocoa—consistency should be of a thick batter.

5. Pour into greased or lined tray or silicon molds.

6. Refrigerate 1–2 hours and serve.

LIKE BEES TO HONEY

CHAPTER ONE

"WHAT IN THE WORLD?" Camellia Hill read over the weekly store sales flyer and winced. "Sugar-free sugar-cookie-flavored coffee creamer?" She shuddered. "I don't know how anyone tolerates that low-calorie, no-flavor stuff as it is. But then they go and add that artificial sweetener and flavoring? All those chemicals can't be good for the taste buds. Not to mention the body." Her mother had had a simple philosophy: if it was made in a laboratory or manufactured in a warehouse, don't eat it. Growing up, their house had always been full of good, homemade food. Camellia tried to keep it that way. "I don't think I'll be using this coupon."

Leif Knudson grinned at her. "People buy that stuff because most of them can't cook like you can. They don't know what real food tastes like."

"He has a point." Her niece Astrid pushed their grocery cart alongside them. "It's sad, really."

"It is," Camellia agreed. "How good could your morning be if that's what you're putting in your coffee?" Camellia was a "one teaspoon of sugar and healthy dollop of cream in her coffee" woman.

"I don't drink coffee so..." Leif shrugged.

"I didn't when I was sixteen, either." She patted the boy's cheek. "Now? I can't imagine going without it."

"I mostly have Pop-Tarts or cereal or frozen waffles

or something easy." Leif paused, frowning. "Guess none of that's real food, either, huh?"

"No." Camellia was horrified at the thought of Leif eating those things for breakfast. "Remind me to make up some sausage rolls and biscuits and cinnamon pull-apart bread for you to take home."

Leif had eaten enough dinners with them for Camellia to see how much the boy could pack away. He was all long limbs, knobby knees and Adam's apple, but teen boys had magical metabolisms. Camellia could barely remember the days when she had anything that resembled a metabolism. She smoothed her blue-and-white floral-print dress over her rounded hips and skimmed over the sheet of coupons. "I can't use any of these."

"Wait? No coupons?" Astrid regarded her with exaggerated surprise, pressing a hand to her chest. Camellia was known for her love of couponing—and her sister and nieces loved teasing her for it. "Are you *sure*? Does this mean…we're going *rogue*?"

Camellia grinned. "That's me." She giggled—out of all the Hill women, she was the least likely to go rogue.

Leif laughed, too.

"At least we have our list to guide us." Astrid sighed, still hamming it up. "All is not lost."

Leif kept on laughing.

"Didn't you request some honey brittle?" Camellia asked her niece. Honey brittle was Astrid's favorite treat—she could eat a whole tin in one sitting.

Astrid stopped. "I'm teasing, you know that." She stooped and wrapped her slender arms around Camellia, hugging her tight. "And, yes, please, on the honey brittle. I'll help, of course."

"Not that I mind being called rogue." Camellia gave

her niece a quick peck on the cheek. "It makes me sound like a superhero. What would my superpower be? I wonder."

Leif didn't ponder his suggestion long. "No one bakes like you. Maybe superbaker?"

"Flatterer. That's why I can't say no to you." Camellia smiled at the boy. "And why I'm making four dozen cookies for you to take to the Junior Beekeepers meeting tonight." She glanced at the slim gold watch strapped to her wrist and sighed. "And why we need to pick up the pace. Leif, you get heavy whipping cream—none of that half-and-half stuff, either. Astrid, go get the flour—make sure it's the all—"

"All-purpose flour." Astrid nodded. "I know. There is no substitution." She hooked arms with Leif. "Let me give you a rundown of the no substitutions list. It'll help for future shopping trips."

Camellia watched the two of them heading off, content. Leif's request for her brown butter honey cookies had been awkward and bumbling, and it'd touched her too much for her to refuse. Leif wasn't a Hill, but he held a special place in her heart. He wouldn't remember, of course, he'd been a baby. But some of her most treasured memories were when he was an infant. Changing his diapers, reading him bedtime stories, watching him take his first steps and kissing away his boo-boos until he was smiling again. For a precious sliver of time, she'd loved him as her own. When her relationship with his father abruptly ended, her time with Leif ended, too. She'd grieved for the boy—oh so much.

But he was back now—in her life and her heart. Since Leif's big brother, Dane, began courting Camellia's other niece Tansy, Leif had become a fixture in the Hill home. Dane said Leif was a totally different boy there, happy and carefree and everything a sixteen-year-old boy should be. At home? Well, Camellia knew things weren't easy for him or Dane. Their father tended to be on the scoundrel side of things.

Speak of the devil. There, walking toward her was the man himself. Harald Knudson. Years ago, her heart would have been bouncing around inside her chest and she'd have been all weak in the knees and tongue-tied. She wasn't the same naive, trusting woman who blindly jumped in—heart first—that she'd once been. And she had Harald Knudson to thank for that.

Still, he was one of the most handsome men she'd ever set eyes on. He wore his age well, just as proud and upright as he'd been as a young man. He was fit and trim, no paunch or hunch to his shoulders. The lines that bracketed his clear blue eyes were, to Camellia, an improvement. He had aged—just right. Like a fine wine, her sister, Mags, would say.

"Miss Camellia Hill." Harald's voice rolled over her. His gaze fixed on her face, those blue, blue eyes holding a familiar spark of enthusiasm.

More like mischief. "Good day, Mr. Knudson." Camellia congratulated herself on keeping her tone casual and bland. There were times, like now, she wished she was more like her sister. Magnolia was the master of intimidation. With one cocked red eyebrow and a few well-delivered barbs, Mags could have someone shaking in their boots—even someone as self-important and egotistical as Harald Knudson.

"Did you paint those galoshes?" he asked, his gaze lingering as his eyes slid over her rain boots and up her thighs and hips.

She'd always been the short, funny, jovial Hill—a "what you see is what you get" sort of woman. And that included her love of food—preparing it *and* eating it. Curves and all, Camellia was comfortable in her own skin. But she wasn't feeling all that comfortable being on the receiving end of such an openly admiring look. Or the stirring of Harald Knudson–related feelings best forgotten.

When Harald's eyes met hers, the corner of his mouth cocked up. "You must have painted them—you and that magic paintbrush."

"I did." Camellia took a deep breath, steadying herself. "You can buy your own pair, if you like. Thirty dollars, at the Honey Hill Boutique. We might have your size. Good day." With a tight smile she brushed past Harald and his all-too-distracting presence. She had a schedule to keep. Leif's cookies weren't going to make themselves. She ticked flour and cream off her list and headed toward the meat department.

"Camellia, nice to see you." Van Kettner stood behind the butcher counter. "I'm betting your gardens are loving all the rain."

"They've perked right up—all green and happy," she agreed. "Which means the bees are happy."

"That's what matters." Van smiled. "Happy hives, happy lives?"

Camellia laughed. She appreciated Van's glass-half-full outlook and ready smile. As far as she was concerned, the more smiles, the better.

He chuckled in response before asking, "What can I get for you?"

"Let's see…" She slid her list to him. "I'm thinking about Sunday dinner."

"What's on the menu?" Harald Knudson's question startled her so, she jumped back—making Harald chuckle. "Didn't see me?"

"No." Camellia was acutely aware of how close he was standing. So close, the familiar scent of his aftershave tickled her nose. She frowned and took one solid step away from him—too pointed to be missed. "You go ahead, Mr. Knudson." She huddled at one end of the counter, giving him plenty of room to peruse the contents of the display case. "I'm not quite ready."

"Oh, I'm in no hurry." Harald chuckled. "Ladies first."

Camellia swallowed her frustration. When she was undecided on meals, she always asked Van. He was quite a chef and he never failed to offer up a useful idea or two. But she'd rather wait than have Harald standing too close, chiming in. "If you're sure."

"You take all the time you need, Camellia." Harald's tone was soft—and unnerving.

She took a deep breath. Harald Knudson loved to tease—he always had. Even now, he had a certain boyish quality to him.

Unlike Van Kettner. Really, there was no comparing the two but Camellia found herself doing it anyway. They were about the same age, both Honey natives, and both were exceedingly handsome, but that was where the similarities ended.

Harald needed to be the center of conversation, he always had. He was charismatic, those blue eyes lively and his crooked smile hinting at the mischief inside. He was all flash and temper, impatience and attitude— with an eye for the ladies. *How many ex-wives does he have now?*

Van was the exact opposite. He put people at ease; they talked to him and he listened. He was soft-spoken and thoughtful and generous with his time. He was a fine upstanding gentleman with a strong whisker-free jaw and thick salt-and-pepper hair. He'd lost his wife years ago and never remarried.

Van was the epitome of a good man and her friend. Harald was not. *And none of this is a surprise.*

She placed her list on the counter and asked Van, "What's fresh? I'm thinking a Sunday roast. Pork or beef?"

"Nothing beats a pork roast." Harald sounded off. "If I remember right, you have a fine honey-glazed pork loin recipe? Along with those real thin sliced potatoes you stack up and cook for hours—with that hint of onions?"

"French onion potato bake?" Camellia couldn't believe he remembered that.

"That." He nodded, patting his stomach. "Oh, and that salad with the nuts and cranberries, too? Mmm-mmm. Nothing compares to your cooking. Nothing." He winked.

Camellia didn't respond. Both the pork and potatoes were time-consuming—something she'd only make for a special occasion. Had she made them both for him? She swallowed, refusing to let a single memory of Harald Knudson at her table rise to the surface. Still, good manners had her saying, "Thank you." Instead of risking a glance at Harald, she focused entirely on Van. "What do you think, Van?"

Van wasn't looking at her or her list, he was looking at Harald. It was some look, too. Almost…angry. Surely not. Van was just about as easygoing a fellow as there was. Usually. Not currently. Camellia glanced back and forth between the two men.

"I guess he's still figuring things out?" The ring of condescension in Harald's voice had her bristling on Van's behalf. "Camellia, I was planning on coming to the farm later—"

"I don't advise that, Harald," Camellia cut in. He might be handsome and charming and smell good but she wouldn't let any of that draw her in—not this time. "Tansy or Mags might feel the need to shoot you for trespassing."

Van's chuckle was unmistakable.

"Even when we're family?" Harald smiled down at her as he crossed his arms over his broad, muscular chest. "Tansy and Dane are all but married."

Camellia shrugged. "I was once told that, until the 'I do's' were exchanged, it doesn't count. And it certainly isn't permanent." She wasn't talking about Dane and Tansy. In her heart, she knew her niece and Harald's son would make it. They loved each other with the sort of devotion and enthusiasm that would stand the test of time. No, she was repeating what Harald had said to her when he'd broken off *their* relationship… A relationship she'd foolishly invested her everything in. She turned from Harald, hoping he'd take the hint and move on. "Now. About my Sunday dinner. What do you think, Van? Pork or beef?"

"I'd say running into you this afternoon was meant to be." Harald *didn't* take the hint. He placed his hand on the countertop, angling his body so she had no choice but to look at him. "I needed to see you but I'd rather not get shot. At least not until I get a chance to clear the air between us." Harald sounded sincere.

"Consider it cleared." Camellia sighed, eyebrows raised. Whatever he was up to, Camellia wanted no part of it. "Now, excuse me. I have to get—"

"That easy?" Harald cleared his throat and stepped forward—too close once again. "Seriously, let's sort this all out. Just you and me." He waited until she was looking at him. "Have dinner with me, Camellia. Lunch. Coffee. You pick."

Camellia stared at the man. She waited for the punch line but Harald stayed quiet. "What…did you fall and hit your head?" She wasn't sure whether to laugh or call an ambulance. There was no way she'd let him make a fool of her again.

Harald had the nerve to grin. "I'm clearheaded. A little slow coming around, I'll grant you that, but I know exactly what I'm doing. You and me, we're meant to be—I see that now. You're good for me, Camellia. You always have been. You've always called me out. Always seen me for who I am and held me accountable. You—"

"Let you into my home to steal from me and my family?" Camellia finished for him. He couldn't be serious, could he? *Does it matter if he is?* "I don't know what you're after, but—"

Harald took her hand. "Time. With you."

Camellia couldn't breathe. She couldn't think. Here she was, in the middle of their tiny local grocery store, with Harald Knudson making some sort of declaration—a declaration that couldn't be real. Why now? Why after all this time?

And why was he holding her hand in front of everyone? No one was moving. No one was shopping. Every single eye was locked on them. She wasn't sure what to do. Her gaze shifted from their rapt audience to Harald's handsome and expectant face. He was serious.

"Aunt Camellia?" Astrid arrived, a large bag of all-purpose flour cradled against her chest. "Is everything all right?"

Leif trailed after her, his expression blank but his posture stiff.

Camellia nodded, pulling her hand from Harald's. Something felt very not right at the moment.

"Dad?" Leif stood straight and tall, looking and sounding older than his sixteen years. "What are you doing?"

"It's a grocery store, son. I'm getting groceries." Harald chuckled and tried to give Leif a clap on the shoulder—but the boy dodged. Harald winced, recovering quickly. "And since I had the good fortune to run into Camellia, I figured now was a good time to ask this lovely lady if she'd like to have dinner with me."

"She would not," Leif said, putting the cream in the cart. "No chance."

Van made a gruff—and oddly approving—sound.

Camellia glanced back at the towering butcher, who was glowering at Harald. It was concerning. Van Kettner was a teddy bear of a man and a dear friend. He never had a mean word to say about anyone, visited his mother every Sunday in her retirement community, donated food and money, and volunteered wherever there was need. And never, in all her fifty-two years, had she seen Van upset. No, not just upset—*angry*. "Van?"

Van's brow eased as he looked at her. The longer he looked at her, the more like himself he became. "Sunday dinner." He cleared his throat. "I've got a fine cut of beef that'd make a mighty tasty roast beef." He glanced at Harald, wavering, before heading into the back.

Camellia stared after him, wondering what had happened. Clearly, Harald Knudson had done something to the man.

"Camellia." Harald took her arm and pulled her gently aside, his voice lowered. "I'm thinking this isn't the time or place for me to pursue this…" He pressed a business card into her hand.

"I have your phone number, Harald." She tried to return the card to him but he held his hand up.

"Keep it." He hesitated, a flicker of uncertainty crossing his handsome face. "I have no right to ask you to give me another chance, Camellia," he whispered. "Hell, to ask you for anything. I know I've been a rat bastard to you. And a damn stubborn fool. But I…I hope you will." He searched her face—looking far too intent and vulnerable for her liking. "All right, I'll leave you alone now." And with that, he turned and walked away.

Camellia blinked, looking down at the card he'd pressed into her hand. On the back, was a note written in blue block-like letters. Harald's handwriting.

Since the day I let you go, I've been missing you. I promise, if you give me another chance, I won't make the same mistake again. Always, Harald.

CHAPTER TWO

"WHAT WAS THAT ABOUT?" Leif practically spat the words out, his face flushed and tight.

Camellia gave him a quick one-armed hug. "With Harald? Who knows? Maybe he thought he was being funny." Camellia forced a grin for Astrid and tucked the business card into her pocket. There was no point in sharing it with them.

Ever since Harald's secret came out, he'd lost quite a few friends. For years, Viking Honey—the Knudsons' honey brand—had been using and selling the Hill family's clover honey recipe as their own. Worse, he'd stolen the recipe when he'd been courting Camellia. To say there was no love lost amongst the Hill women and Harald Knudson was an understatement. But the Bee Girls, her sister and nieces, had rallied and moved on. It was what they did—love and support one another through whatever life threw at them.

Leif was different. Harald was the boy's father—not much of one, according to Dane, but they were blood. No matter what had happened between them, Camellia would never play a part in turning a son against his father.

"It's not funny. You said no, right? He didn't talk you into it? If he did, you can change your mind. You should." Leif sounded almost panicked. "I know he's my dad and I *have* to love him—but that doesn't mean I don't know he's a jerk." Leif sighed, running his fingers through his mop of blond curls. "He is. Just…don't go out with him. He'll screw everything up, for everyone. You deserve better, Camellia," Leif grumbled.

"Sounds like the boy has some strong feelings about the matter, Camellia." Van slid a white-paper-wrapped package on the counter. His brown eyes were searching the store, warily. "Sunday dinner roast. Trimmed up."

"That's kind of you, Van." Camellia smiled her thanks.

"What did he do to you, Mr. Kettner? You looked like you wanted to punch him." Leif slumped forward to rest his elbows on the grocery cart handle, and shot Van a look. "I'm guessing it must have been something bad."

Camellia had been thinking the same thing. Van's anger *was* more than a little unusual.

"I can't rightly say he's ever done a thing to *me*." Van gave a one-shouldered shrug.

Leif frowned. "Then why do you want to punch him?"

"Ah. I hate to disappoint you, Leif, but it's been many a year since I punched a man." Van chuckled. "In my experience, violence doesn't solve a thing, it tends to make things worse."

Camellia appreciated the man's take on things. According to Dane, Leif had been called to the principal's office on more than one occasion for fighting. As much as she'd like to think the boy had learned his lesson, a reminder—from someone like Van—couldn't hurt.

"Sure." Leif rolled his eyes. "Whatever. I'm pretty sure you'd have punched him."

"Leif." Astrid elbowed the boy in the side.

"Sorry," Leif mumbled, his cheeks going pink.

That's my sweet boy. Camellia patted the boy's back while Astrid gave him an approving smile. Apologies didn't come easy for Leif.

"Do we need to get anything else?" Leif looked ready to go.

Camellia couldn't blame him. She was ready for home, some lavender-honey tea and a sit with her feet up. *Except I have four dozen cookies to make in…* She glanced at her watch. "Oh, good gravy, look at the time. You and Astrid run get the condensed milk and powdered sugar? Oh, and some pumpkin spice and cinnamon." She paused, holding up one finger as she scanned her list. "And baking soda. And baking powder."

Astrid and Leif waited.

"That's it." Camellia gave her list a final perusal. "Yes, yes, that's it. I'll get the produce."

"You're sure?" Leif asked, all smiles once more.

"I am." Camellia nodded.

"Best have your phone out." Astrid's whisper wasn't much of a whisper. "I bet she'll text you a handful more things she needs before we even make it to the baking aisle."

The two of them walked off, pushing the cart, laughing.

"Those two are something else," Camellia said to Van, shaking her head. "I think Astrid misses having her little sister around. Having Leif, even if he is that much younger than Rosemary, helps—especially now that Tansy's so wrapped up in Dane."

"It's good you and your nieces have adopted him into the family." Van paused, then added, "Good to see him smiling. And it's nice to see him standing up for you, too."

Camellia was a little caught off guard by the way Van's eyes swept over her face. If she didn't know better, she'd swear those brown eyes of his lingered on her mouth. But of course, she did know better. Van was her friend—and far too practical for lingering glances.

Van cleared his throat, his gaze locking with hers and holding. "I know it's not my place to speak up but, maybe, think about what Leif said." He cleared his throat again and the muscle in his jaw ticked. "About Harald."

Camellia hadn't expected that—not how serious he looked or the intensity of his tone.

"You've got a good head on your shoulders and I'd never tell you what to do." He swallowed, his jaw tightening again. "I'd never do or say a thing to disrespect you. I hope you know that." He paused, his attention dipping—briefly—to her mouth.

The way he was looking at her... Her lungs deflated so suddenly that she feared she'd stop breathing.

"It's *possible* Harald's finally realized the mistake he made." His eyes narrowed briefly. "He might see that he wasted his chance with you and that, if he'd been smart, he should have done anything—*no matter what*—to get you back. It's likely, he regrets all the time with you he can't get back." He stared down at the top of the display case, his hand fisting. "Regret is likely eating him up. It should." He sounded incredulous—and more than a little forceful. Almost as if there was more to what he was saying? But what? What stake did Van have in any of this?

He ran a hand over his face, drawing Camellia's attention to his muscled forearm and his rolled-up sleeve.

Van has a tattoo? She blinked. *Is it warm in here?* Camellia resisted the urge to fan herself or continue staring at Van's tattoo or his muscled forearm. *It was definitely warm.*

When his brown eyes met hers, they sparked with a hint of something deep and warm and toe-curling. Van had never looked at her like this before. And she didn't know what to make of it. She swallowed, hard—a sudden tug in her chest startling her.

"If he's just now figuring out you're one hell of a woman, he's a damn fool." He shook his head, pulling his eyes from her and staring at the contents of the meat cabinet. The muscle in his jaw clenched before he went on. "Excuse me for that."

Van, thankfully, was too busy lifting a large bag of ice to notice how distracted she was by his arms and tattoo. He poured the ice into the tray along the far side of the refrigerated cabinet. He leaned down, reaching forward, his big, strong hands spreading the ice evenly. "He lost the right to court you."

His words had warmth pooling in her stomach, feeding her preoccupation with Van and all his...his manliness. She swallowed.

Van straightened and wiped his hands on his apron. "As Leif said, he's not good enough for you." When his gaze returned to hers, Camellia had no desire to look away. His voice dropped. "You deserve a man who'll treat you right, take an interest in you and be there for you, no matter what. Don't you settle for less, Camellia."

The way he said her name—a delicious mix of gruff and tender—flooded her with heat. *Oh my.*

Until five seconds ago, Camellia would have sworn her encounter with Harald Knudson was one of the more astonishing events in her life. But now *this*... Van Kettner? Camellia's insides were an overheated, topsy-turvy mess.

A deep red stained Van's cheeks. "I didn't mean to carry on." He wiped his hands again. "I overstepped."

Had he? Perhaps, yet everything he'd said was surprising but lovely. *He* was lovely. In a very manly way. She'd never been on the receiving end of such very manly attention—and she liked it. Very much. "Not at all," she managed, her jumbled insides throwing her off-balance. "I appreciate your concern, Van. I'm lucky to have it."

"I'd say I'm the lucky one." The same tone, gravelly and soft and lyrical all rolled into one, sparked another unexpected response in her. His jaw muscle tightened before he added, "To call you a friend and...all."

Camellia held her breath, anticipation pricking up every nerve ending. He had more to say, she could tell. If only she could read his thoughts in those brown eyes of his, she'd know what he was thinking and feeling or if this was all in her head.

His gaze returned to the counter and he shook his head, murmuring something so softly that she didn't hear him.

"What was that?" she asked.

"Nothing." He shook his head again. "Can I get you anything else today?"

"Oh." That was it? She'd expected... What had she expected? Just because she'd had some sort of world-altering revelation that Van was manly and lovely and quite capable of making her weak in the knees didn't change a thing for him. Just because his forearms and hands and tattoo and voice had woken a powerful ache inside her didn't mean it was reciprocated. Van had been a good and loyal friend for years.

"Camellia?" Van repeated, his brow furrowing as he studied her face.

She scanned her grocery list but the words, words she should have memorized by now, seemed blurry. She'd lingered here. Surely, there was a reason? "No." She blinked. "No. I think I have what I need."

"You sure?" he asked, not looking at her. "Nothing else?"

"I'm certain." She tucked her list away. "Thanks again, Van. For…everything."

A harsh sigh slipped from him and he looked up then, one hand resting on the counter. "Camellia…"

She stopped, her heart in her throat, hopeful. "Yes?"

He opened his mouth, closed it, then stared up at the ceiling overhead, tapping the counter with his fingers. "I've got a new recipe for creamy horseradish sauce, if you'd like?"

Horseradish sauce? "Oh, well…thank you, but I'll use my mother's recipe." She smiled, heat creeping into her cheeks. If she needed further confirmation that her internal meltdown was one-sided, here was proof. She was cataloging his every feature and he was offering her a horseradish recipe. It was likely she had a smear of honey butter or powdered sugar on her lip—that was why he'd looked at her mouth.

But Astrid would have told me.

She gave herself a mental shake. "But I like the way you're thinking. A full-on English roast beef dinner."

"Sounds delicious." His warm smile was back. "Give my best to the family."

"Of course." She nodded, appreciating his smile more than ever. "And you give your mother a hello from me, will you? I'll be making some honey fudge soon, and I'll set some aside for her."

"That's thoughtful of you, Camellia." Van shook his head. "Mom will appreciate it. She says nothing tastes better."

Camellia beamed at that. "You just made my day, Van."

"I did?" He chuckled. "That's good to know." He took a deep breath, his smile growing and those brown eyes crinkling at the corners just right. "Good, indeed."

Uma Bumgartner and Ida Popplewell arrived right then, preventing any further conversation. Not that there was anything left to say—not really. And yet, she couldn't entirely dismiss the feeling that things felt... unfinished.

Oh, for Pete's sake. She was making nothing into something. *Enough now.* With a wave and a smile, Camellia moved on to the produce department and whatever else she'd need to make the perfect Sunday roast beef dinner.

But, as she picked some golden potatoes, Camellia was still pondering what had actually happened. The truth was cut-and-dry. Camellia was being courted by a version of Harald Knudson that seemed vulnerable and sincere and very different from the man who had broken her heart and her trust all those years ago. Changed or not, would she be able to forget their past to have a future? Did she want to try?

After all, Harald Knudson was the only man who'd

expressed any interest in her. For all the odd tugs and
breathlessness she'd experienced, Van Kettner and his
warm brown eyes, strong hands and gruffly tender
voice, appeared content being her friend. That was fine,
that was good. Her poor heart had never been lucky in
love, it was unlikely that was going to change now—no
matter how much it ached for more.

CHAPTER THREE

THE WHOLE DRIVE HOME, Camellia had half-heartedly chatted with Astrid and Leif. Now she unpacked the groceries from her canvas shopping bags, handed off each item to Leif or Astrid or whoever stood nearby and was willing to help, and tried to engage in the overlapping conversation that filled the Hill kitchen.

She paused, taking in the scene in the hopes it would ease her sense of disquiet. Gathered around the kitchen was everyone she loved most. Tansy sat in Dane's lap—where she often resided. Dane, pausing to press a kiss to Tansy's temple, was helping Magnolia with a cross-word puzzle she had spread across the kitchen table. On Mags's other side, her daughter, Shelby, sat reading over the tattered copy of Langstroth's beekeeping manual, her baby daughter, Bea, sleeping in the crook of her arm. She was still new to bees, her adoptive family not exactly outdoorsy, but Shelby was determined to learn. She kept a bright stack of sticky tabs within reach to mark important passages. So far, dozens of tabs protruded along the pages' edges. And Astrid sat in the oversize rocking chair, crooning over the cats, Beeswax and Jammie, as they wedged themselves around her for a long cuddle. Leif, who'd assigned himself her grocery helper, was putting away their haul with admirable speed. Lord Byron, Camellia's beloved parrot, snoozed on his perch, the only reason he was silent.

Normally, she loved the chaos and noise and comfort of it all. At the moment, she wished for a quiet kitchen, a cup of tea and time to collect herself.

"I've heard he's a jerk," Leif was saying, taking the bag of chips Camellia handed him. "Like, he was mean to Mr. Diaz."

"Where did you hear this?" Dane asked, holding his hands out.

Leif tossed the bag of chips to his big brother. "Mrs. Svoboda was talking, real loud—"

"Not surprising." Mags looked up from her cross-word puzzle.

"Who are we talking about?" Camellia interjected, uncertain of the particulars.

"Rebecca Wallace's nephew," Mags said, tapping her pencil against the paper. "Mr. Charlie Driver. Apparently, he's here to wrap up her affairs."

"Interesting we've never heard of him until after his aunt's death." Tansy shook her head. "I wonder what he'll do about the property."

"Rumor is he's staying through the summer." Mags shrugged. "But you never can tell."

"Maybe I'll go over and say hello?" Dane offered, tucking Tansy's hair behind her ear. "See if I can figure out his plan?"

"My hero." Tansy smiled up at him. "And determine if he's really a jerk or if Willadeene Svoboda is stirring things up."

Astrid adjusted Beeswax on one leg, then tucked Jammie in close. "Do we know why he was supposedly mean to Mr. Diaz?"

"Because this guy is a jerk." Leif sighed. "Some people are just jerks. Other people are just cool. Perfect example—my dad and Mr. Kettner. Dad's a jerk. Mr. Kettner's chill."

Camellia grinned.

"I mean, Mr. Kettner is old, but still cool." Leif grabbed the handle of the canvas bag. "Where does this go?"

"Old?" Camellia asked. "You think Van is old?"

"Well…yeah." Leif shrugged. "Older than my dad."

By a couple of years, maybe. Old wasn't the word she'd use to describe the man. Hardworking and resourceful. Generous and kind. Now she could add, manly and handsome and, possibly, sexy. *Yes, definitely sexy.* The tattoo and the voice and the hands… Thinking about him that way was pointless. He's a friend. He will only ever be a friend. *My sexy friend.* She grinned.

And Harald? Like it or not, there was a part of her that softened at his note and the uncertainty on his face. She knew Harald was a scoundrel but, once upon a time, he'd been her scoundrel. While she'd tried to lock away all the happy memories they'd made together, she'd never succeeded. And her scoundrel wanted her back?

"Auntie Camellia?" Tansy was standing beside her, the empty kettle in one hand and an odd look on her face. "Are you all right?"

"Of course." She smiled. That was when she realized the room had fallen silent. "I'm sorry. What did I miss?"

Tansy glanced at Astrid, Astrid glanced at Shelby, Shelby glanced at Mags, and Mags stood—eyes narrowing as she crossed the kitchen.

"Leif was telling us who you happened upon at the grocery store. Do not tell me that look has anything to do with Harald Knudson." Magnolia's green eyes bored into Camellia's. "I don't care how irresistible you think he is. Resist."

Camella blinked. Her sister was right. Refusing Harald, tearing up the business card and pretending today hadn't happened made the most sense.

"Look at you." Mags pointed at her. "You're all—" she waved her pointer finger in a circle "—like this."

"Like this?" Camellia echoed, resisting the urge to go down the hall to the gilded framed mirror to see what "like this" meant. "What does that mean?"

"You are sort of staring off into the distance." Tansy nibbled on the inside of her lip.

"And you didn't say much on the way home." Astrid glanced at Leif. "Did she, Leif?"

Leif was frowning. "No."

Camellia threw up her hands. "Oh, for goodness' sake. How about you all get out of the kitchen and occupy yourself with something useful while I get started on these cookies so they'll be ready in time for the Junior Beekeepers' meeting." She handed Leif an apron. "You can help."

Leif took the apron, but he was still frowning. No one else moved.

Camellia groaned, knowing full well no one was going anywhere until this whole mess was put to bed. "Harald Knudson *was* at the grocery store. And, I suppose you could say, something…happened. But nothing exciting, really." Camellia pulled her stand mixer close and pointed at the pantry. "Can you get me the flour, please, Leif?"

Leif did as she asked.

Magnolia was scrutinizing her. For as long as Camellia could remember, Mags had the uncanny ability to give Camellia a head-to-toe sweep and read her like a book. Well, 80 percent of the time anyway. But this…well, these sorts of things didn't happen to Camellia. Ever. The Harald Knudson part *and* the Van Kettner part.

"You could guess," Camellia assured her sister.

This, of course, was met with Mags crossing her slender arms over her chest. "Or you could tell us. Though you're blushing, which isn't a good sign."

Camellia pressed her hands to her cheeks. "Am I?"

Shelby nodded. "You are a bit, Auntie Camellia."

"You are." Tansy wore a curious smile, her head cocked to one side. "Spill the tea, Aunt Camellia."

Dane chuckled. "How about you sit and spill and I'll make some tea?" He came around the table, took the kettle and kissed Tansy's cheek.

"I don't have time for this." Camellia took a deep breath. "I have cookies to make."

"Then you should get right to it." Mags's brows rose. "You went to the grocery store."

Camellia nodded. "I'd sent Astrid and Leif off to get things and Harald came up to me."

"And?" Mags prompted.

They all leaned the tiniest bit forward, eyes widening while they waited.

Camellia laughed. She couldn't help herself.

"That was a synchronized lean, if I've ever seen one." Dane carried her beloved teakettle to the stove and put it on the burner.

Lord Byron woke up, squawked, then echoed, "Synchronized lean."

"We're out of crackers." Shelby shrugged, patting baby Bea's back as the baby stirred.

"Next time you go into town, more crackers." Mags leveled a death glare at the bird. No matter how hard Camellia tried to change their minds, her sister and the parrot refused to play nicely. Lord Byron stole things, tore up the edges of books Mags was reading, and—after one especially unfortunate incident when Mags had reclaimed her sparkle-tipped hair comb—Lord Byron had left parrot poo in one of Mags's favorite high-heeled shoes.

"Or some rat poison." Aunt Mags continued to glare at the bird.

"Anyway." Shelby placed a hand on her mother's arm. "Go on, Aunt Camellia."

Camellia shrugged. "Harald was very charming and gracious and I stayed civil. Then he followed me to the butcher counter—"

"I bet Van loved that." Dane snorted.

Camellia paused. "Why do you say that?"

Dane's eyes went round and he crossed his arms over his chest, flushing just enough to tell Camellia he knew more than he was letting on. "No reason, I guess."

"Anyway. Harald was stalking you and…?" Any sign of Mags's patience was long gone.

"And he asked me to dinner. Or lunch. Or coffee." Camellia shrugged. "My choice." She didn't mention the business card or the rather sweet note he'd written on the back or how utterly sincere he'd seemed.

"Huh." Dane leaned against the kitchen counter.

"Huh?" Leif repeated. "Don't worry, Miss Magnolia, I told my dad no."

Mags's smile was blinding. "I knew I could count on you, Leif."

"But Mr. Kettner seriously wanted to punch Dad. He had that vein thing." Leif pointed at his forehead. "Like you get, when you get mad, Dane. It bulges out."

Tansy smiled sweetly. "Only when you're *really* angry."

Dane pressed a hand to his forehead. "So, Van was *really* angry?" The corner of his mouth cocked up.

Camellia stood. "And that was that." She went around the table. "Now, I've got cookies to bake."

"That's it?" Tansy asked.

"That's it." Camellia was not going to mention her conversation with Van, her unexplainable reaction, or how out of sorts she'd felt since they left Kettner's Family Grocery.

"Well." Leif shrugged. "Everyone was watching. *Everyone.* Like the whole store. And Dad was holding her hand."

"That explains the vein," Dane murmured.

Now that Leif was happily recounting every detail of the exchange, and keeping everyone at the table enthralled, Camellia sidled up to Dane.

"If you've got something to say," Camellia whispered, "say it."

Dane blew out a slow breath. "*I* don't have anything to say."

She frowned.

"It's not my place to say anything." He stared down at her, considering, his blue eyes searching. "What are you thinking? About Dad? A date?" Dane was studying her.

She shrugged. "I haven't given it much thought."

She pulled her recipe book from the shelf. "Too much to do at the moment."

"Right. Cookies." Dane grinned. "Save one for me?"

"I'll think about it." She smiled back. "Come on, Leif. Let's get to baking."

She was elbow deep in flour when the doorbell rang. She glanced around the kitchen. "Of course, *now* everyone's disappeared." She winked at Leif and hurried to the door, wiping her hands on her brightly polka-dot apron and reaching up to tuck in a strawberry blonde curl that'd slipped free from her bun before opening the front door.

"Camellia." Van Kettner stood, taking up most of the doorway, smiling, with a bouquet of flowers in his hand.

"Van?"

"I was in the neighborhood," he murmured, his cheeks flushing.

Had he changed since this morning? His jeans were pressed, he wore a brown button-down shirt—with the sleeves rolled down—and his boots had a high polish to them. The shirt was different, that much she knew.

"I won't keep you, I know you have cookies to make." He offered her the flowers.

Camellia took the flowers. "They're lovely." She glanced at the blooms, then up at him. "Pink camellias?"

His brown eyes settled on her face. "I'm good at talking, Camellia. Most of the time." He cleared his throat. "But when there's something weighing on me, it takes time for me to get the words right."

"Oh." It was all she could manage. Today was turning out to be full of all sorts of surprises.

"Earlier? I should have come right out and said I

don't like Harald Knudson." He ran his fingers through his thick salt-and-pepper hair.

"I picked up on that, Van." She smiled, she had to.

"I figured as much." The corner of his mouth quirked as he shook his head. "Do you remember what I said? About how you deserve a man that will treat you right—"

"Take an interest in me and be there for me, no matter what?" How could she forget what he'd said, or the way he'd said it?

"I should have come right out and said I was talking about…me." Van took a deep breath. "If you'll have me, that is."

Camellia couldn't move. "You?"

"Now you know. I'm not entirely unbiased when it comes to you and Harald Knudson. I felt the need to make that clear. I'll do my best to respect whatever decision you make." His smile was as warm as ever. "I guess I'll let you get back to those cookies now." He turned and ambled toward the steps.

Her head was spinning, her heart clipping along so fast she feared it might burst right out of her chest. *He's leaving.* Camellia sucked in a deep breath. "Were you really in the neighborhood?"

Van paused, turning on the top step. "No." He chuckled. "My nerves got the best of me." He nodded at the camellias. "Those came into the store and I wanted you to have them." The look he gave her almost made her knees give way. "I can't see a camellia without thinking of you, Camellia Hill. And thinking of you makes me smile…always."

Camellia was still standing on the porch, holding the pink camellias, long after Van's truck had disappeared from sight.

CHAPTER FOUR

CAMELLIA SIPPED THE chamomile tea Astrid had made for her, hoping its purported calming benefits would take effect—any minute.

"I think she should wear her hair up." Tansy gathered up Camellia's curls, looking at the reflection in the vanity mirror. "It shows off your neck."

Did she want to show off her neck? Camellia blinked at her reflection.

"I like it down." Astrid shook her head. "She always wears it up. This is…different." She brushed aside her sister's hands. "She has such lovely hair. I mean, your neck is lovely, too, Auntie Camellia."

"Thank you," Camellia murmured. *Different* was the word of the day. *I'm going on a date.* That was definitely different. If thinking the words made her break into a sweat, how would she make it through the date without turning into a nervous puddle?

"I think you should ask her. Shouldn't they, Bea?" Shelby lay sprawled across Camellia's big four-poster bed, Bea cooing and wriggling atop the quilt beside her. "What do you think, Aunt Camellia?"

"I have no idea." Her giggle sounded more like a squeak. She took a sip of tea.

"You don't have to be nervous." Tansy squeezed her shoulder. "It helps that you know he likes you."

"Not that he deserves you." Mags sat on the edge of the bed, interjecting her thoughts on the whole dating thing as she saw fit.

"No one deserves her." Astrid smoothed Camellia's hair. "But a good man, the right man, will never stop trying."

"Which dress did you decide on?" Shelby slid off the bed, Bea on her hip, and held out the skirt of the pink flowered dress, then gave the navy blue dress a once-over. "They're both lovely."

"And new." Mags sighed.

Camellia's gaze met her sister's in the mirror. "You were the one that told me to buy both of them."

"Because you look beautiful in both of them." Mags pushed off the bed and joined Shelby, holding out her hands for Bea. "I just hope you're dressing up for *you*, not him. He'd be lucky to get you in your house slippers and coveralls." She smiled down at Bea. "Wouldn't he, Bea?"

Bea smiled and clapped her hands.

"Now, that would make quite an impression." Tansy laughed.

"We'd have to record his reaction when the door opens so we could send it to Rosemary." Astrid was smiling as she picked up the hair iron and began working Camellia's curls into silky shoulder-length waves.

"I wish she was here." Camellia missed her youngest niece—they all did. "Not that she'd enjoy this much."

Astrid nodded, continuing to run the iron over her hair in slow strokes.

"She'd support my slippers and coveralls take," Mags said. "Rosemary is the most practical of us all, Shelby. I don't think she owns a dress."

"She sounds like she lives a very exciting life in California. I can't wait to meet her." Bit by bit, they were learning about Shelby's life with her adoptive family. Older parents. Her adoptive mother had passed on, but her adoptive father was alive and doted on her—his only child. He'd been against her quest for her birth mother but Shelby persevered. Since she'd arrived at their front door, she'd been learning everything she could about her biological family and their bees. "The bee genome postgraduate study? Insect molecular biology?"

"She's supersmart." Astrid smoothed a hand over Camellia's hair. "Even if she doesn't own a dress." Another slide of the iron. "What do you think of your hair, Aunt Camellia? If you don't like it, we can pin it up."

Camellia stared at her reflection. Between Shelby's makeup, Astrid's hairstyling and Tansy's borrowed dangly honeybee jewelry, the effect was rather dramatic.

"You look like Lucille Ball." Tansy was all smiles. "A sexy Lucille Ball."

Camellia's eyes widened.

"Oh, you do!" Shelby nodded. "He's going to trip over his own feet when he sees you."

Mags snorted, handing Bea back to Shelby.

"I think you look beautiful. But do you like it?" Astrid was watching her, closely, in the mirror.

Camellia leaned forward, blinking her mascara-elongated lashes. "Do I look like…me?"

"Of course, you do." Mags shot her an odd look. "You look just like you. As lovely as ever."

Only her sister could manage to pay her such a wonderful compliment and sound exasperated at the same time. Camellia turned on the stool, smiling at her sister. "Thank you."

She stood, tightening the tie of her robe, and sighed. "I don't know what to wear. You pick."

She'd been excited all day—but still managed to be productive. She'd made a new batch of lavender-honey soap, milked her goats and taught Shelby how to make mason jar beeswax candles all without a hint of nerves. But once she'd showered and they'd all gathered in her bedroom, her stomach had knotted at the realization of what was about to happen.

"You look a little pale, Aunt Camellia." Tansy perched on the edge of the bed. "Nervous?"

"Yes." She nodded. "I'm fifty-two years old and going on a first date." Her smile wavered. "Oh dear. Saying it out loud makes it even worse."

"Nonsense." Mags took the pink flowered dress. "You're not defined by a number, Camellia. You have more energy than most women half your age—that's a fact. You're delightful. Charming. Lovely." She sighed. "No matter how I feel about this, he has exquisite taste in women. Which means he can't be a complete moron. I suppose."

"I second that." Astrid nodded.

"Third." Shelby raised her hand, smiling.

"Same." Tansy unzipped the dress. "Now, let's get you dressed."

By the time Camellia was ready, she was worrying over every little thing. She fidgeted with the decorative buttons down the front of her dress, wondered if her heels would trip her up, and hoped he didn't take one look at her and change his mind.

Mags shooed the nieces out and closed the door behind them. "Breathe." Her green eyes searched Camellia's. "You don't have to do this, you know. It's your choice. All of this."

Camellia nodded.

"What is it, Camellia?" Mags's brow furrowed. Mags, who refused to emote for fear of wrinkles, *was* emoting. "You're worrying me."

"How many men have I dated, Magnolia?" She smoothed her hands over her skirts. "Harry Young in high school. Peter Vaughn in college. Then Nathan Green and Harald. That's all. In all my years."

"And only two of them got lucky." Mags grinned.

"Magnolia!" Camellia was horrified. Doubly so because her sister *was* correct.

"If you were a virgin we'd have cause for concern." Mags shook her head, still grinning. "Relax. Have fun. You're not running off to elope." She gave Camellia a wide-eyed look. "Don't even try it."

Camellia laughed.

Mags nodded. "Good. How about you try…enjoying yourself."

"You don't think I'm being ridiculous?" Camellia instantly regretted asking.

Mags took a deep breath, her face clearing as she seemed to mull over her answer. "No."

Camellia blinked. "No?" She'd been expecting Mags to tell her she was absolutely, irrefutably, ridiculous.

"No." Her sister smoothed a hand over her hair. "This *man*, for whatever reason, has caught your eye. That means something, I suppose. You'd be ridiculous if you ignored it. No one wants to be alone, Camellia. Well, except for maybe me."

"But you have Shelby. And baby Bea." Camellia saw

the hint of sadness in her sister's eyes. "And me. And Tansy and Astrid and Rosemary."

"That's all well and good, but you know what I mean." Mags gave her another head-to-toe inspection. "If you want a man in your life, I say go for it. Apparently, you've got them lining up and waiting. Like bees to honey."

Camellia had to laugh at the imagery.

"But don't you dare set yourself up for that sort of heartache again, Camellia, or I'll wind up in prison for offing the bastard that breaks your heart."

Camellia knew her sister was referring to her breakup with Harald. It had been a nightmare. And Mags had carried her through it. She hugged Mags close. Her big sister wasn't normally a fan of physical affection so Camellia reveled in her sister's tight embrace. "I love you."

"I love you, too." Mags released her.

The steady knock on the front door had them both frozen, staring at each other with wide eyes—before they burst into laughter.

"Come on." Mags grabbed her hand and pulled her across the landing and down the stairs.

Mags was right. About all of it. This was what she wanted. *He* might be everything she wanted. There was only one way to find out. Tonight, was about starting something new and good and full of promise. *No looking back.*

She was fully aware of the audience gathered around the base of the stairs. The girls were there, all smiles. When Dane and Leif had arrived, she didn't know but it wasn't altogether a surprise.

The moment her eyes locked with her handsome date's, however, she was in for a surprise. He looked at her with such pride that Camellia was awestruck. He was proud of her, to be with her, and when his hand took hers—it shook just enough to reassure her she wasn't the only one suffering from nerves.

Neither one of them said a thing. She had so much she wanted to say to him, but she had no idea where to start. They had time, though. There was no need to rush.

"Have fun," Mags said, holding the front door open.

She didn't remember saying goodbye to anyone, only that—somehow—they ended up on the front porch. Alone.

"You look beautiful." He shook his head. "So beautiful."

"Thank you," she whispered. "You're looking pretty handsome yourself."

His gaze fell to their hands and he smiled, as warm as ever. He didn't let go of her as they walked down the steps and along the flagstone path to the gate. "I thought we'd go down to the lake, have a picnic and watch the fireflies. If that's all right with you?"

"It sounds perfect." She squeezed his hand. "If you don't change your mind by the end of the night, maybe you'd like to join us for Sunday dinner? The roast beef was your idea, after all."

He came to a stop, his brown gaze sweeping slowly over her face to linger, most assuredly, on her mouth. "Change my mind? My mind was made up—five or so years ago." Van Kettner shook his head. "I couldn't change my mind, or my heart, even if I wanted to, Camellia. And I don't want to."

Camellia was too breathless to come up with a suitable response, until, "Does that mean you've been wanting to kiss me for half a decade?"

"Give or take a year." He nodded, smiling.

"Oh." She stepped forward and stood on tiptoe, placing her hands on his chest to steady herself. Beneath her palms, she could feel his heart thundering against his chest—echoing the beat of her own. But that was forgotten when he bent and brushed his lips against hers. *Oh.*

Firm and gentle. But as his arms wrapped around her and those big, strong hands pressed her closer, his kiss deepened and Camellia was clinging to him to stay upright. When his head lifted, she was pleased to see he was just as dazed as she felt. "Oh," she murmured again, still holding on to him. "Good gracious."

"I'd say so." His voice was oh so tender as he ran his fingers along the curve of her cheek. "I only wish I'd asked five years ago."

"I think this was exactly the right time for us, Van." She smiled up at him. How had she missed this? He had been there, all along. Something told her he would always be there. *If you'll have me.*

"I'll take it." He smoothed her hair from her shoulder. "I like having you here." His hands pressed against her back. "It feels—"

"Right." She rested her head against his chest, closing her eyes to listen to the steady beat of his heart. "Like this is where I belong."

"I was thinking the same thing." Van's sigh was pure contentment.

"I know you've got plans and all but, maybe, we can stay like this for a few more minutes?" she murmured, burrowing against his chest.

"I'm in no hurry." He pressed a kiss against the top of her head. "I've got what I want."

After years of living with a hole in her heart, she'd accepted it as permanent and made the best of it. But Van's words—his lovely gruff and tender voice—and the strength of his arms around her did the impossible. He filled her heart so full there was no room for holes or aches or hollowness. Just this. Comfort. Strength. Happiness. And love.

* * * * *

GRANNY HILL'S BROWN BUTTER HONEY COOKIES

2 sticks salted butter
1 cup light brown sugar
1 cup sugar (plus 2 tablespoons, optional)
¼ cup honey (plus 2 tablespoons, optional)
2 large eggs
2 teaspoons vanilla extract
3¼ cups all-purpose flour
1½ teaspoons baking soda

1. Melt butter in a saucepan over medium heat, reduce to low heat and allow butter to barely simmer. Cook until milk solids are golden brown (approximately 6 minutes). Set aside to cool. The butter should be liquid but no longer hot.

2. Preheat oven to 350°F. Line two baking sheets with parchment paper.

3. Combine the brown butter, sugars and honey with mixer on low speed until mixture is blended, about 2 minutes. (Note: mixture will look grainy.)

4. Add the eggs one at a time, until mixed in. Add vanilla.

5. In a separate bowl, whisk flour and baking soda. Add flour mixture to sugar mixture and beat until blended.

6. Scoop 1½–tablespoon mounds onto baking sheets, leaving room for spreading between cookies.

7. Bake until golden brown, about 15 minutes. Allow the cookies to rest on the sheet for a few minutes before moving to a cooling rack.

Optional: Drizzle with honey and sugar as desired.

SPECIAL EXCERPT FROM

H HARLEQUIN

SPECIAL EDITION

*Buzz Lafferty's "no kids" policy is to protect his heart.
But Jenna Morris sends Buzz's pulse into overdrive.
The beautiful teacher is raising her four young
siblings…and that's t-r-o-u-b-l-e. If only Jenna's fiery
kisses didn't feel so darn right—and her precocious
siblings weren't so darn lovable. Maybe it's time for the
Morris party of five to become a Lafferty party of six…*

Read on for a sneak peek at
The Rancher's Full House,
*the latest in the Texas Cowboys & K-9s miniseries
by* USA TODAY *bestselling author Sasha Summers!*

It took effort, but Jenna managed not to fall prey to
his crooked smile and flashing eyes. No matter how
charming he was, she didn't want to play this game.
Whatever this game was.

"Maybe I'm just a sweet guy?" Buzz cocked his head
to one side.

She shook her head. "Sweet? No. Infuriating, yes."
Infuriatingly handsome. Or maybe she was so infuriated
because of the way *she* reacted to *him*. Until Buzz, she'd
never been one to daydream or linger over memories or
what-ifs. Now, she spent far too many minutes each day
mulling over that kiss and the still-lingering burn inside
her. For him. This man, sitting on her desk, smiling like
he didn't have a care in the world.

"Why am I infuriating?" He waited.

There was no way she'd admit anything about the daydreams or the aching or wanting to him. No way. Instead, she said, "I've already told you. It's like you're… up to something." She reached for the light switch. "What do you want, Buzz?"

His fingers wrapped around her wrist. "You know what I want. Another kiss. May I?" He turned her hand over and pressed a featherlight kiss to the inside of her wrist. "I'd like to think you want that, too."

The gruff edge to his voice seemed to mute the rational part of her brain. It was the only explanation for her total lack of resistance or restraint. Her gaze wandered from his thumb caressing the inside of her wrist, up the wall of his chest, to the most knee-weakening, gorgeous face she'd ever laid eyes on. *That was the truth.*

But she pressed her lips tight, refusing to let the other far more alarming truth slip free. If she admitted he was right about her wanting his kisses—and so much more— there'd be no turning back. And even though she knew giving in to Buzz Lafferty would likely end in heartbreak, she found herself moving closer to him. What harm could one last kiss cause?

Don't miss
The Rancher's Full House *by Sasha Summers,*
available July 2022 wherever
Harlequin Special Edition books and ebooks are sold.

Harlequin.com

Do you love romance books?

Join the Read Love Repeat Facebook group dedicated to book recommendations, author exclusives, SWOONING and all things romance!

A community made for romance readers by romance readers.

Facebook.com/groups/readloverepeat